Producer & International Distributor
eBookPro Publishing
www.ebook-pro.com

Back from Berlin
Yossi Uzrad

Translation from the Hebrew: Yaron Regev

Contact: yossi@dogtv.com
ISBN: 9781712069875

BACK FROM BERLIN

YOSSI UZRAD

PROLOGUE

Revolutions are not in the habit of giving advance notice, my uncle Kuntz once told me. Kuntz's wise insight was now my reality. Everything that was stable in my life had collapsed. The bright future that I was sure awaited me had vanished. I lost control over my life and was swept away against my will to harsh, distant destinations. A decision formed from that deep despair: I will not surrender, no matter the consequences. I live in a democratic state. This isn't Soviet Russia!

I slowed the car down. The headlights searched the thick fog that had settled on the wet road. Plentiful rains gave hope that 1979 would be a good year for farming. Louis Armstrong was on the radio singing "What a Wonderful World" with his raspy, gravel-filled voice. A lump the size of a tennis ball formed in my throat, and I could no longer hold back my tears. I stopped at an empty bus station and wept silently, frustrated and depressed.

Back then, I could not have imagined that decision would lead me to where I am now. Reality, so it appears, has its own set of rules.

Much water has since flowed through the small river that crosses Kibbutz Mishmar Hatsafon where I was born, and seemingly, nothing has changed.

PART 1

1

In the evening, a thin layer of clouds shrouded the moon. Its faint light flickered like the eyes of a bride seen through her veil.

My father returned from the field, sat down heavily on the front stairs, took a long look at the skies, and thundered, "Just before dawn, a Sharqiya easterly wind will begin to blow, heralding a heat wave. We spent a whole week planting in the orchard's new plot. Now everything will simply dry up and waste away." He unbuttoned and removed his shirt, took off his muddy shoes, and sighed while looking one last time at the moon.

The following day, just as he had prophesied, a strong easterly wind blew in the yard, ushering in a punishing heat. The kibbutz members sat around the Formica tables for lunch in the shared dining hall with the sweat trickling down their necks.

My father wiped his forehead with his hat, and a bead of sweat dropped into his soup. "It will be blazing hot tomorrow, the Sharqiya will dry the seedlings, and they'll die. It won't help even if we fill the pits with water." Just like that, he sentenced the seedlings to death.

Humi Schory, who worked with my father in the orchard, looked up from his soup bowl briefly. He didn't say a word before he re-turned to vigorously dunking bits of rye bread into the goulash soup and gulping them down, slurping loudly.

My father got up from the table, put on his oil-stained hat, and told Humi, "Let's get going. Maybe we can salvage something."

My father had come to the kibbutz following his brother, Moshe Kotzer. Moshe was one of the founding members of our kibbutz, Mishmar Hatsafon. Everyone in the kibbutz called Moshe "Kuntz," a pet name with an undertone of mockery. My uncle was treated with a mixture of respect for his sharp mind and contempt for his opinionated nature and the fact that he always had to have the last say. Kuntz distinguished himself as a man of strong words who, un-like my father, wasn't very good with manual labor, which was of paramount importance in our kibbutz.

Even during my early childhood, I was aware of the pent-up en-mity between the brothers. The two did not exchange a single word unless they absolutely had to, and then their dialogue was brief and to the point. What had led to that troubled relationship — that I did not know. Each time I asked about it, my father gave me a sharp look, making it clear that some matters are better left alone. Still, I became close with my uncle's family, especially my cousins, Haya and Moti. I spent many hours in Henka and Kuntz's apartment to be in the company of Haya and her good friend Nurit Schory. My father was not happy about this, even if he never openly expressed his disapproval.

***

After lunch, Yael Harduf, our nanny, hurried us to shower and get into bed for our usual afternoon nap. Outside, the Sharqiya con-tinued to whirl madly, and the air filled with dust, making it hard to breathe. Nurit Schory, thin and tanned in only her underwear, slipped outside her room. She exited through the rear door and sat on a chunk of black basalt outside the children's house. With an aluminum teaspoon, she dug up a large pile of earth and ate as if it were a steaming bowl of semolina porridge. Slowly, with great concentration, she ground the black earth until she swallowed it all. From the window of my room, I watched her, mesmerized. She was ten, and I was nine.

Our principal teacher, Tova Zisman, who was walking along the path leading to the veterans' neighborhood, saw Nurit and scolded her. "Nurit, get back inside the children's house right now! Everyone needs to be in bed!"

Nurit defiantly placed another spoonful of earth in her mouth.

"Disgusting! Spit that dirt out right now!" Tova shouted at her.

Nurit crossed her arms on her chest, clenched her mouth, and shook her head with a determination that could only mean one thing. Tova lost her composure. With one hand, she pulled my friend up from her stone seat, and with the other, although violence was almost never practiced by the teachers, spanked her. Nurit ignored the blow, stared at Tova, and continued to slowly chew the dirt. Practically enraged, Tova dragged Nurit by the arm to the children's house. Along the way, I watched Nurit swallow the clods of earth in her mouth.

***

I was born in Kibbutz Mishmar Hatsafon in the Upper Galilee. My childhood was circumscribed by clear-cut rules in a social framework that was unlike anything else in the world, but for me it was perfectly natural. As far as I was concerned, this was how all children grew up. Hebrew was the only language spoken there. The Russian songs were soon replaced by those of Israeli military singing groups, which were then discarded in favor of the music of Israeli rock stars Arik Einstein and Shalom Hanoch, which comprised the soundtrack of my life.

We were raised together in two groups named after trees. I was in Cypress, five girls and three boys. My life revolved around the two other male members of my group, Yehiam Gruenwald and Udi Ganani. We grew up together — from the nursery to the army — a strong friendship bound us throughout our childhood.

Both groups, Cypress and Fig, were housed in the same complex, as there were not enough children to justify two buildings. Our lives were lived in crowded conditions. There were strict rules and limits imposed on all kibbutz children, enforced with an iron fist by Tova Zisman, the principal teacher, and Yael Harduf, the nanny, who mainly spoke in pedagogic sentences: "Never eat while standing up; the food might go down to your legs," "Seven olives are the nutritional equivalent of an egg," "He who acts like a beast should live in the cowshed."

Each group had its eccentric member; Nurit Schory was Fig's weirdo. In Cypress it was my best friend, Yehiam Gruenwald, who dared to rebel against the harsh restrictions. Tova and Yael did not regard him kindly. As far as they were concerned, Yehiam was an educational failure, rude and defiant. But even they hesitated to confront him because he was sharp-tongued and was not afraid of them. Yehiam had been blessed with great physical strength and excelled in all sports, easily besting the adults in the kibbutz holiday arm wrestling contests. Fearless, he did not give a damn about the rules, and the adults rarely bothered to punish him.

Once, when Yehiam was late for breakfast, Yael decided to put an end to his insubordination. She punished him with an extra shift of kitchen floor mopping duty, knowing how much he hated it. Yehiam took a full bowl of egg salad from the table, threw it into the garbage can, and furiously left the dining hall.

Yael chased after him, screaming, "You can't throw away food!

There are hungry children in other, less privileged places!"

She grabbed his wrist and sought to return him to the table, but Yehiam pulled with all his strength to release himself from her grip. Yael tumbled to the floor and broke her leg. The education committee unanimously decided that Yehiam Gruenwald would be sent to the "University," as they called the Kibbutz Movement's special education program, established in one of the Sharon area's kibbutzim.

Once every two weeks, on the weekend, Yehiam returned to our kibbutz and walked the sidewalks, angry and intimidating. During his visits he seemed embarrassed and humiliated and avoided contact with nearly everyone. It was during that time that we became close friends. I used to go to his parents' rooms, and together we would go out to play in the kibbutz yard.

When he returned from this forced exile, Yehiam seemed to have become a different person. He was taller and had become withdrawn, distant, difficult to understand. His stubbornness was turned to new avenues. While he had been gone, we'd begun to study English and other subjects. In order to catch up, Yehiam spent his nights memorizing the Hebrew-English dictionary, its pages becoming blackened from use. With the same diligence, he excelled in arithmetic and natural science. He possessed a remarkable memory and knew by heart the dates of major historical events, and by the end of the school year, he had begun to arrogantly correct the teachers' inaccuracies.

***

Udi Ganani was my other friend, a sensitive, introverted child who was perceived by the adults as someone they could rely on. I was the glue that connected Yehiam and Udi. My connection with them joined us into a triangle in which each vertex was entirely different, and somehow, in the end, I would always find myself cast aside. My friendship with Udi was always volatile; I could never really tell what he thought about me. His behavior was enigmatic and unpredictable, and I was his only friend in the Cypress group.

Udi did, however, have a special connection with Max Tishler, one of the kibbutz's veteran members. Max was the kibbutz carpenter and about the same age as Menahem, Udi's father. After school, Udi used to sit in the carpenter's shop for hours on end watching Max build cabinets, beds, and other furniture. He sat on a tall stool with his legs dangling and his feet gently kicking the air to the rhythm of Max's movements when the carpenter vigorously sanded the furniture in preparation for painting. Udi was especially fascinated by a huge band saw that only Max was authorized to operate.

Yael Harduf was suspicious of the unusual relationship between a child and an adult kibbutz member. She had even asked Menahem and Rina, Udi's parents, to keep an eye out to make sure the intimacy between the childless Max and Udi was not too intimate. Yehiam and I had experiences and secrets that we did not share with Udi for fear that he would tell Max. For instance, I was the only one who knew of Yehiam's regular habit of entering the shed where they kept Hercules, the kibbutz's huge bull stud, to feed it hay while stroking its forehead.

***

Moving on to high school also meant distancing ourselves from home. The Educational Institute — or the Institute, for short — ran like any ordinary school during the day. Each age group was housed in a dormitory with a classroom attached to it. The schedule was fairly regular: early wake-up for the first lesson, then breakfast followed by a return to the classroom. At ten o'clock, we had a snack break. The classes continued until lunch in the shared dining hall. At the end of the meal, we boarded a yellow bus that drove up and down the Galilee roads and returned each of us to his own kibbutz for a few hours of labor. A short visit with parents was followed by the return to the Institute in the evening.

Evenings in the Institute were dedicated to social activities, following which we dispersed to our bedrooms. Each room had four beds, and of course there were separate rooms for boys and girls. When the last adult left the Institute grounds, a stream of human traffic began to flow between the rooms. Early in the morning, before the adults returned, there were always several bleary-eyed students who had to hurry back to their rooms. We spent every other weekend in the Institute on our own and without any adult supervision.

The weekends were busy with activities: trips, afternoon classes, and events demanding the participation of all the Institute's students, from the seventh to the twelfth grade. For me, the Institute was a lively place of freedom whose ways and habits I loved dearly. In effect, we each had two homes: one at the Institute and the other in the kibbutz. In Mishmar Hatsafon, my roommate was Yehiam. We lived in a green-painted Swedish hut with a roof made of red asbestos tiles, a remnant from the early days of the kibbutz. The shed in the kibbutz was our home during school vacations and weekends.

***

Nurit Schory continued to not give a damn about convention even after the transition to the Institute. She made few, if any, social contacts. Her alien ways had created an air of mystery and envy around her. Nurit constantly challenged the values of the kibbutz. She was strikingly beautiful and wandered the Institute's paths as well as the kibbutz's yard tanned and barefoot, wearing shorts and a tight t-shirt. Her casual sensuality was in blatant disregard of the kibbutz's sexual conservatism. At night, the kibbutz youngsters would secretly steal their way to the entrance of the clinic where there was a small wooden cabinet containing packets of condoms.

Nurit would brazenly go to the clinic in broad daylight, gather up packets of condoms, and distribute them to those too shy to take them for themselves. I once heard Nurit say to my cousin Haya, her only friend, "Boys have only one thing on their minds, but they don't even have the courage to go to the clinic cabinet."

No one could ignore Nurit; her open attitude toward sexuality was a constant source of unrest. She was the first among us who treated sex with nonchalant indifference. Of course, she knew people were talking about her behind her back but could not care less. The educational staff and the female kibbutz members were furious at her apparent contempt for the community's conservative norms. After repeated failures to rectify her ways, they simply began to feign indifference. Keeping their mouths shut as if they didn't notice her unusual behavior.

I envied her for being so brave and liberated, someone who did not care what people might say. After all, "What would people say?" was one of the driving forces influencing the behavior of every child and adult kibbutz member, an unwritten social code of whose existence we were all constantly aware. Deviating from that code brought about an immediate barrage of gossipy reactions and a lowering of one's social status.

Nurit was the exact opposite of me; I always played by the rules. I think that was her main attraction. During my childhood, I was drawn to Nurit because of her unusual and daring ways, and during our teenage years, for her beauty and blatant sensuality. Her ability to disdain the possibility of condemnation and act freely without any consideration for the mannerisms of the kibbutz aroused my passion. I followed her exploits with a sense of wonder and with the sure knowledge that she would always remain an unobtainable dream.

My cousin Haya was one year my senior, and thanks to her, I could spend time in Nurit's company. During the summer, I would spend hours following Haya and Nurit about. One time, when I refused to go pick raspberries with Yehiam, he yelled at me, "I'm sick and tired of this. You spend all your time with girls." In his mind, and at that age, that statement was a dire insult.

Nurit was particularly popular with strangers who came for brief stays in Mishmar Hatsafon. During the summer, the kibbutz lawns were invaded by naval academy cadets from Acre and volunteers from Scandinavia. Both the cadets and the Scandinavians somehow found their way to her. Of course, there were some kibbutz members who coveted her as well. Today, I know for a fact that some of the adults did more than covet and had used her tender age to their advantage.

***

"Those who refuse to study need to work, our kibbutz has no place for idlers!" Thus, Tova Zisman explained the education committee's decision to suspend Nurit's studies and send her for a week of labor in the orange grove because she had skipped school for a whole day and chose to hang around the Institute's yard instead. At the time, Nurit's mother was experiencing one of her cyclical bouts of depression, during which she lay in bed silently staring at the ceiling for days on end.

Nurit's father, Zeev Schory, called Humi by everyone, was much admired in the kibbutz for investing all his time and energy in his labors. One never heard his opinions about the complex dilemmas facing the community. He maintained a similar silent attitude regarding the frequent problems surrounding Nurit's behavior. Humi preferred to bury his head in the sand, despite his daughter repeatedly embarrassing him among his friends. With marked indifference, he accepted Nurit's harsh punishment. Humi hoarded his anger, walking about the kibbutz sidewalks with a sour face and clinging to his silence either from shame or weakness. He was always early to rise, dress in his blue work coveralls, shamble to the dining hall, sit in the corner, and slowly chew slices of rye bread with jam. Each morning, at exactly five thirty, he plodded sullenly to the tractor shed. At the first light of dawn, he started the tractor engine, harnessed a red plow, and lined the fields with long furrows until darkness fell.

***

Two years before being drafted into the army, during summer vacation, Nurit was late one day for her dining hall duty. She was seventeen then and more rebellious than ever. Chaim Harduf, the kitchen shift supervisor went to look for her. Close to the youth sheds, he noticed a trail of blood drops leading into the showers. Inside, he found Nurit naked on the floor with a box cutter next to her. A trickle of blood slowly flowed through the black tile grooves until finally congealing.

Chaim fled the shower and cried out in the kibbutz main yard, "Nurit has killed herself! Quick, call Dr. Zucker!"

Udi went running off to the showers, and I ran after him. More kibbutz members soon arrived, including Alfred, the dairy farmer. Ten minutes later, the kibbutz physician, Dr. Zucker, arrived, panting and carrying his black bag. He had to clear a path through the curious onlookers.

With a trembling voice he shouted, "Everybody clear off, right now! Move it! You can't stand here!"

The crowd reluctantly took a step back.

Dr. Zucker covered Nurit with a blanket and shouted again, "Go away! This isn't some theater show. Those who don't have anything to do here should leave."

Dr. Zucker leaned over Nurit, looking perplexed. He had spent all his years in the kibbutz as a family doctor specializing in routine pediatric issues — sunburns, minor injuries and sprains, common illnesses. Hesitant, he took another look at Nurit, then, completely out of character, he landed a slap on her cheek.

Nurit regained consciousness and opened her eyes. An ambulance siren was heard down the road, so Alfred picked up Nurit, wrapped in a blood-soaked blanket, and carried her out of the showers. It was only then that Humi, Nurit's father, arrived from the field.

"Your daughter bled more than a cow giving birth," Alfred said to Humi.

Dr. Zucker quickly snapped at Alfred, "Get back to the cowshed, you stupid idiot."

The crowd burst out laughing. As for me, I pitied Nurit and fell even more in love with her. But perhaps that was only because of the beauty of her bare breasts, accidentally on view for all to see.

Perhaps Nurit's suicide attempt was a last desperate cry for help.

***

When the army induction orders started to arrive, Tova, the head teacher gathered us for a talk about the military. "You graduates are setting out on a new road. The army is another hurdle you need to overcome before your inauguration as full kibbutz members. We educators have now completed our task. We have toiled and labored to provide you with broad knowledge, with proper values. You are the jewels in the crown. Go to the army willingly, and use the opportunity to become familiar with all the various aspects of Israeli society. Set out on this new road without fear. We will all be waiting for you here at home, following your postings and knowing you will be at the forefront of every assignment. Don't be led by others; act as leaders. Volunteer to serve as officers and commanders. Use the virtues we have taught you, and serve as the examples during your military service. Be strong and of good courage!"

A few weeks after matriculating, Nurit told the kibbutz secretary she had decided not to serve in the army. Such a dramatic move was unheard of in the kibbutz, and all the members were shocked. As gossip spread, Nurit's mother was committed to an institution in Bat Yam. Then Nurit packed a large backpack, and Humi carried it for her to the kibbutz gate. Before boarding the bus, she gave her father a quick hug, then she was on her way to Sweden with the last volunteer she had met. Her departure left me with a great emptiness and a deep sense of longing.

2

Two weeks after my graduation, I was drafted into the army. The first among my age group. My whole life, I had been called Uri, but from the day I was drafted, everyone in the army called me only by my last name — Dolev. Getting used to the military wasn't easy for me. The first few weeks of training had me suffering: from blisters on my feet, from the harsh discipline, and mainly from the lack of any physical stamina. Many of the officers and soldiers in my company were kibbutz members, and I was afraid I would be thought of as a weakling back home.

A few months later, all my classmates were drafted as well — Udi joined an elite commando unit, Yehiam was an only son, which meant he could choose where to serve. After some deliberation, he decided to follow the herd and chose to serve in a combat unit. He was assigned to the armored corps, finished his basic training with distinction, and successfully completed a tank commander course. The national kibbutz security department pressured Yehiam to take an officer training course, but he refused and blatantly ignored all their persuasion attempts.

Meanwhile, I invested a lot of effort in improving my position in the army, including training even during my brief leaves. Volunteering for combat service was mainly motivated by a wish to be well regarded and to meet the expectations of the kibbutz members.

During the first few months, I counted the days. All I wanted was for the time to pass comfortably until my discharge. I was surprised when I received a summons for officer training. The course lasted six months. When it ended and officer's ranks were placed on my shoulders, something had changed in me — the inexplicable ease with which I had advanced up the military ladder had filled me with a sense of confidence. For the first time in my life I felt successful, especially since I was the first of our class to become an officer. Friends in the kibbutz patted my shoulder and sought my company. I suddenly enjoyed walking around in my uniform, puffing up my chest with pride and occasionally stealing a glance at my shoulders to make sure the insignia were still there. I carried out my duties as a commanding officer enthusiastically and was strongly motivated to be successful. I was enjoying army life and quickly advanced from one senior position to another. Six months before the end of my military service, I was appointed company commander. Success had stoked my ego, and I decided to join the standing army and dedicate my life to the military. I was disappointed that Nurit was in distant Sweden, unaware of my success as an IDF officer.

***

My final position before joining the standing army involved commanding a small outpost in the Golan Heights. One night, Udi surprised me with a visit. After graduation, we had grown distant and barely saw each other during holidays and vacations, each of us preoccupied with his own affairs. Our childhood friendship had slipped, and we found no common ground. During his vacations, Udi was withdrawn and spent most of his time with his girlfriend from the neighboring kibbutz.

Udi had immediately distinguished himself in the army. He possessed extraordinary physical and athletic ability. He had participated in marathons as early as the eleventh grade. No one in the kibbutz was surprised to learn he had graduated from officer training with distinction and returned to serve in the commando unit. In Mishmar Hatsafon, we'd always had a poorly concealed competition about who would be most successful in the army.

The night he surprised me with his visit, Udi opened the door of my quarters and declared, "Uri, we're setting up the unit's stakeout headquarters here with you."

Then without asking permission, he entered with a group of officers from his unit and immediately made himself at home. He unloaded his equipment in the center of the room, tossed his personal weapon on the table, jumped on my bed with his dirty uniform, sprawled out comfortably, and yelled at me, "Dolev, how about some cake and coffee for the guys here?"

Udi's arrogant familiarity made me furious; he treated my room as if it were his own. Udi was waiting for another officer, Dovchek, who was in charge of the special installations deployed by the IDF along the border separating Syria from Israel. Udi told story after story about the legendary Dovchek until I was sick of it.

That same evening, Dovchek arrived wearing oversized army work clothes, unshaved, and with his hair untrimmed. Additionally, he had a nasty habit of vigorously picking his nose at all times. It was hard to believe that disheveled, unkempt man was a standing army officer, and I couldn't understand why Udi was such an avid admirer. Udi and Dovcheck made themselves right at home in my room and carried on a conversation filled with contempt for any army unit other than their own. I sat off to the side, uncomfortable.

Before we went to sleep, Dovchek became restless. He asked Udi to contact the three Dganim stakeout operations to get their reports on the situation in the field and repeated his request every ten minutes. This was when the Dganim had first become operational: ambush teams carrying MAG machine guns equipped with a device that concentrated starlight, allowing night vision.

Dovchek paced back and forth in my room and loudly announced, "It's happening tonight. I can smell it. I have a sixth sense; tonight there's going to be an infiltration from Syria." He told the stakeout commander on the radio, "Tell the guys to stay sharp. They're coming tonight, and I want at least three dead terrorists."

I got caught up in the excitement and decided I wanted to join Dovchek and Udi's company. I overlooked my old friend's infuriating behavior and asked him to allow me to take part in their operation. Udi pulled Dovchek aside, they whispered together, then Dovchek nodded and said, "Dolev, we will let you join us on one condition: you're under my command like any other soldier, regardless of your rank."

I agreed. In my small kitchenette, I made coffee and served it along with some cookies I had left from a package I had received from the kibbutz. I fussed at them like a child who had just received a new toy. Udi told me a little gossip from his vacation in Mishmar Hatsafon, and then we got ready for bed.

A little after midnight, we heard shots being fired and chatter from the radio. It turned out one of Udi's stakeout teams had run into a Fatah squad about a mile and a half from my outpost.

Dovchek shouted, "I told you so! I knew it! Come on, get ready, we're going out there to nail the bastards!"

Udi rushed me as I put on my utility belt, strapped my weapon across my chest, pulled my steel helmet from the shelf, and ran to the jeep after Dovchek. We squeezed all the officers into the equipment-packed jeep, and since there wasn't enough room for me, I had to sit on the radio. With Dovchek behind the wheel, the jeep flew out of the base then down a dirt road that led us across Wadi Ruqqad. Dovchek turned off the headlights and slowed down only a little, driving like someone extremely familiar with the road. When the light of the full moon was augmented by the yellow glow of flares,

Dovchek picked up speed. Red tracer bullets pierced the sky.

I thought we must be very close to the exchange of fire. A small parachute with a yellow flare slowly slalomed its way down, lighting up the sky for a few minutes before extinguishing, leaving a trail of white smoke. Just then, a thick cloud passed over the moon. In the darkness that followed, Dovchek lost sight of the road, and our jeep bounded over the guardrail of a small bridge and fell down the wadi.

I woke up a few minutes later and found myself lying on my back, still wearing my helmet. The pain in my back and hips was intense. Yellow flares continued to light the mountain slopes, and the echoing gunfire sounded close by. Any movement brought excruciating pain, and the chill of the earth seeped into my body, making me shiver. I heard loud groans, and someone whispered, "Dovchek, can you hear me? Hang on, help is on the way."

I realized that one of the young officers who had been with us in the jeep was taking care of an injured Dovchek, but I was afraid to raise my voice to call him; there might have been enemy soldiers in the area. My bladder felt like it was about to explode, but I had to contain myself. Sometime later, I heard someone approaching. I grabbed my weapon and whispered, "It's me, Uri Dolev, I'm hurt, down here in the wadi."

The young officer, whose name I didn't know, bent over to look at me. "Oh, it's you," he said. "Do you have any idea where Udi is?"

I was confused. "Where's the jeep?" I asked with effort, and a sharp pain shot through my head.

The officer leaned toward me and whispered, "I don't know. I only heard it driving off. Maybe Udi went to get help."

I lay on my back like a helpless turtle, my entire body aching. I tried to turn on my side so I could take a leak, but a paralyzing pain overwhelmed me. The firefight continued, and army vehicles quickly passed over the dirt road just a few dozen yards from where I lay on the slope of the wadi. The young officer, who feared our own forces might mistake him for the enemy, preferred running between Dovchek and me to trying to climb up the wadi to return to the road.

An hour later, the firefight was over, but the pain and cold had worsened, making my entire paralyzed body tremble. Up on the road, not far from us, a few vehicles had stopped. I distinctly heard Udi explaining, "Here, right here. The jeep drove across a small bridge, then Dovchek lost control. I think the jeep fell down the wadi. I'm not sure what happened; I was a little dazed. I found myself alone in the jeep. The engine was still running, so I drove to get help. I'm almost certain it all happened right here."

The young officer shouted from the wadi, "Udi, we're down here! We need help! Dovchek and your friend from the kibbutz are hurt, get a doctor!"

Another hour passed before a combat medic arrived. First, he treated Dovchek, who was severely injured. When he finally got to me, he asked me to move my legs. With great difficulty, and only after a strenuous effort, my toes responded. The pain was nearly unbearable.

"You're lucky, it could have ended with complete paralysis," the doctor said matter-of-factly. He cut off my pants, looked for other injuries, covered me with a blanket, and warned the soldiers standing about me, "Don't move him without my permission."

Later, I don't know when, a helicopter landed in the battlefield. The soldiers laid Dovchek and me on stretchers, carried us to the helicopter, and it took off for the Rambam Hospital in Haifa. The flight took about thirty minutes, perhaps more. I was freezing from the wind, but there weren't any extra blankets on board. I also desperately needed to empty my full bladder. I looked at the view below. There wasn't much I could see in the darkness, but I distinctly remember twin flames rising from the maws of two refinery chimneys, just like the picture of Mount Vesuvius that used to hang in our classroom.

When they were taking me out of the helicopter, something went wrong, and my stretcher dropped, hurling me onto the landing strip, where I passed out.

∗∗∗

I came to in the emergency room as they undressed me and covered my naked body with a green sheet. A large team of doctors and nurses flocked and fluttered around me, assessing my condition. From there, I was taken by an orderly down corridors flooded with white fluorescent light and brought to a room where I was transferred from the rolling bed to a stainless steel table with an X-ray camera hanging above it. A technician in a white lab coat carefully pulled the sheet from under me and said, "Don't move now, if you do, the X-rays won't come out well."

What a joker. I couldn't have moved a muscle if I were on fire. The technician adjusted the camera and left. The metal table I lay on felt very cold. A sharp pain its shot across the left side of my back. I waited a few minutes; no one came into the X-ray room. I was left by myself on the icy table. The pain wouldn't stop, my bladder was stretched to capacity, and the bright light stung my eyes. I lay naked with my eyes closed, shivering from the cold. Every muscle spasm brought more pain and my bladder was about to explode. I didn't know what time it was or how long I'd been lying there.

More time passed, and still no one came to the room. The pain in the left side of my back had become excruciating and had even made me forget my burning need to urinate. Time stretched into eternity. I had clearly been forgotten in the X-ray room. I began to scream, hoping someone would hear me. I screamed and screamed until I realized the room must have been soundproofed. I lay there in agony and tried to occupy my mind with other things. Anything besides pain and the need to urinate.

I thought of Nurit and the customary challenge for boys on the last day of ninth grade. The dare was to jump into the Jordan River from one of the highest banks — a kind of annual activity that had turned into a tradition. Only the brave would jump from a great height into the Jordan River, whose water level dropped in the summer. Not far from the Institute, the river had dug a deep, narrow ravine. In one of the river bends, the flow of the water had widened the channel, creating a kind of small pool around which the riverbanks rose to nearly twenty feet. We called that pool "the deeps of hell." At the end of the school year, Nurit urged us to uphold the tradition.

The girls and Nurit led the way, while Yehiam, Udi, and I followed after them. Udi stood first on the riverbank, and with a joyous scream, jumped without hesitation. His body hit the water with a huge splash, he dropped below the surface, then his head emerged, and he waved at us cheerfully, encouraging Yehiam and me to follow his example.

That loud goading had infuriated Yehiam, and he screamed to Udi from the bank, "Only an idiot would jump. Only stupid boys who want to make an impression."

Udi and kept urging me by flailing his hands and screaming, "Uri, jump!"

The girls stood aside, watching us and giggling. I looked at Yehiam and told him defiantly, "Cowards will always find an excuse not to jump. Those who have a pair of balls on them should jump just for the fun of it."

Yehiam glared at me and said, "Don't be an idiot, Uri. Listen to me, no one knows how deep the water is. You shouldn't be influenced by Udi's stupid screaming. Why should you take a chance? What do you need this for, anyway?"

Udi was still screaming from below, "Uri, you coward, jump, come on, let's see you already."

Nurit quietly said to one of the girls, "Uri doesn't have the guts. He just says he'll jump."

I looked down at the river then took a few steps back for momentum.

"Don't be crazy, Uri," one of the girls shouted.

"Don't worry; he's just showing off," Nurit said dismissively.

My heart pounded. I was almost frozen with fear, but I wanted to prove to Nurit that this time she was wrong, that this time I wasn't just talking. I took off with a quick run and jumped headlong from the edge of the cliff with the screams of the girls accompanying my flight all the way down until my body broke the surface of the water.

I felt nothing at first, just a hard blow to the stomach. Then an excruciating pain spread through my hip, and I was barely able to lift my head above water. A red stain appeared in the waters of the Jordan River and began to spread. An old, rusted angle iron embedded in the bottom of the river had torn a four-inch gash into my hip. With great difficulty, I swam toward the bank but was swept away by the swift current. Finally, after a strenuous effort accompanied by unbearable pain, I got close enough to the bank to grab a tree branch and dragged myself out of the water. I was bleeding from the cut in my side, scared out of my wits, pale as a sheet, and barely able to breathe.

I sat on the riverbank and leaned on the trunk of a large Eucalyptus tree. The blood wouldn't stop gushing from my hip, down my leg, and into the water. Udi swam over and helped me to my feet. He took my hand, and we began to slowly climb the slippery, muddy path, with Udi pulling me up as best he could. The wound would not stop bleeding, so I fisted my hand and pressed against the cut as hard as I could. The girls, who had remained on the riverbank, stood huddled together, pale and frightened, waiting for us to reach the top.

When we finally got there, I sat on the ground, looked at Nurit, and tried to act nonchalant. "It's nothing serious, just a little blood. It'll be over as soon as they bandage it."

Yehiam scolded me, "I told you so. And, for your information, rusty metal can cause an infection, you could even get tetanus."

"What's tetanus?" asked Nurit.

"Like rabies, only you die faster," answered Yehiam.

At that, the light-footed Udi quickly ran to get a doctor. The entire gang accompanied me to the Institute clinic. Shivering, I sat on a bench next to the clinic door. I continued to press my fist into my side as hard as I could to stop the bleeding. Dr. Schmerling, the Institute doctor, rode up on his bicycle and opened the clinic for us. He took a white gown off the rack, put it on over his clothes, and ushered me into the treatment room.

I lay on the examination table, and Dr. Schmerling removed my hand from the wound and examined the cut through his thick lenses. Dr. Schmerling knew many languages; Hebrew wasn't one of them. "Well… good now that you tell what happened?"

I explained how I had gotten the injury, and he got upset. "You want be Kamikaze? Well… good now… lucky. If iron get little more into stomach… you finished … kaput."

Dr. Schmerling asked Yehiam to hold down my legs. The nurse, who was still trying to catch her breath, was asked to prepare sterile instruments and to hold my hand to the bed. Then the doctor turned to me and said in a heavy German accent, "Now we stitch real good now… lots of pain… but you Kamikaze… even big hero can cry… as long as not move any, everything is good now."

He took a pair of surgeon's forceps and used them to bring the sides of the cut together. Then he tightened them and closed the wound with five metal clamps. From a special box, he took out a sterile needle and stitched the wound up without anesthetics. I lay with my body tense and my eyes closed, my head facing the wall. I trembled with pain while the stitching went on. I almost lost consciousness but kept telling myself, "Don't cry." I was afraid of what Yehiam would say and what he might tell people later.

When Dr. Schmerling finished stitching, he applied a generous layer of iodine to the wound, making me scream with uncontrollable pain for the first time since I'd landed on the angle iron. Then he placed a large Band-Aid on the cut and finished by wrapping my hip with a gauze bandage.

"Good now… almost done, but tetanus shot first." He pulled down my swimsuit and jabbed my buttocks with a syringe. "I think… you good now… tomorrow I see… good now?"

Once done, Dr. Schmerling took off his white coat and hung it on the back of the door. Then he scolded me in his broken Hebrew. "Kamikaze… what is name? You head knuckle, not good now! Only crazy people jump in water… Well, lucky that you good now… nothing in water but fish shit and people piss."

I left the clinic with a stupid, proud expression that seemed to infuriate Yehiam. "What are you smiling about? Get that stupid grin off your face. You could have killed yourself."

One day later that summer when we were at the swimming pool, Yehiam noticed that while reading the newspaper I was absentmindedly stroking the large scar that looked like a reddish crescent across my hip.

He couldn't help himself and teased me, "What are you rubbing that scar for? That's your gold medal for winning the stupid people's Olympics."

***

In the Rambam Hospital, lying unclothed on a cold stainless steel table in the X-ray room, I didn't want any medals. All I wanted was to urinate to the exclusion of all else. So, I did. I simply didn't care anymore. A pleasant warmth momentarily bathed my left leg. The sharp smell of urine filled the room, but I truly did not care. I tilted my head and watched the yellow liquid expand in puddles on the linoleum floor, tracing odd shapes. I shivered uncontrollably, and every inch of my body ached.

Time elapsed, hours perhaps, I think I must have fallen asleep or passed out. Sometime in the morning, a soldier from the women's auxiliary corps came into the X-ray room. When she saw me lying there naked, she let out a terrified scream.

I woke up and shouted at her, "Why are you standing there like a statue? Get some blankets to cover me with!" I vented all the frustration that had accumulated over the course of the night on that poor soldier's head.

She went running out, and I forced myself not to cry. I felt so ashamed that she had found me in such a miserable and helpless state. I knew that someone else might come into the X-ray room at any moment and didn't want to be seen like that. The soldier came back a minute later with a sheet and a blanket.

"I'm sorry, I had no idea there was anyone in here. I swear, I didn't see anything, really, I'm sorry," she said while covering me with a sheet.

A bony doctor with a gray beard came in soon after. "The X-ray technician thought the orderly was going to return you to the emergency room. Apparently, the orderly went on a break and must have fallen asleep. We'll transfer you to the ward now." There was a hint of an apology in his words, but no actual apology was forthcoming.

They took me back to the emergency room, and it was only around noon that they transferred me to the ward, where I was given a shot of morphine and fell asleep.

∗∗∗

One of the nurses wheeled a cart to my bed with a telephone on it. I heard Udi's voice from the receiver, "Uri, how are you doing?"

I was still sedated and couldn't manage to talk. Udi never bothered to come and visit me in the hospital. Thoughts of the accident continued to occupy my mind for a long time. I tried to understand what had happened, but all the explanations offered were far from convincing. I was angry about Udi's behavior that night. It irritated me that instead of treating us, he had left the field and driven back to base. I had always thought of Udi as a courageous man who could be counted on, but in this case, he had chosen to abandon us. That feeling grew stronger when he didn't visit me in the hospital, not even once. I was hospitalized for three weeks with a concussion. My left kidney was filled with blood, and I had hairline fractures in two vertebrae. I left the hospital in a wheelchair, and my recovery took several months. I was looking forward to an opportunity to delve deeper into this matter with Udi.

Three months later, we ran into each other in the kibbutz during the communal Friday night dinner. We made small talk while we ate, but when he started to get up from the table at the end of the meal, I blurted out, "Could you tell me what happened to you that night?"

Udi paused for a moment then said, "Uri, I need to go. Not now."

I refused to give up. "Just tell me, why did you drive back to base? Why didn't you try to find out what happened to Dovchek and me?"

Udi gave me a hostile look. "Wouldn't you have done the same thing? I got thrown out of the jeep and got hit in the head. I was confused. There was no one around. When I saw the jeep, I thought you'd left me on my own and continued to where the fighting was on foot, so I drove back to base."

"And it never crossed your mind that perhaps we were all wounded or dead?" I insisted.

Udi became furious. "Guns were blazing, flares were up in the sky. I couldn't see anyone. I thought the most sensible thing to do was get help, which was what I ended up doing. If I hadn't gone to get a doctor, Dovchek might not be alive today. Stop being a pain in the ass and leave me alone." He grabbed his tray and left without waiting for my reply.

That uneasy feeling about his conduct that night persisted, and our friendship suffered for it. I saw Udi in a different light from then on. There was a vain attitude about him that I hadn't seen before, and I was very disappointed by his response. Udi's cold reaction made me think that perhaps the army had tainted the values taught us at the kibbutz. Other kibbutz members I knew had also adopted a different set of norms once they became officers, ones that involved an egotistical and alienated approach. But I was careful to keep my opinions to myself.

***

During one of my weekends off, just before finishing my military service, I was sitting with Yehiam on the porch of the hut. Udi's behavior had continued to bother me, and I kept looking for ways to talk to Yehiam about it.

"What are your plans for after the service?" Yehiam suddenly asked me.

"Who said I was leaving the service? I'm thinking about joining the standing army," I answered.

Yehiam was holding a large kitchen knife and using it to slice a big watermelon resting in a bowl of ice. He handed me a piece, and while I bit into it, he said with contempt, "Just look at yourself. See what happens when children like you are given disproportionate power! You and Udi are both drunk with imaginary power. Both flattered by this false status. No wonder you both want to join the standing army. Uri, is this how you pictured your life? As a professional soldier?"

Yehiam's blunt words immediately put me on the defensive. "In the army, unlike the kibbutz, there are strict criteria for gauging performance. You need to carry out your tasks in the best possible way. In the kibbutz, you are appreciated if you merely work long hours.

That's all you need to do to become one of the gang — create the impression that you're working your ass off."

Yehiam took another watermelon slice and sneered. "Every asshole who graduated from officer training thinks he's God. The kibbutz has its fair share of morons who think just like you do. They urge us to do well in the army, but only a blind man wouldn't realize the army is built on a hierarchy that gives a select few an undue amount of power."

"Well," I snapped back, "it seems to me you're jealous of Udi and me for being officers."

Yehiam turned to me then stabbed the watermelon all the way to its heart. His eyes narrowed with contempt and when he spoke his voice dripped with it. "You know what, Uri, just forget it. *Yalla*, join the standing army, walk around with your shiny ranks and make an impression. Just do me a favor, don't wrap that bullshit in cellophane and a ribbon."

Yehiam pulled the knife free from the watermelon and tossed what remained of it among the bushes next to the porch.

A few weeks after that conversation, I was discharged. Yehiam had two more months to serve. On a Friday night, we sat on the porch again, drinking beer and cracking sunflower seeds.

"There's no reason for me to stay in the kibbutz," I said.

"What happened? Suddenly you're giving up that brilliant military career you couldn't stop talking about?"

My plans had gone awry. I was just another simple kibbutz member looking for a future. I poured out what remained of my beer, tossed the bottle against the trunk of a pine tree, and turned to my friend.

"I wanted to sign up for the standing army for another three years, but then it turned out the army wasn't going to honor its side of the bargain. Some stupid shit officer refused to commit to the promotion they had promised me. All my arguments fell on deaf ears, so I just drove to the induction center and got discharged. That's just the way things go in the army. The combat soldiers do all the dirty work, but the pen pushers end up making the decisions for you."

"What do you intend to do now if you're not staying in the kibbutz? How are you going to make a living in the city?" Yehiam, as always, was right. I had no plan.

"I'll find something," I said, trying to hide just how desperate I felt. "What do city people do when they get discharged? They look for a job and get by. Any idiot manages to make a living, so why can't I? Maybe I'll go south to Eilat; there's always work there."

Unlike me, Yehiam had decided to stay in the kibbutz. He needed to finish his high school diploma, and then he planned to go to the university. When I asked him how he intended to pay his tuition, he just stared at me with incomprehension and answered, "How? The kibbutz is going to pay for it. Why shouldn't it pay my tuition?"

He said that last sentence while peeing on a cactus in the garden, and added, "Have you noticed, Uri, how nicely this cactus has been growing?"

"Yeah," I answered, "but it stinks."

***

Udi joined the standing army, and shortly after, in the summer of 1970, stepped on a land mine near the Suez Canal and died. Udi was the first kibbutz member to die in the army. Kuntz told the IDF authorities not to worry about observing the religious rules of ceremony, which were alien to the secular ways of the kibbutz.

Gurnischt, the kibbutz carpenter, went to Udi's parents and told them, "Your son is going to lie in the most beautiful coffin anyone here has ever seen."

He asked his two shop employees to go home. While leaving the carpentry shop, the two heard the radio blasting classical music, loud even above the sound of the industrial saw. He built Udi a coffin made of pinewood with a beechwood lid. Gurnischt, who had always treated Udi like a son, lovingly polished and varnished the coffin. When he was finished, Gurnischt took the thick carpenter's pencil tucked behind his ear and wrote in clumsy letters a note for his sister, whom he had lost in the Holocaust: "Dear sister, I am sending you, to heaven, one of our finest young men. He fell while protecting this country, a loving son and a brave soldier. Take him into your bosom. I loved him just as I loved you." He signed his name and placed the note in the coffin.

The bereft father, Menahem Ganani, noticed the envelope poking from the coffin, read the note inside, and decided to leave it there out of respect for his friend. The story of that note quickly spread throughout the kibbutz.

The funeral at the kibbutz cemetery was attended by the IDF southern command chief, Dovchek, and Udi's army friends. The southern command chief spoke of determination and courage, about Udi's extraordinary self-sacrifice and the brilliant military career that had awaited him. Poetry was then read, accompanied by the live music of a cello and a flute. My uncle Kuntz was next to speak. "Rina and Menahem, my friends, we, your kibbutz brothers and sisters will surround you with love. The kibbutz will carry on the memory of your fallen son. Udi was a son to us all." Thus, Kuntz eulogized Udi and seemed to prophesy the grief that was about to visit his own house.

Six officers wearing red berets carried Udi's coffin to the grave, his brother placed on it the medal Udi won for his first marathon, the kibbutz youths covered the coffin with black soil, and were then joined by Gurnischt, who had arrived at the cemetery with a hoe he'd brought from home. Even once the hole was filled, Gurnischt continued to carefully groom the earth until the mound was a precise rectangle. A white wood slab was lodged in the fresh burial mound, bearing the words: "Lieutenant Udi Ganani, son of Menahem and Rina, fell in battle by the Suez Canal." Major Dovchek, in a starched uniform, took a large piece of steel shrapnel from his backpack, set it on the mound, and said, "He was a man among men, pity that he had to go like that…"

Yehiam snorted in my ear. "Udi was always eager to be first. Here, people rush headlong first and stop to ask questions later."

I remembered going with Udi to borrow a book from the library once. We couldn't decide which book to borrow. The librarian, Rina, Udi's mother, told us, "There's one shelf in this library that we could do without, the memorial bookshelf. I can't recall a single time someone has asked to borrow a memorial book or booklet." Now, Rina would walk around the library knowing that the shunned shelf would bear Udi's memorial book as well, like an unturned stone.

I told Yehiam, "Without Udi, our triangle is gone."

He nodded and we stood, silent. A company of soldiers fired several salute salvos, the kibbutz members wrinkled their noses with distaste as the military cantor sang "*El Malei Rachamim*," and Menahem Ganani, instead of saying the Kaddish, simply whispered an old German nursery rhyme about a rider who fell off his horse:

Hoppe, hoppe, Reiter
Wenn er fällt, dann schreit er
Fällt er in den Graben
Fressen ihn die Raben
Fällt er in den Sumpf
Macht der Reiter plumps!

3

After my discharge, I packed a small backpack and bid my parents farewell. I walked to the kibbutz gate and caught a ride to Rosh Pina. That same night I arrived in the city of Eilat, the southernmost tip of the country. I slept on the beach and the following morning found a temporary job cleaning oil tankers docking at the port. I joined a small team of ex-kibbutz members who had all answered an ad promising high wages and a place to stay.

The contractor employing us distributed yellow coveralls reeking of gasoline and sweat, handed out iron brushes with long handles, and said, "It's a very simple job. Start by cleaning the lamp covers, so you can see what you're doing — it will take you about a week to clean the inside of the tanker. Finish earlier and it's your gain. The tanker docks here for eight days before going back to sea. Any questions? No? Get to it, then!"

We descended stairs leading to the belly of the ship and were welcomed by a murky yellowish light and a terrible stench of fuel oil that got worse the farther down we went. The stuffy air was still, and once my eyes adapted to the darkness, I saw a vast space divided into numerous storage rooms. The smell was unbearable, and I sweated heavily beneath the coveralls. I breathed in the poisoned air and took comfort from the fact that there was good money to be made on this job. We were given a thirty-minute break every two hours.

Each time we emerged from the belly of the tanker, we were required to drink lots of milk to cleanse our lungs. I hated that job from day one but was able to save much more than I had expected. Each day brought me closer to my goal — going abroad.

***

Toward the end of 1970, I left Israel to see the world. I began the European leg of my trip in Sweden, hoping to meet up with Nurit in Stockholm. Before my flight, her father had given me her telephone number. I called her from the airport, and she immediately suggested I come stay with her. Five years had passed since she left Mishmar Hatsafon, and we had not spoken since. I was a stranger invading the home of a young woman who was part of the local scene.

I hardly recognized her when I walked into her small apartment. She was skinnier than I remembered, her black hair was much longer—a single strand was dyed red—and she wore a pair of flower-embroidered jeans and a white Indian fabric shirt exposing a shoulder bearing a tiny winged Little Prince tattoo. There was this air of sex, drugs, and rock and roll about her. Nurit spoke to me in a medley of languages—Hebrew, English, and Swedish—spouted contemporary wisdoms, and demonstrated a hippie "make love not war" detached attitude about Israel in general and the kibbutzim in particular. She had divorced the Swedish volunteer shortly after their wedding. Their marriage allowed her to legally reside in Sweden.

Nurit's studio apartment was decorated with Janis Joplin and Jimmie Hendrix posters. Over her bed hung a *Jesus Christ Superstar* poster. When she caught me looking at it, Nurit told me, "There's something good about Christianity. I went to church a couple of times and felt safe and comfortable there. The music during mass deeply moved me; I even cried. I thought I might give up on the Jewish religion altogether."

On the first evening of my visit, Nurit took me to meet some of her friends. There were about twenty young people in the apartment, all drinking alcohol and speaking Swedish. I couldn't understand a word, of course. I sat apart from everyone, growing weary as Nurit bounded from friend to friend without sparing me a single moment. One of the guys handed me a glass of whiskey. I learned from him that I was at a gathering of the local socialist party members in anticipation of the Swedish general elections.

Nurit continued to make constant rounds among her friends and seemed to have forgotten all about me. This was not at all what I'd expected. I'd flown all the way to Sweden to meet her, and she had absolutely no interest in me. I waited for the evening to end, feeling worthless. I slowly sipped an unfamiliar alcoholic beverage, my anger at her welling up inside. Just before midnight, she sat down next to me, drunk, and wrapped her arm around my shoulder. "Come, Uri, we're leaving. We have a ride back home."

Glad for the opportunity to finally spend some time alone with her, I got into the back seat. The guy behind the wheel talked to Nurit in Swedish the entire ride. When the car stopped at her place, she turned around and handed me a key to her apartment. "Make yourself at home, I put some sheets on the sofa. See you in the morning."

I muttered a good night, closed the car door, and they drove off.

Nurit's apartment contained a dense assortment of items: a double bed in the corner with a drape around it, a tiny kitchenette, a couch, a coffee table, an armchair, and two wooden ladder-back chairs. A large light bulb covered by a red shade dangled from the ceiling, spreading vaguely pink illumination. A record player was on a low shelf with a long row of records next to it. The other shelves were populated by books, mainly in Hebrew. I examined the books and picked up *Hemo, King of Jerusalem* by Yoram Kaniuk. I lay on the sofa and began to read. But I found myself reading the same sentence over and over. All the expectations I'd had for my meeting with

Nurit had melted into thin air. *She has a life of her own*, I excused her behavior to myself. Her kind treatment of me was nothing more than good hospitality.

Just before morning, Nurit came back drunk and agitated. She opened the kitchen cabinet, took out a bottle, and poured herself a glass of whiskey. Then she sat on the couch, crossed her long legs, and said, "All guys are the same. All they care about is fucking. I'm sick and tired of getting up every morning next to a lump of meat for whom I have absolutely no feeling. Lately, it's happening to me way too often."

She took a large swallow, stood, and began to pace about the apartment, huffing and grumbling. "In Sweden, no one makes a big deal out of it."

She stared at me as if I'd made some objection. "What are you not getting? Smoking pot or screwing isn't a big deal here. In Israel, sex is an obscenity, and smoking hashish is criminal. Just like in the Middle Ages."

She took a blanket out of the closet and tossed it in my direction. "For you. It's freezing outside."

She turned on the radio, which instantly blasted loud rock music, went into the bathroom and emerged without her pants. She tossed her shirt onto the chair and continued to undress. I was completely invisible to her. Finally, wearing nothing but her panties, she sat on her bed without even trying to conceal her bare breasts.

She continued to drink, her body slowly swaying to the music. When she noticed me staring at her, she hissed contemptuously, "What are you staring at? Haven't you seen a naked woman before?"

She kept her eyes on me and casually slid the whiskey glass down her chest, looking like she enjoyed embarrassing me. Abruptly, she pulled the blanket up to cover herself.

"This isn't your fault, Uri, I'm just venting. Everything has gone wrong for me today, and I'm in a shitty mood. Come, spoil me. Lie next to me and hug me. Just hugs, though, no fucking; I'm too tired. Come, don't be shy."

I shifted a little but remained seated on the sofa.

"Come on," Nurit said almost gently, "we're like family. We're from the same kibbutz. Please don't be angry, I feel shitty as it is. Come cuddle with me."

I walked the few steps to her bed, hesitantly lifted the blanket, and lay next to her, careful not to touch. She wrapped her hands around my waist and pressed me against her. "You smell good," she said and gave me a kiss on the cheek.

Her skin was warm and smooth, and though I was attracted to her, I refrained from making any movement that might set her off. Finally, I gathered enough courage to draw out one hand to stroke her but found that Nurit had fallen asleep. She stretched her arms above her head and softly sighed. I stole glances at her naked body, growing increasingly uncomfortable with the strange situation. Carefully, I slipped out of bed and went to sleep on the couch.

At noon, Nurit woke up complaining. "I have a splitting headache. Too much to drink last night. I'm hitting the shower. Be a dear and make me some coffee. There's this Turkish coffee they sent me from Israel. No sugar and just a drop of milk."

She emerged from the shower wearing a white robe, water dripping from her hair to the parquet floor. She accepted the coffee cup with both hands and took pleasure in every sip. Nurit returned to being friendly and hyperactive and suggested that we tour the city together.

Outside, a winterish sun spread bright light over the world. The cold penetrated my bones while we toured the old part of Stockholm. Nurit could not stop prattling. But all traces of the previous night's behavior were gone. She was exceedingly nice in a way that deeply irritated me, and her exaggerated cheerfulness embarrassed me. Occasionally, she would hug me for no apparent reason.

Quite suddenly, she drew me to her and kissed me on the mouth. "I have to go to work. I've arranged for you to sleep at a friend's house since my apartment is not really suitable for hosting you. He'll give you your own room and make you feel more comfortable."

She handed me a note with an address and a telephone number, brushed my hair with the tips of her fingers, and said, "Meet me tonight, and we'll go out to have a drink together?"

I nodded, hoping I might solve the riddle of our estrangement. It ended up being a casual meeting, during which we discussed nothing of importance. At the end we said a lukewarm goodbye in the freezing night.

I left the next morning. To my surprise, Nurit insisted on accompanying me to the train station and waited on the platform until the train pulled away from the station. A few months later, I received a postcard from her and replied with a long letter that went unanswered.

4

At the end of September 1973, I traveled from New York to Grandma Fania's house in London.

Grandma Fania represented all the grandparents of the family. She was cast in that role simply because she was the only one who had survived the Holocaust. Back in the day, it was uncommon for kibbutz people to travel abroad unless an emergency or errand on behalf of the kibbutz movement was involved. Fania visited the kibbutz only once every few years, so for all intents and purposes, I grew up without any grandparents.

For me, London was merely a brief and temporary station before another meeting with Nurit. Three years had passed since our previous meeting, when out of the blue, I received a postcard from her. The front was a photograph of a pastoral Scandinavian landscape, and on the back it read: "Come, let's tour Lapland and have fun together." I answered the postcard with three separate letters, just in case one or two got lost in the mail. I couldn't wait to see her again, and hoped that in some paradoxical way the freezing temperatures would help thaw our relationship.

***

I purchased a charter flight ticket from London to Stockholm and had to spend a week in London waiting for the flight. The hole in my pocket and the easy availability led to the same foregone conclusion — I would spend those days in London at Grandma Fania's house. Unfortunately, I had not taken into account that Yom Kippur fell on those exact days. My grandmother was deeply pious. I declined her request to join her in the synagogue but promised I would observe the fast until the end of Yom Kippur. That was our compromise. Then the war broke out.

I was in Grandma's living room watching a rugby match between England and South Africa. The broadcast of the game was interrupted, and a newsman appeared on the television screen and announced, "Heavy fighting in the Middle East. Egyptian and Syrian army forces are attacking Israel." Following the announcement were images of Tel Aviv streets with people running to the shelters while sirens sounded in the background. The footage was repeated several times during the game, and all that time Grandma Fania was in the synagogue.

I wanted to be with Nurit, but at the same time I wanted to get back to Israel and take part in the war. The BBC correspondents reported that the Egyptians and the Syrians were advancing and headed toward a complete conquest of Israel. I could not believe it. I estimated the war would end in a few days with the Arabs' complete defeat. I had missed the Six-Day War, having been drafted after it was over. I was still hungry, despite the news of battles in Sinai and the Golan Heights, but I had promised Grandma Fania I would observe the fast, and I lived up to my promise.

I did not get much sleep that night. I knew there was no chance I could get a refund for the ticket to Stockholm, which I had bought with the last of my money.

In my wallet, I kept a picture of fifteen-year-old Nurit playing the violin. Etched in my mind though was her boyish figure on the day I had last seen her: standing on the Stockholm train station platform, wearing a pair of jeans, wrapped in a sheepskin coat, and waving. I wasn't sure, but I thought I saw her wiping a tear as the train had started moving. That ghostly tear supported my positive outlook regarding a possible future with her, fueling my hope of finally having some sort of meaningful relationship. I'd believed this time we might find our way to each other. I missed her and had hoped this time we would end up together, just me and her. In London, holding that ticket to Stockholm in my hand, I was brimming with excitement. I was so close to fulfilling my dream. Then the war broke out, and all my plans went awry.

I was faced with a difficult decision: miss out on the action or give up on the idea of meeting Nurit again. The dilemma gave me no rest, but deep inside I knew what I had to do.

***

It was a Sunday morning, and the London streets were empty. The city woke up lazily on its day of rest. I looked for information, but all the Israeli establishments in London were closed. I drove to Hyde Park Corner. All the world's would-be saviors, fame cravers, and plain madmen regularly gathered there, hoping to impress accidental tourists with their rhetoric. As I expected, most of the speakers that day were Jews and Arabs.

A large group was gathered around a Jew wearing a black yarmulke. "Soon the desert dunes will be covered with mountains of shoes. Have the Egyptians forgotten the Six-Day War? Anwar Sadat feels like a big hero right now, but just you wait and see; the Egyptian soldiers will roam the Sinai desert like stray dogs. They will crawl under the burnt skeletons of their vehicles in the hope of finding a single drop of water."

A man with a traditional kaffiyeh wrapped around his neck stood on a nearby wooden bench and cried out in a hoarse voice, "With

Allah's aid we have claimed back Sinai and Quneitra, *Allahu Akbar,* *Allahu Akbar.* The Jewish occupation army flees in fear from our hero soldiers and runs straight into the sea."

A young Israeli man I met among those assembled around the speakers told me there was a single flight to Israel scheduled for the next day, and it still had some available seats. I packed that evening. When she saw me with my backpack, Grandma Fania stood with her back to the front door.

"Uri'le, don't be a *meshuggeneh.*" In English mixed with German and Yiddish and peppered with bits of Hebrew, she begged, "You mustn't go. It's safe here, and this is what your mother and father should be doing too, take Yoram and run away from Israel."

I promised Fania I would take care of myself, then I kissed her forehead, and went to the airport. That night I slept on a bench next to the El Al desk.

The following day, an available seat was indeed found for me on the sole flight leaving for Israel. I dropped the few coins I had left into a pay phone and dialed Nurit's number in Stockholm. I wanted to let her know I was going back to Israel and that she shouldn't wait for me. I also wanted to hear her voice. The telephone rang and rang without an answer. The time to board my flight drew nearer and nearer, and I still couldn't reach Nurit. During the final minutes before boarding, I relentlessly dialed and redialed, hoping Nurit might return to her apartment and hear the telephone.

The last call for passengers for the flight to Tel Aviv echoed in the hall. The last of my money had been swallowed by the pay phone. I pounded the device angrily with my fist, cursing my misfortune before giving up. I ran down the corridor and arrived at the boarding gate out of breath. Miserable, I handed the boarding pass to the gate attendant, hoping Nurit would realize it was the war that had made me cancel my plans to meet her. The captain asked us to lower the window shades and congratulated those returning to the Holy Land.

When we landed at 3:00 a.m., the airport was dark and desolate, and no customs inspections were done. I was angry at myself for not taking advantage of the opportunity to smuggle some cigarettes in my suitcase. I had used up all my time before the flight in my futile attempt to call Nurit, and there'd been no time left for shopping.

The airport was under blackout because of the war and empty. No public buses or even taxis were available. I ended up catching a ride to the Arlozorov train station with a private car that came to pick up one of the passengers. The streetlights were off, the buildings were all dark, and the roads were nearly deserted. Arranging my luggage around me, I took a nap on one of the station benches. At the crack of dawn, I stood on the road until I caught a ride to my reserve unit headquarters near the Qastina intersection. When I arrived at the base at noon, I found out my unit had already left for Sinai. I put on some jeans, a red-and-blue plaid flannel shirt, and a pair of Converse All Star sneakers I'd bought in Rome. The military base's Shekem kiosk was closed, but I was able to find the vendor. For the five pounds I had miraculously found in my wallet, he agreed to sell me officer's ranks and a pack of chocolate wafers. From the Qastina camp, I continued to thumb rides. Wartime made drivers feel generous, and I easily hitched my way to the Kerem Shalom kibbutz. From there, I called Mishmar Hatsafon. Max Gurnischt, who was on duty in the dining hall, picked up the telephone — there were only two phones in the kibbutz, the second one was in the administration office.

"It's me, Uri Dolev," I said. "I'm back from abroad."

"For the war?" asked Gurnischt.

"Yes, the war. I'm on my way to Sinai. Tell my parents I'm back and that I'm fine, and they shouldn't worry."

Gurnischt was silent for a moment, then he said, "Goddamn those anti-Semites, we need to teach them a lesson they'll never forget."

"Don't worry, Max," I answered, "we'll teach them a lesson."

5

I was still looking for a way to get to the front. There was a road grader by the Kerem Shalom gate. The reservist driving the machine had been summoned to clear some roads, but the clumsy vehicle was so slow he had lost the rest of his convoy. He stood helplessly by the grader, which looked like a yellow grasshopper with oversized arms.

I suggested to the reservist that I join him in chasing the lost convoy. He was more than happy to have me accompany him on the grader but was disappointed that I had no weapon. I sat on the fender of the large wheel, and we set out. After what felt like two years of riding on top of the grader wing down a bumpy road, my backside was burning with pain. As night fell, against all logic, the driver increased his speed, convinced that going faster would reduce the risks. I held on to the wing of the wheel as best I could, already imagining the headlines: "First Lieutenant Uri Dolev from Kibbutz Mishmar Hatsafon Fell from a Road Grader and Perished in the Line of Duty." We drove along Lake Bardawil and reached the Baluza military base just before midnight.

***

I'd had an exhausting twenty-four hours getting from London to the Sinai desert. I was tired and hungry when an Egyptian bombardment served as my welcome to Baluza. The grader driver stopped and ran to find cover. I wasn't bothered by the sparse shelling and looked for a good place to sleep. The storage room of the base's abandoned dining room served all my needs. I ate some canned food and fell asleep on two rice sacks that molded themselves to the shape of my body.

I slept for several hours. It was still dark when I was woken up by the loud blast of a shell falling close by. My rear end was still painful, and my entire body was sore from sleeping on the rice. I left the storage room, and an officer I chanced to meet told me that my division was south of there, in the area of Tasa, by the central section of the Suez Canal. With the first light of dawn, I tried to hitch a ride on the cross Sinai road. Following two nights of driving without an opportunity to bathe, I was undoubtedly the strangest hitchhiker in the wilderness: long, curly hair that fell down to my shoulders, several days' worth of stubble, backpack on my back, a camera empty of film, a pack of Marlboro cigarettes, a small book of Alterman poetry, and lots of chocolate wafers.

***

A military bus with the following words painted on its side: "Torah and Tradition — The Military Rabbinate" stopped beside me. The driver poked his head out the window and asked my destination. I boarded the bus. There was a sergeant-major-ranked rabbi sitting in the front seat. The rest of the passengers were religiously observant reservists called up for duty.

"Where are you headed?" I asked.

The rabbi tugged on his long beard and scratched his head under a broad-brimmed green hat. He untangled his thick beard from the hat's chin cord and answered me in long, convoluted sentences.

"All the kosher food supervisors here have been drafted per order of the chief military rabbi. We have a task of the utmost importance to perform — by tomorrow, we need to prepare the kitchens of the armored division, which I have been seeking for many hours."

The rabbi spread a large map on his knees. "I don't know where we are or where the division is. They are supposed to be somewhere in this area," he said, pointing at the map, "between Baluza and Tasa. God willing, we will find them. Perhaps you could help us?"

I handed my officer ID to the rabbi and said in a whisper, "I need you to get me to Tasa, to the division command headquarters."

The rabbi inspected my ID, stroked his beard, and didn't reply.

I faced the yarmulke-wearing passengers. "Listen, I am an IDF officer, and I have an urgent task to carry out. This bus needs to go to Tasa now. Once I reach the division headquarters, you will be able to continue with your own important task."

The sergeant major surrendered and vacated the front seat for me. My takeover was successfully completed. The kosher food supervisors obediently accepted my authority and returned to reading their psalms. The bus drove off, and I found myself sitting in the front seat of a rabbinate bus, a hippy kibbutz member.

I ordered the driver to drive as fast as possible to the Tasa military base, where I instructed my own private religious army to remain seated and wait for me while I went to look for the commando unit. On a low dune in front of the base basketball court, I was confronted with an unusual sight. Major General Ariel Sharon, his oversized body stuffed uncomfortably into a new khaki uniform, was standing at the top of a hill giving a briefing about the course of the fighting. Hundreds of soldiers sat wide-eyed, listening. An older man walked between the rows of attentive soldiers, wearing an unkempt military uniform with blue tags on the shoulder straps: "Military Correspondent."

I went to him and asked, "Do you happen to know where the Avraham Bern division headquarters is?"

The reservist correspondent stopped the spinning reels of his tape recorder, stepped aside, and from the edge of the sandy mound pointed at the desert. "See this dune? Go back to the road and drive all the way there. Behind the dune, you will find a large armored corps encampment. Go off-road and keep driving west down the gravel road until you see the ruins of the only building in the area. Just follow the tire tracks from there. There's no other way, about… three… four kilometers, maybe… All roads lead to Rome, you'll find them."

After receiving his directions, I still hadn't the faintest idea where the Bern Division was. I returned to the bus, clapped the rabbi on the shoulder, and in an official tone told him, "Sergeant Major, the bus is under your command once more. You have done well thus far. Now be quick and drive to prepare the armored corps battalion headquarters and make it kosher."

The rabbi nodded and saluted me. "Thank you, officer," he said feebly. Then he took out a tiny book of psalms from his shirt pocket and handed it to me. "Here, for you, keep it safe, and He will keep you safe in turn."

***

I stood on the road again, a colorful blob in the desert, and waited to hitch a ride.

A patrol jeep bearing three soldiers stopped next to me. All three bellowed with laughter. It took me a moment to realize why they were laughing at me; they were soldiers from my unit. They showered my back with affectionate slaps, and I jumped up on the jeep, which crossed the desert in a straight line accompanied by a cloud of dust, all the way to the unit's gathering point. When the rest of the guys saw me getting off the jeep in civilian clothing, another wave of laughter followed.

Binder, the commando unit's chief officer, measured me with amused eyes. "Take a look at yourself, Dolev. You call yourself a soldier? Yalla, get a grip and get ready, you're in Sinai now, not Europe. Take charge of your soldiers. An hour from now we're going out to get a briefing at division headquarters."

Gidi Turner checked the pocket of his plaid flannel shirt. "Marco Polo, you good for nothing, you couldn't even get the guys some cigarettes from abroad?"

But the giddy atmosphere was abruptly interrupted when a tank about a hundred meters away started burning, and the crew ran away in a panic. After two and a half days on the road, I had finally reached the front.

★★★

The first night, I was plagued by the thought that Nurit had waited hours for me at the airport. I kept thinking she would never want to see me again. I sat on the sand, and by the faint light of the jeep's headlights I wrote her a letter of explanation and apology.

Binder was suddenly standing over me. "Dolev, get a grip. What are you doing sitting here? You just arrived two seconds ago, and you're already writing love letters? Get yourself a weapon. This is war, not junior high. I don't care if it's a pistol or an Uzi, so long as it fires. Move your ass, otherwise you're just an extra load on the jeep."

Binder got up on the jeep and told Gidi, "Yalla, let's get a move on. You guys follow me. Let's try to get Dolev a weapon from the armory. If we don't find any there, we'll try at the division headquarters."

I tucked my letter to Nurit in my shirt pocket, hoping I would find an opportunity to mail it. A dark, starless night descended over the Sinai. We couldn't find the armory tent, and Gidi told Binder, "Don't waste your time here. Go on to the briefing, we'll manage."

Gidi drove our jeep to the kitchen tent, jumped out of it, and struck a menacing pose in front of the cook on duty. Moments before, he had attached improvised paper tags to his shoulder straps bearing the words "Major General." He had cut the paper tags from the wrapper of a chocolate bar thus named, adequately distributed in our battle rations.

Major General Gidi Turner explained to the frightened cook, "We're from the special forces, give us your Uzi submachine gun, we need it for an urgent special mission."

The panicked cook looked at the fake Major General with me standing beside him in a pair of jeans, with a flowing mane of hair, and a red bandana wrapped around my neck. Our strange appearance must have added to the credibility of the demand. The cook handed us his weapon uncertainly. In return, Gidi gave him a note of authorization stating that his weapon had been taken for a secret mission. Gidi signed as "Major General Shmuel Gorodish." Throughout the exchange, Hatuka stood off to the side, clutching his stomach with both hands and barely suppressing his laughter. Before leaving, Hatuka went to the stunned cook, who had returned to his dishwashing, and loudly recited a sentence that would later become his motto: "Remember, soldier boy, nothing is stronger than water. Don't ever forget who taught you that, my name is Shlomi Hatuka, nothing is stronger than water."

And so, I set out for the Yom Kippur War equipped with an Uzi submachine gun and two magazines of bullets.

6

We took up position in a dugout shelter to camp for the night. We still did not really feel the war. The sun slowly sank in the desert, and in the dim remaining light we saw a few unidentified figures marching in the sand toward us. Three, we counted as they drew a little closer. We tensed for what might follow. All weapons were aimed at them. As they came even closer, we recognized them as IDF soldiers. One of them had a badly injured arm, which was tied up in a makeshift sling.

The second was sooty and barefoot, his weapon slung across his body and his eyes filled with terror. He screamed at us, "Why are you standing there staring like that? Get a doctor. There are more injured in the field." Then he lay down — possibly unconscious — on his back.

The third soldier was a pudgy man whose face was flushed and washed with perspiration from the strain of walking. He didn't utter a word, just went to the jeep, took the water jerrycan, and drank.

The cheerful atmosphere among the commando unit warriors became quickly subdued. The three armored corpsmen all belonged to the same team. Their tank had been hit by an Egyptian missile. The gunman was severely injured. They had left him in the tank and fled.

One of them, possibly their commanding officer, justified their actions. "We left him because we all would have died otherwise. There was nothing to do but run."

We drove off to see if the abandoned gunman could be rescued.

"His name is Shimon Ohana," the pudgy one shouted.

We saw the silhouette of the tank in the last vestiges of sunlight, resting in the desert, unmoving and in complete solitude. A menacing silence filled the air, and no movement could be discerned. I climbed from the jeep with my crew. Carefully and vigilantly, we advanced toward the tank. The rest of my unit lay on the ground to cover us in case we ran into enemy forces. We found the gunman dead, seated inside the tank. With great effort, we managed to extract his body and haul it onto the jeep. Hatuka quickly dismantled the tank's deck machine gun, picked up the dead soldier's weapon, then ran again to the tank to collect the combat rations. The unit regrouped for a long and silent night of reflection — death was fast coming closer and becoming more tangible.

The war continued in the morning. Jeeps etched the desert sand with tire marks resembling the feet of little insects. The desert was in a turmoil. Army units appeared only to vanish behind the yellow dunes or beyond the yellow horizon. Tanks, guns, and halftracks barreled across the field. Dense convoys of military and civilian trucks moved along the main roads.

We drove back and forth for over a week without actually changing our position. Even the enthusiasm of the combat-eager reservists had cooled off. Everyone's mood had changed upon realizing this war was far from over. The Egyptian artillery corps covered large areas with dense shelling. Egyptian warplanes attacked IDF convoys every day. The desert filled with the incessant noise of exploding artillery and gunfire. Sirens blared as ambulances rushed the injured to improvised landing strips where helicopters waited to evacuate them to the hospital. The dead were wrapped in blankets and piled aside until the bodies could be loaded onto a civilian truck headed north. During the respites we ate Spam, canned peas, and goulash. We all felt like shit.

***

Instead of the customary eight jeeps, the commando unit went out to war with the only four that could be found in the emergency warehouses. Not a one was fully equipped. Only one jeep had a deck machine gun, the one salvaged from the destroyed tank, two had no radio communication, and none were equipped with a tire iron. They had run out of flak jackets at the supply base, so we had to fight without them. Sometime later, we were joined by two ancient command cars that weren't suited to our missions. We spent most of our time aimlessly driving dozens of kilometers across the desert, back and forth. We received new operation orders every day, most of which remained unachieved or were canceled.

During the day, Egyptian shelling was sparse, but as soon as darkness fell, the artillery fire escalated. The Egyptians competent-ly targeted the division's improvised camp, so at night, the division gathered in the open spaces for protection. The rain of shells caused panic and injuries, completely extinguishing the upbeat mood of the first few days. Within a week, everyone's nerves had become frayed, and our desperation increased. We all looked forward to a turn-around, which finally happened when we received orders to cross the Suez Canal.

In preparation for the crossing, we advanced through the night and took up position near the intersection of two roads code named Spider and Hazing. We were close enough to the Egyptian side of the canal to see the palm trees growing there. The Glilim bridge stretched by the side of the road like a black centipede. While wait-ing, we endured an especially harsh shelling attack, which began in the darkness and continued long after dawn. Each of us lay quietly and alone in a ditch he had dug for himself. I stayed alert for the sound of the shell leaving the barrel of the Egyptian cannon and silently counted the twenty-four seconds until the landing.

We each responded to the nonstop shelling in different ways. Hatuka dug a deep ditch and in the morning stood inside it and began to sing Oum Kalthoum's "Enta Omri" at the top of his lungs. "Only now did I begin to love my life, only now, to fear they would run away from me…" He remained erect and singing, and only lay down mere seconds before a shell fell with an explosion. That ritual repeated itself until Kadmi told Hatuka that unless the Arabic music stopped he would start singing arias from *The Marriage of Figaro*, the only opera Kadmi knew.

The shelling continued during the day. Mitleman, one of the unit soldiers, complained of pains in his chest and severe headaches. We took advantage of a brief pause in the shelling and drove Mitleman to the nearest battalion aid station. We returned to pick him up an hour later, but Mitleman, it turned out, had needed no medical assistance. He had simply snuck inside a passing milk truck going back to Israel and deserted the front. For me, that was one of the war's hardest moments — knowing that one of my soldiers had run away and left us behind made my stomach churn.

That night when we endured another shelling attack, I buried my head in the sand and waited. Gidi crawled to me with a transistor radio and together we listened to a Joe Cocker marathon broadcast on the army radio station. The unit stationed next to ours sustained a direct hit. The screaming of the wounded mixed with the sounds of *Sheffield Steel* and "With a Little Help from My Friends."

Later, our reconnaissance unit joined Arik Sharon's division. During the night, we moved in an endless line of vehicles toward the Suez Canal to cross to the Egyptian side. We drove on the sand next to the main roads to get past the long convoys blocking the way to the canal. During the pitch-black night, the jeep bounded over a dune with only its "cat lights" on then bumped over something and came to an abrupt halt. We heard a muffled sound, like the rustle of an old engine making its final few spins before a stop. Hatuka jumped off the jeep to see what had happened and immediately burst into screams. "*Shema Yisrael*! Oh, dear God! We're sorry!"

It turned out our jeep had run over the body of one of our soldiers left in the field, and the weight of the vehicle had crushed the remaining air out of his lungs. We didn't know what to do with the body, and we were forbidden from talking on the radio because radio silence had been ordered. Kadmi reversed the jeep, cautiously getting off the dead man's stomach. We placed the body by the side of the road and stuck a marking pole in the ground beside it. We continued the drive in complete silence, each of us lost in his own thoughts.

By then we were very close to the canal and did not want to miss the crossing. The convoy of vehicles standing bumper to bumper stretched for miles. Every few minutes, we crawled a few meters forward only to come to stop again. That was how we slowly advanced toward the canal. By noon, we'd had enough, so we took some air out of the tires and began to drive down the dunes, bypassing the endless line of vehicles. Our jeep drove past a small hill, and we saw a column of infantry soldiers walking on the sand toward the Chinese Farm. The hot desert sun lashed at the equipment-laden soldiers, who quietly marched, one after the other at well-spaced intervals. Those were the paratroopers of the 890th battalion.

"Stupid," I muttered to myself, as I couldn't possibly know the bloody outcome of the Battle of the Chinese Farm.

I sought out my brother, Yoram, knowing he should be among them. Hatuka, who came from the rival Golani battalion, shouted at the paratroopers, "Fresh meat, fresh meat," and Kadmi smacked his helmet to silence him. I didn't find my brother.

✳✳✳

We crossed the canal on October 18 in Dawar-sawar. My jeep was hauled onto a *timsach* — a Gillois amphibious tank carrier — to cross the canal to the Egyptian side. When the tank carrier sailed, Hatuka cried out, "There is nothing stronger than water. There is nothing stronger than water," and everyone laughed.

"A glass of wine keeps your penis strong and fine," Kadmi retorted with a motto of his own, and a sense of euphoria settled over us. When we finally reached the Egyptian side, we broke into a cacophony of screams and howls that is almost impossible to describe.

"Nothing is stronger than water — we've won the war," Hatuka rejoiced.

The vehicles landing on the Egyptian side were being directed by a bareheaded young paratrooper brigade officer, bony and swarthy of skin. A small piece of iron shrapnel was embedded in his forehead, reaching up like a little rhinoceros horn. He stopped our jeeps with a wide smile.

"Just keep going straight until you see the next marker. Be careful, there are still some Egyptian commandos out there."

As I passed by him, I shouted, "Why haven't you taken that shrapnel out of your forehead?"

The officer flashed a white-toothed smile and answered, "I can't. It's my lucky charm. We got shelled yesterday, and one shell fell right next to me. If the shrapnel had struck a few more centimeters to one side I would have lost my eye. But this? This is nothing, it just stings a little, like my mother's hot sauce. I'm not taking it out until the end of the war."

The reconnaissance unit led the way, and the tanks were arrayed in the field, driving carefully in battle formation. Gunfire skirmishes flared up here and there as the Egyptian army retreated in a disorderly manner. Fired up by our recent successes, we broke into a military base near the town of Fayid. Hundreds of Egyptian soldiers came out to meet us, waving their weapons cheerfully in greeting. Kadmi threw the jeep into reverse, and we escaped the crowd before they realized we were Israeli soldiers.

The light jeeps hurtled across the desert toward the Jinpa Mountains. From there, we slid our way down to the outskirts of Suez City. I thought that was it, that the war was over. We stopped to rest, then over the radio I received an order to turn around and drive back to the canal, cross it, and go to the Refidim base. A convoy of armed ammunition trucks was waiting there for us to escort it across the canal. I almost refused the order. The last thing we wanted was to head back to Sinai.

The division's second-in-command stopped by my jeep and yelled at us. "Get a move on! Quickly! Go to Refidim. My tanks and cannons are driving on empty stomachs without a single shell."

Reluctantly, we began to make our way back. On the Egyptian side of the canal my jeep boarded the tank carrier, and the timsach motored back toward Sinai. When the carrier was in the middle of the Suez Canal, brown Egyptian helicopters emerged from the east and dropped barrels of burning gasoline into the water. Two Israeli warplanes appeared on the horizon, reduced altitude, and launched missiles at the enemy choppers. The helicopters smashed into bits, which scattered in every direction. The Suez Canal was lip up with flames. In the heat of battle, the helmsmen abandoned their positions, and our giant tank carrier began to drift with the slow current of the burning canal.

Hatuka stood up on the deck firing futile volleys at the sky and screaming, "Like I told you, nothing is stronger than water!"

"Shut up already!" I shouted, but he continued firing into the air and screaming, "Nothing is stronger than water" like a man possessed.

The helmsmen regained control of the carrier, and it clung to the wall of the canal in the crossing area, appropriately called Dawar-Sawar — Death's Backyard. We were welcomed by massive volleys of Katyusha rockets and precise shelling. We cowered in our jeep as Kadmi carefully drove it off the carrier, continued for a few meters, then stopped. We jumped out and threw ourselves on the sand beside a truck. I flattened myself on the ground, buried my head in the sand, and hoped for the best. The shells continued to explode, and the moments between barrages were filled with the screaming of the wounded. We lay in the besieged terrain for about an hour, and all that time Hatuka went on like a broken record: "Nothing is stronger than water. Nothing is stronger than water."

In one of the longer breaks between shelling onslaughts, Gidi Turner shouted to me, "We need to get out of here. It's now or never."

I got up from the sand and screamed at Kadmi and Hatuka, "Let's go. Everyone up on the jeep. We're getting the hell out of here."

The jeep's radio antenna had been cut in two, and the sides of the vehicle were riddled with ugly tears inflicted by flying metal. Kadmi, a mechanical engineer in his civilian life, jammed the gas pedal to the floor and honked for Hatuka to hurry up. The jeep bounded forward, leapt across the hills of the dune, jumped over wadis and additional obstacles leaving a trail of dust behind it until we finally escaped the shelling. Not long after, we found out that the truck we'd sheltered under was loaded with ammunition — one direct hit would have spelled our doom.

***

We reached the Refidim base in the early evening. A mere half hour from the Suez Canal, it seemed like the war did not even exist. Kadmi turned off the jeep's engine, and I immediately heard music and singing voices. I moved closer and saw the most surreal scene. An accordionist with a goatee was sitting in the center of the dining room surrounded by a circle of men and women dancing merrily, oblivious to the battle raging just a few dozen kilometers away.

We went to the Shekem kiosk to get an army hamburger. We stood in the long line — Gidi, Kadmi, Hatuka, and I — exhausted and filthy after ten days of combat without a drop of water to clean ourselves with. Our uniforms gave off a foul stench made up of perspiration and gun oil. We were unshaven, our faces caked with a thick coating of sand and dust.

Gidi angrily turned to the pencil pusher behind the counter. "Hurry up, we don't have time for this, we need to get back to the Egyptian side!"

The Shekem vendor took the abuse in stride. "You guys want me to actually fry your burgers, or do you prefer your meat raw?"

We didn't laugh. Kadmi climbed on the counter and nearly throttled the guy.

***

In one of the offices, we asked the secretary if we could call home. She shook her head and continued smoking her cigarette.

Hatuka pleaded with her, "Come on, soldier girl, just a quick call, I swear to God. Just to tell my mom that I'm fine. Just connect me to the operator, will you?"

The secretary puckered her lips and blew smoke rings in Hatuka's face, then tapped the ashes of her cigarette onto the floor and stood her ground. "Just look at yourself, your uniform is disgusting, and you stink! Is that any way to be coming into my office? And besides, you know the rules, this is war — no private calls. Don't you understand plain Hebrew?"

Kadmi exploded again, and Gidi held him back. Hatuka came to me and said, "Dolev, come on, you're an officer, talk to the stupid cow."

I pulled Hatuka back to the jeep, and we returned to the canal. In Refidim, it seemed, the war was already over.

***

We crossed the canal again that night. We immediately felt the momentum of the war was on our side. Over the next few days, the Egyptian army camps emptied, and the Egyptian soldiers traipsed around without a shepherd. All that was left in the field were traces of battles that had taken place just a few hours earlier. On one of the Fayid airport runways, an IDF jeep that had been hit by a Stinger missile stood smoking.

We drove on to the city of Suez. The battle over that city had claimed many casualties. We drove carefully through the burning metropolis and stopped at the port. We sought cover from the Egyptian snipers firing from the tall buildings. Later, we joined the armored divisions surrounding the Egyptian Third Army. Our unit took up positions on a small hill overlooking the Third Army soldiers on the other side of the canal. Just after dark, three Egyptian soldiers swam across the canal from Sinai, hoping to join the retreating Egyptian army. The three were shot at close range.

Toward dawn, a pack of stray dogs arrived and began to eat the corpses. We tried to chase them away, but they were relentless and kept coming back. It was another typical October heat wave. We were sweating profusely, and the hot wind carried the terrible stench of putrefaction and sunbaked corpses. I leaned against the jeep and vomited, despite it having been hours since we had eaten. Gidi became furious and started shooting at the dogs. They scattered but ten minutes later returned to the corpses, bloated under the furious sun, and continued to tear at them.

Gidi was the first to give in to his hunger despite the disgusting circumstances. He listlessly took tin cans of goulash and peas from the jeep, sat on the sand, and opened them. Hatuka hesitated, muttered the proper blessing, and dug his spoon deep into the goulash. Gidi came to me with an open can. My nausea worsened.

"How can you eat with that stench?" I asked.

Gidi gave me a bemused look, stuffed a spoonful of meat into his mouth, and spoke to me while chewing. "Marco Polo, this isn't America, it's the Middle East, get used to it. You eat what you can, when you can. Try it, it won't kill you."

***

The cease-fire went into effect, and we were sitting pretty much idle near the Fayid airport on the Egyptian side of the Suez Canal. We'd had two quiet days of relaxation. In the morning, we got word of a driver who went into an Egyptian bunker to loot it and was shot by the Egyptian soldiers hiding there. His friend had come running to us for help. Binder, the unit commanding officer, decided there was no reason for us to risk our hides for some pen pusher out seeking souvenirs. We called for a doctor with a full set of medical equipment to come with us then carefully made our preparations. We knew we had to finish the extraction before dark or risk firing at our own forces in the area.

Kadmi suggested to Binder, "Let's use our prisoners. Why should we risk ourselves? Let's get a few fucking Egyptians into the bunker and have them bring out our injured guy."

Binder deliberated briefly then agreed. Hatuka and Gidi joined Kadmi, and they went to look for candidates among the dozens of Egyptian soldiers tramping the desert in search of water. A short time later, the jeep returned with Gidi, Hatuka, and Kadmi cheering like schoolboys. Two Egyptian soldiers were sitting tied up on the hood.

"We brought two. We could have brought thousands; they're

everywhere," Kadmi announced.

The two prisoners, downcast and humiliated, were pulled off the jeep to sit on the sand. The unit soldiers surrounded them. One was tall, bony, bearded, and bald. The other one was short with a hefty potbelly; he clung to the jeep while his eyes darted around anxiously. Gidi, in broken Arabic, tried to explain to the two prisoners that they must go into the bunker and bring out the wounded Israeli soldier. Gidi's lame Arabic gave us all a good laugh, especially Hatuka, who spoke fluent Arabic. He particularly enjoyed letting Gidi twist his tongue up with his awful high school Arabic. The timid prisoners sat frightened on the sand staring blankly at Gidi.

Binder lost his patience and screamed at Hatuka, "Come on, tell them to start moving their asses."

Hatuka burst into a series of screams accompanied by plenty of urgent gestures. "Yalla, get up! Go into the bunker and bring out the Israeli soldier. Tell all the Egyptians inside to come out and surrender!"

The tall prisoner, upon realizing what was demanded of him, started crying and pleading with Hatuka to take pity on him.

Kadmi raised his rifle and directed the barrel straight at the taller prisoner's head. "*Uskut, ya ibn kalb*," he ordered him. Be quiet, you son of a dog. Then he added, "Asshole! *Ruh min hon!*" and pointed at the bunker entrance. The skinny soldier began to walk on faltering legs toward the bunker while keeping an eye on the barrel of Kadmi's rifle. Before disappearing into the depths of the bunker, he began to scream, hoping the Egyptians in the bunker wouldn't open fire on him. "*Ana masri! Ana masri!*" I'm an Egyptian!

We lay down around the bunker opening and waited tensely with our weapons at the ready. The prisoner emerged first, his hands high in the air above his bald head. An Egyptian soldier slowly followed, dressed in a camouflage commando uniform. They stood by the bunker with their hands raised, waiting for instructions. We thought that was it, but another Egyptian soldier suddenly emerged from the bunker. He threw himself to the sand and began firing an Uzi submachine gun with great sweeping motions. Within seconds, the desert filled with the deafening sound of automatic weapons as our men returned fire.

The shooting continued for some time, until Binder raised his weapon in the air like a conductor's baton and silenced the orchestra. The clouds of dust slowly began to disperse. On the sandy mound by the bunker, lay the three Egyptian soldiers. We saw a slow and cautious movement as the tall prisoner stood with his hands high in the air. His pants were wet front and back, as he'd lost control of his bladder and bowels, his clothes were caked with dust, and his white beard was full of sand. With the slow movements of a man resigned to his fate, he dropped his hands and lowered his head, waiting for the bullet that would strike the back of his neck. All the while, he continued to whimper pathetically. Seeing his miserable state, even Kadmi had a little sympathy for him.

"You guys are worthless," Binder shouted. "You've shot a million bullets, and not even one hit him. This Egyptian is one lucky dog."

The body of the Israeli soldier was taken out of the bunker. All the combat medic could do was pronounce his death. Hatuka took a pair of dry IDF pants from his backpack and handed them to the trembling bald prisoner. The pants were much too short for him, and he looked ridiculous. Hatuka gave the man a canteen and tried to calm him down in his bizarre Arabic as he led him to the back seat of the jeep and apologized while Kadmi cuffed his hands. I remained in the field with another reconnaissance officer, waiting for an evacuation vehicle to come for the dead Israeli soldier. The body of the Egyptian officer who had fired at us lay near the opening to the bunker. The Egyptian commando was sprawled beside him, still alive despite a severe injury. He lay on his back, a large bloodstain spreading on his shirt, breathing heavily and apparently unconscious. I took the military ID card out of his sticky shirt pocket; between the pages was a family picture of a wife and two small children against the background of the pyramids.

The reconnaissance officer with me did not utter a word, he simply took his pistol from its holster and fired a single shot at the injured man's carotid artery, as if shooting a horse that had broken its leg. "He's done for, zero chance of survival," he dryly commented as he slowly placed the pistol back in its holster. "That's just the way it goes. War gets dirty whether you like it or not."

A trickle of blood oozed steadily from the soldier's neck and stubbornly refused to be absorbed by the sand. The thin drizzle coursed its way to create a spreading red fan, rivulets that entwined together to form a braid of blood resting on the golden sand.

7

My cousin Moti died during the retaking of Mount Hermon. Four days later, Yoel Harduf, son of Yael, our former nanny, died as well. The deaths came as a great shock to the members of Mishmar Hatsafon. My brother, Yoram, was severely injured on the Egyptian front. All these bad tidings were late reaching me; I heard them only after the war was over.

My unit was stationed close to the town of Fayid in Egypt, where I waited impatiently to go home. In a parcel my parents sent me I found the kibbutz newsletter. It was full of items about the deep grief that had claimed the kibbutz. Rina, Udi's bereaved mother, wrote:

Strong gusts of Sharqiya wind washed over the kibbutz on October 17, 1973. The easterly wind brought hot air that flew down the slopes of the Bashan Mountains, raising clouds of dust that stung the eyes and made it almost impossible to breathe. The Sharqiya painted the air with shades of gray and brown, made the bushes bow their branches, struck at the shutters, ruffled the hair, grated every rusty hinge. A wild gust, singing a tune all its own through the tops of the trees, gathered clusters of thorns, then rolled and swirled them in the air. Currents of hot air disturbed the trash remains lying in neglected corners and whipped the tree trunks and the walls of the houses.

The Sharqiya moved things that had rested in the same place for many years, blew newspapers into the air, breathed momentary life into old plastic bags, and scattered dust and leaves that dirtied Mishmar Hatsafon. A whirlwind of dust spun across the kibbutz until it was finally blocked by the dining hall's wall. Right then, a military command car stopped by the kitchen ramp. A male reserve officer and a female soldier emerged from the vehicle. The Sharqiya lashed hot, humid air at them. The officer and the soldier struggled against the wind and stepped into the dining hall as fast as they could. They asked the kitchen supervisor on call about the kibbutz secretary and where the Kotzer family lived.

***

Later, my mother told me the events from her point of view. "I was standing at the apartment complex's access path with a broom and dustpan to clear the dirt the Sharqiya had piled up. Shmulik Finklestein, his hair a mess from the wind, approached me accompanied by the officer and the soldier. When I saw Shmulik, my heart froze in my chest. A day earlier, Grandma Fania had called from London sounding concerned. She'd read in the *Jewish Chronicle* an item about a soldier named Uri who had fallen in combat. Your father sent a telegram to her house: 'Everything is fine with us. There is nothing to worry about.' When Shmulik drew closer, I had a very bad feeling, and I thought that Dad's unemotional attitude wouldn't help this time. Shmulik, his face ashen, placed a single hand over his head to try and contain his hair, which raged in the wind. 'You're the kibbutz nurse and a relative as well. Come with me to Henka and Kuntz.'

"I am ashamed to tell you, Uri, that I was relieved it wasn't you. I burst into tears of joy and deep grief. The small delegation marched on to the apartment and stopped at the Kotzer family's door. Shmulik knocked reluctantly. Henka opened the door wearing a robe. There was this brief moment of uncertainty, and then Henka..." My mother's voice cracked. "It was terrible, as you can imagine. Kuntz came running from the shower, his hair wet, wearing nothing but a pair of gray underwear and holding a towel in his hand. The officer, who was probably accustomed to such situations, went in room first, and Shmulik and I followed. He gave Henka and Kuntz the news in a dry voice, something like, 'The IDF bows its head with grief,' and that 'Moti was killed yesterday in the battle for retaking Mount Hermon.' The officer told them Moti had been temporarily buried in a cemetery next to Kibbutz Lohamei HaGeta'ot."

My mother told me Henka collapsed on the sofa in their small living room. "Kuntz dropped the towel and just stood there in the middle of the living room in his gray underwear. Then he came to his senses and bent over Henka, hugging her and stroking her hair. Shmulik, an Auschwitz survivor, who had lost his eldest son a few years earlier, remained focused. He immediately took charge and brought Kuntz a pair of pants and a shirt from the closet. While Kuntz got dressed, Shmulik tried to calm Henka, who had rested her head on my shoulder and would not stop crying. The officer and the soldier finished their duty as fast as they could and left for their next assignment.

"I don't envy them," my mother told me.

***

The news quickly spread throughout Mishmar Hatsafon. Moti Kotzer was only nineteen, in the middle of his active service. Haya came home from Givatayim.

I tried to picture my father's reaction. The brothers rarely spoke to each other. I imagined my father entering Henka and Kuntz's home unsure about what to do. Did he hug Kuntz? Did the brothers find the emotional strength to get over the ancient falling out between them?

Rina Ganani signed off her piece in the kibbutz newsletter:

My Udi was killed three years ago. Back then, I thought we had had our fill of disaster. Today, Udi was joined by two sons, Moti Kotzer and Yoel Harduf, both honest and possessed of beautiful souls. They died while battling to defend their homeland. The kibbutz is overwhelmed with sorrow at their passing.

In the evening, the Sharqiya ceased in the same way it had come, abruptly. In its absence, the air turned murky and nearly unbreathable, and the sorrow was unbearable. The trees in the kibbutz farm lowered their heads, and the dust in the air refused to scatter. All work in the kibbutz ceased. At night, a rain began to fall, bringing with it the hope of recovery and regeneration.

***

Many days later, I received the long-yearned-for approval for a few days' leave. I slept on the bus for most of the drive from Fayid to Jerusalem. With a heavy heart I walked down the corridors of the Hadassah Hospital. In the orthopedic department I found my brother bearded and scrawny. Yoram welcomed me with a wide smile that turned into a grimace of pain with each wrong movement. Both his legs had grave injuries. His paratrooper platoon had gotten into trouble in some Egyptian village not far from the canal, and he was hit by a bullet in each leg.

One leg, in a cast, was suspended from the ceiling in a sling. There was an opening around the knee through which the wound could be seen, blackened with blood and oozing pus.

We had not seen each other since my trip to Europe. I shook my brother's hand and then, with atypical familiarity, tousled his curly hair. I sat at Yoram's beside for a few hours catching up. Yoram wanted to know how I was doing and asked where my unit was stationed. He said nothing about his injury. A foul odor hung in the air. When I complained, Yoram just laughed.

"You get used to it. This is what it smells like when your leg is rotting."

I told him, "Choose the finest wood for your leg; you don't want any worms in it."

My All Stars were about to fall apart from too much wear and tear, so I asked Yoram to lend me his combat boots. He called the nurse, who explained that his equipment was in the hospital storeroom. I went to the basement and after some searching found Yoram's combat boots, stiff with caked blood. I returned to his room with his shoes in a plastic bag.

"Just tell me when you need to return them to the quartermaster, and I'll fetch them back to you right away." I shoved the plastic bag with his shoes in my backpack and promised to visit him on my next leave.

From the Hadassah Hospital I drove straight to the Tel HaShomer Hospital to visit my friend Benny Dvir. He'd been hit by a single bullet — friendly fire, no less —and was paralyzed from the waist down. I found him in a dreary mood, hardly able to offer even a slight smile.

"Hello, Uri, thanks for coming to visit," he managed in a voice barely above a whisper.

"How are you feeling?" I stupidly asked.

Benny was sprawled unmoving on the bed. He tried to rise and dryly said, "I wish I could feel anything. I'm alive, but my legs are dead. Everyone here is paraplegic; I need a nurse to help me every time I want to move my ass."

I sat by Benny's bed and unintentionally drifted to sleep. When I woke, embarrassed, about half an hour later, I apologized and said I was in a hurry to get to the kibbutz.

I headed out to hitch a ride north. The roads were packed with military vehicles that considerably slowed down the drive. Fall is a season of beautiful sunsets, and that night produced a spectacular one that is etched in my memory. Toward evening, close to the Gome Junction, I ran into my old classmate Yehiam, who was also on leave. We hitched a ride with a military command car that drove us all the way to Mishmar Hatsafon's northern gate.

Walking down the entrance road leading to the veterans' neighborhood, I told Yehiam, "In the kibbutz, life goes on as usual. As if there were never any war."

Yehiam grunted. "Uri, life stops for nothing. This will sink in with you as well, and in a week or two everything will be the same as it was. How's Yoram?"

I told Yehiam about my brother's injury and about my friend Benny Dvir. "For us, the war is over. For them, it is only beginning."

On the sidewalk by the kibbutz yard, we met our old nanny, Yael, and her husband, Chaim. Their oldest son, Yoel, had been killed in the fighting. She came over and hugged me. I was suddenly unable to control my emotions and burst into tears. Yael stroked my head warmly, and her husband joined her and wrapped me in a bearlike hug. Instead of comforting Chaim for the death of his son, I found myself being comforted by him. I could not help but think of an embarrassing incident I'd had involving Chaim many years before.

I was ten and a half, walking from the children's house up the path to the northern tower at the edge of the kibbutz on my way to our neighborhood. I had almost reached the tower when I heard a noise. I paused for a moment, and in the twilight, I saw a man and a woman on the concrete base of the tower, which was surrounded by bushes. They were intertwined, leaning against the tower wall. I hid behind some shrubs, frightened and curious.

The man had his back to me, and his pants were down around his ankles. In front of him was a young female soldier. I looked on in bewilderment at the two rubbing their bodies together. For a moment, the man turned toward me, and in the faint light still clinging to the sky, I recognized Chaim, our nanny's husband. I froze, not knowing what to do. I wanted to run, but I remained stooped over behind the bush. I looked on from between the branches at Chaim and the soldier going at it. In such situations primal instincts take charge — even when we don't actually see anyone, we can somehow sense when we're being observed, as if the eyes send out invisible rays.

My gaze must have struck that soldier, and she reacted like a frightened doe trapped in the headlights of a passing car. A shiver passed through her, and she released herself from Chaim, who could not at first understand what had gone wrong.

She looked in my direction and said softly, "I think there's someone there."

I didn't know if she had seen me, so I held my breath and dared not move. I was sure they could hear my heart as it beat wildly with shame and fear. Chaim angrily pulled up his pants.

She whispered to him, "There, behind the bush," and she pointed in my direction. With four long strides, Chaim made it to my bush. Like a flushed partridge, I bounded off and ran away as fast as I could. I was hoping Chaim didn't recognize me in the dim light. I ran and ran until I could hardly breathe. I finally stopped behind the dining room. I was sweating like crazy, and my face was wet with tears.

When I settled down a bit, I walked in the dark to my parents' apartment, wiping the tears with my sleeve before entering their room. When my mother saw me she asked if I was okay. I told her it was nothing. That I'd just run all the way from the children's house.

In many ways, that event had toppled the structure of family values right before my eyes. I was angry at myself for having seen Chaim cheating on his wife. I felt myself at fault for having been exposed to a forbidden secret. I kept the incident to myself, and it burdened me for many years to come. After that evening, I began to see Yael Harduf in a completely different light. I wanted to tell her that her husband was cheating on her and avoided looking into her eyes when she spoke to me. I felt sorry for their son, Yoel.

In the dining hall during Friday dinners, I used to watch the Hardufs sitting together like the rest of the kibbutz families. The lie just kept resurfacing. I never knew whether Chaim had recognized me. I was sure he had but preferred to ignore it. Each time he looked at me, I was sure that he knew I knew, and he expected me to keep his secret.

The years had passed, we had all grown older, and Yoel had died in combat. On the main path of the kibbutz, Chaim hugged me, and I fell apart. I couldn't stop crying, mainly because of his fatherly embrace. I thought of Yoel and of his father, who hugged me as if I were his son. Did Yoel's death erase the betrayal? Chaim's embrace made me realize that as far as he was concerned, that awkward incident had been forgotten, or perhaps Chaim had forgiven my weakness because I had witnessed his.

Yehiam yanked me away from Chaim and Yael. "Pull yourself together," he hissed and helped me straighten my uniform. "Go to your room, shower, and put on some civilian clothes. We'll go together to visit Henka and Kuntz."

When Yehiam and I entered the Kotzer family's small apartment, it was still teeming with callers, who had kept coming many days after *shiva* was done. When Kuntz saw me, he rose clumsily from the sofa, waded his way through the people, and clasped my hand with both of his for a full minute or so. The only thing he said was, "Moti loved you so much."

He offered me his spot on the couch then walked with weary steps to the kitchen. He pulled a chair from the dining table, set it by the couch, and sat down heavily.

Kuntz welcomed visitors with a handshake and a tilt of the head, like a branch swaying under the weight of a wintry wind. I went over to my cousin Haya and sat beside her. She looked at me with green eyes framed by masses of long chestnut hair, settled her head on my shoulder, and said nothing. A large picture of Moti was displayed in the living room. He was dressed in his uniform with his jump wings prominent on his chest. His blond hair was wavy, and his wide smile exposed the white teeth of a man in the prime of his youth.

The atmosphere was tense and awkward. Henka stared into space, sitting on the sofa like one more pillow that had lost its shape after years of overuse. I went to her, and she leaned a little forward and stroked my hand with hers without uttering a word. I felt ill, so I went to the bathroom and smoked a cigarette to calm down and try and regain my self-control.

When I returned, my mother leaned toward me and whispered, "You just couldn't help yourself, could you? You think a cigarette will solve the problem? You're smoking too much as it is."

Kuntz got up every few minutes to serve the callers cake and fruit. I clung to Haya, comfortable next to her. Sometimes she looked beautiful, other times a little less, and she'd always struggled with her weight. We had formed a beautiful friendship, and she was like a big sister to me. During the years before my military service, we had worked together for a time in the chicken coop.

"What will happen to them now?" I asked Haya.

"I don't know. Dad's going to be fine, he'll get over it. Mom's done for."

There was something loving and kind and soothing about my cousin's eyes. They held the hope that these hard days would melt away and everything would turn out all right. I thought Haya was the thread that bound her parents together and that perhaps she could mend the rift that had been torn in the family. I knew for sure that it would be impossible without her.

Moti was six years his sister's junior. Haya had left Mishmar Hatsafon when he had just started high school. He was flighty back then and did not do well in his studies. Kuntz was disappointed by his son's dislike of fine literature and poetry. At the time, the age difference between brother and sister did not encourage them to be close. Their relationship had blossomed only after Moti had been drafted. Haya understood him. She too felt she had not lived up to her father's expectations. She had given up on her university studies and found a job as a secretary for a building materials marketing firm in Tel Aviv. Moti preferred to spend his vacations with his sister rather than in the kibbutz.

Before his army service, he had asked my advice regarding where he should volunteer. I urged him to go to a combat unit or one of the reconnaissance commando units. Kuntz had expected Moti to prove himself in the army, to fulfill the values taught him by the kibbutz. Kuntz was adamant about proving to everyone that his son understood what was demanded of the young kibbutz members. When Moti was admitted to the Golani reconnaissance commando unit, Kuntz boasted about it. Kuntz's attitude upset Henka, who had a bad feeling about her son's assignment. Moti had a slight build and had to handle the immense physical strains posed by the elite unit he had selected. He was strongly motivated to successfully complete the unit's training, but his outward displays of masculinity belied his gentle nature. On one of his vacations, he had told me he was about to be released from the commando unit. I suggested he ask for another position, one that would utilize his skills.

Moti was indeed released from the commando unit, but his superiors decided to keep him in the Golani Brigade, and he was assigned as a noncommissioned officer to one of the brigade's battalions. Kuntz saw Moti's release from the commando unit as a personal failure and did not hide his disappointment.

Henka and Kuntz's relationship had gone awry long before Moti died. They had drifted apart over the years and found it difficult to agree on almost any subject. Once their relationship had soured, they busied themselves with their own affairs. Moti's death had simply served to further unravel the bond that was almost impossible to mend as it was.

Henka told me, "Moti's willingness to volunteer for every mission was a futile attempt to win his father's love. His wish to prove himself a good soldier cost him his life."

***

During the war I'd sent Nurit Schory letters but did not receive even a single reply. Still, I was hopeful with each mail delivery. The echoes of war began to fade. We spent a few more months on reserve duty. I wrote another letter full of longing to Nurit, detailing how I had desperately tried to reach her before leaving England. I apologized for not meeting her as we had scheduled and hoped she would understand I had to go defend our homeland. I couldn't stop thinking about her and the fact that I had missed a golden opportunity to renew our relationship. Not a single postcard came from Nurit.

8

In Israel, life returned to normal, while some of us were still on reserve duty. My unit lay on mattresses in a tent near the town of Fayid. There was little routine activity. A black cable snaked its way to our tent, connected to a field phone with which we could call a remote operator at one of the bases. Kadmi took charge of the telephone whenever the line was actually working. He sat on the sand, Indian style, pressed the telephone to his bosom, and screamed instructions to his employees back home. Once done with that, he would call his girlfriend and dictate a long list of tasks in anticipation of their impending wedding. At night, Gidi taught us everything there was to know about the constellations. Shalom Hatuka got on everyone's nerves. Eventually, Binder persuaded the brigade commander to offer Hatuka a long leave so he could help his family at home. And so we sat idle next to the town of Fayid in the middle of the desert with nothing to do. Everyone began to get restless. While many units had been discharged, we were told to prepare for a long stay until the end of the cease-fire negotiations.

On my next leave, I visited Henka and Kuntz. Kuntz was still unshaven, even though more than a month had passed since the death of his son. The white beard completely changed his appearance.

"How long do you intend on growing a beard?" I asked.

"I don't know, Uri, until I'm done grieving. The beard reminds me of Moti." A few months later he returned to shaving every day.

"It's time you know where you came from, and where you are headed," Kuntz told me during that visit. Then he asked, "What do you even know about your family?"

To be honest, I knew very little, but I wasn't in the mood. "Are you sure this is the right time for this?" I replied with a question of my own.

Kuntz interpreted my reply as a sign that I would listen to what he had to say. "Your grandfather left Poland and passed through the gates of Berlin in the beginning of 1919," Kuntz began with a dramatic flair. "He was dressed in a long overcoat and a top hat and had all his belongings in a small wooden suitcase. In his other hand he carried a leather bag containing all the tools a shoemaker required. He told me he had reached Berlin on the day Rosa Luxemburg's body was found floating in the stream crossing the Tiergarten. Red Rosa's murder had provoked much tension in the streets of Berlin. Police forces were deployed on every street corner for fear of a civil war erupting. Distrust and nervousness were everywhere. The police arrested anyone who seemed even remotely suspicious to them." Kuntz took a deep breath.

"Young Martin Kuntzmacher, your grandfather, spoke fluent German. He found a small room to live in, in the Mitte borough, on a street inhabited by hardworking laborers and peddlers. In Poland, he had served as a cobbler's apprentice for a few years, but in Berlin he immediately opened a small shop for the sewing of shoes, boots, and custom-made coats. He proved to be a skilled craftsman, and his prices were reasonable. The scope of his work increased daily, and there was no shortage of it. His reputation grew, and he even won a contract to sew shoes for the German army. His business expanded — he employed ten laborers who sewed military shoes — until he finally stopped doing handwork and dealt only with the management of the business."

As Kuntz continued to speak, he clasped his hands behind his back and paced back and forth in the narrow living room. "Your grandfather married Vera, that was your grandmother's name. I wish you could have met her; she was a rare woman. She was born in Berlin to a family that had emigrated from Warsaw."

I remembered that one of my father's photo albums contained a picture taken on their wedding day. My grandfather appeared in it as an elegant groom wearing a black suit and a top hat, a bow tie adorning his white collar, and gold-rimmed thin spectacles framing his eyes. Vera stood beside her husband, slightly taller than him, dressed in a white lace dress, a white hat encircled with a ribbon on her head, and her white-gloved hands holding a bouquet of gladiolas. My grandmother was a very beautiful woman.

Kuntz continued the story, his voice full of tender reminiscence and longing. "Family life revolved around a large table that occupied most of the living room. During Shabbat dinners, we would all gather around the table with other relatives. The fine Rosenthal dinnerware and crystal glasses were taken out of the cupboard, and a snow-white embroidered tablecloth was spread on the table.

"Life in Berlin was good and beautiful. We had a well-organized, clean house and Mother would keep it in order, prepare food, and see to disciplining us. Father was never involved in any of the household chores. Mother was aided by a nanny, who cared for me and your father.

"Your grandfather was strict and orderly. On the weekend, he would wear a three-piece suit and a top hat and go to the synagogue like that. I remember that on one such Saturday, I mistakenly touched Father's white shirt with a dirty hand. The little stain nearly drove him out of his mind. His face turned crimson, and he screamed at me. I ran into my mother's arms, terrified. Father tried to get the stain out with a hand towel soaked with lukewarm water, failed, and became even angrier. He took out his watch, peeked at it, and realized the hour grew late. It was nearly Shabbat.

"He hurried to the closet, took out a clean white shirt and dressed in the living room. Mother urged him to hurry so we wouldn't be late. Perhaps it was the pressure, but he was unable to fasten the last button. He pressed the shirt collar against his neck, trying to push the rebellious button into place, but it continued to resist. The effort and anger had Father's face covered with sweat. Mother handed him a handkerchief to wipe it off and offered to close the button for him. He reluctantly gave in. Then he pulled at the hem of the shirt, straightened its creases, tucked it into his pants, and tightened them with a thin leather belt. After that, he masterfully straightened the collar of his new shirt and put on a light-blue, white-striped tie. Following that incident, I was always careful not to dirty my own clothes because I had seen how much it had angered Father."

Reality in Germany changed in April 1930. When Kuntz told me about that period, the flow of his speech slowed down, and it was apparent he found it difficult to speak. "I went shopping for Passover with Mother. On our way back, she had to carry two heavy baskets. Despite the cold weather, she was perspiring and found it hard to breathe. We stopped several times to rest until finally we reached the train station. The streetcar had just stopped at the station. Mother picked up the two baskets and then simply collapsed on the sidewalk. The baskets dropped from her hands and their contents spilled to the sidewalk: a box of matzo, a jar of jam, carrots, beets, and potatoes rolled on the sidewalk. I didn't know what do to, care for Mother or pick up the scattered food.

"Passersby gathered around Mother, also unsure what they should do. A vendor working at a nearby store stopped a passing car. Helped by a few passersby, he placed my unconscious mother in the car, which took her to the hospital. The man accompanied me on foot to our house, which wasn't too far. At the hospital, a young doctor pronounced her dead." Kuntz sat in his armchair and supported his head with both hands.

"Father only learned of his wife's death a few hours later. He was completely grief-stricken. Your grandfather refused to take comfort even when the mourning period was over. His mind was occupied with troubling thoughts, and he hardly noticed us children. He distractedly prepared the meals and was silent most of the time. At night, he restlessly walked about the house. The burden of taking care of us was beyond his endurance."

Kuntz suddenly stopped speaking. He looked up at the sky for the span of a few breaths and muttered. I thought he was talking to himself, like many old people do, but then he said to me, "You know, Uri, until then, I believed in God with all my heart, but after Mother's death came the doubts. So, you see, I had stopped believing in the Almighty even before the war, and its atrocities merely served to confirm my opinion."

Vera's death had completely changed life in the house. Martin Kuntzmacher entrusted the care of his children to Vera's relatives for a meager sum. Kuntz was nine, and my father was five. Sometime later, a permanent situation was found for the children — they were placed in the home of a neighbor whose children had grown and moved out. Martin returned to work but was a changed man. He let himself go. His hair had turned gray, his beard grew wild, and he paid no attention to how he dressed. He no longer wore a suit and a tie every day. Each morning he would wake up despondent and wear whatever was available in the closet. Often, he would arrive in the workshop wearing shirts that needed ironing or laundering.

His business began to decline, simple repairs remained undone, orders were not fulfilled, and the clientele quickly dwindled. When work became scarce, Martin was forced to fire most of his employees. He tried to hold on to the workshop for a little while longer, with the few loyal clients he had remaining. Finally, he had to sell the business at a ridiculously low price and found work as a hired shoemaker for another shop.

"I had to go with Father to work one day. He explained to the shop owner that no other arrangement was available for me. Then he had me sit on a tall chair, while he sat in front of a large pile of shoes that needed repair. Father worked with mechanical motions, hunched over a large, black sewing machine. He avoided the shop's leather storeroom; after the death of my mother, he had become sensitive to the stench. At the end of the day, he placed his finished work on the shop owner's table. In the evenings, he would come home exhausted, depressed, and drained of energy."

Kuntz sighed and turned silent, I thought he might be grieving over his father more than he was grieving his son.

"Your grandfather," Kuntz continued, "taught me to play chess when I was five. First, he let me feel each piece with my hand. The first piece he chose was the knight. He placed it on the appropriate chessboard square, showed me how it could move during the game, and explained its importance. The first game was held only after I was introduced to all the various pieces and the rules of the game. Father set the board and let me play with the black pieces. 'Think carefully before each move,' he said and marched a white pawn two squares forward. He defeated me with a few simple moves. 'Remember this loss,' he said to me, 'never let anyone defeat you with a scholar's mate.'

"I loved playing chess, which allowed us to spend a lot of time together. I noticed that Father regularly chose to sacrifice the queen for an inferior piece. A knight, a bishop, or a rook. Sometimes, this sacrifice move was senseless and did nothing to improve his situation on the chessboard. As this repeated itself, I asked him why he sacrificed his queen every single game. Father took a deep breath then finally said, 'You can sacrifice any piece for the sake of winning. A good player knows that sacrifice moves hold a great deal of risk, but sometimes this risk is turned into an advantage that ultimately leads to winning.' My guess is that Father sacrificed his queen to give me an advantage in the game. By the age of twelve I was already his equal, so I found my own ways of losing a rook or a bishop, not wanting to take advantage of Father's deliberate sacrifices."

A few years after Martin's wife had passed, he was matched with a childless widow a few years older than him. The two met several times, and their loneliness and desire to get back to a normal family life served as the glue that brought them together. The widow visited Martin's apartment and he got the impression she was a decent woman who would treat his children kindly. Six months after they met, my grandfather asked for the widow's hand in marriage. They married in a modest ceremony at the local synagogue.

Kuntz described their marriage in the following way: "This was a marriage that brought the couple little joy, but much mutual benefit." The new wife took over the housekeeping chores, brought order and discipline into the household, and, indeed, took good care of Martin's children. Her presence added to the family atmosphere in the house. The food improved, thanks to the widow's brother, who was a butcher. "From the moment Father remarried, there was never any shortage of meat on the table," Kuntz mentioned.

As a child, Kuntz felt his mother's absence in a painful and tangible way, especially on Shabbat eve dinners. "When our stepmother lit the candles and prayed, I would remember the scent of my own mother's cooking. At the end of the prayer, Father would break the challah bread and distribute it among us. I would chew the bit of challah Father gave me as long as possible; this was my way of bringing back a little of my mother."

***

As the Nazi party continued to gain strength and popularity, brown-uniformed hoodlums prowled the streets, and the simple act of going to school had become dangerous.

"Father transferred me to the more easily accessed Jewish school in Grosse Hamburger Strasse. Jews were being hunted in the streets; one of our relatives was jailed and sent to the Oranienburg camp. Father chose to ignore it all and continued to go to work as usual, but his salary was reduced."

In the Jewish school, Kuntz became acquainted with the HaShomer Hatzair movement. His classmates invited him to attend one of the group's activities, and the movement's branch in Sophienstrasse turned into the center of his life. Kuntz always arrived at the youth movement center riding an old bicycle he used for his work as a delivery boy. The money he earned was an essential part of the meager family household budget. He spent most of his time doing various odd jobs. His school studies had taken a back seat to everything else. He went to the movement center whenever he could, and it became his second home.

In HaShomer Hatzair, Kuntz found an orderly structure for his life; a world full of passionate ideology; evenings full of dancing and singing, discussions, and the study of Zionism and the history of the Jewish people. During movement activities, Kuntz forgot all about the difficulties of providing for the family, his father's depression, and having to live crowded with his brother in the one small room. In HaShomer Hatzair, Kuntz made some good friends: Tzvi Cohen, Menahem Baumgarten, Zeev Schwartz, Hilda Heisendorf, and Max Tishler.

"Every Sunday, early in the morning, I would ride my bicycle to HaShomer Hatzair; Sundays were normally dedicated to trips. I made all my preparations in utter silence, so as not to wake the rest of the family. I put on my sturdy hiking boots only at the door. I usually settled for a large black bread sandwich with a little butter and cheese."

Kuntz had turned passionate as he told me about the movement life in Berlin. He recalled one trip where, after a strenuous walk, the cadets sat down for a noontime rest: "The instructor asked all the cadets to place the sandwiches they had brought from home in a single pile. 'The most important group values have to do with sharing and solidarity. If each cadet gives up his own sandwich and accepts a random sandwich from the pile, we will express our group's spirit of equality,' the instructor told us. The group happily accepted his idea. Each cadet put his sandwich into a pile. Then the instructor distributed the sandwiches.

"I received a sandwich wrapped in parchment paper. It was made of sweet Shabbat challah spread with a thick layer of mayonnaise. In between were several slices of fine salami, tomatoes, and parsley. I was embarrassed because the sandwich I had brought was plain compared to the one I had received. After I ate, I couldn't contain myself and apologized to Zeev Schwartz, who had gotten my sandwich. Zeev told me that it was actually very tasty, and he had enjoyed it because his family never bought black bread, but only the white bread that spoiled rich families eat. I was happy with Zeev's answer because it seemed to confirm the fact that I was truly a part of the group.

"During one of the group talks, Menahem Baumgarten turned to me in front of everyone and suggested that I lose some weight. I was offended of course, but Menahem quickly explained he had not meant to be insulting. He said that in the land of Israel conditions were harsh, the work was excruciating, and the climate warm and humid." After that my uncle stopped taking public transportation and rode his bicycle to try to lose weight.

"During one of our field trips the instructor asked us to empty our water canteens and then took us on a quick march through the groves surrounding the city for a few hours. I found the walking to be extremely difficult and soon felt dehydrated. When we finally reached the water tap, the instructor stopped us before giving us permission to drink. 'The land of Israel is nothing like Europe,' he said. 'The desert has claimed many parts of it, a shortage of water is a common thing. The HaShomer Hatzair cadets should also know the taste of thirst. This will help you cope with the difficulties inherent in pioneering.'

That summer, the Nazi party flags were taken down, and the battalions of soldiers that regularly marched through the city vanished, bringing a nice respite from the constant sound of boots stomping in the streets. Banners announcing the 1936 Berlin Olympic Games were hung on every lamppost. Kuntz described the Berlin streets to me, how they were filled with the flags of every participating country. Countless tourists filled the city with a cacophony of foreign languages.

"For the first time in my life, I saw people whose skin was black. The black athletes received a lot of attention as they walked in the streets of Berlin. On the games' opening night, the Berlin streets were completely deserted. Father came home early, showered, and dressed in our finest clothes. We sat down for a quick dinner, then the whole family gathered around the radio. We all eagerly anticipated the broadcast of the opening ceremony.

"When the radio announcer began to speak, Father asked us to be completely quiet and threatened to send us to bed if we disobeyed. His threat worked like a charm. Silence settled on the living room, except for the voice from the radio. The announcer described the way the Chancellor Adolf Hitler's car entered the stadium. The deafening cheering of the audience drowned out the announcer's words, and the loud applause continued until Hitler sat down in the State Box.

"During the Olympic Games, Father avidly followed the various competitions. Most were dominated by the German athletes, and he was proud they outshined the Americans. During the games, the house schedule completely changed. Each evening, Father would sit next to the big radio in the living room and closely follow the activities in the stadium. The chess board remained orphaned on the table. Dinners were brief. Sometimes, we would eat only a hard-boiled egg and a slice of buttered bread and drink a cup of tea.

"Father wouldn't miss a single broadcast. When the track and field finals began, he left the table in the middle of dinner and dragged his chair over to sit by the radio. He asked everyone to be completely silent so he would not miss a single word of the ecstatic German announcer's account. German athlete Luz Long was leading the long jump competition. The American competitor, Jesse Owens — a black man — disqualified his first five jumps, leaving only one attempt remaining. Owens set out with a quick run and leaped over the sand pit for a measurement of eight point zero six meters. With his only legal jump, Jesse Owens won the gold medal. Luz Long went over to the black athlete and gave him a warm hug right in front of Chancellor Adolf Hitler.

"The next day was the hundred-meter dash. My father seemed very agitated before the starting gun sounded. He bit his nails, leaned on the table with his eyes glued to the radio, and his hands clasped on his head. Silence fell over the stadium. This was one of the rare times I saw my father lose his usual composure. After Jesse Owens won the race, he forgot all about his manners and screamed, 'That negro beast has shamed them all!'

"After the war, I had no sympathy for the Germans, of course," Kuntz added, "but I was still sorry to hear, while I was here in Israel, that the Berlin silver long jump medalist, Luz Long, was among the German soldiers killed in Italy."

***

The brief respite brought by the Olympic Games vanished with the closing ceremony fireworks. Martin took the advice of his older brother, who had relocated to Argentina, to try to join him. He went to the Polish consulate to arrange the necessary family reunification paperwork. The Polish official found that it had expired and that Martin did not have German citizenship. He asked for a Polish passport so he could emigrate from Germany. The official wondered why Martin's last name was Kuntzmacher, while his brother's last name was Seltzer.

"Our great-grandmother was very sick," Kuntz explained. "On her deathbed, she asked the family to preserve her last name for future generations. To honor her request, Martin changed his last name from Seltzer to Kuntzmacher. But the Polish official refused to accept Martin's desperate explanations, even though they were true. He did not believe Father and refused to approve his family reunification request."

Having no choice, Martin traveled to Poland to get an official copy of his birth certificate, issued under the name of Martin Seltzer. It took a few trips and quite a bit of money to accomplish it. Once, he even took Kuntz and my father with him so they could meet their relatives in Poland. Due to his frequent absences, Martin was fired from his job.

"Father never gave up looking for ways to leave Germany. With his new birth certificate, he went to the Paraguayan consulate in Berlin and asked for help. Father handed the consul an envelope with money. In return he received an official travel certificate from the Paraguay government. Once more, there was hope of escaping Germany.

"Father sold what little property he had and his wife's jewelry to pay for boat tickets. The sailing date was the end of December 1937. We spent several months with our suitcases packed and ready. During the long wait, Father traveled one more time to the Polish consulate in an attempt to obtain a Polish passport. This was a tragic mistake. The Polish consul decided that Father's new birth certificate looked suspicious and suspected it had been forged. Father returned home that day without any paperwork. He traveled to Poland one last time to obtain a new certificate. While Father was in Poland, the Gestapo came to our apartment looking for him. I told them he had gone to Poland for his mother's funeral. The detectives left a warrant ordering Martin Kuntzmacher to report to the nearest police station without delay."

***

Henrietta Szold, the representative of the Jewish Agency, visited Berlin. Kuntz met her with his friends from the HaShomer Hatzair, and she convinced them to leave Germany and emigrate to Israel. Martin objected to splitting up the family, but seventeen-year-old Kuntz would not listen to him. He sold his bicycle and told everyone he was leaving for Israel.

"When we said goodbye, Father took off the gold watch that was always connected with a chain to his waistcoat pocket, handed it to me, and asked that I keep it safe. It is the only reminder I have left of my father."

Kuntz left his home in Berlin and traveled to Trieste in Italy along with the rest of the Youth Aliyah group. A short time later, they boarded a ship that sailed to Israel.

"When the ship was in the middle of the sea, I looked at the foam of the waves and the seagulls, I took out the pocket watch Father had given me, opened the gold cover, reset it to show the time in Israel, and returned it to my backpack. In my notebook, I wrote: 'A dream come true! A few more days and we will reach the shores of the homeland. I am ready for whatever tasks will be required of me. The preparation stage is over, now comes the time of our trial. To fulfill the values of a cooperative life and of equality, and to redeem the land of Israel.'"

As Kuntz told me about that voyage, I saw, for the first time, a film of tears forming in his eyes.

***

Martin Kuntzmacher had managed to rescue Kuntz's little brother — my father — by sending him from Germany to Denmark with a group of children. His cousin, Eva Stein, was also sent there with the same group. My father, so Kuntz told me, had managed to convince the people in charge of the group that Eva was his little sister who had lost her paperwork, thus saving her. Only Martin and his wife remained in Berlin. Toward the end of the war, my father somehow managed to get to Israel with his cousin Eva. Eva found it difficult to get used to the warm country and emigrated to America.

***

Kuntz measured his small room with his heavy footsteps, pacing from end to end. He moved a large hand over his bald head as if smoothing down hair and seemed to be talking to himself.

"The Second World War was in full swing. For several years I heard nothing from Father and his wife and hadn't the faintest idea what had happened to them. Here and there, we heard of the mass murder of Jews. Truth be told, we were focused on what was going on here in Israel rather than the occurrences in Europe."

Kuntz opened a small cabinet and took out a dusty bottle of cognac. He filled two small glasses and placed one in front of me, and continued to hold on to the bottle. Martin Kuntzmacher must have seen the events of Kristallnacht, on November 9, 1938, from his apartment by the Central Synagogue. The Gestapo had gathered the Jews from all over Berlin.

After a long sip from his glass, Kuntz grew even more melancholy.

"To this very day, I still don't know what exactly happened to your grandfather after I left Berlin. The war had changed him, and we drifted apart. Conversations became almost impossible. He had become introverted and refused to speak about what happened to him during the war.

"All I know is that Martin and his wife were led to the Grunewald train station, to platform seventeen. They were ushered into a cattle car. Another shipment of Jews was being sent to Eastern Europe, and that time, my father did not miss it."

9

The seemingly endless posting of our unit near the Fayid airfield isolated us from the rest of the army. The war was over, there was hardly any military activity, yet we remained in the field, huddled together in a large tent that was still too small to hold us comfortably. Little by little we created a kind of village for ourselves. Besides the tent, we fixed ourselves a dining area. Every Saturday night, we sat together for a communal meal using tables and chairs we'd found by combing the desert for furniture of any type. We stretched a camouflage net above the dining room, a cover from the scorching sun. In addition to the dining room, we had a picnic corner for smoking and drinking between meals. We erected a reading corner: armchairs arranged beneath a faded yellow patio umbrella taken from the quarters of an Egyptian officer who appreciated fake splendor. A broken refrigerator tossed into the desert served as our card and backgammon table. We had improvised closets full of groceries, canned, and nonperishable foods. Our settlement in the land of Egypt took the shape and form of a temporary refugee camp. We did not adhere to any military dress code and spent most of our time in and around the tent in our underwear. Discipline wavered, to say the least. Through unspoken agreement, we abandoned basic grooming, becoming long-haired and bearded. This "stylistic rebellion" became a protest against the military structure that had overstayed its welcome. Once a week, a supply truck brought us fresh supplies and combat rations. The canned food we hadn't used began to pile up beside the tent — mounds of Spam, goulash, corn, peas, and grapefruit slices. Most of the time, we lay idly in the tent, bored out of our wits. Everyone grew tired of backgammon and card games.

One day, Hatuka stood in the middle of the tent and announced, "Let's see which one of you can solve a riddle I invented."

Kadmi roared back, "Enough with your bullshit, Hatuka. Shut up or I'll strangle you with my bare hands."

Hatuka did not relent. "Come on, Kadmi, let's see how intelligent you really are. There's no way you're going to solve this riddle, no way!"

Gidi Turner chimed in, "All right, Hatuka, my main man, let's hear it."

Hatuka cleared his throat and stood up straight like a great orator. "Hear me now, this is my riddle for you. I am robbed by robbers. The water all trickled away through the holes, and I am on the verge of death, who am I?"

Even Binder, our tough commander, burst into laughter.

"Hatuka," Kadmi snapped, "please go slower. I didn't get it all."

With a squeaky voice, and his usual thick accent, Hatuka repeated his riddle.

Kadmi was laughing so hard he could barely breathe. "Hatuka… come on, slower…" His voice faltered with each laughing fit. "Hatuka… come on… slower, please… one more time…"

The laughter had become infectious, and everyone in the tent was in an uproar. Hatuka stood calmly in the center of the tent wearing nothing but his underwear, swarthy and skinny, his legs like two matchsticks, the hairs of his thin beard lining his serious face like wrinkles. "Laugh and mock if you'd like, none of you are wise enough to solve my riddle. I am robbed by robbers…" Hatuka repeated his riddle.

Kadmi's enormous body shook with uncontrollable spasms of laughter. He rolled on his mattress, clutching his stomach. "Hatuka… cut it out, I can't take it anymore… you're killing me… Hatuka… come on… bring us something to drink… so we can all calm down…"

All at once, everyone began to shout in a chorus, "Nothing is stronger than water. Nothing is stronger than water."

Gidi threw a pillow at Hatuka, who threw it right back at him. A pillow fight ensued, and the air filled with flying objects and thick clouds of dust. Gidi escaped from the tent and went outside in his underwear to get some fresh air. Casually at first, then with increasing intensity, he began to sort and arrange the hundreds of tin cans scattered around the tent. By the evening, Gidi had completed his creation, an entire wall comprised of canned corn. A new wall made entirely of Spam cans began rise beside it. Other army units passing through the area noticed the neat piles and began to offload their extra cans next to our tent. We'd found a new occupation.

Each day, additional cans were added to the creation. Kadmi, the engineer, drafted a plan for constructing a pyramid out of tin cans. The pyramid grew taller by the day and quickly became a tourist attraction for soldiers passing by. Gidi and Hatuka served as tour guides, offering visitors a lecture about this new archeological discovery in Egypt. At the end of the speech, each visitor had the honor of adding a tin can, and the pyramid was soon over six feet tall. Kadmi drafted an additional plan for widening the pyramid base to build it even higher.

Word of the tin can pyramid had reached division headquarters, and the division quartermaster called us on the radio to say that trucks would be arriving to collect the extra tin cans. "Someone way up high gave the order to dismantle it."

A general sense of resentment settled among the reconnaissance commando unit soldiers. At dusk, four jeeps took position on a starting line about half a mile from the edge of the camp. Binder fired his pistol in the air, and the jeeps set off at tremendous speed. The drivers pressed their gas pedals to the floor, and with a deafening crash, the jeeps plowed into the tin can pyramid. The air filled with red jets of tomato sauce mixed with bits of goulash, corn, and grapefruit slices. The sand was littered with crushed cans surrounded by scattered peas, meatloaf, and halvah.

"They said dismantle it, didn't they? An order's an order." Binder was rather pleased with himself.

The division quartermaster arrived the following day in a REO truck. He walked into our tent and said, "Guys, where are the extra cans of food?"

No one said a word. Binder, wearing nothing but his underwear, winked at Gidi. All eyes turned to him as he rummaged in a duffel bag and theatrically fished out a can of corn. He tossed it to the quartermaster. "Do me a favor, deliver that to the division commander. A personal gift from me."

The commandos shook with laughter, setting the tent to trembling. Two soldiers sent from division headquarters worked a full day sifting through the scattered cans to pick out the few intact ones and load them onto the truck. In the evening, when the two soldiers went to the tent to shower, we quickly loaded something extra onto the truck — the putrid remains of two Egyptians that had been left in the field. This prank cost us dearly: the division commander canceled our ration of flight tickets to Israel. Fresh food continued to arrive, but the combat ration supply was stopped. The division adjutancy let us know that the promotions planned for after the war had been canceled for all reconnaissance unit officers, and so it was. None of these punishments did anything to wipe the smiles off our faces for a very long time.

***

The cease-fire continued.

Mitleman, who had gone to see a doctor in the middle of the war and never returned, showed up at our tent one day in a fresh, clean uniform and said cheerfully, "Guys, I'm back. I was in the hospital with a severe infection, then they sent me home to rest."

Binder, in his underwear (his new uniform), slowly rose from the mattress on the sand and raised his Kalashnikov. A tense silence ensued, and the embarrassed Mitleman lowered his backpack from his shoulder.

"All right, hang on a minute, sir. I have a whole lot of treats for you guys here: chorizo, some fine salami, Dutch cheese, I even brought some arak, cognac, and lots of candy." Mitleman moved quickly to take the delicacies out and spread them on a blanket in the middle of the tent. He wiped the sweat off his forehead and put a big smile on his face.

Binder cocked his weapon and aimed the barrel at Mitleman. We froze. Our commanding officer lowered the barrel until it was directed straight at Mitleman's crotch then spat out his words with a husky voice. "That's just great, Mitleman. You think you can buy us with some sausage? You chickenshit lowlife, get the fuck out of my face or I'll take off your balls."

Mitleman hesitated for a moment, seeking any sign of sympathy in the tent, especially from Hatuka and Kadmi, his friends. Their expressions made it clear that no help would come from them. He quickly gathered his backpack and took off running toward the Fayid airstrip. All that time Binder stood there in his underwear pointing the Kalashnikov at his back.

***

Reserve duty had a strange and debasing effect. The moment they stepped through the base gate, everyone's manner of speech would change completely. A monotonous cycle of predictable talk about sex, income tax, and work issues. The immediacy with which we fell back into this lowly lingo — the sentences peppered with profanities, the unstructured language filled with street talk —made me uncomfortable every single time. All codes of politeness and proper behavior were trampled in a matter of minutes. Reserve duty made my friends act like fools — childish, smug, and cynical. Personal neglect became the norm; suffocating stench of perspiration and gun oil issued from our uniforms. Each of the guys adjusted his behavior to fit the role expected of him. Binder — the tough commander, Hatuka — a clown against his will, Kadmi — a short-fused aggressive man, and Gidi Turner — the smart-ass who brought everyone together and united them into one big family, to which I did not want to belong most of the time. The constant and relentless scheming of the reconnaissance commando unit soldiers, the desire to be separate from and to have better conditions than other units made me sick to my stomach. Still, I always managed to fit in and be one of the gang.

***

When the Yom Kippur War ended, I found myself jobless, without a penny in my pocket, and no idea where I would live. I never thought of returning to the kibbutz, even for a moment. I was discharged from reserve duty in April 1974, destitute, depressed, and embittered. My reserve duty had lasted for six months and social security did not deem it necessary to pay me for that period. They excused their refusal with the fact that I had not paid my social security taxes during my stay abroad. I was trapped in a situation that deeply frustrated me. I returned my equipment to the quartermaster, other than a military mattress that I used as a temporary bed while sleeping at my friend's house in Tel Aviv. I provided for myself by doing various odd jobs: I washed cars in a gas station, I operated a metal bending machine and worked as a general laborer for a construction contractor. I managed.

I saw a small ad from the Jewish Agency in the newspaper; they were looking for counselors for their US Jewish community summer camps. I got the job and spent a couple of months in America. At the summer camp, I met an Israeli who had finished her service as a broadcaster with IDF Radio. She couldn't get over the fact that I could remember each news story in great detail. "With your kind of memory and knowledge, you simply must try to get into the Army Radio, they're looking for people like you at the station."

Her diagnosis amused me, and I deduced that journalists knew very little about a lot of things. Still, when I returned to Israel, I tried my luck. My passion for trivia proved to be valuable; on the application test, I easily answered questions about politics, sports, crime, and art. Thanks to that radio announcer, I began work for the Army Radio news as a freelance reporter. I quickly fit in and was given the status of a temporary civilian army employee. As far as I was concerned, I was on the right track. IDF Radio seemed like the natural place for me. I felt the same sense of pride and satisfaction I had after matriculating from my officer training.

About a year after the war ended my first reserve duty order came in the mail. Things were back to the old, familiar routine of one month's reserve duty a year. As far as that was concerned, nothing had changed.

PART 2

10

About five years after the Yom Kippur War, we were called for a routine division drill. I went to perform my reserve duty feeling more relaxed than usual. I comforted myself — just one week in the field then I'd be back at the radio station. I didn't expect much from a routine army drill; we all knew our jobs. It took just a few hours from the time we put on our uniforms for everyone to fall back into the military mentality. My commando unit friends came in a good mood; they all loved their reserve duty service. For them, it was a welcome change, a way of escaping their mundane lives. As for me, I no longer felt at ease in that environment.

At dusk we finished setting up, ate dinner, and went out to the field. That night in November 1978 was cold and rainy. My patrol jeep led a long convoy of tanks, cannons, armored personnel carriers, and trucks. The headlights of the jeep were barely able to light up the narrow road leading from Ma'ale Adumim to Jericho. It took a high level of attention and vigilance to drive safely through the sharp bends of the road to reach the area designated for the division drill.

We reached our destination in the wee hours of the night, wet, tired, and nervous. We killed the engines and spread canvas tarps between the jeeps to keep out a little of the rain, which came down in a steady drizzle.

"Nothing is stronger than water," Hatuka desperately shouted into the cold night air.

"Grow up already," Kadmi answered and urged Gidi to hurry and finish setting up camp so the guys would be able to get a few hours of sleep. I hurried to squeeze into my sleeping bag, took off my shoes, and tried to catch a short nap on the muddy ground. While trying to find a comfortable position to sleep in, I wondered why Hatuka clung to his mantra of "nothing is stronger than water," resorting to chanting it during every crisis. How had that trivial sentence become the commando unit's slogan during the Yom Kippur War? I had come up with no answer by the time I fell asleep under the rainy sky in the desert not far from Jericho.

I slept an hour, maybe. Hatuka, who was on guard duty, shook my sleeping bag. "Dolev, get up. The division commander wants to see you in his tent. Urgently. Get up, nothing is stronger than water." Hatuka continued muttering his signature sentence over and over to the rhythm of the rain drumming against the tent.

I cursed under my breath, put on my wet shoes, and shuffled my way through the mud to the Colonel Gershon's temporary office. The division commander stood next a map of the reserve duty drill area dotted with colored pins and bizarre code names and decorating the entire wall of the tent. A small generator coughed in a monotonous rhythm, forcing everyone to raise their voices to be heard above the noise. Colonel Gershon, full of vigorous energy, stood by the map tapping a silver pointer at a specific location on the map. In his other hand he held a green plastic cup and drank hot tea from it with measured gulps. When he saw my head poking through the tent flaps, a wide smile curved his lips. He came closer and clapped my back with exaggerated theatrical kindness.

"The entire army is taking part in this drill! You're the only soldier who's being discharged. Way to go, Dolev. Yalla, pack your personal gear and go home. Good for you."

He winked at the officers around him. "This guy has connections on top of his connections. What a sly dog. Don't underestimate him. Dolev manages to surprise me every time." He continued talking to the rest of the officers over my head. "The southern command major general has personally asked me to discharge him. Well done. Who needs favoritism when you have connections, right? Now seriously, Dolev, that's an order — you have till noon to report to the army radio commander's office. Yalla, take your gear and get the hell out of here."

His announcement of my early discharge came as a complete surprise. I woke Binder, who grunted from inside his sleeping bag, "What do you want from me now?"

I apologized, reported that I was transferring command of the team to Gidi, and at 5:30 a.m., the crack of dawn, wet and tired, I went out to Highway 90 to try to catch a ride back to Tel Aviv.

***

I wiped my shoes on the doormat in front of the iron gate at the station entrance. It was 1:00 p.m. I stood there, tired and unshaved, in front of the gate sentry, who blocked the entrance in his starched and pressed uniform.

"Uri Dolev. I work here," I offhandedly told the guard, who clearly didn't recognize me.

"Wait here, I need to get approval from the master sergeant."

I dropped my duffel bag on the ground and hung my personal weapon over my shoulder. Kabesa, the army radio's veteran drill sergeant came out and measured me with his eyes; it was the first time he'd seen me in uniform.

"Dolev, you're a mess. Is this any way for an IDF captain to look? Don't ruin the discipline here for me, at least put some rubber bands in your pants."

I smiled. "Kabesa, is this really the army? Everyone here is a pen pusher, holding a microphone and a broom instead of a rifle!"

I hurried by him up the worn-out stairway to the station commander's office on the third floor. The receptionist gave me a quick look and nodded to indicate I could go in. The army radio commander, who was usually full of smiles, completely ignored my presence and continued to scribble on the paper in front of him. I lowered my weapon from my shoulder and leaned against the conference table. If I was going to wait, I decided to take advantage of the break. A blue plastic plate in the center of the table was laden with biscuits; an additional plate held apples, and there was a pot of coffee. I sat at the table and poured a cup of lukewarm coffee. I was tired and nervous while I waited for the station commander.

He eventually dropped his pen, leaned back in his chair, shifted uncomfortably, pushed the biscuit plate in my direction, and said, "Uri, there's something serious we need to discuss."

I didn't touch the military-style refreshments and waited for him to continue.

"I see that you were pulled straight from the field. You want the cook to prepare something for you to eat? Something warm?"

I shook my head and waited for him to continue.

"All right… I wanted you to know, I got an order. You're no longer working here. It isn't final yet, and I hope I can still reverse the decision. This information needs to stay between the two of us, right here in this room. Is that clear? Not a word. Strictly for your ears; it's best for all of us at this stage." His words were spoken without an iota of emotion.

I thought it was a joke at first and waited to hear the reason I was discharged from the division exercise. The thunderous silence and the commander's grim expression left no room for doubt — he had meant every word. "Did something happen?"

He made himself comfortable in his chair and looked me straight in the eye. "What do you think? I've been waiting here impatiently for days to hear your explanation. I was surprised too, and I still don't have a clue what's going on. I was hoping you'd know."

The commander leaned forward, grabbed hold of one of the metal spheres of the Newton's cradle resting on his desk and let it go, setting the other spheres in motion. He kept looking at me, waiting for an answer.

"What explanation? I'm being fired, and you don't even know why? What, you haven't been told? You're the army radio commander, not some ground soldier getting instructions," I snapped back.

The commander shifted uncomfortably in his chair again, looking pissed off. He turned his gaze toward the street, rubbed his chin, stood up, and immediately sat down again. "Look, Uri, not everything in the army comes with an explanation, but the army doesn't just fire someone for no reason. Especially not a civilian army employee who is also a reserve IDF captain, and in a combat unit, no less. I guess there are things I just don't know, but normally, where there's smoke, there's fire."

"What are you talking about? What smoke and what fire? Don't you think I deserve an explanation?"

The commander considered the matter. He picked up a biscuit, dipped it in his coffee and muttered, "That's just the way it goes. Unfortunately, I'm unable to offer you any more details. The army has made up its mind. I'm just here to inform you of the decision." He sounded impatient by the time he reached his last sentence.

"Explain something to me," I said and placed my M16 assault rifle on the floor. "Was it so urgent that they had to discharge me from reserve duty? You needed the southern command major general to personally intervene?"

"Dolev, you just need to accept it. Believe me when I tell you that the order came from way up high. Remember, your status as a temporary employee expires in a month. As of now, we don't have authorization to give you permanent status. So, no matter how you look at it, you can't work here anymore, got it?"

I was surprised yet amused at the same time. The whole conversation seemed surreal. I tried one more time. "Is it possible that in a few days we'll find out this order from way up high was a mistake?"

"I don't think so. There's a conscious decision here; this isn't a mistake." He pressed the intercom button. "Tell the department heads to come for our meeting, we're late as it is," he ordered the office manager. As far as he was concerned, our conversation was over. He'd received a mission, and he'd carried it out.

"That's it, I wanted you to know where things stand. This isn't carved in stone. I'm taking care of it, trust me. You need to give me some time to check things out. In the meantime, I ask you again not to say a word to anyone. Keep this information to yourself, Dolev."

Standing at the door of his office, I couldn't help myself anymore. "If this isn't a joke, then I came into your office as Uri D., and I'm leaving it as Josef K."

The commander glared at me. "I happen to have a literature degree, and I think you're blowing this all out of proportion. This isn't remotely Kafkaesque."

The station's news manager, who was also a friend, was waiting for me in the hallway. He took me to his office, locked the door, and told me, "Dolev, this isn't a laughing matter. This is serious. If you've gotten yourself involved in something, now's the time to say so. This is very important, listen well, the demand to have you fired is serious, this isn't a game. This came directly from the chief of staff's office, and they asked us to keep it under wraps.

"If you have connections, now's the time to have them pull some strings. I have no idea what this is about, but let me give you a little advice. Get a lawyer, and go figure out where this thing might lead."

"Lawyer? Why would I need a lawyer? Aren't you taking this whole thing too far?"

The news manager drew closer and whispered, "Listen to me, Dolev, you need a lawyer. And not just any lawyer — a top-caliber one. Now, go home, shower, change your clothes, get some sleep, and ask yourself why. Think back, perhaps you've done something that—"

"I haven't done anything. I really don't know what you want from me!" I answered in frustration.

With his quiet voice, the news manager repeated his advice. "Dolev, for your own good, go home. Think hard, look deep into your past. At least that way you'll know what to expect and what you'll need to explain."

I stood there perplexed, upset, tired, and filthy. I counted on one hand all the stupid things I'd done that came to mind. "Look, I've done a few dumb things but nothing too serious. I swiped tractors from the kibbutz garage a couple of times before getting my driver's license. I stole watermelons with my friend Yehiam Gruenwald from the neighboring kibbutz's fields. Once, after my army service, I drove with Kushi from the paratrooper's brigade to visit his friend in the hospital. On the way, Kushi stopped by a peach orchard and filled a couple of crates, even though there was a 'Private Property' sign right in front of us. I told Kushi it was daylight robbery. He responded by opening the glove compartment, taking out his unlicensed gun, and shooting at the sign. That's it. These are the only times I can think of when I broke the law."

The news manager nodded. "That's it? You're sure?"

I stared at the ceiling and tried to dredge up other events. "I participated in a Black Panthers demonstration and a couple of Peace Now demonstrations after the Yom Kippur War. I drove to Jerusalem to visit Moti Ashkenazi's protest tent. You think that's why they decided to fire me?"

"Look, I don't have a clue, and I'm convinced you're the only one who can get to the bottom of this. Right now, I just can't help you. That's the order we got. I suggest you try to review your every action over the past few years. Look for a reason. Trust me, it will help you down the road."

I left in a grim mood and drove home. I showered, slept for a few hours, and drove to the reserve duty base to return my gear to the quartermaster.

11

Two nerve-racking weeks passed.

Binder called me. "Pen pusher, you managed to escape reserve duty, but you can't get away from this one. Gidi Turner's mother passed away yesterday. Funeral's tomorrow, and everyone is coming. Promise me you'll come too."

After the war, I tried to refrain from going to funerals as much as possible. I attended only the few that I absolutely had to. Mostly, I stood off to the side as an indifferent onlooker. The traumas of war had not hardened my heart — I covered my emotions with a thin layer of cynicism mixed with indifference — but this time I felt an obligation to attend. I knew the deceased only in passing, but since the war, my friendship with Gidi had deepened, and we would meet from time to time outside of reserve duty.

A group of family and friends was gathered in the Rehovot Cemetery. I said hi to my friends from the unit and stepped away to find a shady spot. The *chevra kadisha* undertakers began to cover the grave with brown clods of earth, and I found myself staring at those around me. As was my habit, I started with the shoes, trying to guess what kind of man or woman wore them. An elderly man stood beside me, leaning on a walking stick and wearing a flat cap. My view of the open grave was blocked by the wide back of a tall man whose long blond hair was tied back with a black elastic hairband.

To his left stood a swarthy, gaunt man, probably of Jewish Yemenite descent, wearing an oversized skullcap from which two long coiled sidelocks emerged. An old man sat in a wheelchair, the wind scattering his thinning hair in an unexpected dance. Two men, one fortyish and wearing an elegant suit, the other younger and wearing a t-shirt, observed the funeral happenings from atop a small mound of earth.

I looked at the unfamiliar crowd and was surprised to see that all the men I just described were wearing the same shoes: black moccasins with bright crepe soles. Two white stitches adorned the shoes, one on each side. Strange and ugly shoes. I was amazed by this unreasonable coincidence. I could find nothing that could possibly connect these men other than their shoes. On the surface, they had nothing to do with each other, yet still, they had all come to the same funeral wearing the same shoes. This coincidence gave me no rest.

The funeral was over, but I was still busy trying to solve the riddle of the moccasins. The crowd of mourners was making its way to the parking lot, but I continued to stand there, pondering the coincidences that surprise us at the most unexpected of moments. Coincidences often separated by the same thin line that divides life and death. Six people had relayed the same message or maybe not. And I, the onlooker, received their message but was unable to decipher it.

My thoughts then drifted to completely different realms. I thought of our kibbutz group, the Cypress group, eight children born in the same place. Eight children raised together in the same kibbutz with the exact same conditions and education. Now, nothing remained to connect us.

***

When the days of *shiva* ended, I called Gidi and asked to see him. He welcomed me to his small house in Rehovot with a smile and the reddish beard he'd had since the war. I sat in a chair in the kitchen not knowing where to start. My dismissal from my job with the army radio and my conversation with the station commander now seemed to me like a fevered delusion. Despite the radio commander's strict admonition, I decided to consult with Gidi. I searched my mind for the right opening.

Gidi waited and stroked his beard. "Dolev, are you feeling unwell?"

I didn't answer. I didn't know where to begin or what I was allowed to tell him. Gidi took a bottle of arak from the freezer, stuffed with sage leaves and mixed with honey, and poured me a small glass. A few sips later, I managed to ease up a little.

"This is top secret! Everything I'm about to tell you. On your mother's grave, Gidi, this isn't a laughing matter, this story can't get out," I pleaded with him.

Gidi listened, he looked serious at first, then burst into smug laughter. "Drink some arak, Dolev, it'll make it all go away. Your story sounds like a whole lot of horseshit to me, some stupid prank pulled by the information security department. You're lucky this isn't the Shin Bet. Tell me, those leftist friends of yours from the radio, can't they help you?"

He was being obnoxious, and I wanted to just get up and leave, but then Gidi continued. "I have an idea; let's ask Herzberg, my uncle, he's a reserve colonel and a retired judge, let me talk to him."

I agreed. What did I have to lose?

A few days later I met with Gidi again. This time he made no jokes. "Herzberg told me you're in trouble. If he thinks so, then it means it's serious. Herzberg isn't just anyone. He knows what he's talking about. He—"

"How does your uncle know about this? I don't even know anything. I've no idea what they want from me!"

Gidi went to the refrigerator and took out the arak bottle.

"This isn't the time to be drinking arak," I said.

Gidi didn't listen and poured two glasses. "Herzberg has been working with the security forces for years. Trust me, his word is solid. The bad news is that Herzberg is convinced, without even knowing you, that you'll be gone from the army radio much sooner than you thought. He thinks they'll let you go in a month, or by the end of the year at the latest. To use Herzberg's words: 'Now your friend is in the cooking and softening up stage. These guys have patience. They're grilling him nice and slow for now, then they'll turn up the flames.'"

Gidi scratched his beard and didn't take his eyes off me.

"And how come this Herzberg knows everything?"

"I trust Herzberg. He's got connections and a lot of experience," Gidi said. "He's seen similar cases. He thinks the easiest and best thing to do is to just let it go and go home, then there's a chance they'll lay off your case."

I jumped from my chair. "Let this Herzberg resign if he wants to. I haven't done anything. Really, Gidi, why should I resign? Tell me, I just started to make it there."

Gidi looked away, unwilling to meet my eyes. "You always have the option of fighting it. Herzberg believes that your chances are slight, even if you happen to be right."

I dropped to the couch, pulled the glass of arak from the table, and drained it. I was suddenly very tired.

Gidi sat next to me and added, "According to Herzberg, the security services don't have enough proof right now and are still gathering evidence. Firing you is a scare tactic; sometimes that's enough. Time passes, the date comes, the dismissal goes into effect, and the case is closed. By the way, Herzberg was surprised they hadn't interrogated you yet."

I motioned for Gidi to refill my glass.

"Understand, you're up to your neck here," Gidi said and filled both glasses. "You think they have nothing on you, but you can't really be sure. Your uncertainty works in their favor."

I rubbed my temples, but it did nothing to ease my headache. "I can already see the headlines: 'Uri Dolev from the army radio is arrested.' Next they'll say I'm a leper with syphilis. "

Gidi took small sips of his arak and said, "All is not lost. In my conversation with Herzberg, he mentioned that the guys in the media are the biggest cowards. To quote him: 'Even the biggest sumo wrestler will lose his balance and tumble when pushed in just the right place.'"

I slept at Gidi's that night after we demolished a bottle and a half of arak. I woke up late with a headache and a roiling stomach.

Before I left his apartment, Gidi told me, "I'll call Binder today and have him bring the guys from the unit to demonstrate in front of the Ministry of Defense office. We'll sell copies of Kafka's *The Trial*. If Binder says the word, the whole reconnaissance commando unit will be there. Even a right-wing extremist like Hatuka will come. You're not alone, Dolev, always remember that."

For a moment, I allowed myself to be carried away by his enthusiasm. "You're right. The security services walk around with a stick up their asses when it comes to the media. They know that dirty laundry washed in public stays dirty no matter how much bleach they use. All the guys there know they'll have to go back into the real world one day." But then I got scared by the idea of a demonstration and pleaded with Gidi not to talk to Binder and, most importantly, not to make too much noise.

***

The World Today weekly magazine published a small item with the title: "Army radio editor suspected of state security felonies." Even though my name was not mentioned, I was stunned. At last, the reason for my dismissal was made known. Publicly. Agitated, I drove to the station to speak to the army radio commander. During the drive, my mood shifted from anger to anxiety. *They tell me to keep my mouth shut then leak prejudicial information to the media.* I was being toyed with and had no idea how I had even gotten involved in this hellish dance.

I bounded up the stairwell and rushed past the secretary without even acknowledging her presence. I stormed into the station commander's office, interrupting a staff meeting, and waved *The World Today* magazine at him.

"State security felonies? What are we even talking about? How come the media knows about it, and no one has said a word to me?"

The employees left their seats uncomfortable and embarrassed and walked out of the room. Even I was a little amazed by my outburst.

"Stay calm, Dolev, I'm taking care of this," the army radio commander snapped at me. "Anger isn't going to solve anything. Remember what I told you? Sit tight, don't talk to anyone. So why can't you keep your mouth shut? Why are you stirring up trouble You got some good advice, why don't you use it?"

An icy chill came over me. "You think I leaked this to the media?" I raised my voice. "Give me one good reason why on earth I would do that. You know perfectly well that I'm being harassed for no reason."

The radio station commander motioned for me to lower my voice. "Trust me, Dolev, you're in over your head. What did you need to go to the media for? I wasn't born yesterday; such stories don't just get to a magazine by accident. Look at your own actions before blaming other people."

"It definitely didn't come from me, and I've no idea how this got to the magazine."

"You think the security organizations would just invent such accusations out of the blue? They must have a reason. I don't understand why you keep saying you don't know what this is all about.

Something must have happened, right? Who did you tell about it? Maybe that's who leaked this to the press."

"This does nothing but hurt me. Someone wanted to bad-mouth me, to threaten and intimidate me, can't you see that? I wasn't the one who leaked this to the media." I was nearly shouting again by the time I finished.

"You reporters always rush to make things public, and think of the consequences only when the damage is done."

I realized I wasn't going to get any help from him.

"I'm being falsely accused, and this is what you have to say to me? That I'm behind the leak?"

"I hope you know what you're doing. As far as I can see, going to the media with this will only make things worse for you. Let me give you some personal advice. Stay away from reporters, at least for the foreseeable future. Keep your mouth under lock and key. 'No comment,' that's your best answer."

"I've been sitting on my ass doing nothing, and what good did it do me? *The World Today* writes that I'm a spy! Great strategy you got there for me." I spat out those last few sentences with any commas or periods and completely ran out of breath.

"I need a few more days," he said calmly. "Understand, Dolev, this whole business had gotten a little complicated and out of hand. Give me some time to figure out which way the wind blows. I'm taking care of this for you, I promise."

I went back home feeling depressed. Racking my brain, I eventually came up with an avenue to explore. The prime minister's military adjutant, a brigadier general, had been my company commander during my officer training, and we had kept in touch. I didn't have too many options left, so I played my last card. I called the prime minister's office and asked to speak with the military adjutant. I told the girl who answered the phone that this was personal and gave her my name. Much to my surprise, the adjutant answered immediately.

116 | Yossi Uzrad

I told him about my dismissal, the news item in *The World Today*, and asked him to find out what it was all about.

He listened patiently then said kindly, "It'll be all right. Give me a few days, and we'll see what happened there." Then he added, "Take it easy, Dolev, we don't take people out to the firing squad so quickly." He promised to get back to me in a few days.

I felt relieved after the conversation. The adjutant was in a position to know things, so I assumed that if he was calm, I shouldn't be too excited. Three or four days passed, and I didn't hear back from him. About ten days after our conversation, I called the prime minister's office again. This time the military adjutant's voice was cold and sharp.

"Listen well, Uri Dolev, don't you dare call here again. Ever. You're not my friend, got it?" Then he slammed down the receiver.

12

The kibbutz cowshed was the domain of Alfred and Hercules the bull, his pride and joy. Alfred had bought Hercules when he was just a little calf. That calf had grown to become a monster of a bull. His body was light brown with white spots, his head was covered with curly white hair, his horns were wide and sharp, and in his nose, a thick copper ring glistened.

Alfred attributed remarkable qualities to Hercules, and the bull's reputation as a stud was known throughout the Hula Valley. Hercules, without knowing it, was the subject of great interest not only to Alfred, but to Yehiam as well. Their mutual affection for Hercules had merely served to create a mutual suspicion. A strange and silent rivalry had developed between Alfred the adult and Yehiam the child. Alfred had been the kibbutz's dairy farmer for many years, and it provided him with countless stories that irritated Yehiam, who once told me, "Alfred is a sack of shit. I saw him once, beating Hercules with a stick."

Alfred used to walk about the farmyard barefoot and wearing nothing but shorts. During the winter, he wore a few extra pieces of clothing consisting of a gray tank top and leather sandals. Every child in Mishmar Hatsafon was afraid of him. Except for Yehiam, that is.

There was a rumor in the settlements of the valley that Hercules' balls were the largest in the Middle East. Alfred, of course, had started the rumor. The locals regularly stopped by to get an eyeful of the remarkable bull. Curious onlookers would stop by the shed to stare at Hercules as he trod the muddy bull pen, his giant testicles swinging from side to side as he walked. The beast was mostly indifferent to the attention, going hither and thither proudly, raising his head from time to time and shaking it to brush off the flies, scattering drops of saliva in every direction. Most of the day, the bull would just lie in the shed, slowly munching on the hay and alfalfa in his trough. Sometimes he would stop chewing, give those outside the pen a sad look, then snort and paw the muddy soil with his hoofs.

Whenever a crowd would gather, Alfred would rush over and relate the same old tired story. "I have a special method that always works. First, I prevent Hercules from having his way with the cows for at least ten days. Then I choose cows that are in heat and put them in the shed next to his just to tease him, make sure he starts to get all worked up. A few days later, when he is at his peak, I call the vet to have Hercules' sperm extracted. The results are always of the highest quality.

"Once, when Hercules saw the veterinarian approaching, he began to go wild and started charging the bull pen's iron fence. The force of his headbutting was such that the echoes reached all the homes in the valley. The vet was afraid to get into the pen, so I had to take the bull by the horns, as they say." He always stopped to laugh at his own joke here.

"I grabbed a horn with one hand, and with the other, pulled on the ring in his nose to stun him. I shoved his head under my arm, just like they taught us in the Palmach, gave a hard yank and a thrust, and threw Hercules to the ground. It was only then that the vet managed to draw the sperm from him." At that point, Alfred would grab one of the listeners beside him in a Nelson hold and pin the surprised victim to the ground as if he were Hercules.

Yehiam deeply disliked Alfred's stories and was convinced they were merely vehicles for bragging about himself. "For Alfred, Hercules is just a trophy to take pride in. All his fussing about Hercules stops the moment no one is around to tell his tall tales to," he once said to me.

Hercules' reputation spread far and wide. The Ministry of Agriculture organized tours for dairy farmers from all over the country so they could witness the phenomenon. Alfred, in his short pants, rubber boots, and gray tank top, would present himself before the dairy farmers to tell of Hercules' exploits.

"Our vet from Rosh Pina is a four-eyed weakling," Alfred would start out, "and he slipped on some cow shit once. One of the kibbutz children, Hilik Zisman, was standing by the pen and burst into laughter when he saw the vet wallowing in mud and dung. The vet got pissed off and smacked Hilik in the face with a shit-smeared hand. Hilik decided to get his revenge on the vet. During the vet's next visit, Hilik, who was quite the imp, mixed some vanilla ice cream in Hercules' sperm collection tubes.

"The veterinarian didn't notice and conducted the insemination with sperm mixed with ice cream. When the vet was finished, the little devil offered the tired man a cup of coffee and an oversized cone of vanilla ice cream laced with Hercules' special ingredient. The vet, who could hardly see anything even with his glasses on, ate the ice cream down to the last bite and even asked for a refill."

Alfred would burst into wild laughter and swear before everyone present, "There were a lot more births in the cowshed that year. That imbecile veterinarian walked about the cowshed with his chest puffed up and his face beaming, as if it had been his own sperm."

Alfred would then open the cowshed refrigerator and offer his dairy farmer friends a taste of that special ice cream.

***

Despite the tight-knit group mentality, Yehiam and I had managed to create a sort of subgroup all our own. We spent our free time together roaming the kibbutz yard, having long conversations. Other than me, Hercules the bull was the only who received such favored treatment from Yehiam. When the bull noticed Yehiam approaching, he would rush at him like a happy pet, stand by the fence, wave his tail to chase away the flies, and give him an affectionate look. Yehiam would offer the beloved bull some fresh hay, and while Hercules was chewing, he would stroke the bull's giant head and speak words of endearment in his ears. Between bites, Hercules would stick out a pink tongue and lick Yehiam's hand.

Yehiam Gruenwald led the way, and I followed after. He was tall and strong for his age, and he spoke very little. A gifted athlete, he was the star of the kibbutz volleyball team. I was never too important to the team but was liked by everyone. Alfred mockingly called us Max and Moritz, after a book about two mischievous boys. Our friendship lasted for many years. Together, we huddled next to the radio when Nehemiah Ben Avraham broadcast the Israeli soccer team games and jumped with joy when Nahum Stelmach scored a goal with a header against Lev Yashin, the Soviet Union team's famous goalkeeper.

***

When the Eichmann trial began, it seemed that life in the kibbutz came to a halt. Throughout the four months of the trial, Yehiam and I listened to the radio broadcasts together.

"The State of Israel is settling the score with a Nazi war criminal, with the whole world as a witness. Never forget this day," my father told me.

Yehiam and I spent whole days listening to the broadcasts. A few days after the horrifying testimony began, Tova Zisman, our homeroom teacher, stopped coming to school. At night, we could hear wailing coming from her room. Her crying fits lasted for hours, and she refused to open her door to anyone. At the end of the testimony stage she returned to the classroom as if nothing had happened. One of the kibbutz members, Shmulik Finklestein, testified at the trial, and we were extremely proud that our kibbutz was contributing to the effort of convicting Eichmann. The stories that Holocaust survivors told during the trial became the main topic of conversation in the kibbutz. Alfred the dairy farmer walked about the kibbutz yard with a pitchfork, saying, "We need to smoke all the Nazis out of their holes and kill them one by one."

***

As far back as my early childhood, I discovered that I remembered everything, that no detail was ever lost from my memory. In my mind, each event was neatly filed in its appropriate drawer, down to the minutest details. My memory had served my Cypress group companions as a substitute for a group diary. Yehiam would tease me and constantly test my ability to remember negligible bits of information by asking questions such as: "Who was fourth in the four-hundred-meter swim finals in the Tokyo Olympics?" "How many states voted in favor of the establishment of the State of Israel in the United Nations General Assembly?" "How high is Mount Hermon?" And I, like a robot, would recite my answers, down to the last tiring detail, and win Yehiam's appreciation along with a hint of ridicule. The more I tried to erase some of the information that had accumulated in my head, the more firmly the details were etched into it, refusing to fade away.

***

During the first few years after I left the kibbutz, I used to meet with Yehiam every time I'd come for a visit. After dinner, we would sit on outdoor recliners in the shade of the old carob tree in front of the veterans' neighborhood, where our parents lived, and catch up. My mother would spoil us with coffee and homemade pastries. Sometimes she even added an apple, sliced just like the ones we used to get in the children's house. Each meeting with Yehiam would eventually drift to days gone by, and since he too possessed an exceptional memory, we were constantly pulled back to our childhood, recreating the events with a more sober and adult perspective.

More than once, the memories took me back to places I had no wish to revisit, especially during sleepless nights. Many times the events of the Yom Kippur War inundated my thoughts and refused to leave. During one of my visits in the kibbutz I met with Yehiam on a Saturday afternoon. We descended the path and crossed a small Japanese-style wooden bridge over the stream flowing through the center of the kibbutz. Its water ran in a steady trickle all through the year, and gathered into a small ornamental pool by the northern tower, which during the Independence War had served as a guard post.

Yehiam walked around the pool, looking to see if it still had carp and goldfish swimming in it. I looked at the watchtower, one of the last remnants from the kibbutz's early days. A cultivated garden surrounded it, and its bare concrete walls were covered with moss and black lichen. Bullets had pockmarked the gray concrete in the Independence War during the attack on the kibbutz. It was siesta time in the kibbutz yard. It was restful in that secluded place, surrounded by tall trees. And a nice breeze passed through the branches of the bamboo jungle Menahem Ganani had planted many years ago. From a distance, we heard the wailing of a baby, which mingled well with the sloshing sound of the water flowing through the narrow channel of the stream. Those sounds were joined, then soon overwhelmed, by a metallic drumming coming from the south.

Into the cloudless blue sky emerged a pair of helicopters, flying low, clawing their way through the tranquility with a raspy, pulsating echo of engines. They were headed toward Lebanon. The black helicopters quickly moved away, eventually turning into two indistinguishable specks before disappearing completely.

"Look at them," I told Yehiam, "two tiny storks that lost the flock on its way back to the colder regions."

Yehiam kept staring at the sky long after the helicopters were gone from view. "It's amazing how quiet it is here. It's like living in a big bubble. My dad once sat me in a tractor tire and pushed it into the center of the swimming pool. It floated aimlessly on the water, and I sat in it with my eyes closed, without any fear in my heart. Despite being so close to the Syrian border, there was an untroubled air to our childhood here. Such peace and quiet were not to be taken for granted."

We stood and looked around the old watchtower. Two victims killed in the attack on the kibbutz during the Independence War were buried there. The graves were hastily dug, and the bodies buried during a brief respite in fighting. Tall trees grew around the graves, and their branches created a vast canopy with beauty and intimacy beneath it.

"Just like in European towns, the center of the kibbutz has a small, secluded cemetery. The kind in which lovers can walk, enjoy the tranquil air and imagine themselves to be in some romantic place. In Europe, cemeteries are also tourist attractions, and they don't carry the sense of grief and pain that hangs over nearly all the graveyards here in Israel," I said to Yehiam.

I looked up at the scars the bullets had left in the concrete walls of the tower. I slowly walked around the burial plot, pulling a few weeds that had grown by one of the gravestones. The northern tower looked much smaller and lower than I had remembered it.

"Do you remember when you lost your childhood innocence?"

Yehiam asked. "Childhood's end, that moment of realization, is always tied to one specific event, often an inconsequential one. Do you remember Baruch the electrician?"

Of course I did, and Yehiam continued as we went back through time together, "What about Yitzhak the barber? Joseph the cobbler?"

I told him that yes, I distinctly remembered all three, who worked as salaried employees in the kibbutz, outsiders.

"All right, this isn't what I wanted to say," Yehiam continued. "Udi and I used to play at being Tarzan on top of a Margosa tree by the main sidewalk leading to the old dining room. We tied a thick rope and jumped from one branch to another, howling wildly as we went. We thought that was Tarzan's call, like Johnny Weissmuller in the movies. We screamed as hard as we could.

"Baruch, the electrician, happened to be walking on the sidewalk one day. He stopped for a moment and said out loud, as if speaking to himself, 'I never knew the trees had asses in them.' His words immediately offended me. Udi kept playing at being Tarzan, but I turned crimson from shame, suddenly realizing just how ridiculous I looked. In an instant, Tarzan, my childhood hero, was transformed into this inconsequential boy wearing shorts, a green t-shirt, and single-strap sandals.

"I climbed down from the tree, ashamed and embarrassed. That was the moment I lost my childhood," Yehiam summed up.

We sat in silence on the stone bench by the old watchtower. A single ray of sunlight shone between the gravestones. Two leaves slowly swirled down from the trees then were swept away by the current of the stream until steadying like miniature boats in the middle of the pool. A solitary goldfish tried to nibble one of the leaves. The braying of an ass was heard from the petting farm on the outskirts of the kibbutz. Dozens of black snails latched on to the concrete sides of the pool. The subtle sound of the water murmuring in the gentle stream merged with the background noises then eventually faded away.

13

When the situation became complicated, and the sword of employment termination was about to descend on my head, I decided to talk to the radio station's union representative. My mysterious dismissal had been the talk of the station for quite some time.

The union representative, a famous radio anchor, spoke to me in his velvety voice, emphasizing each word with irksome slowness. "The rumors around the station aren't exactly flattering, to say the least. What do you have to say about that?" He took a pipe and a cleaning kit from his jacket pocket, letting me know he had all the time in the world.

"I took you for a serious-minded journalist who doesn't base his opinions on gossip. I came here to seek the union's protection, not to listen to more groundless accusations." I came off more hostile than I intended.

The radio anchor stuffed his pipe with tobacco. I was surprised when he responded to my aggressive reaction with understanding. "I apologize, I didn't mean to insult you, but there is a technical issue preventing me from helping out. The union is authorized to represent only regular radio employees, and since you are a temp, we are procedurally unable to represent you. We are seeking a way to overcome this technical hindrance. I will personally speak with Dova'le Hershko. As chairman of our worker's organization, I'm sure he'll want to have his say."

A few days later, Dova'le Hershko received me in his office. His silver hair was neatly combed, he wore blue Dacron pants, and a jungle of white chest hair burst out of his white shirt. Something about his appearance reminded me of my father. A naive picture of the kibbutz farmyard hung on his office wall, painted by Yohanan Simon: a water tower, a woman wearing a headscarf sitting on the grass holding a baby, a group of boys playing basketball in the background, a towering cypress tree with a white cloud hanging over it. The kibbutz had never looked more cheerful and full of hope.

Dova'le Hershko interrupted my train of thought. "Yes, young man, how can I help you?"

Dova'le's prominent position in the party and the labor federation marked him as a sure candidate for the federation's future chairman. Dova'le was known as a man of mystery, someone pulling the strings far from the prying eyes of the media. His connections extended well beyond his own party. Dova'le had a lot of influence in all the other major political parties, and government ministers often consulted with him because of this.

His secretary came into the room and set a cup of tea and a bagel on a plate in front of him. She offered me a glass of orange juice, which I accepted. When she had gone, as succinctly as I could, I told Dova'le about my coming dismissal. He listened patiently. Finally, he casually asked his secretary to get him the defense minister's office on the line.

"All right, young man, rumors about some unpleasant business related to you reached my desk a few weeks ago. I wonder what Mot'ke has to say about this. We've been friends for many years, but he keeps track of every little favor I ask from him.

"Mot'ke is no sucker. Some time will pass and then, out of the blue, he will call and ask me to get something done for him in return. This is just the way it works. Sometimes I need a favor from him, other times he needs a favor from me."

The secretary poked her head through the door and said, "Mot'ke is out of the office. I left him a message."

Dova'le beckoned his secretary to come to his desk, glanced at his calendar, and said to me, "Come back in about three days. The guys from the radio station asked me to help. Nicely. So, I'll see what I can do."

Next, he took a bottle of cognac and two small glasses from his desk drawer. "This is a traditional remedy that always helps. One shot, young man, will make you feel much better, trust me. It takes patience to unravel such a tangle. Surely you know how slowly the wheels of justice turn." He pronounced the cliché as if he'd just thought of it and drank the cognac in a single gulp.

I walked out of the office and slowly walked down the corridor. Paintings by Israel's most prominent artists hung on its walls. I was struck by contradiction of the paintings of Joseph Zaritsky, Mordecai Ardon, Yehezkel Streichman, and many others gracing the walls of the world's most boring office building.

***

A few days later, I found a brown envelope with no return address in my mailbox. Inside, was a torn notebook page with the following brief message: *Mr. Dolev, I have something important for you. You can meet me every day between the hours of two and four, 12 Kaplan Street, fourth floor. You won't regret it, Rachel Tenenboim.* The postmark indicated that the letter had been mailed from Tel Aviv three days before.

The following morning, I drove to 12 Kaplan Street to meet the mysterious Rachel Tenenboim. I skipped the elevator and climbed the four flights of the Jewish Agency building. I walked up and down the corridor until I spotted a small sign: Rachel Tenenboim,

Accounting. I tentatively knocked on the door.

"Come in." The woman's voice was hoarse from too much smoking. A fiery-haired woman sat behind a simple office desk, wearing a simple Bedouin dress. She glanced at me over her glasses.

"Uri Dolev…?" I said.

"Oh, it's you." She came out from behind her desk and placed a finger on her lips to indicate that I shouldn't talk. She came closer and said in a low voice, "Not here, Uri. There are nicer places, right? Let's go to a coffee shop."

Of all the coffee shops in the world she had to choose the one at the Israel Journalists Association building — Beit Sokolov. It was apparent that Rachel knew the place well. With an easy movement, she freed a newspaper from a long wooden pole and sat in the farthest corner with her back to the wall, eyeing the few people sitting at the tables.

She leaned toward me and said in her cigarette-stained voice, "I just want to help you, yes? I have sympathy for people who come from the kibbutz, especially from Mishmar Hatsafon. They told me you're a good guy, yes? And I thought I might be able to help a little."

I was still getting over my surprise at the meeting. The woman in front of me was nothing at all like the one I had imagined. "Excuse me, what are you talking about?"

"You come from Mishmar Hatsafon, right? My sources are never wrong."

"Where do you know me from?" I really had no idea what was going on.

"That's the thing… I… don't. But I know a little about you. It's a long story, and it isn't that important. Let's just say that I have connections and sources, not just in your kibbutz. You are on everyone's lips. People are talking about you in the dining hall. The word is that you're all right, and it is too bad you left, yes? Not everyone believes the stories circulating in the kibbutz right now."

She was getting me all wound up. Curious as well. "What are they saying about me in the kibbutz?"

"Well, as you can imagine, they have you guilty of a little of this and a little of that: embezzlement, spying for enemy countries. You know how it is in the kibbutz, no one has any secrets."

I heard her, but I couldn't believe my ears. "What are you talking about? I'm a traitor now?" I erupted at her.

"I'm neither a prosecutor nor a judge; this is the gossip in your kibbutz. So... I did my own research, well, not me exactly, but my younger brother, who is the brightest in our family."

She looked about her suspiciously to make sure no one was listening and whispered to me, "My brother, let's just say he has a position in the right places... In the civil service, yes? Now do you get it? He's... on the inside."

I shuddered, sitting on the edge of my seat, listening to a woman I had never met or even seen before.

"Believe me, Uri, I am hoping I'm not making the mistake of a lifetime here, maybe I'm sticking my nose in the wrong place. My gut instinct tells me: Rachel, dear, just sit tight and don't interfere, yes? But I have a very good friend in your kibbutz, and he pressured me to do it, so I went to speak with my younger brother, and it turned out he is very familiar with the stories about you, yes?

"Normally, you need a pair of pliers to get a single word out of my brother's mouth. But with a story like yours..." She shrugged. "As they say, shit floats on water, yes? Here, it got published in that magazine, right? Everyone in your kibbutz knows that it was about you."

I cringed in my chair, barely able to breathe. "How do they know about this in the kibbutz? I haven't even spoken to my parents about this."

Rachel was barely able to hold back her laughter. "Two guys arrived in Mishmar Hatsafon. You know what they say, two are better than one, yes? They came to ask around about you. They met with the kibbutz secretary, with a few other members, maybe. Well, rumors soon spread like wildfire. The curiosity was killing me, so I asked my brother. He was as silent as a fish until I spelled out your name, and he… gave me this slight motion of his head. Bingo, I knew I wasn't wrong."

Rachel Tenenboim had managed to raise my anxiety levels to the verge of dread. I wondered who could have gone to Mishmar Hatsafon in search of information about me.

Rachel leaned toward my ear and said, "And my brother hinted to me that is all just a load of fluff, yes? He didn't say much, only that someone snitched on you. I may look stupid, but I have good instincts. I realized the snot-nosed official in charge of your case is just jabbering. This is all hogwash…"

She looked both ways again to make sure no one was listening and said, "I guess you stepped on the wrong toes, yes? This little shithead… one of your friends in the army radio ratted you out to get back at you. Trust me on this…"

I was glued to my seat. Shocked. I racked my brain trying to think which of my friends at the radio station might have implicated me.

"Uri, here's some free advice from a Jewish Agency accountant, tread on your tiptoes, yes? You hear me? Don't blow any horns, keep quiet, keep your head down. Once the storm passes, you can resurface. Where my brothers works, they eat people like you for breakfast, and I hope I'm making myself perfectly clear."

I remained silent, and Rachel continued preaching to me. "Tell me, Uri, why did you have to go and tell your troubles to that scumbag… what's his name? It's on the tip of my tongue, the one with the white beard who sells communism in his magazine, wrapped with pictures of naked girls. That was the wrong move. The guys in the organization really don't like this tabloid — this is what you media people call this kind of newspaper, right?"

Two people came into the sleepy coffee shop and sat at the table next to ours. I moved my chair closer to Rachel's and angrily hissed, "Who cares what they wrote in that magazine? Why is it even important? It didn't come from me."

Rachel wasn't swayed. "Someone spoke with the magazine, and this publication only added fuel to the fire. In the organization, they think they know everything, that they're the only ones with any sense, that they're always right, yes? You're not one of them, understand? They have no sympathy for someone like you, even if you haven't done anything, yes?

"I planned on saying a single sentence to you, and I ended up reciting a whole book. Remember, I never spoke to you, and I don't even know you." Rachel closed the newspaper, slung her bag over her shoulder and exited without even having touched her coffee.

I remained there, shocked and confused. The thought occurred to me that Rachel Tenenboim might also be a part of the conspiracy against me.

***

That week, the army radio commander handed me an official termination letter. It included a laconic message stating that from the moment the letter was handed to me I was forbidden from broadcasting. I was asked to return my press card and any other equipment belonging to the station. I was also asked to refrain from entering the station building, which was officially a military area. The brief, emotionless phrasing hurt me more than the termination letter itself. The army radio wasn't just a workplace I loved; the station was a home for me, one that gave me status and a sense of belonging.

The cold wind blowing from between the lines matched the winter days of December 1978. The simply worded instructions gave me the feeling that the main objective was not the termination, but my public humiliation. I read and reread the official document and knew that I mustn't give up. The atmosphere around me was chilly and hostile. I initiated a meeting with a select group of friends, senior reporters from the station. Following the conversation, some of them decided to help me with my struggle. I found some comfort in that, a little encouragement for my demoralized heart.

***

From the army radio building in Jaffa, I drove to meet Dova'le Hershko again. While driving down HaYarkon Street, I noticed a white Ford Escort driving close behind me. I turned onto Ben-Gurion Boulevard, and the Escort turned after me. *They're following me. And they are not even trying to hide it.*

I continued to drive down the boulevard with the Escort hot on my tail. Stressed, I accelerated, going through the Dizengoff Street traffic light a split second before it turned red. The Ford remained glued to my bumper. I slowed down and stopped by the side of the road. The white Escort, with two young men in sunglasses inside, sped past my car and kept going. I tried to relax by taking deep breaths, and after a few minutes of waiting, pulled back into traffic. On Ibn Gabirol Street, I saw that the Escort was behind me again. I was convinced this would end with an attempt to hurt me.

"Don't lose your grip here, Dolev. Stay calm, and don't do anything stupid." Hearing the words out loud helped a little.

I took comfort in the fact that the sidewalks were brimming with pedestrians, and the roads were jammed with traffic. Still, my heart pounded in my chest. On Ibn Gabirol Street, I stopped by a crowded bus station. I opened a window and asked directions to the Worker's Organization building on Arlozorov Street. I knew the way, I just wanted to talk to someone.

Back on the road, I glanced at my watch and cursed; it was already time for my meeting with Dova'le Hershko. I continued down

Ibn Gabirol, then turned sharply into Arlozorov. When I got close enough, I pulled a U-turn, then came to a shuddering halt at the guard booth for the Worker's Organization building. I opened my window, presented my press pass, and said, "The secretary general is waiting for me, I'm late."

The guard immediately opened the gate, and I took the first open spot in the parking lot. I looked back at the street and saw no trace of the white Escort. I ran to the entrance door, and instead of waiting for the elevator, I took the stairs two at a time to the fifth floor. Panting, I went straight to Dova'le Hershko's office. The secretary smiled at me and led me to Hershko's room.

He stood up and came to greet me, reaching out to grip my shoulder as if we were old friends. Immediately and unceremoniously he said, "Listen well, Mr. Dolev. When I mentioned your name to Mot'ke, he said, and I'm quoting, 'Uri Dolev from the army radio? You should know that this guy is considered a hardcore extremist, a spy, worse than Udi Adiv. Maybe they told you he is a nice guy, I don't know. But our guys are sure this little punk of yours is one of the heads of this country's most extreme left-wing organizations.'"

For a moment, I thought I'd faint. I sat down, wheezing, and poured myself some orange juice from the carafe on the table. After I swallowed, I looked at Dova'le. Once again, I noticed how much he resembled my father, even his facial expressions. "Is that what the Minister of Defense told you?" My voice was trembling. "That I betrayed my own country like Udi Adiv? Do you believe that?"

Dova'le rolled up his shirtsleeves while he answered. "This is what Mot'ke said. Personally, I don't know anything." By then he was back behind his desk.

I drank the remaining orange juice in my glass in a single gulp. "You're comparing me to Udi Adiv? A man who traveled to Syria and, of his own free will, handed the Syrians information that could harm our country? Udi Adiv was convicted of spying against Israel and is now in prison. Udi Adiv cooperated with the enemy and handed them state security secrets for ideological reasons.

"They are completely out of their minds. I still don't even know what this whole thing is about." I tried to push back the tears stuck in my throat. "Tell me, if any of this is true, why am I not in a Shin Bet interrogation room right now? Do you think such serious allegations would result merely in losing my job at the army radio?"

Hershko leaned across his desk and continued, unperturbed. "I know Mot'ke down to the soles of his shoes. We happen to wear the same size. We've both come a long way in politics, two old foxes, in and out of the vineyard, we've eaten our fair share of grapes together. Mot'ke is a stubborn old mule with a lot of experience who's been plodding his way forward since forever. I have a lot of respect for him, and I'm convinced there is nothing personal going on against you." He shrugged.

"Maybe the service guys took it a little too far; it happens. Someone kicked a table too hard, and a vase fell unintentionally. Let me, Uri Dolev, give you a little bit of advice: just leave the radio station and don't make a fuss about it. You'll see that things aren't as bad as they seem. You're a young man with a good head on your shoulders.

"Do as I ask and be patient. Unravelling unnecessary entanglements is my specialty. I'll sit with Mot'ke, and we'll come to some arrangement that will make everyone happy. We'll appoint you as a foreman in one of our factories, one that has nothing to do with state security, we'll find you a job in one of our supermarkets. Life will go on, and everyone will be happy."

14

The first time I went to visit Tel Aviv, my mother took me to the city zoo. It was surrounded by a high wall, and we were required to buy admission tickets. Paying to watch animals had seemed completely illogical to me at the time. I admired the cages with the bears, lions, tigers, giraffes, elephants, and monkeys. In my pants pocket, I found the remains of a pink coconut snack my mother had bought me. I approached one of the cages and extended the snack beyond the safety net. Two baboons quickly bounded toward me to win the food. One quickly snatched the snack, and the other bit my hand. I yelped, and my mother jumped up from her seat on the bench.

"Why? Why are these things always happening to you? Get away from that cage! Can't you ever do what you're told?" My mother, the kibbutz nurse, looked at the bleeding bite wound. "It isn't serious, we'll find a first aid kit and dress it up for you."

I held back my tears. People crowded around us and wanted to see what had happened to me.

A woman said to my mother, "Ma'am, I'm sure they'll have a first aid kit in the office."

My mother grabbed my other hand and practically pulled me to the administration office. She carefully cleaned the wound, applied some iodine, and shook yellow Dermatol powder over it. She placed a pad of gauze on the wound and wrapped my hand with a bandage.

"We'll need to see Dr. Zucker when we get back to the kibbutz; you may need a rabies shot."

The events of that summer vacation left physical reminders: the monkey bite scar and fourteen red, itchy dots from the rabies shots that circled my bellybutton.

I preferred our kibbutz petting zoo to the Tel Aviv one. Our animals were small and never very rare, but we developed a personal attachment to them. Each of us had to work in the petting zoo once a week. We took care of the animals on our own, gave them fresh water, fed them, and cleaned the cages. Each day in the petting zoo came with some new surprise: a warm egg recently laid, a new litter of guinea pigs, or a rabbit that had died in its cage.

One afternoon, when I went to feed the animals, Nurit Schory was supposed to be on duty with me but was late as usual. The peacock cage had accidentally been left open, and a single peacock found himself in the goose yard. The flock of geese approached the intruder with loud honks and flapping wings. The peacock spread his colorful tail to frighten his attackers. The geese were unimpressed and surrounded the peacock and attacked him. The peacock folded his feathers and tried to escape. The geese closed in on him from every direction in a coordinated assault.

Moments later, the poor peacock collapsed to the ground, and his beautiful feathers scattered. I stood, fascinated, beyond the fence and looked on at the cruel sight without doing anything. The geese continued to peck at the peacock and trample him with their feet.

When I left the place running, I bumped into Alfred and muttered excitedly, "I think that… the geese are killing the peacock."

Alfred gave me a hard look, lowered the scythe from his shoulder, and said. "Well, and did you chase away the geese?"

I stood shamefaced and shook my head. Alfred spat on the scythe, and a few tiny drops of spit splattered on my face. Then he took a whetstone from his pocket and passed it over the blade of the scythe several times. He wiped his hands on his undershirt, fixed the sunglasses on his forehead, and returned the scythe to his shoulder. He gave me a little push on the back, and we set off for the petting zoo with me doing my best to keep up with him.

"Come, little man, let's see what we can do. Aren't you ashamed of being afraid of geese? They just make a lot of noise. One kick and you could have scattered them all to hell."

He opened the goose pen gate with a kick and went inside. The entire flock ran toward him with loud honking. Alfred stood in the middle of the pen among the geese, waved his scythe, and scattered the birds back to their cages. He picked up the dead peacock from the muddy ground and slung him across his shoulder. He gave me a scornful look as he went out of the pen. Before leaving the petting zoo, he gave my backside a mighty kick.

I sat on the petting zoo bench, ashamed down to my bones. I pitied myself more than I mourned the dead peacock, and the tears dropped down on my cheeks all on their own. That's when Nurit arrived.

"What happened to you?"

I swiped at the tears with my sleeve. "Alfred kicked me," I said and pointed at my backside.

"And are you going to tell on him?" Nurit asked.

"I don't think so. It doesn't hurt like before."

I wiped my face, then Nurit and I returned to the children's house, which made me feel much better.

***

The routine of our lives in the kibbutz was comprised of studying, working on the farm, and taking part in social activities. There was only one place we were not allowed to work — the pigsty. Only adults worked there. The pigsty was built on the outer edges of the kibbutz with a small slaughterhouse beside it. The pigs were fed kitchen refuse.

After each meal, food scraps were gathered into large containers then poured into an improvised feeding trough, which was simply a metal barrel cut in half. The pigs would storm the garbage and dig into it squealing and snorting until the barrel trough was empty. Once a month, normally on a Tuesday afternoon, the gate of the path leading to the pigsty was locked. That was the day a butcher from Kiryat Shmona would come in a blue pickup truck.

The pigs set aside for the slaughter would be taken to a small yard paved with concrete, where they were washed using hoses. The pigs, as if aware of their impending demise, emitted deafening squeals the whole time. When they were clean, the butcher's assistant would tie a rope around a pig's head and drag it to the butchering station. Using a block and tackle, the pig was picked up by its hind legs. The butcher would pass the large knife one last time over the grinding machine and with a single swift movement slit the squealing pig's throat. Blood splattered in every direction, and when it stopped spurting, his assistant, wearing butcher's boots, washed the blood off the concrete floor with a powerful stream of water. The butcher tugged at the chains, and the carcass was lifted until it was suspended in the air. Then he slit the pig's belly, after which his assistant quickly washed the floor again. When the job was done, the assistant would load the meat cuts onto the blue pickup truck, and they would drive off until the next time.

***

Hilik, our schoolteacher Tova Zisman's son, was one year older than me and was in Nurit and Haya's class. For years, Tova had instilled in us the values of morality, discipline, and the fair treatment of others. But the values she had impressed upon us did not take root in her son. From an early age, Hilik worked in the dairy farm with Alfred, who fondly called the youth a "little punk." At night, Hilik would scour the kibbutz yard for stray cats. The he'd put them in a sack and place them in the old bread slicer that stood abandoned by the dairy farm.

Hilik routinely came up with insanely cruel pranks. Everyone in the kibbutz knew the story of how he had once gone out with two teenagers from the city who had come to see the cows in pasture. Hilik pointed at the fence marking the cows' grazing area and dared the teenagers to piss on the fence wires. Of course, the teenagers had no idea that the fence was electrified with a low-voltage current to deter the cows from trying to cross it. One of the teenagers accepted the challenge and was hit with an electric jolt straight to his privates. He rolled on the ground for the next five minutes, wailing with pain, and clutching his testicles. Hilik was extremely proud of this prank.

***

Over the course of six months, prisoners from the military confinement base "Prison 6" dug communication trenches for the kibbutz's protection. While digging the trenches next to the pigsty, the remains of a Byzantine-era settlement were discovered. In the winter, after rainy days, one could find potsherds and copper coins there. One day, Udi and I were walking to the pigsty together. On the way we met Haya and Nurit and told them we were going to look for antiquities.

"Hilik is going there too," Nurit said. "Be careful. If he does something to you, just let me know and I'll teach him a lesson. Things never end well when Hilik's around."

By the dairy barn we met Hilik, who was equipped with a rake and rubber boots. "Alfred has two Roman coins and a broken oil lamp in his room," he said. "It was raining all week. Come to the pigsty with me, and we'll search for antiquities together. If we hurry, we might even get to watch the pigs being slaughtered, then we'll go searching for artifacts in the communication ditches."

"I'm not coming if they're slaughtering pigs," said Udi, who had a special fondness for animals.

Hilik looked at Udi contemptuously. "You guys are so slow that I bet the butchers have already finished. They came early today, and I probably missed the slaughter of our biggest pig."

We went with Hilik and passed by the granary. Udi noticed a sparrow nest that had fallen off a eucalyptus tree. Inside it were three hatchlings. Their bodies were transparent and their beaks small and yellow. Hilik picked up one of the birds, held it by its little leg and hurled it against the granary, leaving behind a brown-red smear on the whitewashed wall. He went to wipe his hand on his pants and noticed one of the hatchling's little legs had torn off and was stuck to his fingers. He tossed the torn leg to the ground and stomped it with his boot.

When he picked up another hatchling from the nest, Udi screamed at him. "No! Come on, Hilik, take pity on him. I'll raise them. Hilik, let me raise the baby sparrows."

Hilik sneered at Udi. Smugly, he held the second bird by the leg, swung it in the air a few times, then hurled it at the granary wall. "Stop whining over the stupid sparrows," he said to Udi, who stood there rooted to the ground, appalled. "Alfred told me this is how the Nazis used to kill children. There's a reason I'm killing them; it's because of the vipers in the granary."

"What do these hatchlings have to do with vipers in the granary?" I protested.

Hilik chuckled scornfully. "You're just a bunch of little kids who don't know anything, and I don't feel like explaining." Hilik picked up the last baby bird and prepared to hurl it to the wall as well.

Udi burst into tears and begged him. "Please, Hilik, don't. I'll give you whatever you want; I have lots of marbles."

Hilik hesitated for a moment, swung the hatchling back and forth and said, "Who needs your stinking marbles? Look at these birds, sitting around all day pecking at the grain sacks. It's because of them that the grain scatters. Then mice and rats come to the granary, and everyone knows where there's mice, there's vipers. This is why you need to kill as many sparrows as possible."

Hilik threw the last hatchling, and its body exploded on the wall. "You two are too small and don't know anything yet. Come to think of it, I don't need you. I'm going to look for antiquities on my own."

15

After much deliberation, I decided to share what had happened to me with my parents since there was no point in hiding it from them anymore. More and more people in the kibbutz were talking about it, and I assumed it was only a matter of time before my name would be mentioned in the media in an unflattering way.

I went to Mishmar Hatsafon for the weekend. For a little bit, I felt like I was home again: the festive Shabbat eve dinner in the communal dining hall, the kibbutz members all wearing their khaki pants and white shirts, and the sight of familiar faces filled me with warmth and comfort. Friends came to greet me, and even Alfred clapped my shoulder, and whispered, "We're not crazy about leftists or righties here, but we'll help you out. We've already spoken with all the right people to make sure you're treated fairly. Trust me, you're in good hands."

Others ignored my presence and passed by me as if I were invisible. At one end of the dining room, at a table set apart from the rest, sat the bachelors and widowers, with Max Tishler, AKA Gurnischt, prominent among them in his blue work shirt. I went over and said hello to him.

He raised his eyes from the chicken soup. "Life in the city isn't that great. Over there, every man is his own lone wolf. Here, you can't spend five minutes alone in your doghouse without people coming to check how you are doing."

Hilik came to me holding a food tray. "Personally, I wasn't surprised in the least when I heard the stories about you. I knew that day would come. You were always a self-righteous Arab lover. You think I forgot about that night-navigation exercise near Nablus during our officer's training course? Because of you, we had to walk an extra five kilometers. We could have crossed a watermelon field for a shortcut, but you threatened us that you'd file a complaint with the course commander. Even back then I knew you had a thing for camel jockeys. Kuntz is just like you, same family. The apple didn't fall far from the tree."

After dinner, in my parents' room, I told them what was going on. I tried to minimize it as much as possible so as not to worry them too much. My mother was concerned only with the idea that someone wanted to fire her gifted son from the army radio.

My father remained unconcerned. "Just explain to them that they're wrong," he said while leafing through the newspaper. "Overall, we're talking about a serious-minded lot that takes care of our national security. But they can make mistakes too. If they didn't understand the first time, just explain it to them again."

My mother suggested I consult with Kuntz because of his connections with the party's parliament members. My father raised his eyes from the newspaper and grunted. "Moshe talks a lot and does very little."

I'd been under the impression that my father had forgiven his brother since the latter had lost his son, but apparently, their relationship had settled back into the old cold, reserved mold. Later that evening, I went to visit Henka and Kuntz. I told my uncle about the suspicions against me and that I had been fired. Kuntz listened attentively, growing angrier and more agitated as my story progressed. When I finished, he stood up with his head held high, appearing ready to set out and strike at the enemy. He grabbed a sheet of paper from his desk and waved it like an orator facing a crowd of true believers.

"Those right-wing idiots are a bunch of shitheads. Crooks who always go looking in all the wrong places. A deadly combination of stupidity and misguided diligence."

Even before I could react, he continued heatedly, "Listen to me well, Uri. "Don't be naïve. Here in Israel, this is the way the system has worked since forever. Do you remember that sad story with Aharonchik Cohen from Kibbutz Sha'ar HaAmakim? A true Renaissance man, a brilliant scholar, an expert in Middle Eastern affairs. So Isser Harel's Shin Bet security services decided he was spying for the Russians and threw him in prison.

"It's no secret that Aharonchik was a different kind of man, strange and aloof, working on his own. His causes were noble, of that I have no doubt. He kept stirring the pot until everything got burned. And what did he want? Just to promote his academic research about the Arab countries. No espionage was ever involved, I can tell you that much with certainty."

My uncle paused briefly, probably to catch his breath, then continued his tirade with renewed vigor.

"I know Aharonchik well — a stickler who leaves no stone unturned, all in the name of his research. He was stupid now and then. I won't argue with that. To this day I still don't understand why he had to hang around with that Russian guy. But a spy? Isser's guys were looking for a scapegoat, why? Because Ben-Gurion wanted to screw Meir Yaari. Isser's hoodlums from the Shin Bet ambushed Aharonchik then bragged about catching a big, fat fish. Isser Harel's shitheads knew that the Russian cultural attaché was working for the KGB. The Shin Bet stood aside and let Aharonchik step right into the trap. Isser never bothered to warn Aharonchik about that Russian guy. Get it? He was set up, all to make the leaders of the rival United Workers Party look bad. And what did Aharonchik really do? Just had tea with the Russian embassy's cultural attaché. And what did they talk about? Nasser, Pushkin, and Lenin. Then they accused him of betraying state secrets to an enemy country and endangering national security!

"Look, Uri, this is just the way Ben-Gurion's Workers' Party of the Land of Israel used to work. He invented the system. Menahem Begin's Herut merely improved it. Nothing ever changes in this country. There's no difference between Begin and Ben-Gurion, understand? It's like comparing twin evils. Still, I prefer the Workers' Party of the Land of Israel hypocrites to the fascists from the Lehi and the Irgun. Just look at them now that they are running this country, disguising their hoodlum ways under the cover of Begin's polite European mannerisms. But patience, Uri, the truth will eventually come to light, just like in Aharonchik Cohen's case."

I finally got a chance to speak. "Great, but even if your impressive theory is correct, what good did it do to Aharonchik? He ended up in prison for years."

Kuntz paced back and forth, and I was sure he was still busy with his own words rather than the fact I had just laid before him. "So, Aharonchik did a little prison time, no big deal. He ate at the taxpayer's expense, used his time in jail to his advantage, continued to write up his research, and published a very nice book. The party and Kibbutz Sha'ar HaAmakim supported his ideological struggle, and thanks to Aharonchik's sacrifice, they changed the law."

While Kuntz fervently spoke on, Henka sat on the sofa and knitted. Before I left, she raised her head from the wool sleeve and quietly said, "Remember, Uri, there is no shortage of evil men in our world. Give anyone a little power, and the stick-bearing kapo in him will come out in a second."

16

The termination of my employment at the army radio became a reality. The fighting spirit that had motivated me in the beginning gradually faded, and I sank deeper and deeper into long bouts of melancholy and chronic fatigue. I was close to despair and about to give up.

My associates, perhaps out of fear, mostly refrained from encouraging or supporting me. When I walked around the station, there were those who stared at me, openly displaying their disdain. Others lowered their heads, tried to hide behind a wall, or slip away unnoticed. I felt like a leper. My every word was questioned and doubted. My integrity, the source of my pride, was sullied. I felt unwanted, as my presence created a general sense of discomfort and embarrassment. I suspected everyone and preferred to trust no one. My thoughts revolved around trying to recreate my every past action, but I couldn't find a single thing that could justify the sanctions against me.

Among the few who still believed in me was the radio's political correspondent, who turned, of his own volition, to the prime minister's office, no less. In his roundabout way, the office head answered the political correspondent in the following manner. "There was once a pious man who was sent to a butcher's shop to buy a chicken on Shabbat eve. Upon reaching the shop, the Hassid saw a long line of patrons waiting for the butcher. The pious man feared his wife might not be able to prepare the chicken soup in time for Shabbat. Abandoning his teachings, he crossed the road and bought a non-kosher chicken from the gentiles' shop."

The office head never bothered to give my friend the interpretation of his fable. Who was I in this story? The pious man? His wife? The butcher? Or was I the chicken to be cooked?

***

My mood darkened. I felt lost and helpless. I stopped by a falafel stand on Ben Yehuda Street, took a bite but couldn't bring myself to eat, frustration eating at me instead. I threw my food in the garbage. I continued walking, all the way to Café Mersand. It was early afternoon, but I was tired and the coffee shop was almost empty. I sank into a chair, and Mike, the owner, pushed a table closer to me. I didn't need to say a word to him. Mike had known me for years, ever since I had arrived in Tel Aviv. He returned a few minutes later with a cappuccino and a slice of cheesecake.

He studied my face carefully for a moment then said, "How about a small glass of vodka? On the house."

I politely refused. I slowly drank my coffee and took a bite of the delicious cake. I sat there for half an hour, staring at the passersby. I paid and thanked Mike, who gave me a friendly pat on the back. I continued walking until I reached Allenby Street. From there, my feet led me on their own to the Carmel Market. I bought some apples at the first fruit stand. I bit into an apple and tossed it away after a few bites.

Every little mishap in my life had taken on monstrous proportions. My nerves were shot. One Saturday evening, I went to buy tickets at the movie theater on Dizengoff Square. An overgrown hoodlum pushed past the line and cut in front of me.

When I called him on it, he raised his hand threateningly and said, "Get out of here. Who do you think you are?" Then he spat, "Fuck you" and stepped closer so his face was an inch from my own, waiting for my reaction.

The crowd accepted this with indifference; ignoring things is an art form in our neck of the woods. I couldn't shake the feeling this was another intentional act of harassment and devised an elaborate theory. This act of provocation was intended to drag me into a physical confrontation to frame me. I gritted my teeth, overwhelmed with frustration, and stepped aside so as not to give the jerk any reason to continue to pester me.

***

Days passed. The lack of certainty, the tension, and the idleness served to worsen my constant state of fatigue. One evening, following yet another uneventful day, I tiredly sank into the couch and stared at the television. The newscaster, Haim Yavin, peered at me from the screen. I couldn't get a word of what he was saying. I'd lost any interest in the news. Yavin's deep voice echoed like distant thunder from the apartment walls. I looked at the flickering images, unable to focus. A white piece of paper sticking out among the books on the bookcase caught my eye. I had no idea what it was doing there, so I struggled to find some strength then rose to put it where it belonged.

To my surprise, the paper turned out to be a thin booklet with a title in Hebrew and Arabic: *The Palestinian National Covenant*, which I could not recall ever seeing before. An identical booklet was on the kitchen table. The bedroom contained another one in English, on the bookcase next to my bed. I was horrified. That was the last thing I needed — PLO-printed booklets in my apartment. I racked my brain trying to figure out where they had come from. In a panic, I searched the apartment and found several more copies. I gathered them all and tossed them in the wastebasket.

I was, of course, positive they had been planted in my apartment. I looked for signs of a break-in and found none. The fact that no valuables were missing bothered me and served to further enhance my anxiety. I sat on the edge of the bed. *This is definitely an escalation.* No more hoodlums waiting in line outside the movie theater. I didn't know what to do. I was scared, but who could I turn to? The police? Who could I talk to about this? It suddenly dawned on me that I was being watched and followed. How come I hadn't seriously considered that before?

That night, I went to bed without even brushing my teeth. I hid under the covers, still in my clothes. I lay curled up like a man about to get a fist to the stomach, until I finally fell asleep.

Following that night, I changed many of my regular habits. I stopped using the pay phone by my apartment building, as I assumed it had been tapped. I left little, insignificant markers around the apartment so I could tell if someone had been there in my absence — a sock lying by the front door or a sweater carelessly hanging on the bedroom door. I placed the newspaper on the dining table, opened to the sports section. Each evening I checked and double-checked that nothing had been moved. I always kept the apartment shutters closed. At night, I left the living room lights on. During the day, the radio was always turned on.

***

One morning, while leaving my house, I discovered the front tire of my Renault 5 had been punctured. A few days later, my car radio antenna was broken and the pieces were on the hood. Someone was sending me messages. There was no point in filing a police report. These little acts of sabotage to my car and the PLO booklets I had found in my apartment made me wonder what might follow. I found even more damage the following morning: a long scratch on the driver's side and a large cross etched on the hood.

My anger turned to fear. I lost my confidence. Every time I left my house, I was overwhelmed with dread that after they finished with my car, it was my turn to be marked. Anxiety made me act suspiciously, with uncalculated frenzy. My every thought revolved about what might be coming next. Outwardly, I kept a normal routine, but inside, I was on the verge of a breakdown. My patience was wearing thin, and the constant stress made me act like a paranoid, always nervous and quick to erupt into impulsive and unnecessary outbursts.

***

The new year, 1979, was just around the corner. My official status was still shrouded in mystery. I didn't know what to do next. I asked for a personal meeting, outside the station, with the radio commander. He offered to see me at his home in Ramat Efal at 9:30 one night.

His wife opened the door wearing an unreadable smile. She sat me down in the living room and went to call her husband. He came downstairs wearing a blue tracksuit and slippers and shook my hand heartily. He sat in the armchair facing me, spread his legs, and leaned back.

"How are you, Dolev?" His politeness sounded phony.

On the television, flickered the image of Prime Minister Menahem Begin, pale and grim. Begin was explaining some political issue to reporters in anticipation of his trip to Washington to continue his talks with Jimmy Carter.

"It was only this morning that I received authorization to assign a reporter and a technician to accompany the prime minister," the radio commander told me with obvious pride. "The chief human resources officer nearly drove me crazy before approving this trip."

"Did you get a chance to talk to him about my case as well?" I wondered aloud.

The commander was suddenly a little less comfortable. He turned to his wife and abruptly asked, "Are you going to make us something to drink?" Then he shifted in his seat until she came back, clearly using the time to craft his response.

After his wife came and went, leaving a glass of tea for him and a pitcher of orange juice on the table, he finally spoke again. "Look, this isn't so simple, the human resources office is very busy. My request made it to the major general's desk; that's the way it works. Putting too much pressure in a case like yours won't help."

The commander stole a glance at the television, where Begin explained with large gestures his position regarding the international border and sustainable security agreements.

"Did he at least offer you an explanation of why I have been fired?" I persisted.

The commander poured me some orange juice and sipped from his tea. Occasionally, his eyes wandered over to the television. But he said nothing.

"You need to understand; I can't continue to sit and wait much longer. Nothing is happening."

The commander, sensing a veiled threat in my words, turned his attention away from the TV and said, "Your temporary employment period ended. As of now, we have no intention of offering you tenure, which is why your employment has been terminated." He announced that last sentence with great finality. As far as he was concerned, our meeting was at an end.

He peeked at the television screen again then added, "Unfortunately, I have nothing new to relay to you. Like I already told you, patience is the name of the game."

I felt like getting up and turning down the television, which seemed to interest him much more than I did. "That's your excuse? Tenure?"

I got up and stood in front of the television, blocking his view. "Where did you come up with that lame excuse? Do you actually believe that nonsense?"

In the brief silence that followed my outburst, I heard Menahem Begin's voice behind me as he continued to emphatically speak about the importance of peace in the Middle East.

The station commander laced his fingers behind his head and leaned back in his chair. His blank expression made it clear that the aim of my visit completely eluded him.

I continued to stand in front of the TV and said, "In the end, I will have no choice but to turn to the Supreme Court."

As soon as he heard the words "Supreme Court," his entire body tensed. "As a friend, I suggest that you immediately set aside the idea of turning to the Supreme Court. What happens if the court rejects your request?"

He got up from his chair and stood in front of me. "You will need to face the military and the defense ministry's attorneys. Should you lose the case, your name will be tarnished forever, a cloud of suspicion will constantly hover over you. This is a small country, where everyone knows everyone else. Are you willing to take this risk?

"Think carefully. If you turn to the Supreme Court, I'm stepping out of the picture. No one knows how far this thing might go should you choose to go down that path."

A long silence followed. His wife entered the living room with a tray laden with fruit and cake. When she saw us facing each other like that, she paused as well, deliberating what to do next. Her presence broke the stalemate.

"You know I haven't done anything," I said before moving to the front door.

The commander pulled up his pants and scratched the corner of his eye, seeking the right words. "I don't know anymore. Maybe you pulled a fast one on me. How do I know you're not lying to me?

People way up high in the system have told me some things about you that were difficult to hear. It turns out you're not as pure and blameless as you present yourself to be."

Hearing her husband's harsh tone, his wife turned on her heel and walked back to the kitchen with the refreshment tray. I felt much freer with her gone.

"So you do know! What are you hiding from me? What did the higher-ups tell you? What's the big secret? You all know what this is about. I'm the only one without a clue. Don't you think it's time to tell me why I am being fired?"

The commander raised his glass of cold tea from the table, took a small sip, and dryly said, "Be precise, Dolev. You're not being fired. Your temporary employment will expire at the end of the year, and it was decided not to offer you tenure. The IDF has a right to do that, same as any other employer."

I left the commander's house angrier and more confused than when I'd arrived. I was upset, and an irksome drizzle fell from the sky. I started the car and sat behind the wheel for a few minutes, depressed and on the verge of tears. Finally, I regained my composure, hit the gas pedal, and headed for home. On the highway, I heard Louis Armstrong on the radio singing "What a Wonderful World," and it sent me over the edge. I stopped at a dark bus station and quietly wept. I had to do something.

I turned toward Holon from the highway, drove through the Jesse Cohen neighborhood, and stopped by a pay phone. I knew I had to somehow stop this insanity, but I had no idea how. Despite the late hour, I called my old friend Yehiam to talk it over with him. There was no answer. I couldn't reach Gidi Turner either. I wanted someone to hug me and thought of Nurit, who had vanished from my life.

The hour drew closer to midnight. I ended up calling the radio's news manager. He was surprised by my late-night call but still patiently listened to what I had to say and did not rush me even once.

"I've reached a dead end and have no choice but to turn to the Supreme Court," I said in a choked voice.

He cleared his throat and said, "Listen, Dolev, turning to the Supreme Court isn't that simple. You may be right, but you don't stand a chance, and let me explain to you why. The army and Shin Bet may not have anything genuine to point to. On the other hand, it is unlikely they are just out to get you for no good reason.

"Remember, the army has every right to dismiss you without offering any explanations. As an employer, they have the option of terminating your temporary employment and not offering you tenure. It is a standard clause in your contract. Come to the station tomorrow. We'll figure out together what you should do."

***

One of the rear tires on my car had been punctured again. That was how the next morning started. My mood, already dark, immediately got worse. The lug nuts were impossible to unscrew; it was cold, and the wind numbed my fingers. I struggled with the cap removal tool, taking out the flat tire. My sweat-stained shirt was glued to my body. When I pulled the wheel from the axle my shirt was smeared with black oil. I cursed furiously. I had bought the shirt only a few days earlier and was wearing it for the very first time.

The mechanic I brought my car to examined the tire. "Sorry, I just ran out. Come back in three hours."

I washed my face and hands in the shop sink. I tried to wash the oil out of my shirt but merely managed to spread it further. My disposition was as dismal and dreary as the day. The whole world had turned against me.

I had three hours to kill, and the Holon industrial area seemed desolate. I walked the streets until I found a small blue-collar restaurant. The place was empty. A swarthy, slender waitress stood looking bored and fiddling with her dark her. Her handsome face ended with a high forehead sprinkled with teenage acne. It was 10:00 a.m.

I sat in the corner and asked for a Coke. She brought me a can of Coke and a glass of ice. "What would you like to eat?" she asked.

I wasn't hungry, but I felt the need for some human contact. "What would you suggest?"

"We have everything on the menu: shakshuka, omelets, salad, pastrami sandwich…" She detailed the various dishes while leaning on the armrest of the opposite chair.

"Is the shakshuka spicy?" I asked.

The waitress responded with a flick of her hand. "We can make it any way you like," she said and brushed an errant lock of hair from her acne-riddled forehead.

"Fine, get me a shakshuka, then, but not too spicy. And… order yourself a coffee… on me," I added with sudden embarrassment.

"So, shakshuka and coffee?"

I cringed. "Never mind, just shakshuka," I said and turned crimson.

My embarrassment apparently made her understand. "I'm not allowed to sit with the customers, sorry. The owner will be coming any moment."

She walked off to the kitchen and returned a few minutes later. She placed a plate of shakshuka on my table without saying a word.

While I ate my shakshuka without any real appetite, she quietly sat across from me and placed a small glass of black coffee on the table. When I raised my eyes from the plate, she lowered her gaze and examined my reaction from the corner of her eye. There is no way to exaggerate the ensuing discomfort; I felt that even the faded surface of the table blushed with me. I set the knife and fork next to my plate, excused myself, paid the check, and went away shamefaced.

***

The IDF radio station was awash with rumor. One music editor passionately claimed among his friends that, "This is all about state security secrets and contact with a foreign Lebanese agent working for the Syrians." He told his friends he had obtained the information from a reliable source.

As it goes with rumors, whispers of bribes and favors followed: call girls, drug use, large deposits in foreign bank accounts. What could I possibly have done to stop those rumors? I kept silent, and my silence undermined the confidence of the few who still believed in me. Most of my friends abandoned me, never explicitly saying as much. They simply vanished and avoided me, offering no explanations, sliding out of my life as if by coincidence. From their point of view, the state couldn't possibly persecute one of its citizens for no good reason.

I had no one to share my troubles with. Gidi Turner, who usually served as a shoulder to lean on, was traveling abroad for ten days on a business trip. Of course, I suspected that he too was attempting to avoid and keep a safe distance from me. Without even realizing it, I became completely paranoid. I suspected everyone, and everyone suspected me, or so I thought. I became habitually leery of those around me, and the few social contacts I still had soon disappeared.

Having no other recourse, I went to the office of the only lawyer I was personally familiar with, a distant relative. I called his house from a pay phone, and he agreed to see me the following day. His office was on King Solomon Street in Tel Aviv. Scraps of garbage thrown from the upper floors were caught among the branches of the bushes by the narrow path. At the end of the walkway I was faced with a peeling brown wooden door bearing an ancient plaque: "Giora Giron, Attorney and Notary." I rang the doorbell, and Giora, wearing a brown suit that matched his peeling door, answered it.

"I'm on my own today," Giora declared. "The secretary took the day off."

Perhaps he wanted me to have the impression that his office was normally much busier.

"How are you? Come on in," Giora continued heartily. He pulled his pants up over his sizeable belly and smoothed what little remained of his oily hair with his fingers. With a quick step, he marched me through a kitchenette to the single room that served as his office. A desk took up most of the small space. A dust-coated lamp spread faint light over the surface of the desk, almost completely covered by a tilting tower of folders. An Olivetti typewriter lay dormant beside the files next to a chipped mug used for holding pencils and pens. A large stapler, a perforator, and a box of tacks were scattered chaotically.

Giora plopped down behind the desk, straightened his black tie, which didn't match his brown suit, took a pen from the mug, flipped to a new page on a yellow notepad, and began with a question. "Well, young man, what brings you to me?" He took a sip from a glass of water, wiped a bead of sweat from his forehead with a thick finger, and squinted at me from under his thick, black eyebrows.

"I'm being fired from the army radio… I think… I need to turn to the Supreme Court," I hesitatingly began.

Giora pulled himself up in his chair, and a spark flared in his puffy eyes. "The Supreme Court? My young friend, turning to the Supreme Court is a complicated thing. What makes you think you require the Supreme Court's particular assistance?"

He took a plastic bag from one of his drawers and placed a sandwich wrapped in greaseproof paper on the desk. He peeled back the paper, held the base of the sandwich in his thick hand, and took a hearty bite. With his other hand, he motioned for me to continue speaking. While he was busy chewing, I recounted my tale.

In the middle of my story, he took a wrinkled handkerchief from his pocket, wiped his mouth, and shoved it back in his pants pocket. "You didn't say anything that convinced me. I don't think we have enough meat on this bone to justify turning to the Supreme Court.

Let me put it this way, do you have the right of standing? In this particular case, I highly doubt it," he said. "Perhaps you should seek out a way around the Supreme Court, by turning to the regional labor court."

The pathetic office and its pathetic owner cooled the flames of my enthusiasm. "What is… the right of standing?"

"Indeed, an excellent question," said Giora. He pushed back from his desk, went to the kitchenette, and returned holding a glass of water. "Without a reason for the dismissal, it is unclear what stew we could concoct to serve to the honorable court. We would have to scrape the bottom of the pot. We must find a proper reason, allowing the venerable judges a sturdy ground to stand on." While speaking, he brushed the oily remains of the sandwich from his brown jacket.

"I'm being fired without an explanation. Isn't that a good enough reason?" I suggested.

"The answer to this question is — maybe. The fact that you are ignorant of the dismissal's reason, does not mean that it does not exist. We need to delve into the root of the matter. If that is the case, we would have no choice but to remove the cat from the bag by the process of elimination," Giora announced with indisputable authority.

"Excuse me, what exactly do you mean by that?" I asked, despite the fact that by then I mainly just wanted to leave his office.

"Another excellent question. We will claim before the court that you are a model employee. We will convince the honorable judges that your dismissal is tainted by extraneous and irrelevant considerations. Corruption, perhaps. You throw an anonymous man to the dogs in order to get someone with all the right connections in his stead. Someone whose political views correspond to the ones currently favored by the government."

Giora scribbled something on one of the papers scattered before him then looked at me. "So, what do you have to say?"

I took a deep breath and told the lawyer, "I have no idea about the reason for my dismissal. I have no explanations. No facts. That is what I have to say."

Giora collected the crumbs and crumpled greaseproof paper from his desk, piled them together, and tossed them in a wastebasket near his feet. "The facts, my young friend, are not always the determining factor. Putting up a good show in the courtroom is often more important. The judges are flesh and blood too. They are naturally inclined to support the weak. From their lofty vantage point, they strongly dislike unknown elements, such as shadowy government bodies and organizations. They are suspicious of those pulling the strings and those determining fates with a mere scribble of their pen. This is, my dear, everything there is to know in a nutshell."

I remained unsure, still, I had no choice but to trust him. "What do I need to do now?" I asked.

The lawyer shifted a folder, opened a drawer, and finally found a blank white sheet of paper. He recited as he wrote. "First, we'll need some written affidavits to support your version. We will ask your superiors to provide written and signed statements making it clear that your dismissal was carried out against their opinion. To do that, they would need to make the effort of coming to my office with their identity cards, preferably as soon as tomorrow. Without the affidavits, we stand no chance of success."

That evening, I called the news manager, told him of my meeting with the lawyer and asked him to sign an affidavit. The news manager showed up at Giora's office and signed an affidavit stating that no fault had been found in my professional conduct and that I had been diligently and successfully doing my job. Additionally, he declared that the dismissal order had come without any explanation. The news manager's signature on the affidavit cheered me up immensely. I was delighted to find out that some of my friends remained loyal to the basic principles of justice, even if they knew their support could put them at risk.

17

At 5:00 a.m., loud knocking on my front door woke me up. When I opened, I found myself faced with a policeman and two men wearing civilian clothes. One of them, tall, wearing a leather jacket and a black t-shirt, violently pushed the door open, waved a sheet of paper in my face, and asked, "Uri Dolev?"

"Yes," I replied in a feeble voice.

"We have a search warrant and an arrest warrant."

The other one, a husky man with bearlike features, grabbed my arms, pulled a pair of handcuffs from his belt, and cuffed my hands behind my back. The policeman stayed outside my door while the two civilians looked around my apartment. One of them closed the shutters and turned on the lights in all the rooms. The bear-faced civilian led me to the kitchen, placed his hand on my head and forced me to sit down.

"Sit right here in this chair and don't move, understand?"

The two civilians searched the apartment, methodically going from room to room, emptying the closets, spilling the contents of the drawers on the floor, and wreaking general havoc. They collected some documents and placed them in a large paper bag. A few hours later, when the search was finally complete, the apartment looked like the insides of an oversized garbage bag. I didn't even get the chance to pack a bag with some personal belongings. The two turned off the lights and accompanied me with my hands cuffed to the parking lot, where a white civilian car was waiting.

I was ushered into the back seat, where I sat between the policeman and the tall civilian. The bear-faced man sped the car to the national precinct in Jaffa. I should have expected it, but I still could not believe this was happening to me. At the police station, the policeman led me to a sort of reception room. They took my watch, my wallet, my leather belt, and my apartment keys. Then I was taken to an interrogation room. The policeman sat me in front of a wooden table, uncuffed me, and left the room. Sometime later, the bear man stepped inside, accompanied by another, much taller man. Bear face was about thirty-five, wearing a pair of jeans and a yellow shirt, his hair trimmed short and his cheeks smoothly shaved.

He sat at the other end of the table and addressed me in a comfortable, pleasant tone. "Hello, Uri Dolev, my name is Amos. I suggest that you cooperate with us. Try to answer every question. That way, there's a chance it'll all be over quickly. Up to you."

"What do you want from me?" I asked, scared out of my wits.

"Shut up!" — the tall one pushed off the wall and stopped nibbling on the toothpick in his mouth — "We're the ones asking the questions here!"

He took a little step toward me, took out the toothpick and waved it like a tiny sword. "You talk only when spoken to. You'll get your chance to talk soon enough... and you'll talk all right... don't worry. Now listen to what Amos has to say, and answer his questions nicely and without any wisecracking." I immediately classified the two interrogators as a bear and a fox.

Amos opened a cardboard file, placed a notepad on the table, took out a pen from his shirt pocket, and asked me to answer his questions slowly so he could write down every word. "Do you know why we arrested you?"

"I haven't the faintest idea!"

Amos stayed calm and unmoved by my utter conviction. He took another look at the cardboard file, squinted his bearish eyes, and began to ask a series of trivial questions: my ID number, the names of my parents and relatives. He asked many questions about my personal history. I cooperated fully. I told him of my time with the HaShomer Hatzair youth movement, my military and reserve service. I willingly replied to all his inquiries. The interrogation was slow going, with Amos writing down every word. An hour passed, maybe more. The tension I felt began to fade. But then Amos changed directions.

In the same relaxed tone, he suddenly asked, "All right, what's the name of your contact person?"

I think I even smiled at that. "Come on, what contact person? Why are you even interrogating me? I think you know this is all a big mistake."

The other interrogator seemed to wake up. He smoothed his hand over his beard and hair, unbuttoned his jacket, and spat the tooth-pick out. With a feline movement, he came closer and leaned his weight on the back of my chair. "I'm warning you, this isn't the radio station. We eat wiseasses like you for breakfast every day of the week. Stop lying and start cooperating, or your situation here is going to get much worse! You get me? Or do I need to speak some other language besides Hebrew to make you understand?"

I felt paralyzed by the tall investigator's aggressiveness and rumbling voice. I turned to Amos, who, despite his appearance, apparently served as the "good cop." "What does he want from me? I haven't done anything. I've no idea what you guys are talking about."

Amos shook his big head and the fox, "the bad cop," stepped back and returned to his former place by the wall. Amos left the room, and the fox paced up and down the wall, stroking his beard and hair. I was afraid of what might come next.

Two minutes later, Amos returned and handed me a cup of

coffee. Then he sat back down across from me. "I assume," he said, in that mellow tone of his, "that you have a developed political consciousness. Are you or were you a political activist?" Amos spread his hands on the table, brought his face closer to mine, and gazed straight into my eyes.

"I have political views just like anyone else, but I've never been a member of any political party or organization," I replied.

Amos shifted in his chair with obvious discontent. He took a printed list of names from his briefcase, placed it in front of me, and asked if I was familiar with any of them. Most of the names belonged to students in my theater class, many of whom did not bother to hide their left-wing political views. Amos put a tiny checkmark next to each of the names I indicated was an acquaintance. I never imagined the fact I was familiar with someone might harm him. Amos continued asking questions about demonstrations and protest activities. I mentioned that I had participated in a few Peace Now demonstrations, a single Black Panthers demonstration in Dizengoff Square, and the protests over the government failures after the Yom Kippur War.

"What about the Matzpen socialist organization? Have you ever participated in any of their demonstrations?" Amos asked, although they sounded more like statements.

"I never had anything to do with Matzpen," I said firmly. I wasn't lying, I really had nothing to do with that revolutionary socialist and anti-Zionist organization.

The foxlike interrogator took a few long strides toward the table until his head loomed over mine and then barked at me, "You can get a few years in the can for lying to us. This is your only chance to tell it all. Continue to deny the facts we already know, and you'll spend your finest years in prison." His foul breath made me sick to my stomach.

Amos offered me a cigarette and another cup of coffee. I refused.

He leaned back in his chair. "Uri Dolev," he said in his soothing voice, "we could have ended this interrogation an hour ago. Instead of digging yourself deeper into trouble and being stubborn, why don't you shift gears and help us make this whole thing easy. Just start talking. Tell us everything from your point of view, and we'll write your testimony together. You'll read it, sign it, and be done with it. Trust me, it'll make you feel a whole lot better. All that dead weight burdening your conscience will go away. Let's do this my way; it'll be best for you.

"What I want to know is very simple: When were you drafted? Who did you meet? What information or documents did you turn over?"

I began shaking my head, unable to believe what was happening.

"Look me in the eye. I believe you when you say you never meant to hurt anyone! We can take that into consideration. I'm on your side; let me help you. Just cooperate. Trust me, I have a lot of connections in the state prosecutor's office. A good word from me will help you get out of this with a light sentence. Keep denying everything, and your situation is just going to get worse."

The tall interrogator approached me from behind and whispered in my ear, "You should listen to Amos. This is the best offer you're going to get. Come on, stop being a tough guy, and spit it out. You're lucky to have Amos here. I wouldn't have offered you jack shit."

Silence settled in the interrogation room, with each side trying to assess the situation. Amos shifted in his chair, fished out another printed page from his briefcase, and started reading names from it. After each name, Amos paused, waiting to see my reaction. At the end he asked, "Do you know any of the people whose names I just read?"

I considered how to answer. Some of the names weren't familiar at all. Others I only recognized from the media. There was one name on the list that I knew well — Yaki Cohen. After some hesitation, I pointed at his name in the middle of the list. I was a little worried because Yaki Cohen was related to Aharonchik Cohen from Kibbutz Sha'ar HaAmakim, who had been convicted of espionage years ago.

A small smile grew on Amos' lips. "How long have you two known each other?"

"We've known each other for years. Yaki was in high school with me. We hardly saw each other once I went into the army and have no contact today."

Judging by the bear's and the fox's reactions, I realized they hadn't made the connection between Yaki Cohen and Aharonchik Cohen's espionage affair. After all, Cohen was the most common last name in Israel. Amos started to lose his patience. He stood and placed another sheet of paper before me. This time it was a list of Arabic names. I had no idea who any of them were. I reacted involuntarily with a frightened, embarrassed laugh.

In the blink of an eye, the fox grabbed my hand, tugged at my shirt collar, pulled me up from my chair, and shook me. His black stubble nearly scratched my face, and his breath filled my nose with its stench as he spoke. "What do you think we are, stupid? You're a nobody! A two-bit reporter. You're nothing but a cockroach here, got it?" He illustrated his words by stamping a foot on the floor to crush an imaginary bug.

"You think we don't have proof? We know everything about you. We weren't born yesterday. You can sit here and keep denying everything until you're blue in the face. We'll put you in solitary confinement for a few days. See how brave you are." He let go and pushed me back into my chair, looming over me as he carried on.

"Everyone cracks and starts singing at the end. Enough people have already sung about you, believe me. In here, everyone thinks about his own ass and forgets all about his friends. You think any of them really care about you? Find me a single Arab who wouldn't sell his own mother for the right price. To them, you're nothing but another Jew boy. They already snitched on you. Threw mud and shit all over your face. You wouldn't believe how much filth we have on you!" He pounded his fist on a briefcase sitting on the table.

"Trust me, we have enough material for a couple of indictments. So far, we've given you the white glove treatment, offered you the opportunity to cooperate. This is your last chance. Keep messing with us and you'll get into a world of trouble. Just to remind you, you're looking at fifteen years in prison, maybe more."

I was intimidated down to my bones. Still, when the fox finished screaming, I told him, "You have nothing. You're just making empty threats."

Amos pushed back from the table and left the room. The fox grabbed me and pinned me to his chest. I was sure he was about to headbutt me, but he grabbed my cheek with his fingers, pinched hard, and hissed, "You freeloader… you piece of human garbage, I'm going to stuff your mouth with shit unless you talk. You have no idea what I'm capable of doing to people who piss me off." Then he let go of me with a light shove.

My cheek stung, and I wanted to vomit and urinate so badly I could barely hold back. When the treatment was over, Amos returned to the room.

I pleaded with him, "I need to take a leak. I can't hold it much longer."

"You little piece of shit! Start talking," the fox yelled, "then we'll see!"

Amos ran his hand over his giant head. "Let's start over. Who knows, maybe you've suddenly regained your memory."

"I've got to pee," I repeated.

The fox laughed. "You can pee in your pants for all I care."

The two interrogators left the room. I knew that urinating in the room would be considered an act of submission. I tried to distract myself by thinking of other things, but that didn't work. I doubled up in the corner of the room and, God only knows why, found myself repeating, "Nothing is stronger than water. Nothing is stronger than water."

After some time, perhaps an hour and a half, the door opened, and Amos came inside holding a glass of water. He motioned for me to sit down at the table, and I sat with my legs crossed. He pushed the glass at me. I managed to smile so he'd understand his stunt was too obvious.

Amos clumsily took out a paper pad from his briefcase, marked the time and the date, and repeated the questions as if asking them for the first time. I answered all his questions with the same reply: "I'm not talking without a lawyer. I have to go to the restroom urgently."

At a certain point, I sensed Amos had had enough too and realized that concentrating on not wetting myself had made me stop listening to him. Time seemed to stand still. I had no idea how much had elapsed since the interrogation began. I couldn't begin to guess what time it was. I sat in my chair, doubled over from the pain of tensing my muscles to maintain control of my bladder. All my thoughts focused on that one thing.

At last, Amos stood up, cuffed my hands, and motioned for me to follow him. I could barely stand and was afraid I would lose control when I started to walk. Amos and the fox accompanied me down a long, narrow corridor and led me to a small restroom. The fox gave me a push on the back, and I found myself in front of a reeking squat toilet. They left the door open, and the fox stood by and watched me. I quickly pulled down my pants, but the strain of holding off for so long had made me unable to let go. I had to focus for at least two minutes to perform the simple act of urinating. When the floodgates finally opened, I felt dizzy. My entire body went weak, and I felt I was about to faint. I trembled all over, drops of perspiration dripped down my forehead and the back of my neck, huge sweat stains collected under my armpits, and I was washed with cold sweat. I leaned my cuffed hands against the filthy wall until I had completely emptied myself.

A few minutes later, I came to and felt a great sense of relief. Amos led me down the hallway and took me to another wing in the building. Two men in civilian clothes took Amos aside and exchanged a few words with him. He walked off, and the two accompanied me to a tiny holding cell. Inside was a prisoner who looked about forty years old. He spoke with a thick Russian accent, presented himself as Mikhail, and was interested to know what I had been arrested for. I was in no mood for small talk, so I ignored him. Mikhail told me he had been arrested for embezzlement and asked me again why I was there. I thought he might be a plant placed in the cell with me. I was drained and just wanted to get some sleep.

I lay on the mattress and fell asleep immediately. I dreamt I was lying on the Acre beach. The sea was calm, I swam with large, slow movements, and the waves carried me far from the beach. A young woman in a blue bikini paddled on a sea mattress, moving closer to me. Her face was speckled with freckles, and she kept smiling. She spoke to me in English, and I couldn't understand a word of what she was saying. She continued smiling, reached out a long, shapely arm, and pulled me to her mattress. We kissed and hugged. She took off her bikini top, revealing a boyish, freckled chest.

The girl slid off the mattress, and she suddenly had two yellow oxygen tanks strapped on her naked back. She circled me, kicking the flippers on her feet, and wrapping an arm around me. Her strange smile now seemed intimidating, and I thought she might be a mermaid. All at once, she pulled me into the depths of the sea. Huge fish swam across our path and looked at us through human eyes. I was running out of air. A faceless, long-haired man with a white beard walked through the water as if he were walking on land. I screamed at him, but he simply kept walking. I tried to open my mouth and breathe like a fish. The salt stung my eyes and my mouth, and I felt myself drowning. A giant ship propeller circled above and quickly moved closer, emitting a terrifying sound.

I woke up to the sound of the prison guard knocking loudly on the cell door and hurrying us to get up. It was extremely cold. Flashes of lightning and echoes of thunder filled the room. Through the narrow window, I could see it was pouring outside. My hands and feet were bound once more, and I was led to the same chilly interrogation room. I hadn't brushed my teeth, my hair was glued to my scalp, and my clothes were rumpled from sleeping in them. Amos walked in looking fresh in a pair of blue jeans, a green shirt, and a black hoodie. A wide smile was spread across his large face.

"Good morning, Mr. Dolev, I hope you've used the time to get some rest and to pee. Did you have a good night's sleep in our hotel?"

Amos continued the interrogation, repeating the same old questions, while I offered him the briefest possible responses. Noon came, and I was losing my patience. At one point, I came to my senses and loudly declared, "I want to talk to a lawyer."

The bear's face turned serious. Without saying another word, Amos left the room. The fox came in wearing a buttoned shirt, a leather jacket, a pair of jeans, and work shoes. He stood in the doorway, fisted his hands, and cracked his knuckles. Then he began to pace around the interrogation room with an evil smile. After a couple of minutes of that, he ran his hand over his beard and studied me.

"All right, the party's over. Amos thought we could manage without this, but if you insist on acting like a stubborn ass, we'll just have to do it my way. The hard way. If that's what you want, that's fine by me.

"Come on, let's get up close and personal. Strip search time. It's standard procedure. Let's do a thorough examination and then see what's next. Let's see how much of a hero you've got in you. Come on, sweet cheeks, take it all off so I can search you. We'll soon find out what you have hidden in all those deep, dark places."

I had not anticipated such a humiliation. I took off my shirt and pants and stood on the cold floor in nothing but my underwear. The tall interrogator walked around me in a steady orbit, looking at me intently. He continued to alternately clench and flex his hands.

"You're used to communal showers in the kibbutz, so why are you still wearing your underwear?" He took two thin medical gloves from his pocket and slowly put them on. "Well, what are you waiting for? Take it all off. Haven't you ever had a rectal exam?"

I stood in front of the fox, naked, ashamed, and frightened. When I began shivering, a wide smile of contentment settled on his face. "I have to say, you're not very well equipped down there," he said in a quiet tone I hadn't heard from him before. "What's the matter, you're so scared that your balls have shriveled into marbles? Now stand with your face against the wall, raise your head, just like that, easy does it, hands up in the air, stretch them as far as you can go. Spread your legs, wider, a little more, good. Now bend over slowly, hands straight and touching the wall, further down, very good, now we're finally getting somewhere."

I stood there, bent over, my head hanging down, my arms stretched, and my hands touching the wall. I waited. A few minutes passed. The fox paced about the room, and my muscles began to ache. I expected the worst. "Can I go to the restroom first?" I asked.

"Again? We should get you a diaper." The fox laughed as a violent tremor passed through my legs, and a sharp cramp stabbed through my hamstrings. "Come on, what's the big deal? You're a kibbutznik, a country guy. I'm sure you've seen how cows take a piss with their legs spread, just like this," he continued, mocking me.

I straightened up a bit and urinated on the wall. The sharp odor filled the room, and the interrogator recoiled. "I hope you're not going to shit in here too."

He moved closer and kicked me right in the ass. He lost his balance and nearly fell into the spreading puddle of urine. "Fuck this shit," he grumbled. "Look at the kind of stench that can come out of a man when he's afraid. Aren't you ashamed? You're disgusting." He took off the gloves and tossed them in the urine puddle.

"Get dressed, wiseass," he ordered. "We have all the time in the world. We can have the rectal exam later, when the right opportunity presents itself."

The fox left, and I got dressed.

Amos came in next, and the smell made him twist his bearish face with distaste. When he saw the puddle on the floor, he tugged me by the sleeve and pounded on the door. It opened, and Amos led me to another interrogation room, where he kept asking the same questions and I kept refusing to answer. Many hours passed.

At dusk, I was led to a holding cell with four bunk beds, all of them occupied. A fluorescent bulb gave off some faint light. I stood at the entrance for a moment, holding a dusty blanket and a mattress. I placed the mattress on the floor and prepared for sleep.

One of the inmates woke up and screamed at me, "Quiet! Be quiet or I'll fucking kill you!"

I woke up early in the morning to loud knocking on the cell door. I was tired, sticky, reeking, and depressed. A guard handed each of us an over brewed cup of tea, a hard-boiled egg, half a tomato, and some bread and butter.

When he'd gone, the inmates asked me what I had been arrested for. I told them I didn't know. One of them, a short, nervous-looking bully, walked up to me. He stood very close and loudly hissed at me, "I smell a snitch. I'm warning you, say something, and I'll kill you with my bare hands."

Later, I was taken for another interrogation. Amos walked into the room smelling like cologne. With a ridiculously phony pleasant tone, he read me a list of names. Most of them were new to me. I refused to cooperate. The interrogation lost its momentum. Amos asked, and I answered, "I maintain my right to remain silent."

This game continued for some time, and Amos patiently

documented his questions and my laconic and repetitive reply.

When he finished asking questions, Amos handed me several sheets of paper. "Read it and sign. This is your testimony."

My detailed testimony was written there in his handwriting. Next to many questions, he mentioned that the interrogee had refused to cooperate. I read and reread the written testimony several times and couldn't find anything that might be used against me.

I told Amos, "Add that I've been humiliated, kicked, cursed at, prevented from going to the lavatory, and denied my right to speak to an attorney."

Amos looked at me and replied, "I've no idea what you're talking about."

I refused to sign the interrogation form. Amos shrugged, signed, took the scribbled pages, and left.

***

Following two days of incarceration, I was released without any explanation. I was told to report every day to the Holon police precinct to sign my name.

As I went out to the street, I heard a rusty tune emerging from an old speaker, and a monotonous voice crying out, "Ragpicker… ragpicker… refrigerators… washing machines… furniture… buying and selling… ragpicker…"

A thick-bodied ragpicker wearing a brown flat cap, rode a cart loaded with his wares, lashing his scrawny horse. The horse struggled to draw the cart, which was full to the brim with a disorderly pile of used objects. The horse and the cart slowly passed by. I wanted to ask the ragpicker to pick me up and toss me on his cart as well. I felt like I was about to be tossed in the trash anyway. I was exhausted, reeking of sweat and urine, but mainly, I was desperate. I had reached rock bottom.

18

The game of kings was extremely popular among the members of Mishmar Hatsafon. We all learned to play chess at an early age, just as we had played Monopoly, which taught us about the exploitative nature of urban capitalism. My uncle Kuntz was the driving force behind the beginner's chess class. In our first class, Kuntz took a handful of sand from his pocket and scattered it on the floor.

"Take a look at these grains of sand. Can we count them? The same can be said about the game of chess. The possibilities inherent in it are as innumerable as the grains of sand on the beach."

Then Kuntz took out the game pieces from a purple velvet bag and placed them on the board. He lifted each piece in turn and explained its role.

***

Nineteen sixty-one saw the first Chess Olympiad in Israel. There was great excitement in the kibbutz when it was learned that grand master László Szabó, from the Hungarian team, had agreed to come to Mishmar Hatsafon after the Olympiad and conduct a simultaneous multiplayer chess game.

Tables were moved together in the dining hall to form a long, rectangular surface. Sixty-two players from Mishmar Hatsafon and the neighboring kibbutzim had come to try their skill against the famous player. Grand master Szabó walked into the dining hall wearing a gray suit, a white shirt, and a blue tie. He was a tall, chubby man, and his black hair was smoothed back with brilliantine.

Kuntz nodded at the guest, addressed the crowd, and explained the rules of the contest. "First, we will be very strict about the 'you touch it; you use it' rule. Touching any piece means that you must move it off the square. Szabó will be playing the white pieces, and we will be playing the black. Is everything clear? I ask that all members present maintain absolute silence." Kuntz finished his introduction and theatrically sat behind the first chessboard.

Szabó regarded the players vigilantly waiting behind the chessboards, then simply said, "Good luck." He stood in front of Kuntz and moved the white pawn before the king two squares up, took a step to face the second opponent and marched the pawn before the queen two squares up. The grand master spent little time with any player during those first rounds. He made his move then continued to the next board with a strange gait: his left foot moved sideways, then his right dragged him along until he was steady.

A large crowd peeked from beyond the players' shoulders — advice givers, and curious onlookers. Szabó quickly moved from board to board, occasionally looking with bewilderment at a stupid move made by one of his opponents, and usually beating that player a few rounds later. An hour passed, Szabó easily defeated most of the contestants. Only a few of us remained. The youngest was eleven-year-old Amotz Finklestein, then there was me — twelve and a half years old — and thirteen-year-old Yehiam. Only two adults were left: my uncle Kuntz and Shalom, Yehiam's father. At that stage, Szabó lingered with each of the remaining contestants. He arrived at my chessboard, looked at me, gave me a light pat on the head, complimented me for my game, and suggested that I yield. I accepted his offer. I have never been a great chess player, and the fact that I had been one of the last contestants filled me with a great sense of pride. Yehiam lost not long after.

Shalom Gruenwald, who was considered the best player in the kibbutz, found himself in a losing position. He laid his king on the chessboard with a sharp movement then gave Szabó a long handshake. Of all the contestants, only Amotz Finklestein and my uncle Kuntz remained. Amotz, the youngest contestant, was considered a genius and a bit of an odd duck. He earned a lengthy round of applause when he was able to score a draw against the Hungarian grand master.

Many members went over to Amotz to congratulate and hug him. The boy pushed them all away with tears in his eyes. He avoided contact with the crowd and nervously twisted a strand of hair between his fingers. Barely able to refrain from bursting into tears, he left the dining hall running, not even waiting to see the outcome of the only game remaining, between Szabó and Kuntz.

The tension in the dining room simmered. Kuntz was in a superior position over the grand master. The kibbutz members were hoping Kuntz would at least manage an honorary victory against the Hungarian. Szabó stood with his legs spread wide in front of Kuntz's board, one hand supporting his chin. He examined the chessboard. He picked up a rook and moved it to threaten Kuntz's queen. Then he leaned on the table and continued to look at the pieces. Kuntz deliberated and shifted in his chair for a little bit, and a hushed murmur passed through the crowd around the chessboard. Kuntz raised his hand and let it wander over the chessboard. Finally, he picked up the black queen and with a swift and unexpected movement struck Szabó's rook.

For a few moments, the Hungarian supported his head with both hands, trying to understand the logic behind Kuntz's dramatic move. A small, relieved smile finally curled his lips. He lightly tapped his forehead with his finger, picked up the knight defending the rook and left Kuntz without his queen. Szabó stood straight up, bowed to Kuntz, extended his hand, and told him in Hungarian, "Pity, you played beautifully up to this point."

Visibly excited, Kuntz rose from his chair, warmly shook Laszlo Szabó's hand and gave him several polite bows. "Thank you, thank you," he said in Hungarian.

Kuntz's queen sacrifice had proved to be a terrible mistake. But despite his loss, Kuntz appeared pleased.

Alfred the dairy farmer went over to Kuntz and said, "You had a chance to nail that gentile bugger. Why did you have to give him your queen? I would have beaten him, but you had to turn the other cheek like a weakling and ended up getting your face slapped." He gave Kuntz a hard push on the shoulder and my uncle nearly lost his footing.

To the people still standing about, Alfred shouted, "Idiots, you really thought Kuntz could win? You should have asked me; I knew he was going to lose. Anything that has to do with Kuntz eventually turns to shit. That's just the way it is. You can't trust anyone in this kibbutz anymore." And with that final statement, Alfred stomped out of the dining hall.

Other members surrounded Kuntz, shook his hand, and expressed their disappointment over his loss. I patiently waited for my father to leave the dining hall, then went closer to Kuntz, tugged on his sleeve, and asked, "Why did you sacrifice the queen for a rook? That was a stupid move. You had lots of better options."

Kuntz placed his hand on my shoulder and said, "Uri, you need to understand, I played just like your grandfather would have played. When I was a child, your grandfather had this habit of sacrificing his queen. I think it was his way of helping me. Your grandfather... he was incomplete, a king without a queen. Throughout the game, I sought an opportunity to use my father's trick. I lost because I was eager to imitate and honor him. I didn't win, but Szabó appreciated my courage, and I've earned something just as important — I lit a candle in my father's memory."

I remarked to myself that Kuntz had lost the game and emerged happy, while Amotz Finklestein, who had scored a draw, had left the dining hall in tears, disappointed down to the very depths of his soul.

***

Amotz's father, Shmulik Finklestein, enjoyed special status in and outside of our kibbutz. Occasionally, he published a guest editorial in *Al HaMishmar* —a daily newspaper — and was highly regarded for it. Shmulik was indeed a man of stature. His books about the Holocaust, written from the vantage point of someone who had survived the horror of the death camps, served as living proof of the spirit of man and his ability to withstand even the most inhuman cruelty.

Shmulik had been a follower of Mordechai Anielewicz, the leader of the Jewish Fighting Organization, which led the Warsaw Ghetto Uprising. Shmulik had participated in the ghetto uprising and survived Auschwitz. When WWII ended, Shmulik was twenty-four and weighed thirty-six kilograms — about eighty pounds. As long as he lived, he had a habit that was impossible to ignore. Each time a fresh, warm loaf of bread was served to his table, Shmulik would look at it, take a little bite, and tears would pour from his eyes. Shmulik always kept a handkerchief in his pocket. He would wipe his tears then blow his nose with a trumpetlike sound before settling down. The kibbutz members said that in his pocket, he had not only a handkerchief, but a dry piece of bread, so he would never forget those days.

Once, on Holocaust Memorial Day, we asked him why he cried whenever he ate fresh bread, and he frankly told us, "In the ghetto, and later on in the camps, I yearned for the taste of fresh bread just one more time. That yearning has not let go of me since. The urge to eat in order to survive was stronger than anything else. The hunger hurt even more than the loss of my parents."

Shmulik started a family in Mishmar Hatsafon and named his firstborn Amotz, a name befitting a proud Sabra, a native-born son of the new Jewish country. But the boy was very far removed from the tough, coarse image of the typical Sabra. Amotz was a skinny boy, clumsy of movement, and pale skinned. His black hair was parted on the side. His large, curious eyes darted about with the uneasiness of a frightened animal's. He traveled the paths of the kibbutz on his own, always twisting a strand of hair between his fingers.

When he was with the group, he always trudged a few steps behind and always walked on the left side of the path. When he entered a room, he was glued to the left wall and gently touched it with his fingers as he walked. Amotz Finklestein never adhered to the typical kibbutz fashion of wearing sandals, shorts, and a white tank top. Even during the hottest days of summer, he walked around in ankle-high brown shoes, long pants, and a long-sleeved shirt. While the other children were splashing in the swimming pool, he sat on the grass reading a book. He spoke little with the other children, and when he did his words were always well chosen and pointed. He was cynical and often intentionally harsh and offensive. He had skipped a grade, and being the youngest child in class combined with his strange ways to make his day-to-day life extremely difficult.

Amotz had a hard time waking up in the morning. By the time he got his clothes on, breakfast was almost over. He never took part in any sports played on the grass, and his pale skin stood out among the tanned children of the kibbutz. His entire appearance spoke of the diaspora, and his urban style and behavior were held in contempt.

The boy actively disliked his own mother. He always treated her harshly and rejected any effort she made to try and protect him. The more she tried to get closer to him, the more he would push her

away. When Amotz was nine, he walked up to the work coordina-
tor's table in the dining hall and with utter seriousness asked the
man to find him a substitute mother.

Amotz was perceived as an exceptional and sharp-minded child.
The teachers chose not to confront him and left him to his own de-
vices. He spent most of his time studying on his own in the library.
There, he fully mastered the English and German languages. For
his own amusement, he translated Orwell's *Animal Farm* and other
works of classic literature. Those who knew something about literature said his translations were exceptional. He read mathematics
books as others would read light novels. Occasionally, he sent *Al
HaMishmar* complicated chess puzzles that were always published.

Before his induction into the IDF, one of the kibbutz nurses alerted
the proper military authorities that the youth might not be capable
of coping with the difficulties of military service. During that year,
Amotz's classmates were drafted into the paratroopers' brigade, the
various commando reconnaissance units, and the finest elite combat
units. That was the norm in Mishmar Hatsafon. The drafting officer
examined the information from the kibbutz nurse, and the military
exempted Amotz from military service.

For Shmulik, the army was the symbol of Jewish post-Holocaust
revival. For him, the IDF was a crushing counterblow to Nazism.
Shmulik Finklestein would sing the praises of military service at
every opportunity, claiming the Israeli army served as a testament
to the Jewish people's strength and endurance. He urged young kibbutz members to choose combat service in order to protect a free
and democratic country defending the natural rights of its people.
Shmulik had very high expectations of his own son, Amotz, and
fervently wanted him to play a significant role in the army. So of
course he was furious over the army's decision to exempt his son
from active duty.

Shmulik used all his connections among decision makers to try to get the military authorities to overturn their decision regarding his son. When he found out the army's decision was based on information provided by the kibbutz nurse, his fury turned into burning rage. He demanded the immediate intervention of the kibbutz authorities. Shmulik Finklestein claimed that a kibbutz member was not allowed to make use of personal information obtained in the course of her work. It was his opinion that the nurse had divulged sensitive information to the Israeli security forces, thus compromising his son's privacy. The nurse, so he claimed, had unraveled the communal fabric of kibbutz society in which all members support and mutually trust one another by choice. As far as Shmulik was concerned, she had crossed the line. He demanded that the nurse's privileges as a kibbutz member be stripped away. He threatened that unless the nurse left, he would take his own family and go away.

Shmulik's special status and the outrage the affair had aroused caused the nurse to temporarily relocate to another kibbutz while her family remained in Mishmar Hatsafon. A year later, Shmulik succeeded in his task — his son was finally inducted into the IDF. Amotz coped well with the challenges of boot camp, following which he was assigned a top secret role in the air force. There was a spirit of optimism in the letters he wrote home, even enthusiasm for his military service. Following one year of training, he was integrated into a small air force unit in a role that required much knowledge and involved important responsibilities. One night, Amotz was on guard duty, patrolling the fences surrounding his military base somewhere in central Israel. He was found dead in the morning — a single bullet had pierced his head. No one had heard the shot during that rainy winter's night.

His parents were beside themselves with grief. Amotz was their hope, the rekindled ember of a dying past. The rifle bullet had shattered both the son's skull and the new world the father had toiled so hard to build. The bereaved Shmulik deemed the roots of the tragedy lay with his son's initial rejection from the army. He thought the kibbutz had not properly shielded and nurtured his son.

At the end of the mourning period, three chess puzzles were published in *Al HaMishmar*'s chess section in Amotz Finklestein's memory. The puzzles were penned by Yehiam Gruenwald. Shmulik Finklestein was deeply moved. He wrote Yehiam a long, emotional thank-you note. A few years later, the Finklestein family left the kibbutz. As far as Shmulik was concerned, Mishmar Hatsafon had ceased to be his home.

***

Many years later, I spoke with Yehiam about Amotz's death.

"Amotz did not kill himself; he chose death as an experiment," Yehiam pronounced. He theorized that sometime during that fatal night on guard duty, the young genius had decided to understand the true nature of death once and for all. He wanted to know the meaning of that abstract concept about which entire philosophies revolved and numerous books had been written, to get nearer to the death that had so often crept by his father's door — the death his father had managed to escape time and again.

Yehiam came up with a hypothesis that Amotz had coped with the question of death by regarding it like a complex chess puzzle. "Perhaps he thought that the right move across the chessboard of life would allow him to solve death's riddle. All the philosophies Amotz had read offered no conclusive proof regarding its true nature. That slippery, elusive essence of death remained unsolved until he shot himself that night to better understand it. Amotz had used his weapon just like he would use a chess piece: he sacrificed the king, himself, thus solving the riddle of his father's survival with his own death."

19

I could find no rest while I waited for the Supreme Court's decision. My petition received wide coverage in the media, and several newspapers printed my name and picture. The process of my employment termination had meanwhile been completed. I was officially unemployed and sat idly at home. The days went by in a slow crawl as I waited for good tidings from the court. But nothing happened. I had no plans. I couldn't bring myself to think of what to do next. I still bore a certain hope that the court would instruct the army radio to reinstate me but knew the chances of that happening were slim.

One morning, I heard my apartment doorbell, looked through the peephole, and saw a bespectacled young soldier. I opened the door, and the soldier handed me an envelope. "This is from the army radio commander," he said.

The envelope contained a handwritten note summoning me to an urgent meeting.

***

Uncertainly, I entered the building from which I had been banished a mere few months before. The filthy corridors welcomed me back with indifference. I was no longer a household member, but a guest. I climbed the three flights to the radio commander's office. His secretary's embarrassment upon seeing me was apparent, despite the fact we knew each other well. For a moment, I was overcome with fear that I might be stepping into another trap. I took a deep breath, and all my senses were alert as I walked into the commander's office.

In a flat, emotionless voice, he said, "Dolev, what are you standing there for? Grab a chair and sit down. There are a few matters I'd like to discuss with you."

I pulled over a chair and sat as far as possible from his desk. "Yes…?"

The commander drummed the surface of his desk with his fingers. "It appears there is a certain opportunity for us to get you back to work." He continued his nervous drumming, looked at me, and added, "In order for that to happen, you need to withdraw the petition you submitted to the Supreme Court. Also, you need to terminate all workers' union activities on your behalf. You need to change your attitude. Good will and flexibility are the order of the day. Get it? We need to straighten things out and clear the air. The system expects a written commitment from you that you won't act against it in the future." His words came as a complete surprise.

"They want me not to act against the system? It's the system that's been acting against me. I still don't even know what they want!"

My aggression was received by the commander with a certain level of surprise. "Look, officially, your file is still open. But there is a certain reluctant willingness to meet you halfway. Such a move would be almost unprecedented. Don't expect any apologies or explanations. Do what I ask, and I'll see what I can do to get you back to work. Just look at this whole thing as … a malfunction that's been fixed, a little dent in the fender."

I noticed that he was just as tense as I was, eager to hear my reply. Inwardly, I rejoiced, although I had no idea whether this was a complete surrender or one more act of diversion. I was suspicious. "What do you mean? You want me to withdraw the petition and cancel the legal process? And then what, no more interrogations, and I get my old job back?"

The commander sat up straighter up in his chair. "I can't promise you anything; you need to trust me. I received certain indications that a particular agreement could be reached with you."

What did that even mean? "What sort of agreement? Will I be allowed to go back to work? Will the accusations against me be erased?"

The station commander was now visibly agitated. "Like I said, I can't promise you anything. You need to make up your mind, just don't expect too much. Still, I think everything will turn out all right. On the other hand, don't forget, your termination is still in effect. Take some time to think, but my personal opinion is that the Supreme Court will not interfere with the considerations of the security forces. This, by the way, is also the opinion of the legal advisors familiar with your case.

"Look, the system did not raise any specific claims against you. The army radio received instructions to terminate your employment when your temp period ended. You had a contract, it was decided not to renew it, and now it's expired. This is a legal position you'd have a hard time refuting. Personally, I suggest you start thinking in another direction. Now's the time to be smart, not right. Just think about it."

***

The army radio commander presented me with both an opportunity and a dilemma. I did not know how I should proceed. Seeking consultation, I called the parliament member, and he summoned me for a meeting that evening. I told him about the message I had received from the army radio commander.

"Interesting, no one bothered to update me, or even give me a hint. Good, I'm glad that the head has reached the right decision."

"Who is the head?" I asked.

"That's just what we call the head of the Shin Bet. By the way, two weeks ago I met him at the Foreign Affairs and Defense Committee meeting. Afterwards, we sat to have coffee, and I asked him to look into your story. He got back to me and admitted that some of the information they'd received about you was a little exaggerated. Reading between the lines, I was able to gather that they didn't have enough concrete evidence to file an indictment. Nevertheless, they decided to take no chances. They found some technical clause allowing the termination of your employment at the army radio. The head summed up this case in his typical picturesque manner: 'Where trees are felled, chips will fly.'"

"What was I even suspected of?"

He lit a cigarette and somewhat heavily sat in his armchair. "It began with someone informing on you, I assume it was someone close to you. Do you remember telling me about that article you wrote for that political left-wing newspaper? The newspaper's editor lives on Zrubavel Street in south Tel Aviv, and you walked into his apartment with the shittiest possible timing. That evening he had a gathering of ultra-left-wing extremists there. One of the attendees was a Shin Bet informer, and he gave your name as one of the activists present.

"An undercover surveillance operation to monitor your actions began. They searched here and they dug there, and the information they unearthed was enough to tag you with a high-risk profile, a man with a radical left-wing ideology. In other words, you were a potential spy. The Shin Bet was bothered by the fact that you were with the radio and exposed to a lot of classified information. Reliable information had been received that you are an independent type, one who would walk over hot coals for the sake of a principle, a hard-headed man. That same source described you as having an infinite memory, a bottomless well that never loses a drop, a walking computer! That description raised another red flag. In fact, that scared them most of all.

"I'm sure you remember that embarrassing incident during the Yom Kippur War, when a junior intelligence officer was captured by the Syrians at the Mount Hermon outpost. That officer provided the Syrians more information about the IDF than you could ever imagine. The damage he caused to the security of Israel was almost inconceivable. That particular ordeal had a lot of influence on your case. The Shin Bet put the Mossad in the loop. Unfortunately for you, the two intelligence organizations began to squabble over who would handle your case. The Mossad claimed your file must be handed over to them, while the Shin Bet claimed they had first dibs. Because of their dispute, your case began to receive a lot more attention from everyone involved. This undoubtedly worked against you. That's what it's like when two powerful organizations want to eat the same slice of cake, get it?"

I just sat there, stunned by the information. "Someone informed on me, they found nothing, but decided to throw me to the dogs anyway?"

The parliament member flashed a fatherly smile. "You know what it's like. Some official, probably one of the lesser lights, put two and two together and came up with five." He shrugged and chuckled at his own joke. "He assembled a profile of you: youth organization member, demonstrations, peace movement connections. Now add to this stew your service in a combat unit with knowledge of top secret military information followed by access to the media through the army radio. That diligent pen pusher gathered all the facts in your file into a neat pile then wove them together into a nightmarish theory. Doubtless, the potential damage was way overestimated. So, they started looking for ways to eliminate you as a threat. Your security clearance and permanent employment forms happened to come their way. Someone high up wanted to cover his ass and

recommended that you be removed from your job. Sounds sophisti-
cated, but it's just sheer stupidity."

"Is this how it works? They just remove you from the chessboard
like a pawn? Instead of getting a grain of sand out of the sock, they
toss away the shoe?" The nonsense I'd heard was truly astounding.

"In your case, there were several other factors at play. They found
an excuse: your indirect connection to a left-wing extremist organization member who was in contact with a foreign Syrian agent.
They reached the conclusion that you must be related to that agent,
currently sitting in Paris. The Mossad was looped in and immediately demanded that the case be transferred to its care. The dispute
between the two organizations turned your problem from bad to
worse. Everyone's a suspect with the Shin Bet and the Mossad, always! Especially leftists like you. They don't trust anyone or take any
chances. These people never wear their pants without suspenders.
Always on the safe side.

"Your permanent employment status was just an excuse. They
sniffed an opportunity and used it, sure you were going to fold.
One more of many assessments they got wrong. You insisted, stood
your ground, didn't offer them a shred of information. But the worst
thing for them was when your story went public. Too much noise.
This was why they took you to be interrogated. People do stupid
things in interrogations; they break down and invent stories just to
buy some time, get their asses out of the fire. Luckily for you, you
kept it together. They wanted a steak and barely got some cookie
crumbs for dessert, but they kept looking.

"They ended up dumping you from the radio station because
they preferred to get rid of the problem instead of handling it." He
paused for a breath and looked me straight in the eye. "Even if my
description isn't a hundred percent accurate, this is how these cases play themselves out. In my opinion, you have nothing to worry
about. Just withdraw the Supreme Court petition. They want this

screwup of theirs to disappear quietly."

For a few minutes, I sat silently, digesting this absurd tale. "Is there a chance I can get my job back?" I finally asked.

"There are enough smart people there who'd recognize an opportunity to settle this to everyone's advantage. It might take some time, and I can't guarantee it, but I think they'll take you back. For me, the important thing is the mere fact that you were able to shake the tree. You never meant to do that, but you did. These organizations will think twice before pestering you again."

The audience over, he walked me to the door. He turned to me before reaching for the handle, and I found myself putting my arms around him. He was surprised by this unexpected embrace but returned it warmly.

***

Almost six months had passed since the army radio commander summoned me for that first meeting to the day the affair supposedly ended. Those were undoubtedly some of the longest, most excruciating months of my life. On the surface, it appeared I had won. A short time later, I received authorization to return to my old post at the army radio. It was all done very quietly. The army radio commander politely suggested, "Should anyone ask, perhaps you could say you took an unpaid leave to take care of some personal issue."

I didn't like his request but decided to let it pass. I never received an official — or unofficial — apology. The case was never officially closed either, but the entire thing seemed to have melted into thin air. The whole job termination farce had perished without anyone having to be held accountable. It was all gone and buried, still, I felt marked and tainted. At a certain point, I asked to receive an official document, a sort of certificate of integrity, stating that my conduct had been found to be beyond reproach. The army manpower directorate made it clear such a document would never be issued.

That same week, probably not by coincidence, I was summoned to the Ministry of Defense. At the gate, I was directed to the main building. In a graceless, utilitarian office, I was met by a man who presented himself as Yehiel. Without bothering to state his official rank or position, he explained things to me in a cold, impersonal tone.

"Please bear in mind that this meeting is not official. As far as I am concerned, it never happened. You just happened to walk into my room." Yehiel proceeded to issue a warning couched in precise legal terminology and a request that I keep a low profile.

Before I left, Yehiel added with a smile, "Do you know the fable about the bird that was on the verge of freezing to death in the snowy plains, then a cow shat on its head and saved its life? You listen to me, Uri Dolev, you keep quiet and don't sing too loud. Don't do anything rash. Should you decide to open your mouth… well, you know how it goes… there's always a chance some hungry coyote might hear the bird singing and decide to gobble it up."

Still smiling, Yehiel added one more barely veiled threat. "You're innocent, but only for the time being and only because our suspicions were not proven."

My meeting with Yehiel lasted about fifteen minutes. I emerged from it rattled. Scared, even. Over the years that followed this sad affair, I became a skeptic and a cynic. I remained disappointed, firmly believing there were others across the length and breadth of this country who also carried the burden of scars and humiliations, people that no one has ever heard of.

***

I returned to my old post at the radio as if nothing had ever happened. Since then, I have advanced in my career and won much praise and appreciation from my peers. But I lived in constant trepidation during those years, even though the suspicions against me had been supposedly refuted, and my life went on as usual.

In addition to my job at the radio, I also did some part-time television work. Outwardly, everything was going well, but deep inside, I was terrified and uncertain. I couldn't stop thinking that I had lost my country and it, in turn, had lost me.

I decided it was time to lead my life elsewhere but did nothing to further that goal.

PART 3

20

In the mid-nineties, I was offered the opportunity to join a new media venture. It was a tempting position — a television development manager for an American company expanding its activities to the European continent. The company had set up its European headquarters in Berlin. A promising career was outlined for me, but I was reluctant about relocating to a foreign country. I conducted a lengthy conversation with the company's personnel manager. I was initially deterred by the foreign management culture and mainly by my poor command of the German language. I was relieved to learn the company would be managed in English. Yet still, and despite the high salary and additional bonuses promised, I remained ambivalent. To determine the seriousness of the offer, I sent a long list of demands. Much to my surprise, the American company accepted them all.

About three weeks after the assassination of Israeli Prime Minister Yitzhak Rabin, in November 1995, I boarded a plane with two suitcases and relocated to Berlin.

I can't explain why, but I was filled with a sense of great relief.

***

My months of settling in Berlin were full of intense activity, which greatly improved my mood. Accompanied by a local real estate agent, with whom I scoured the city, I found a beautiful apartment not far from my office in the Charlottenburg-Wilmersdorf borough. My employment contract included several pleasant perks: stock options, a company vehicle, a lavishly designed office, a laptop, and a generous personal expense budget. Additionally, the company provided me with a German-language private tutor. For the first time in my life, I was driving a brand-new automobile, a Japanese sports car. My CEO raised an eyebrow, but because I had not exceeded the budget allotted me, he settled for a cynical remark: "I just hope your performance matches the car's."

***

My love affair with Berlin had begun years earlier. My first visit was to East Berlin in 1986, to attend an international film and theater convention. I had completed my studies in the field during my time with the army radio. The invitation I'd received had been sent by the East German government ministry of culture, and I saw the trip as an interesting journalistic opportunity. The city was still divided by the wall, and East Berlin was almost completely off-limits to Westerners. The radio station's news manager hesitated. He checked with the Israeli military authorities, who found no reason to prevent me from traveling to East Berlin. As all my travel expenses were to be paid by the inviting party, the news manager authorized the trip.

I found a flight from Tel Aviv to Munich and from there took a train to Berlin. At the train station, I flagged a taxi and asked the driver to drop me off at Checkpoint Charlie. Christmas was approaching, and the Berlin streets were decorated for the season. The border checkpoint area was nearly empty; only police and military personnel were hanging around. A tourist group stood off to the side and took pictures of the gray concrete booth and the sandbag wall. I paid the taxi driver and walked to the border checkpoint with my suitcase. The process of leaving West Berlin was surprisingly quick and easy. I crossed the distance separating the two border checkpoints on foot. I was excited, knowing I would soon leave the safe, Western part of the city and move to the communist side of Berlin. On the eastern side, I was welcomed by a gaunt young policeman wearing a green uniform and an army flat cap adorned with a strip of red fabric. His reddish face was speckled with moles. His uniform was several sizes too large, and he looked like a teenager wearing a Halloween costume. The smile that this image provoked vanished under his scrutiny. He inspected me with cold detachment, turned the passport this way and that until finally finding the proper direction, and then, with a gesture, asked me to remove my sunglasses. He returned to examining the passport and carefully studied my face then took my documents to an officer nearby. The officer looked at the passport and paperwork and whispered something into the policeman's ear. I began to fear that something was wrong. The pink-faced youth returned and asked to know the purpose of my visit. Barely able to understand his German, I replied in English, emphasizing the words "convention" and "theater." Then I added the word "journalist." The officer, who stood within earshot, nodded, and the policeman stamped my passport.

The entire process lasted about fifteen minutes, at the end of which I began to march eastward. I walked until I decided I was far enough from the border checkpoint, then I stopped and searched for a taxi. I looked up and down the street for quite some time but did not see a single taxi. I picked a direction at random and walked until I reached a bus stop. A woman of about forty-five stood there alone. She wore a coarse wool coat over a dress that looked like the plain work gowns worn by the women in the kibbutz. On her feet were rough work shoes, and in her hands were two plastic bags stuffed with groceries.

The woman recognized that I was a foreigner and offered her help. I showed her my invitation to the convention with the name of the hotel and the address. I took out a few dollars to show that I had only Western money in my wallet. She thought I was offering her the dollars as payment for her help and firmly rejected my money. She pointed at a sign with various bus line numbers, took a pen from her bag, scribbled the right number on a crumpled bit of paper, and gave me a few coins for purchasing the ticket.

I automatically thanked her in Hebrew. "*Toda raba.*"

We waited at the bus stop for twenty minutes or more, during which the woman kept looking over at me anxiously. Finally, she asked me in a whisper, "Israel?"

I nodded.

Hesitantly, she took out a newspaper from one of her plastic bags, fished out a photograph from her wallet, and placed it between the pages of the newspaper. She looked both ways suspiciously and asked me with a silent nod to look at the photograph. It showed a young woman wearing a floral evening dress. Her melancholy eyes stared straight at me. I noticed that the picture had been taken in front of the Habima national theater in Tel Aviv.

The woman in the work gown said to me in broken English, "This is my sister from Tel Aviv… you know?"

The face of the young woman from Tel Aviv was completely unfamiliar to me. With my miserable German, I tried to explain that I had no idea who the woman in the photograph was. In my heart, I resented my parents for having refrained from speaking German in my presence all those years, thus preventing me from mastering the language. I took another look at the photo and an additional detail caught my eye: next to the woman, leaning on a bus stop shelter, was a young man wearing an IDF uniform, and he was very familiar to me. It was Yehiam Gruenwald, my classmate from the kibbutz! I pointed at the soldier in the picture and tried to tell the East German woman that I did not know her sister, but I was good friends with the soldier standing next to her. The woman did not understand a word of what I said. After that, we waited for the bus in silence.

I was thrilled and surprised by the freak coincidence, which seemed even more remarkable as the date was December 21, Yehiam's birthday. What were the odds of a stranger in East Berlin, a woman I had never seen before, showing me a photograph of my friend? And on his birthday, no less! I yearned to speak with Yehiam to tell him about it, but during those long-gone years, calling from abroad was almost an impossibility.

***

It was a stark and pleasant transition from the gray, derelict East Berlin street to the luxurious Forum Hotel. In the lobby was a gaily decorated Christmas tree. The junior hotel employees wore their finest uniforms, and the senior ones were in elegant suits. The Forum was a showcase hotel intended to impress tourists from the West. My suitcase was carried by a young man wearing a blue uniform and a small service cap. He led me to a room designed in a decidedly European style and full of massive furniture. I wanted to give him a modest tip and once again had to apologize for not having any local money. I gave him a dollar bill. He smiled, looked both ways, gave a little thankful bow, and quickly tucked the bill in his pocket.

My room had a large, luxurious bathtub. I turned on the faucets, set the water temperature, and emptied the liquid from the small flasks into the tub. I undressed and slid into the warm, soapy water. I think my passion for bathtubs came from growing up without one. Bathing was an entirely functional activity in the kibbutz. To enjoy ourselves in the water, we had to climb to the reservoir pool, take a dip in the Jordan River, or be "lucky" enough to be confined to the infirmary's isolation ward, which contained the sole bathtub in the kibbutz. I remembered the isolation ward as place one could be pampered, a rarity in the kibbutz. I often hoped to catch some kind of throat infection — any illness that would ensure an entry ticket to the coveted isolation ward. In time, an additional tub was installed in Gurnischt's room, as he suffered from rheumatism. The kibbutz health committee had approved the installation of a tub in his room at the expense of his annual vacation budget, which he would always use to take a dip in the Dead Sea. Once Gurnischt had the tub installed, Alfred and several more members suddenly complained of rheumatism to the kibbutz doctor.

∗∗∗

Many memories resurfaced during that East Berlin convention. My parents, like most kibbutz founders, had emigrated from Germany and were great theater enthusiasts. Plays performed by the kibbutz members were the highlight of our cultural activity. Some years saw as many as two different theater productions. As far as I know, we put on more plays than any other kibbutz in the world. One play was particularly etched into my memory — *Till Eulenspiegel*.

For several days, a yellow bulldozer with a huge iron bucket leveled an area of about half a square kilometer outside the kibbutz fence. This graded area would serve as our amphitheater. Volunteer carpenters, orchestrated by Max Tishler, erected a large stage in the leveled area. The stage set boasted an impressive European-style castle. The children were asked to behave, and in return we would be allowed to see the play despite the late hour. And indeed, we behaved like model children. On the Friday preceding the play, we all made sure to clean our ears with a thin cottonwood cylinder soaked with paraffin oil. Before our afternoon nap, per the instructions of Dr. Zucker, we swallowed our spoonful of fish oil without a word of complaint. On the evening of the play, the whole Cypress group, wearing our best clothes — brown shoes, blue pants, and white shirts — and carefully combed and scrubbed — set out for the amphitheater. The play, as befitting a kibbutz full of German Jews, began at eight thirty on the dot.

I recalled one unexpected scene that earned the actors a thunderous round of applause. A white horse harnessed to a wagon proudly trotted onstage. It stood in the center of the stage and, uninterested in its surroundings, raised its tail and emptied its bowels. The audience burst into laughter that lasted several minutes. At the end of the first act, while the stagehands changed the set and cleaned the horse droppings, our nanny, Yael Harduf, declared, "For you, the children of the Cypress group, the show is over. Time to go to bed. Little children shouldn't be up and about at night."

All our pleas were to no avail; Yael was hardly affected by our tears. The show went on, while we were ushered back to the children's house.

***

I still don't understand why I chose not to tell my parents about my trip to East Berlin. They had never spoken of their past, and I had never pried. But in East Berlin, perhaps for the first time in my life, I distinctly felt their absence. I walked along Friedrichstrasse and Oranienburger Strasse all the way to Hackescher Markt, the heart of what had once been the Jewish area. I wanted to get to the Wedding District, where my mother's family had lived before the war, but I couldn't find the time and was very frustrated by that missed opportunity.

Wintry weather accompanied my visit to East Berlin. The air in the city streets was dry and cold. The remains of snow had turned into muddy piles that collected beside the houses, and the main streets had a faded, dreary look that filled me with melancholy. Only the areas where there were government buildings and those of the tourist hotels were decorated for Christmas. But that desperate attempt to beautify such places only served to emphasize the many years of neglect of the rest of the city.

I cared little for the convention meetings and lectures. I preferred to walk the streets of East Berlin for hours on end. The hosts had gone out of their way to ensure that Western participants would receive only positive impressions. They arranged a trip to Weimar, where the poet Heinrich Heine had lived, as well as the beautiful forest bordering it. We were also given a guided tour of Bertolt Brecht's house on Chausseestrasse in the middle of the Mitte borough, next to the small Dorotheenstadt Cemetery, where Brecht and his wife, Helene Weigel, are interred. While exploring the house, I discovered that Brecht had had a great view of the cemetery in which he is buried. The government tourist guide told us that the playwright had purposefully rented an apartment close to the cemetery because he needed a quiet spot. Brecht and his wife maintained separate bedrooms. She lived on the ground floor, which had an adjacent garden, while he lived on the upper floor room overlooking the cemetery.

21

Four years following that first visit to Berlin, I returned to it, but this time to its western side. Unlike the east, West Berlin was a bustling, tumultuous metropolis. I did not have the luxury of a tourist's schedule. I wanted the freedom to meander about the foreign city streets and look at passersby. For many months before the trip, I had been assailed with bouts of depression that I carefully kept hidden from friends and colleagues. Outwardly, I acted and functioned as usual, but my actions left a bitter taste that remained with me no matter what I did to rid myself of it. In my sleep, I was haunted by the same repetitive nightmare: I stand before a group of enemy soldiers. I know they intend to kill me, but the weapon in my hands is jammed, so I cannot fire at them. I would wake in a panic, sit up in bed, turn on the lights, and try to read. Even while reading, my thoughts gave me no rest. On the days following that dream I was tired and mentally drained. I often felt like a dead man walking. I hoped that in Berlin, an unfamiliar European city, I would be able to get lost in the streets and forget what needed forgetting in order to escape my melancholy.

A few hours after I had settled in my hotel for the night, not far from the Kurfürstendamm shopping district, I heard a commotion and loud screaming coming from outside. The main street was filled with a multitude of people who seemed to be celebrating. I went down to the hotel lobby and asked the receptionist what happened. The girl leaned across the reception desk, kissed me, and declared, "The Berlin Wall has fallen!"

Once again, I recalled my uncle Kuntz's wise saying: "Revolutions are not in the habit of giving advance notice." I went out to the streets and mingled with the celebrants. The human stream pushed me toward the Brandenburg Gate. Youngsters holding beer bottles and champagne noisily celebrated the happy event. The excitement around me continued to rise as the hours passed. I squeezed my way through the masses, who wanted to be as close as possible to the gateposts that had become Berlin's most famous icon. The Germans were as excited as we Israelis were when our paratroopers liberated the Western Wall during the Six-Day War.

The following day, the streets were teeming with East Berlin residents. They were easily identifiable by their clothing as well as the fear in their eyes. They were afraid the magic might vanish at any moment. The unexpected tourists filled the department stores and emerged laden with plastic bags stuffed with basic foodstuffs, fruits, and various delicacies. They were dazzled by the new plenitude that surrounded them. One could see men and women carrying heavy loads on their backs in baskets or in simple cloth sacks. Faltering Trabants — cars of an East German make — were suddenly seen around town.

The festive atmosphere lasted for over a week. The supply of bananas in West Berlin gradually dwindled until not a single one could be found. When the food hoarding eased up, the new city residents turned their minds to other attractions. Large waves of visitors shamelessly frequented the sex stores scattered around the city. East Berliners flocked to witness that wonder of the liberal world. Recognizing the profit potential, prostitutes from all over Europe descended on Berlin to fill its bars and clubs. The bacchanalia continued day and night. Drunks rolled in the gutters. In those few days, the city of Berlin changed forever. In addition to the wall, many other barriers had fallen. People would burst into tears in the middle of the street for no apparent reason. Hope reigned in the city, the hope of a better world. And I, who wanted a laid-back vacation more than anything else, had suddenly found myself in a maelstrom of activity and change.

I had traveled from my home to a place where no one would know me. I had traveled to look for myself, to be as far as possible from the perpetual noise that accompanied my life in Israel. All I'd wanted were a few moments of peace and relaxation. Now I found myself in the world's most vibrant city. I wanted some quiet and was instead swept away by the swirl of history. I walked about the streets and squares, excited and overwhelmed by the many experiences offered me by the city. I called my parents to share this extraordinary experience with them. My father picked up the phone. There wasn't a shred of happiness in his voice.

"I've seen it all on TV. As far as I'm concerned, Germans are Germans, no matter what side of the wall they are on. When they're happy, I'm sad, no matter the reason. The fallen wall is just an excuse for them to drink more beer.

"Look, Uri, they get to forget all about Kristallnacht; now they have a new reason to dance and get drunk on November ninth under the Brandenburg Gate."

Strangely enough, and despite my father's words, I felt at home in the very city where my parents' childhoods had abruptly ended and from which their families had been banished. I avoided the question of why Berlin of all places. The harsh sound of the German language was familiar and reminded me of Grandma Fania's visits to the kibbutz. I'd felt at ease from my first day in the city. Curious, I allowed myself to walk its streets wherever they led but constantly reminded myself that many of its aging inhabitants could have been part of that vile racist machine of destruction. Entranced, I roamed the city and watched its overjoyed people relishing the new winds of hope and freedom. The fall of the Berlin Wall and the dramatic events that followed persuaded me to extend my stay in Berlin. I even considered the possibility of permanently relocating there; I had simply fallen in love with the city.

***

Adjusting to my new workplace and permanent residency in Berlin wasn't easy. Israel was still rife with unrest after the assassination of Prime Minister Yitzhak Rabin and I, whose whole career had revolved around the media, now found myself very far from the stormy center of the events that were changing the face of Israeli society. In Germany, news of the assassination simply came and went. After work, I sat by myself and tried to master the German language. I cared little for television. I was isolated, an immigrant living in the city of my parents' childhood. At night, when the streets grew cold, I stayed in my apartment, warmed some instant soup, and stirred it in a pot much longer than necessary, anything to postpone sitting at the table all alone.

On the weekends, I explored Kurfürstendamm — known locally as the Ku'damm. I was careful not to skip a single floor of the famous KaDeWe department store. I walked along the street that sprawled from Tauentzienstrasse all the way to the heart of the Charlottenburg district. Each time I passed the Gedächtniskirche — the Kaiser Wilhelm Memorial Church, I felt a wave of gloating satisfaction. Of course, I kept my feelings to myself. I wandered the streets like an unleashed dog. I expanded my tours and reached Wilmersdorf and the Rüdesheimer Platz.

Naturally, I was attracted to the old Jewish neighborhoods. During one of my forays, I visited the Wedding District and searched until I found Muller Street. I stopped in front of No. 13, where my mother's family had lived before the war. I stood there like a tourist, peering at the well-preserved apartment house. I went inside the adjacent tea shop and told the proprietor that my family had once lived there. She took a large key out of her apron pocket and led me to the front door, offering me the chance to look inside. I tried to imagine what it was like to live your life there in Nazi Germany of the thirties.

***

The years passed, and I gradually began to feel more comfortable. The German language seemed to be coming to me more easily, and I no longer had to chase it. Words and phrases I had fleetingly heard in my childhood resurfaced as if they had never left. I spoke adequately, and gradually I considerably improved my writing skills. All those years, I never stopped touring the city and exploring its various neighborhoods and districts. I especially enjoyed wandering through the Mitte borough, walking into the small stores, not to buy anything, but only to look at the young people crowding them. I visited the galleries, fascinated by the thriving local art scene. That beautiful area, mostly populated by Jews in the past, was now filled with lively shops, restaurants, cafés, and galleries.

I also fell in love with the Kreuzberg borough, which was populated mostly by Turkish immigrants. The atmosphere made me feel at home. There, I found Mediterranean restaurants very much like the ones in Israel, a bohemian atmosphere, and the flavors of other places. Most of the borough's residents were foreigners, and I was one of them. Whenever the chill would bite into my bones, I would sit in a café, eat the cakes, and slowly sip a cappuccino. I looked at the couples around me. I was envious, even of the couples who sat across from each other without exchanging a single word. I tried to imagine their relationships, and then my mind would inevitably drift to Nurit Schory, lost to me for so many years.

In Berlin, I felt free from all my worries. I had found what I'd been looking for when I'd left Israel: time for myself. There, I had as much time as I wanted, but I did not know what to do with it.

22

Almost unnoticed, my stay in Berlin had grown from months to years. I rarely visited Israel, and when I did, I refrained from going to Mishmar Hatsafon. I would meet my parents only in Tel Aviv. In the kibbutz, no one had really taken an interest as to why I lived in Germany. I built an impenetrable bubble for myself, keeping my distance from everything that had tied me to Israel — my friends, the culture, and the views of the country, so dear to my heart in childhood. I willingly sentenced myself to this detachment, especially from the kibbutz. I felt comfortable with this isolation.

I formed a small circle of friends, mainly other Israelis who had relocated to Berlin. Occasionally, I indulged in a brief romantic affair, but I dedicated most of my time to my work, and my efforts were greatly appreciated. My work-related duties expanded and included a good bit of traveling around Europe. One of my trips took me to Stockholm. I hesitated then thought, *What have you got to lose?* I called Nurit's apartment and found out she had left it years before. Disappointed, I returned to Berlin.

Two weeks later, I called the same telephone number, and the new tenant told me he had found Nurit's new address. I went to see her unannounced. I was barely able to recognize the woman who opened the door. Nurit's raven hair had mostly turned white. Old age had claimed the beautiful girl of my dreams. Her boyish body

had thickened, the smile was gone from her lips. Her face had broad-
ened, her skin was pockmarked, and one of her front teeth was broken. We stood there, facing each other like two people seeing each
other for the first time.

"It's me... Uri Dolev. From Mishmar Hatsafon."

A spark of understanding brightened Nurit's eyes. She put her
arms around me, and tears welled up. She took my hand and led
me into her apartment. She placed a plate with some sliced cake on
the table and offered me coffee. All that was left of the wild-spirited
Nurit I had loved was a sad, faded remnant, like a piece of clothing
washed too many times. I invited her to have dinner with me in the
Old Town, and Nurit immediately agreed. She dressed in a pair of
jeans, a loose shirt, and a bulky wool sweater. For a moment, a cold
ember of her former beauty glimmered.

The wine we poured further improved her disposition. Nurit
wouldn't stop talking, just like in the old days. She told me everything
that had happened to her since we had last met, but there was no
real conversation. She spoke in an unending monologue, interrupted only by occasional visits from the waiter. Dryly, monotonously,
she told me of the harsh years in which she had become addicted to
drugs. It was a shorthand version of events, recited without emotion
or attempts to conceal or beautify. She had been found unconscious
in the street and taken to the hospital. Once her condition had been
stabilized, she was sent to a rehabilitation center in a village a few
hundred kilometers from Stockholm. It had taken two years of treatment for her to recover.

While Nurit spoke on, I pecked at my food, looking at her once
beautiful face. I saw no trace of the uninhibited girl I had loved so
much.

Upon leaving the rehabilitation center, she had decided to remain
in the village. She found work at a flower nursery, met a young man,
and spent three happy, quiet years with him. That enchanted period

had ended abruptly; her companion was run over while riding his bicycle. Nurit left the village and returned to Stockholm. She'd found a low-paying job in a customer service call center.

Just before the end of the meal, Nurit told me, "I'm tired of being here. It's always so sad and cold. I'm going back to the kibbutz to live near my mother. Back to the landscapes of my childhood." A moment later, she said, "Tell me, Uri, why did you leave Israel? And why Germany, of all places?"

I dismissed her with a casual reply. "There's no point in trying to explain… you wouldn't understand anyway."

Yet Nurit's question continued to bother me long after we parted. I recalled how, as a child, I had asked my father why he and Kuntz never spoke to each other. He dryly replied, "There's no point in trying to explain… you wouldn't understand anyway."

My meeting with Nurit had left me drained and exhausted. I returned to my hotel room in a pensive and melancholy mood. Time has no mercy, and it marks us all. I felt sorry for Nurit and angry at myself for not being there for her when she had needed my help. For the first time, I began to realize that we would probably never be together. Tired and disappointed, I returned to Berlin.

***

On a cold and dreary afternoon, the CEO of my company convened an urgent management meeting. The CEO held a sheet of paper in his hand and read the following statement: "The company board of directors has accepted the shareholders' offer to issue the company on the New York Stock Exchange over the course of the following months." I calculated my steps and decided to wait until the stock was issued. Happily, the public offering was very successful, so I took advantage of the opportunity and sold all the options I had been given over the years. The stock I sold was worth a fortune.

One could say I had become rich overnight.

This dramatic change in my financial situation encouraged me to quit my job, with which I had already lost interest. I patiently waited six months, as required by my contract. When the time came, I left my beautiful office without regret and embarked on a new path. I considered buying an apartment in the Kreuzberg quarter, home to Turkish immigrants and artists, but ended up buying a nice apartment on Kollwitzstrasse, in the eastern part of town, a place where many young people lived.

23

I was woken by the insistent ringing of the telephone by my bed.

"God damn it," I cursed and grudgingly picked up the receiver.

A woman, with the husky voice of a lifelong smoker, spoke to me. "May I speak with Uri Dolev? This this Ruhale from Mishmar Hatsafon."

I stretched and sat up in bed. "Did something happen?" I drowsily growled as if emerging from a nightmare.

"What are you doing, sleeping so late? You know, Uri, everyone here has been working for hours, yes? It wouldn't hurt you to see the sunrise now and then."

That last sentence made me recall those early wakeups during apple harvesting season, the stale taste of communal dining room tea, sitting on the edges of a wagon harnessed to a red tractor, slowly driving in the morning cold with your legs dangling in the air. Each of us keeping to himself, snuggled in the remains of dreams disturbed by the abrupt waking. Like palm fronds, our bodies bobbed up and down, silently echoing every bump on the road as we desperately tried to hold on to another precious moment of sleep. Half an hour of a dazed drive accompanied by the strained grumbling of the tractor engine as the wheels struggled with the rugged road. The engine cover rattled noisily but not hard enough to dislodge the thick layer of dust clinging to the metal in a coating of oil and diesel fuel.

In the orchard we heard the scream of the foreman. "We're here! Everyone down! Get yourselves shears, a ladder, and a basket. Today we're harvesting the Jonathan, Alexander, and Orleans apples. Wake up! We're late already! Breakfast is in two hours!"

I sat higher up in bed and pulled the comforter over me. "Look, what did you say your name was…. Ruhale? It's six in the morning here in Germany, we don't work on Sunday, and there's a two-hour time difference," I said in a voice still hoarse with sleep. Rain trickled outside my window, and a grim morning crept into my room.

"Oh… I see… So, you in Germany are still sleeping at this hour? Perhaps you remember me? We met many years ago, before you moved to Germany. Well, what does it matter? I'm the kibbutz secretary now."

"Ruhale, you said we met a long time ago. When was that?" I was still in bed.

"Try to remember on your own. How many Ruhales do you know, Uri? But let's not go around in circles, yes? Let's get straight to the point. We're preparing to celebrate the kibbutz's sixtieth birthday. The members of the kibbutz had the idea that you should write the play for us. A history of our kibbutz… yes? A musical drama reenactment. Well… what do you say?

"Look, Uri, you may have left the kibbutz, yes? But the kibbutz has never left you. See what happened? You left, while I came back from the big city to Mishmar Hatsafon; we switched places. You do see the irony, yes? So, like I said, you know the kibbutz like the back of your hand. Nothing has changed here. Lazy people say, 'Go to the ant to seek her aid, then you can easily sit in the shade.' But here, most of the members are still diligent, know how to roll up their sleeves and offer a helping hand when they need to… yes? The sons that left us often do that and come back to help.

"Your parents live in the kibbutz, and I'm sure they'd be pleased if you'd do your share in pulling the collective wagon."

I hated the preachy, pedantic tone of her voice and tried to unearth it from my memory… Ruhale? But it was no use. I still had no idea who this kibbutz secretary was.

"How did you even get to the kibbutz?" I hoped that her answer might give me a clue.

"Oh… that's a very long story, and we're on an expensive international call that costs the members a lot of money, yes? In short, I want an answer. Time flies, and we have less than a year before the happy anniversary day. You know the way it works with us people, you can resist, object, argue, and be angry, but at the end of the day everyone needs to bow his head before the collective will. I'm writing in my little notebook that you've agreed to help us, yes?"

It took me a second or two to come to my senses. "Let me think this over. Please understand, I haven't even been to the kibbutz in a long time. Give me a week to sleep on it."

"I think you've slept enough, Uri Dolev. It's time for you to wake up, yes? Pull yourself together, we don't have time for hesitation or deliberation. Oh my… this is quite the rhyme, yes?" That was how Ruhale concluded the conversation.

**

Quiet returned to my beautiful apartment on Kollwitzstrasse Berlin. I snuggled under the covers and tried to go back to sleep, but I remained unsettled by that bizarre phone call. Long-forgotten anxieties bubbled up from some inner depth. I racked my brain to remember who the hell Ruhale from Mishmar Hatsafon was. While tossing in bed, I tried to recreate the details of the conversation. I was flattered the kibbutz had remembered my existence so many years after I had left. I considered and reconsidered the matter as if it were some mental Rubik's cube. I got out of bed, prepared myself a cup of instant coffee, and stood by the window looking at the rain lashing at the panes.

24

An item published in a Berlin newspaper caught my attention. The headline was: "*Man found hanged in Berlin Jewish Museum Restroom.*" The article stated that a note had been found in the deceased's pocket: "*The memory of the Holocaust has passed from the world. Antisemitism is raising its ugly head, and no one is doing anything about it.* Gurnischt mit gurnischt. *Nothing with nothing. I doubt that the death of an old Jewish man like myself will make a difference. Nothing will ever change.*"

I flipped through the newspaper to read the rest of the article. "*A key was found on the deceased's body. It led police investigators to a small pension in the Mitte quarter. The pension manager told the investigators that an Israeli tourist had rented the room a few days before and had not returned last night. The investigators found an old suitcase with clothes and a few other belongings, and an Israeli passport in the name of Max Tishler, born 1921 in Berlin, Germany.*"

I read the name over and over. A dull ache of sadness began to spread in my chest. Long before I read the last line, I knew that the hanged man, Max Tishler, was none other than Gurnischt, one of our kibbutz founders. From the newspaper, I learned that on his last morning, Max Tishler had bought a rope from a hardware store close to the pension. He had purchased a ticket to the museum about an hour before closing. After entering the museum, he must have hidden in the restroom. When the last of the museum employees had gone, he took the rope out of his bag and tied it to a hook on the ceiling. He set a trash can on a toilet bowl, climbed on top of it, put his neck in the noose, kicked the can, and hanged himself to death.

***

During the early years of the kibbutz, Max was still a central figure and had even served several times as the secretary. His attempts to get elected as the kibbutz representative to the various party institutions repeatedly failed, however. His wife had passed away at a young age, leaving him a childless widower. Max was always considered an odd bird in Mishmar Hatsafon. Of all the kibbutz children, my friend Udi Ganani was the only to find common ground with him, and Max treated the child like his own. In my mind, I saw a distant image of Max, a memory of how, following Udi's death, he had left his carpentry workshop and dedicated himself to filing and collecting documents for the kibbutz archive, which had turned into the center of his world. I could see Max sitting behind his desk in the tiny room, cutting clippings from *Al HaMishmar* to be filed for the benefit of future generations. There were those in the kibbutz who thought Gurnischt mourned Udi's death even more than his own parents, Menahem and Rina.

My father had never cared much for Gurnischt. He and Max had an ongoing argument regarding who had founded Aliyat Hanoar, the youth immigration department of the Jewish Agency. Max heatedly claimed Henrietta Szold was the founder, while my father insisted it was Recha Freier. I once heard my father derisively referring to Max, after another one of their disagreements. "That *schmendrick* may know how to build cabinets and closets in his shop, but he doesn't know the first thing about history."

My father declared that Gurnischt's obsession with the archive was fueled by his desire to rewrite the kibbutz history to glorify his own name. He based his claim on the fact that every word Max had ever said during the general or secretariat kibbutz meetings was scrupulously documented in the archive like God's own truth. My father, like many other kibbutz veterans, did not like Gurnischt treating the kibbutz archive like his private property.

Over the years, Max's rheumatism worsened. He complained of backaches and stopped working in the carpentry shop altogether. When people inquired about his occupation, Max would reply, "I used to be a carpenter. Now I'm an archivist, documenting the history of the kibbutz."

And indeed, Max spent all his time preserving and expanding the kibbutz archive. This behavior was frowned upon by many kibbutz members who regarded his work in the archive as nonproductive and of no use to the collective.

***

Max's suicide brought some unexpected momentary publicity to Kibbutz Mishmar Hatsafon. A German reporter from *Der Spiegel* spoke with Ruhale, the kibbutz secretary. She said that the suicide had come as a complete surprise to all the kibbutz members. In the article, the reporter mentioned that some were of the opinion Max had taken this final drastic step because of a decision to cut the archive budget and transfer it to a much smaller room.

The secretary dismissed such theories. "The kibbutz sees great importance in preserving its history. There was never any intention of interfering with Max Tishler's life's work."

The reporter interviewed Alfred too, as one of the kibbutz veterans. Alfred was depicted as a model kibbutznik: an oversized, bald man working in the dairy barn, walking about barefoot wearing nothing but his shorts, and flailing his hands while speaking flowery

German in a thunderous voice. "I, for one, was not surprised at all to hear that he killed himself. Gurnischt regularly hid notes in the coffins he built in his carpentry shop. The first we found in a coffin he prepared for Ronnie Schory, one of the kibbutz children who died of an illness when he was only three. When we placed the child in the coffin, we found an envelope containing a letter in German addressed to Max's parents and sister, who perished in the Holocaust. Gurnischt wrote that he knew little Ronnie's soul would reach heaven. He never forgave himself for abandoning his family in Germany in 1938 and emigrating to Israel by himself. Everyone knew that without his family, Max Tishler's life in the kibbutz was *gurnischt mit gurnischt*, nothing with nothing."

To sum things up, Alfred added, "Little Ronnie Schory's father took pity on Max Tishler and decided to leave the letter in his son's coffin."

25

Mishmar Hatsafon had its own set of rules. Those unwritten guidelines included one that involved concealing the past — my parents had never told me of their lives in Germany. To be honest, I didn't especially care about their past at the time. Life in the kibbutz was beautiful, washed with perpetual sunlight. The adults tried to protect us from any unwanted "intrusion" that might undermine this serenity. The Holocaust hovered over our heads but in some far-off, hidden place. Perhaps on the highest shelf of the wardrobe, where instant coffee boxes and fine chocolates were tucked away as well, treats that regularly arrived from London wrapped in brown paper, sent by Grandma Fania every six months. Bit by bit, the larger picture became clear to me, mainly during brief conversations with my uncle Kuntz.

My parents never divulged anything, but unlike them, Kuntz was eager to tell me everything. When I was young, I had avoided speaking to Kuntz because of the hostility between the brothers. As I grew older, Kuntz would bide his time and wait for opportunities when my father wasn't around to tell me a little more about our family history.

***

"While Hitler's soldiers were conquering Czechoslovakia and Poland, we in the kibbutz continued to deal with fulfilling the ideals of the HaShomer Hatzair Jewish youth movement and reinventing the Hebrew language. The echoes of the fast-approaching war gradually seeped into our world until claiming a central place in our lives," Kuntz explained to me.

"Your grandfather, Martin Kuntzmacher, managed to survive the death camps. In 1947, he arrived in Mishmar Hatsafon in a bus that stopped by the front gate. It was a warm day in the month of June. He was fifty-six, and all his possessions were in two battered suitcases he had brought with him. Menahem Ganani brought him to the communal dining room to sit and rest. A noisy ceiling fan blew hot, humid air at him. Menahem gave him a glass of water then ran to look for your father and me.

"When I entered the dining room," Kuntz continued, "I saw an old man who looked like a piece of anchovy on a slice of dried bread. His shirt was tattered, dark lakes spread under his armpits, and a brown fedora rested on his head. I hardly recognized him. He stared at me and could not tell who I was right away.

"When he finally recognized me, he stood up, adjusted his tie, put on his jacket and said, 'Moishe'le… is it you?' and shook his head in disbelief. The dining room was full of kibbutz members wearing shorts, tanks tops, and sandals. And there was my father, with his fedora, a striped brown suit, a tie, and shiny leather shoes. He looked like a visitor from outer space. He forced a smile, and we shook hands. After so many years apart, we didn't even exchange a hug."

***

WWII broke out shortly after Kuntz left Berlin. By the time the war ended, his father was a different man. Ten years after he had left Berlin, Kuntz, his son, was an Israeli in every respect. Father and son barely found a common language. Martin Kuntzmacher became withdrawn, retreating into long silences and refusing to speak. But one time, with my father present as well, he suddenly told us, without a shred of emotion, about the stepmother who had died in the camps. Kuntz's attempts to learn from his father how he had survived yielded no clear answers.

"You could never understand what went on there," Martin said to his sons.

Martin Kuntzmacher spoke German and Polish, while both his sons made sure to speak only Hebrew. Their conversations with him were always brief. The father was unable to understand why his sons chose to live in such a remote location at the far edges of the country, in harsh conditions, and why they had relinquished the financial possibilities life in the city would have offered. He thought he might be able to open a small business in Haifa and was hoping that one of his sons would share in the realization of his dream. The great intimacy he had once shared with his eldest son, Kuntz, had vanished. As far as Kuntz was concerned, his reunion with his father served as final confirmation that his past in Germany had been erased, and the door to his childhood country was permanently closed.

The young Mishmar Hatsafon members weren't too keen to absorb members' relatives who came from Europe after the war and asked to join the kibbutz. My aunt Henka thought differently and even turned to the kibbutz secretariat members, demanding that Mishmar Hatsafon open its gates to Holocaust survivors. She believed the kibbutz mustn't think of financial considerations in this matter. Henka insisted the kibbutz was morally obligated to welcome those who had come destitute from Europe.

"She was right, but we were young and not always willing to accept the dictates of reason," Kuntz told me.

The accepted view was that the kibbutz was not a place that should accept just anybody. Only those who were willing to accept and endorse the movement's doctrine and ideals should become members. And Kuntz supported that belief.

"The collective ideology was not merely a slogan. It was the flag that proudly flew over our heads. Philosophically speaking, parents who wanted to live close to their children in the kibbutz had to accept the principles of the collective authority. At least that was what we thought back then."

When a request was presented before the kibbutz's general assembly to accept Martin Kuntzmacher as a kibbutz member, there were those who claimed the collective ways of the kibbutz were alien to the Berlin shoemaker. As far as the kibbutz members were concerned, Martin was a useless old man. They thought he merely intended to buy himself some time in the kibbutz until he could resettle in the big city. Additional claims were that he had rejected every productive work opportunity offered him. The members doubted the authenticity of his various ailments, which had caused frequent absences from work and required frequent treatment in the city, all paid for by the kibbutz.

Kuntz and my father remained silent during the discussion concerning Martin's kibbutz membership request. Martin himself did not bother to attend the vote that took place in the dining hall. Kuntz told me that during that assembly, he and my father sat on opposite sides of the room. Both brothers believed that the kibbutz should make a calculated, logical decision without taking the emotional and personal aspects of the matter into consideration.

Henka, who rarely spoke in kibbutz general assemblies, stood up and said, "The kibbutz must admit any Holocaust survivor who wants to become a member."

During the vote, she was among the few supporting my grandfather's membership request. Kuntz and my father abstained. Following that assembly, a bitter argument broke out between Henka and Kuntz. Henka was furious over her husband's and his brother's silence, over the fact that they had accepted with equanimity the kibbutz's decision to reject their own father.

Henka's harsh words were etched into Kuntz's memory. "Shame on you! You were both silent like a pair of fish! You chose to hide behind this make-believe democratic righteousness. Is this your Zionist dream? You, who pride yourselves on being true pioneers upholding the ideals of integrity and basic human rights, have no shred of respect for the weak and the different. When I came to the kibbutz as a war refugee, all I heard from you were heroic tales about clearing fields along with whining about mosquito bites and malaria. What have you done to try to save your families in Europe?"

My grandfather took his few personal possessions and relocated to Haifa. He felt lonely and worthless in his new country. No one in Haifa needed a shoemaker who had long ago lost the nimble use of his fingers. He knew no other trade. Years of severe cold and hunger in the camps had left him with many ailments. All he wanted was to find some clerical work, but his poor Hebrew hindered all attempts to find that sort of employment. He tried his hand at several odd jobs, applied for positions here and there and was repeatedly rejected. He spent hours sitting by himself in the various city cafés, wearing a suit, tie, and his fedora. For a brief period, Martin Kuntzmacher worked as a waiter in one of the cafés he frequented. The service he offered was slow and clumsy, and his poor Hebrew was yet again his undoing. The head waiter, a former Berliner, did the best he could to cover for Martin's mistakes, but in the end the café owner lost his patience and fired him.

Following a long period of unemployment, Martin found a job as a street cleaner for the Haifa municipality. In the morning, he would get up early and go out to the streets equipped with a broom and a garbage cart, praying that he would not come across any of his few acquaintances. In the evening, he would wear his finest suit and go sit in a café in the Hadar HaCarmel district, where he would while away his time reading old German newspapers.

One day, in an alley in the lower city, not far from the Haifa Port, Martin collected a scrap of metal into his garbage cart. It was an old shell from the War of Independence. The bouncing of the rickety cart jostled the fuse. The deafening blast that followed was heard all over lower Haifa. Martin was mortally injured and died before he was moved to the hospital. I was born several months after his death.

26

Max Tishler's suicide had interrupted my laid-back life in Berlin. In Mishmar Hatsafon, Ruhale, the secretary, impatiently waited for my reply regarding the writing of the festive play commemorating the kibbutz's sixtieth anniversary. I promised her I would decide in a few days and get back to her with a reply but continued to delay. The nights began to haunt me again. I had naively assumed I was fully healed from the nightmares of the past.

I woke up in a panic early one morning. Snowy winter weather reigned outside. I got out of bed, stepped into the shower, and stood beneath the stream of hot water. I closed my eyes, allowing the water to cleanse my body. I thoroughly shampooed my head then rubbed some of the remaining shampoo on my face and began to shave lethargically. A blind shave. Careful not to injure myself with an uncalculated movement, I stretched my facial skin with my left hand, and with my right moved the razor with slow, skillful strokes. Many years ago, in boot camp, a group of recruits stood outside together by the drinking fountain and shaved. Someone beside me said, "See this shaving motion, Dolev? It takes all the toxins out of the body."

I did not believe that special shaving motion had any effect on toxins, but it had turned into a habit anyway.

I ran my hands over my cheeks under the running water then checked for rebellious clusters of stubble on my chin and down my neck. I turned off the faucet and dried myself with a towel. I wrapped myself in a bathrobe that always made me look odd and descended one flight of stairs to pick up the newspaper from the mailbox. I began with the sports section, not skipping a single word.

I prepared another cup of instant coffee and flipped through the newspaper between sips. I skipped the main headline and went straight to the inner sections. While reading, I remembered that when in Israel, I had never missed an opportunity to read the obituaries, but I knew no one in Berlin. From my upper floor window in the last building on Kollwitzstrasse, I could see the steady traffic flowing through Danziger Strasse bordering on Ernst-Thälmann Park. I loved standing by the window and looking at the tree-lined boulevard. Since it was winter, the plane trees were naked. Only a few rust-colored leaves clung to their branches, refusing to accept nature's decree and fall. That boulevard always reminded me of the plane trees my father had planted in Mishmar Hatsafon.

While in this pensive mood, I heard the phone ring. I didn't expect a phone call at such an early hour, and I assumed the kibbutz secretary, Ruhale, had called to demand an answer. I let the phone continue to ring for a few minutes before finally stopping. My relief was short-lived. A second later, the shrill sound of the telephone again filled the apartment.

I recognized my brother's voice as soon as I picked up the receiver. "Uri, Dad's been severely injured in an accident. I'm on my way to the hospital in Safed, can't talk much, I don't have a speakerphone in my car. Get here as soon as possible, we're waiting for you."

My brother's call had caught me unprepared, but then again, was it possible to prepare yourself for such a situation? I paused to pull myself together then I asked him about my father's condition. A whirlwind of calculations and horrific images were already swirling in my head.

"I've been told only that Dad's badly injured. I'll be at the hospital soon, and then we'll see. Mom's already there. I have to hang up now, Uri, the last thing I need is some cop pulling me over for talking on the phone while driving. I'll call as soon as I get to the hospital. Meanwhile, find the earliest flight and get over here. I need you to do that."

I thought about my mother and wondered who was taking care of her. As a nurse, she was used to taking care of others. I assumed she was in a bit of a state and needed her children beside her. As soon as I finished talking to Yoram, I called my mother's cell phone, which was turned off, as usual. I called my travel agency to find me the first flight to Tel Aviv, a sense of dread churning in me. While I waited for a call back, a flurry of thoughts flooded my head, most of them involving various horrific scenarios. I did my best to repress these. *Patience, you don't have any facts or details.*

***

The light from my reading lamp reflected through the glass surface of my table and flooded the apartment with a cold, pale light. A black crow, wet with snow, settled on a utility pole outside my window. It shook its feathers, and I could hear its loud caws. The crow puffed itself up to keep its body heat in and kept watching the traffic on Danziger Strasse. Occasionally, and for no apparent reason, the crow tilted its head and emitted a shrill, disturbing cry. The black bird continued to perch on top of the pole, patiently waiting for food scraps to be tossed from the window of a passing car.

A steady wind was blowing outside, and the temperature dropped to minus three Celsius. A small, long-tailed squirrel bounded from among the trees by the road. The squirrel stopped, looked about with jerky movements, deciding where it should turn to next. The noise of an approaching speeding car made the squirrel leap with a start straight into the bumper of another car rushing from the other side. The squirrel's crushed body was quickly hidden under a thin blanket of snow. A sudden, powerful gust sent a tremor through the plane trees, bringing a sense of restlessness to my street.

I continued to watch the crow, admiring its magnificent ability to dive at the squirrel's body, plunge its beak into the bleeding flesh, and fly away unharmed every time another car passed by. *Nothing is ever wasted. One creature gets run over; another devours it. A cycle of a sort*, I thought.

***

My father had survived several injuries in the past: a rifle bullet that passed through his shin during a Palmach combat training exercise, a stone shard that smashed his cheek and knocked out many of his teeth following the detonation of an explosive device leaving a scar on his jaw. Before I moved to Berlin, he had a severe heart attack, and none of his doctors believed he would recover.

It was late at night, and my father was watching his favorite TV show. My mother was getting ready to take a shower. At the hospital, my mother had told the story from her point of view. "You know how it is with us, the showers are connected to a central steam boiler, and during the winter it takes time for the hot water to start coming. I was standing in the shower, shivering and waiting. I shouted at your dad to turn off the television and go to sleep already. After all, he has to get up at five in the morning. He didn't answer. Then the hot water came at last.

"When I got out of the shower, I found him sprawled on the carpet by the bed. I did what they taught me in nursing school — gave him a strong blow to the chest and mouth-to-mouth resuscitation."

It worked just like in the textbooks. My mother's CPR had brought my father back to life.

Back then, when I had walked into his room in the intensive care unit of the Safed Hospital, I was surprised how skinny he looked in his pajamas, which were a few sizes too big. He lay unconscious in a bed surrounded by a silvery frame. A green mask covered much of his unshaven face, connected to a ventilator. Monotonous sounds issued from the device, reminding me of the songs of whales I had once heard in a documentary. Red and green lines flickered on the monitor like snakes moving in a series of tangled coils, rising and falling according to some unquiet regularity governing human heartbeats and blood pressure. An IV bag provided liquids through a transparent plastic tube straight into the vein of my father's hand, a hand that had withstood many years of sunlight and hard labor. Over the years, the skin had turned into a thick parchment covered with brown spots and striped with the gray-bluish veins of old age.

But that had happened years ago. Ten days later, he had fully recovered from that severe heart attack. A short while later, my father had returned to his gardening work and cultivated the kibbutz's flower beds and gardens every day. Very quickly, he had returned to all his old habits, except for one. He did give up the pleasure of smoking cigarettes.

***

In my Berlin apartment, I imagined to myself that despite the experience she had accumulated over the years as a nurse, my mother was now unable to help. No nursing course could have prepared her to deal with this situation. I pictured her sitting in the Safed Hospital emergency room, helpless, measuring every doctor and nurse that passed by. As a retired nurse, she would be very familiar with hospital priorities. Younger patients were treated first; older ones had to wait. The elderly were treated merely as a formality. She would be concerned that the doctors and nurses wouldn't make too much of an effort to save an old kibbutznik. Not consciously but because of human nature. After all, the lives of those at the end of their journey in this world were worth less.

The nurses who walked by would give a momentary glance to the man lying under the harsh lights, his mouth open, fighting his last battle. The nurses had no idea what that old man had gone through in his life. As far as they were concerned, he was just another old man they had to treat. An old man struggling to live just a little longer in a world so unlike the one he had dreamt of. Only my mother wouldn't give up, carefully making sure he got his medication, the doctors' care and attention, the proper treatment. She'd be sitting next to my father's bed for hours on end, stroking his hand and waiting for him to wake up and open his eyes. And when he finally did, she would scold him, "At your age, there's no need for you to show off and act like a maniac anymore." But she would say it with love.

***

I still had hours before my flight. I tried to read the newspaper with little success.

Yoram called me. "Uri, do you have any idea when you'll get here?"

"Not yet, but there's a flight in a few hours, and I'll try to get on it. Tell me, how's Mom?"

Yoram evaded my question. "You've nothing to worry about, Mom's fine. Dad's unconscious. He's in intensive care. Just get here," he said tiredly and hung up.

***

I wondered whether Kuntz had gone to the hospital to be by his brother's side.

A political dispute from their first years in the kibbutz had torn the brothers apart. None of them had ever bothered mentioning the details of the dispute with me. During his first years in the kibbutz, my father had kept his last name, Kuntzmacher, despite the fact that his older brother Moshe had changed his to Kotzer. My father, who wanted no connection whatsoever with his brother, Hebraized his last name to Dolev; he wanted everyone to know he and his brother were nothing alike. We lived in the same housing complex as Henka and Kuntz, but as my father would barely exchange the occasional cold greeting with my uncle, nothing but the echoes of a troubled relationship remained. The family connection was reserved strictly for disasters and emergencies. Unfortunately, these frequently struck at Kuntz's family.

***

On my way to the airport, I called Yoram again to check on my father's condition.

"No change. He's still in critical condition. The doctors aren't giving us too much information." I sensed an undertone of desperation in his voice.

The road to Schönefeld Airport was relatively clear of traffic, and I arrived at the terminal in plenty of time. I passed through the airport security checkpoint and haphazardly explored the duty-free stores. I felt embarrassed that I was looking for gifts, but I thought it would be inappropriate to go empty-handed. I bought my father a new watch, perfume and a chocolate-brown silk scarf for my mother. For Yoram, I picked up a bottle of whiskey and a few boxes of chocolate for his children. I made sure all the presents were nicely wrapped and stuffed them in my carry-on bag, whose weight had doubled.

Boarding was delayed, and time seemed to drag. My anxiousness had made me forget to eat, and my stomach churned with hunger.

I paced back and forth in the gate area, staring at the passengers walking by, until I finally heard the call for boarding. I gave the El Al flight attendant my boarding pass, and she directed me to my row in business class. I sank into my seat, fastened the seat belt, took off my shoes, and closed my eyes. Up in the air, above the clouds, I thought about Henka and Kuntz.

I missed my cousin Haya. We had reinforced our blood tie with a friendship so powerful we did not need words or regular meetings. I would always feel safe with her. She shielded me without doing anything at all. Haya had helped me bond with the older kibbutz children, especially with Nurit. As we grew up, we shared common experiences and unashamedly conducted intimate conversations about any subject under the sun.

"Does Nurit have a boyfriend?" I had once asked, and Haya laughed.

"Nurit doesn't have a boyfriend, but she has a lot of friends."

Haya was like the older sister I never had.

When I had decided to go to Germany, she asked without waiting for a reply, "When you come back… will we still be friends like before?"

***

Haya was diagnosed with cancer and treated with chemotherapy. She rapidly lost weight, her hair fell out, and reddish splotches flared all over her beautiful face. First, she was hospitalized at the Beilinson Hospital in Petah Tikva. When her condition worsened, the doctors transferred her to the Tel HaShomer Hospital. The treatments did not help, and Kuntz, through his various connections, had her transferred to the Hadassah Hospital in Jerusalem.

When I heard of Haya's severe illness, I bought a plane ticket and went to visit her. I did my best to conceal my shock at her appearance.

My cousin was lying in bed completely bald, her face swollen from medication, her arms stick thin, and her eyes sunken in gray sockets. She looked at me, gave a shriveled smile, and said, "Thanks for coming, cousin, take good care of my parents. I can't say that I really trust the kibbutz to do that."

Haya's struggle lasted eight months before she died.

The funeral, quiet and sad, was held in the Kiryat Shaul Cemetery. Two buses brought a few dozen kibbutz members who had come to support Henka and Kuntz. For a short time, our family was reunited. My father hugged Kuntz, and my mother hugged Henka. Haya's children were glued to her bereft husband. Kuntz led the way; Yoram and I followed. Distant from each other, Henka and Kuntz stood in front of the open grave, with the rest of the nuclear family surrounding it. Behind them in a wider circle, stood Haya's friends and the kibbutz members, who looked distinctly out of place in the urban environment. There was no chatter, no words at all; only the sound of muffled sobs accompanied the burial ceremony. Eulogies were brief. Kuntz, who was regarded as a skilled eulogizer in the kibbutz had preferred to remain silent at his daughter's funeral. Everyone in the cemetery felt the magnitude of the parents' helplessness before the cruel fate that had robbed them of both their children. With their hearts broken, the funeral attendees dispersed, finding their way among the countless gravestones, gathering themselves, getting back to their lives, and leaving Kuntz and Henka behind. My aunt was nearly prostrate with grief.

"Let me lie down next to Haya, I want to die… I have no more reason to live," she pleaded over and over.

Henka's and Kuntz's lives had withered after Moti died in the Yom Kippur War. With Haya's death, Henka lost her will to live, her taste for life. She stopped going to the dining hall, stayed clear of the kibbutz cultural events, and lost all interest in friends and in her husband. She dedicated all her time to her orphaned grandchildren.

***

Many of the kibbutz founders were stereotyped based on the stories they had brought from Europe. Even before the death of her children, people in the kibbutz had spoken about Henka in hushed voices while stealing sideways glances. Her beauty was exceptional, her hair long and fair. Two dimples bestowed upon her an enchanting, eternally youthful appearance. Her winning smile and green eyes concealed what was in her heart. But a gossipy cloud hovered over Henka's head in the kibbutz.

When she worked in the cowshed, tension and arguments between her and Alfred were part of the daily routine. She found it difficult to accept his authority and detested his vulgar language and ways. The quick-tempered Alfred would scold Henka over every little trifle. Mostly, she would hold back and keep silent.

During one argument, Alfred was completely beside himself and spat out, "Everyone here knows you were a *kurva*, during the war. Prostitutes never change. A whore always remains a whore!"

Henka burst into tears, kicked over a milk container on her way out, and never returned to work in the cowshed again. From that day on, she had not spoken another word to Alfred.

***

Minute vibrations rattled the plane. The captain asked the passengers to remain in their seats and to fasten their seat belts. I dozed off again.

A single image returned to haunt me. A black-and-white photograph I recalled from our photo album: my father standing on top of the hill, where the kibbutz was founded. His eyes are set on the Hula Valley. A gray flat cap rests on his head, his shirtsleeves are pushed up over his elbows. His light-colored shirt is dappled with large stains and tucked into khaki shorts cinched by a thick leather belt. His feet are clad in work shoes and leg warmers sewn in our workshop. A huge smile is spread on his lips. He is holding me in his arms — a chubby, smiling baby. The contrast between my clean clothes and his dirty flat cap and stained shirt is nothing short of amazing. The photograph captured a tiny bit of a world still full of optimism and hope, the world of the kibbutz's first days.

"Can I set the table?" asked the flight attendant cheerfully, interrupting my train of thought.

Skillfully, she spread a white cloth on the seat back table to give the pretense of a high-end airborne restaurant. At the end of the meal, I fell into a light sleep and woke only when the plane descended for landing. I found myself unexpectedly excited and eager to reunite with my family, whom I had not seen in a long while. I had no doubt my father would recover from his injury and be back on his feet soon. I imagined that when he woke in the hospital, he'd casually ask for a cup of coffee and a newspaper and command all those huddled by the bed, "Stop making a fuss over every little thing," and with a flick of his hand dismiss the unnecessary commotion.

The plane landed in Israel after midnight, and when I exited the jet bridge in the terminal, I admired the new airport building. A cold, clear night welcomed me; the time was almost 1:00 a.m. I collected my suitcase and found a taxi. While settling into the back seat, my cell phone rang.

The driver turned his head and asked in broken English and with a cunning look in his eyes, "Mister… you… go… Tel Aviv?" A large black yarmulke covered his head, and his furrowed face was shaded in coal-black stubble streaked white with old age only in the center of his square jaw.

The cell phone continued to ring in my bag. I fumbled for it until I managed to unearth it from the bottom of the bag. Yoram immediately said, "Uri, where are you?"

Before I was able to reply, the taxi driver said to me, "Mister… you… go… to Jerusalem?" The same sly smile remained on his face.

"The Hilton Hotel, Tel Aviv, please," I replied in Hebrew.

"The Hilton?" I heard Yoram's voice coming from the cell phone. "Uri, have you gone crazy? What's going on?"

The taxi driver, realizing I was a local and not a tourist, dispensed with what little politeness he reserved for foreigners. "Sir, flat price or do I put the meter on?"

I waved my hand at the driver, signaling for him to keep quiet. "Hold on a second, Yoram," and to the taxi driver I said, "Meter, put the meter on."

Then to Yoram, "I landed only half an hour ago. I'm in a taxi now, on my way to the hotel. I'll just drop my bag there and continue straight to the hospital."

The taxi driver chose to ignore the fact that I was on the phone. "Listen, pal… you don't want me to put the meter on. It'll save you a lot of money to go with a flat price. I'll charge you a hundred and thirty, suitcase included. I can take you straight to the hospital if you'd like. Which one: Tel HaShomer or Ichilov?"

I heard the driver buzzing in one ear and Yoram speaking in the other.

"Dad's still unconscious. I don't know if there's any point in going to Safed now. Mom went back to the kibbutz, and I'll be sleeping in the hospital tonight. Maybe it'll be better if you catch some sleep and come visit in the morning."

The taxi driver continued to question me. "What's it going to be? Meter or flat price?" He started the engine and began driving without waiting for an answer.

"Hold on, Yoram, just a sec…" I covered the phone with one hand and snapped at the driver, "Leave me alone. My dad's in the hospital. I don't care what you charge me… meter… flat price… just get me to the Hilton without talking… all right?"

"Sorry, mister, I couldn't have known, could I? What, you just got here and heard the bad news? All right… I'm putting the meter on."

I nodded at the driver and told Yoram, "I'm on my way to the hotel. I'll talk to you as soon as I get to my room."

Finally, there was an almost complete silence. Only the soft humming of the tires on the road and the rattling of the taxi's diesel engine mixed with the muted voice of some announcer on the radio. The driver peered at me in the rearview mirror and turned around once to make sure I was all right.

There wasn't too much traffic, and the taxi quickly covered the distance between the airport and Tel Aviv. Half an hour later we stopped at the Hilton on HaYarkon Street. The taxi driver took my suitcase out of the trunk, set it on the sidewalk, and said in a buttery tone, "Don't worry, mister, God willing, everything will be just fine. I'll pray for him. And don't be shy if you need to get somewhere else, buddy, I can drive you anywhere in the country."

I paid the fare. The driver stuffed the bills in his pocket after counting them three times. "So, mister, which hospital? I'm available to take you anywhere in the country. Here's my number, you never know when you might need me…"

I took his card.

"It'll be fine. It's all in God's hands, praise the Lord. Don't be angry. My advice? Pray regularly and put on *tefillin* every morning. Trust me, buddy, believe in the Almighty, and everything else will just fall into place. I myself put on tefillin every morning; I'm getting closer to God. But it can get hard on Shabbat. It's the no smoking thing, you see?" He shrugged.

"I'll give you a special discount, just because I like you… good health to you and yours, buddy."

It was 3:00 a.m. by the time I got to my hotel room. After a moment of hesitation, I called my mother at the kibbutz. There was no answer. I left a message on the answering machine, got into bed, and fell asleep immediately.

27

Early in the morning, I woke up with a splitting headache.

"The mind is the only organ in the body that investigates itself."
I spared a small smile as I recalled another of Kuntz's pronounce-
ments. I prepared a mental list of possible causes: meningitis, a terminal illness, stress, or simple fatigue. It was 5:00 a.m., and my body
was issuing desperate distress signals of exhaustion. I swallowed two
painkillers and tried to sleep some more, unsuccessfully. At 6:00 I
got up and showered.

Down in the hotel dining room, I drank some tasteless coffee.
I checked out of the hotel and was handed the keys to the car I'd
rented in advance. At 7:30 I left the Hilton and began a slow drive up
north. My headache gradually faded, and my driving became more
confident. I leisurely drove past Ramat Aviv and Herzliya. Drivers
sped past me, cutting from lane to lane, honking for no apparent
reason. The country's nervous, agitated road culture reminded me I
was home again. The coastal highway between Netanya and Hadera
was congested. One driver gave me the finger while speeding past
me. I had no idea what had angered him. He opened his window
and added a juicy curse. I continued with my casual driving in the
right-hand lane.

I was very familiar with the road leading to the Upper Galilee.
Over the years, I had taken it hundreds of times. Now, almost a

tourist, I curiously looked around to see what had changed. As the road turned downhill near Zikhron Ya'akov, just before Wadi Milk, traffic decreased, and I took pleasure in the leisurely drive. I thought about making a coffee stop in Moshav Bat Shlomo but recalled the circumstances and decided against it. A beautiful cloud hung above the mountains of Menashe Forest. Even the gray and dreary city of Yokneam seemed pastoral and appealing. Passing HaTishbi Junction opposite Kfar Yehoshua, I studied the view in front of me. A white dirt road carved a path that coiled between the green fields. It snaked its way up the hill, echoing a painting I once saw in The Museum of Modern Art in New York. By the side of the road, not far from Beit She'arim, lupine fields graced the view with a blazing blue. A Judas tree grew in a forest clearing , alone and in full bloom, with the Sheikh Bureik hill towering behind it.

***

Once, on a school trip, we drove to the hill to see the statue of Alexander Zaïd, one of the founders of two Jewish defense organizations, mounted on his horse. Sitting in the statue's shadow we had a picnic, and in between bites, our teacher, Tova Zisman, told us stories about that brave protector of the fields. Udi and Yehiam argued heatedly about who was braver, Zaïd or paratrooper Hannah Szenes.

Yehiam was adamant. "How could you even compare the two? Of course Hannah Szenes was braver. She parachuted on her own, with the German army all around her."

Hilik Zisman picked up a stone and crushed a grasshopper unlucky enough to have landed next to him, and Nurit angrily punched him in the shoulder. "Why must you kill everything you touch?" It was one of many fond memories of her.

Driving up north, I found myself missing Nurit, the unobtainable girl. We had not kept in contact since our last meeting in Stockholm.

All I knew was that she had returned to live in the kibbutz. I had barely spoken to Yehiam either in the past few years. He was born on December 21, the shortest day of the year, while I was born exactly six months after him, on June 21. He had winter in his bones and character: calculated, introverted, and aloof in his relationships. I recalled with a smile how he used to cover the distance between the children's house and the dining hall by walking on his hands. Secretly, I had always been jealous of him. Every year, even while in Germany, I would call and wish him a happy birthday. I had called him this year as well. After exchanging the usual polite trivialities, he apologized and said he had to hang up, that he was busy at work. Driving on, my mind wandered back to those beautiful times and how our friendship had withered and turned into fragments of casual conversations.

***

Acacia trees bloomed in yellow on both sides of the road leading to Alon HaGalil. Chrysanthemums filled the fields and mustard flowers reigned in yellow all the way to the horizon. To my north, beyond that sea of yellow, the Eshkol Reservoir appeared, its water a vast blue bonnet resting between the fields. A western wind sent little ripples across its surface.

I turned north at the Golani Interchange, and when I passed by the road sign for Mitzpe Netofa, I remembered how, years ago, I had driven with a new girlfriend up the road leading to the hilltop settlement through a dense pine forest. We climbed the iron ladder to the top of the watchtower and took in the view of the entire area from Mount Tur'an. The sun began to set, flooding the Beit Netofa Valley with a soft, reddish light. We stood snuggled together, alone on top of the watchtower. It was one of those magical moments, and a newfound love ignited the primeval need that bonds men and women.

Without a word, we shed our clothes and lay together on the watch-tower's wooden platform, a cold wind stroking our naked bodies.

Just after the Kadarim Junction, the cliffs of Mount Arbel and the Sea of Galilee came into view. A large flock of storks swirled and glided on the air currents, tracing in the sky a path of longing for distant lands. My cell phone rang. I slowed down and pulled over by the side of the road.

Yoram was on the line, and his voice had an odd tone. "Uri, where are you? Well, it doesn't matter, it's over... The doctors said there was nothing more they could do. At least he didn't suffer — Dad is dead." The last three words, "Dad is dead," were uttered in a feeble, faltering voice, as if his batteries had run down.

"What a stupid way to go," Yoram continued a moment later. "He took the turn by the chicken coops too fast. The weight of the wagon pulled the tractor off the road, he lost control, and it turned over."

"Dad is dead." Three short words defining such a life-changing event. I realized Yoram was still on the line, waiting to hear my reaction.

"When...?"

"About ten minutes ago. I'm still here... There are some things I need to take care of."

"And Mom... how is she?" I asked.

"She's fine... sort of... Rina and Menahem Ganani took her back to the kibbutz. The hospital nurse gave her a tranquilizer. I need to sign all the forms. Mom insisted that the funeral be held today. The kibbutz is arranging everything. Just drive straight to Mishmar Hatsafon, that's it, nothing more to do here in the hospital. I'll manage. We need to let all the relatives know. There's not much time before the funeral." By the time my brother had finished speaking, his voice had taken on a no-nonsense, matter-of-fact tone.

***

It was a beautiful day. Wide fields of green sprawled along the highway, blending beautifully with the yellow blossoms. Brown patches pockmarked the green and yellow skin, the first traces of wilting hinting at the coming seasonal death.

"Are you all right?" I asked him.

For the first time in the conversation, impatience colored my brother's words. "Do me a favor, Uri, get a move on and get to the kibbutz already. The funeral's today at three, and there's lots more that needs to be done." Yoram disconnected, and the silence spread in me and turned into a vast emptiness.

I killed the engine and sat in the car trying to envision my father's face after not seeing him for several years. I wanted to continue to sit like that, doing nothing. An overpowering fatigue overwhelmed me, a sense that the day would never end. I felt gravity tugging at me with every motion. I started the car, grabbed the wheel until my knuckles went white and encouraged myself with hollow words. "It'll be fine…"

The day dragged on, even though it was only 9:00 in the morning. I was tired after my abbreviated night. I wanted to leave everything behind and sleep. The car carried me past Moshav Elifelet. A new, two-lane road bypassed the town of Rosh Pina. The Egged buses used to make a brief stop at the Rosh Pina station. When I was a child, my father would always get off the bus and buy me a pink coconut snack at the kiosk, my favorite treat. I swooshed past the entrance to Hatzor and at the junction near Kibbutz Mahanayim turned off the main road leading to Kiryat Shmona and took the narrow road passing through Kibbutz Gadot, a route that shortened my trip by a few kilometers.

A piercing migraine suddenly exploded in my head. I pulled over by the entrance to Kibbutz Mahanayim, turned off the engine, and adjusted the back of my seat until I was almost lying down. I took two more painkillers and made excuses for myself. Now that my father was gone, I had no reason to hurry. I closed my eyes and gently rubbed my scalp and temples to try and ease the pain. I knew that I couldn't linger for long. I turned on the radio and idly wondered if I was allowed to listen to music in the time of mourning. Unbidden, came a memory of Yankel Rozen, our kibbutz music teacher, how he had once dropped his little baton, come very close to me and whispered impatiently, "Why do you keep coming to choir lessons? Why won't you go and play soccer instead? What am I to do with you, Uri?"

I remembered shrugging, as if I didn't know why either.

"Well, just go stand in the last row, as far as possible from me. You're off key, and it is driving me insane. And *piano* when you sing — which is quietly — get it? You're not exactly Caruso. Back in Russia, they'd put singers like you in prison to punish the criminals."

***

It took another twenty minutes or so for me to recover enough to drive. The narrow winding road leading to Mishmar Hatsafon led me forward turn after turn. Until June 1967 the road had been used as a patrol route for military vehicles guarding the border with Syria. On the hills kissing the road I saw the remains of the abandoned villages of Dardara and Darbashiya. Before the Six-Day War, the Syrian army had taken up position in the villages. Syrian soldiers would hide between the houses and fire at farmers in the fields and passing vehicles. To protect the drivers and their passengers, dense rows of eucalyptus trees were planted along the road with fig and carob trees among them. The trees also served as a camouflage wall for the patrols moving across the border. A few weeks before the Six-Day War I drove up the patrol road on a tractor pulling a wagon full of hay bales. In one of the bends, a few volleys were fired at me from the Syrian town of Darbashiya. I stopped the tractor and jumped into a ditch by the roadside. I lay there frightened, while the whistling of bullets went on for about two hours.

Eventually, two IDF half-tracks accompanied by a white UN jeep with a pale blue flag drove down the road. I jumped out of the ditch, and the vehicles stopped. One of the soldiers drove the tractor, and I sat in the back seat of the jeep between two UN soldiers from Denmark. We drove to the kibbutz in a convoy: the UN vehicle led the way, followed by my tractor dragging a wagon of hay and an IDF half-track at the back. When the convoy passed through the kibbutz gate, we were welcomed with cheers and applause.

Now the Syrian Heights gazed at with a tranquil air, numerous trees scattered down its slopes and a wide, beautiful road twisting its way upward and cutting the wild scenery. I slowed down as I got closer to Mishmar Hatsafon, perhaps subconsciously postponing my unavoidable, sad meeting with my mother. Eventually, though, my car stood at the kibbutz gate. I was home.

PART 4

28

The iron gate, marked with remains of old yellow paint, screeched loudly as it moved open slowly along its track. I was immediately welcomed by the fish warehouse — a massive lump of concrete notable for its height and awkward shape — marring the kibbutz's entrance. A stream of water gushed from a pipe into the concrete pool. Several tons of carp lazily swam in dense schools toward their destiny— lying on plates as patties topped with a slice of carrot, a must for every Jewish holiday. Rusty scraps of farm machinery stood by the warehouse. A grass-strewn field spread alongside the entrance road. Two brown horses munched on the grass, occasionally flicking their tails to chase away the flies. I drove past the long dairy cowshed. The lime was peeling off the walls of the defunct milking parlor. The road led me to the dining hall parking lot. A new sidewalk had been built, its cleanliness in stark contrast to the access road, spattered with dried clods of mud ground to dust by vehicle tires. Countless cars lined the inner road in my parents' neighborhood, and I was forced to park far from home. I looked around to see what was new. On the surface, nothing had changed in all those years I was away.

But my father had died.

I walked a few dozen meters then was disturbed by the thought that I might have forgotten to lock my car. I walked on with the constant gnawing feeling that I had forgotten to perform some essential action. *I'm in the kibbutz*, I reminded myself. *No one is going to steal my car here.* Still, I stopped and tried to recreate my actions in my mind. *Everything is fine*, I kept repeating to myself, realizing how stupid that sounded under the circumstances. Once more, I reviewed my actions, which only served to exacerbate my insecurity. Finally, I stopped, muttered an angry, "Oh, for fuck's sake," and trotted back to the car, only to discover what I already knew — it was locked, and the lights were off.

I knocked lightly on my parents' door and walked inside without waiting for a reply. My mother burst into tears as soon as she saw me. I cupped her face in my hands and brushed away the tears running down her cheeks.

"Your father came home at ten… just to take a little break. He drank his coffee and read the paper, then he drove back to the nursery… and then… on his way there…" She burst into a new bout of sobs.

My mother's apartment was full of kibbutz members. I saw Henka, sitting apart and aloof, staring into space. She did not even greet me. Perhaps she did not recognize me because of her deteriorating mental health. My uncle Kuntz was leaning on the bookcase. He hurried toward me and shook my hand. One of the women served me a cup of instant coffee and a few cookies on a porcelain plate from an old set Grandma Fania had brought us as a gift.

Yoram left the sofa and hugged me.

"How's everything?" I asked him.

He slung his arm over my shoulder and tiredly said, "Fine… It'll be all right…" He was wearing jeans and an old brown sweater he must have bought at least ten years earlier. "Mom wants us to say the

Kaddish prayer together," he whispered in my ear.

"Kaddish prayer?" I cried out loud.

"She wants us to say Kaddish, and now is not the time for arguments. If it's too hard for you, then I'll say Kaddish on my own."

"I don't get it. Mom wants a religious funeral service?"

Yoram clenched his jaw then hissed back at me, "Religious, nothing. Mom just wants us to say Kaddish, that's all. Do me a favor, Uri, don't make a scene here. It's the last thing we need."

But I couldn't stop the argument's momentum. "Prayers and Kaddish are the last thing Dad would have wanted. I just don't get you. Let me make myself clear — I'm not going to put a yarmulke on my head or tear my shirt."

Yoram grabbed me by the hand and pulled me out of the room. "Come on, Uri," he said when we were out of earshot, "get a grip. You need to meet us halfway. Mom just wants us to say Kaddish, nothing more. You didn't give a damn about what's been going on here for years. Now's not the time to show up and start fighting for your principles." My brother suddenly sounded like he was the head of the household.

At two thirty we headed to the dining hall. The coffin was on two tables that were pushed together and covered with a green tablecloth. The kibbutz secretary, Ruhale, eulogized my father: "He was a working man who, in recent years, dedicated his all to the cultivation of the kibbutz's landscape. For years, he helped kibbutz members receive their reparations from Germany. These funds allowed our kibbutz to get by and survive lean and difficult years."

Ruhale continued to read a jumble of facts from a sheet of paper without an iota of emotion. I looked at the kibbutz secretary, trying to understand why she looked so familiar. My mother wasn't even listening. Yoram stood by the coffin and looked around like a foreman making sure everything was in order.

Finishing her recitation, Ruhale said, "Friends, let us now go together to the new cemetery."

A few younger members carried the coffin from the dining hall and loaded it onto an open pickup truck. My mother and Kuntz walked close behind the truck as it moved slowly down the road. Yoram, his wife and children and I walked beside my mother. A long trail of kibbutz members and guests from neighboring kibbutzim ambled along behind us. Some kibbutz members joined the convoy with their mobility scooters, while three cars transported others with mobility issues. There was even a cluster of people on bicycles. Henka had been brought back to the nursing home. I looked at the crowd accompanying my father on his last journey and almost smiled to see that the kibbutz's German tradition of order and punctuality had vanished. The crowd following the coffin was a hodgepodge of people wearing working clothes without form or distinction. The mobility scooters weaved around those marching on their feet and gave the funeral procession the appearance of a band of colorful gypsies right out of an Emir Kusturica movie.

They buried my father between two pine trees, beside the graves of other veteran kibbutz members. A larger crowd than I had anticipated gathered around the fresh grave mound of black, basalt-rich earth. My mother stood beside me and gripped my hand.

Kuntz approached the grave and eulogized his brother. "My little brother... not many know of your escape route from Germany to Denmark, the hardships you had to endure... my little brother demonstrated extraordinary resourcefulness during the war. After the war, he obtained forged documents and dressed up as a British soldier, without speaking a single word of English. That was how he crossed the whole of the European continent until he finally reached Israel."

Kuntz continued and spoke of the establishment of the kibbutz, about the Palmach fighting force, and how my father had taken part in drying the Hula marshlands. The service was supposed to be brief, but his eulogy speech continued, and there appeared to be no end in sight.

Yoram went over to Kuntz, gripped his arm, and whispered to him.

Kuntz pulled away from his nephew, raised his voice, and carried on. "Enough, no more." There was no escaping the bitterness of the words as they spat from his mouth. "There were always those who wanted to silence me. Now… I won't be silent anymore. My two children are no longer among the living. My brother is dead and my wife… she lost all interest in reality years ago…." My brother reached out a tentative hand.

"Yoram, don't rush me. No one knows this cemetery better than I do, and I am ashamed of nothing. For years, I've sentenced myself to silence, out of respect to everyone around me, but no more. No one will prevent me from speaking anymore. This is the final reckoning between me and my brother. We had a stupid argument concerning conflicting ideologies… We hadn't exchanged a word in decades. But I wasn't wrong. I was among those who sobered up early from the drunken worship of Russia and Stalin. The communists… they are the ones who betrayed the core, the basic principles."

Kuntz's voice had grown even louder, and the mourners had begun looking around and shifting their feet uncomfortably.

"Don't let anyone tell you any stories. I've heard them with my own ears… my friend Yaakov Riftin from Kibbutz Ein Shemer publicly declaring that the hand raised against the centers of Soviet power must be cut off the body."

Yoram went back to Kuntz and placed a hand on his shoulder. Kuntz shook it off once more, and when he spoke again, he was nearly shouting.

"Listen well, Yoram… and you too, Uri… your father… and many other members of Mishmar Hatsafon were blind followers of communism. They regarded any twisted declaration coming out of Russia as the words of the living God. They relinquished Zionism, but

I forgave them. Today, everybody knows that my brother and his friends were wrong, while I was right, and for that, he did not forgive me until his very last day."

The embarrassed murmurs in the crowd intensified, and my mother could no longer contain herself. She elbowed Kuntz in the side, moving him away from the grave. Then she turned to her brother-in-law and in a trembling voice said, "Kuntz, that's enough! There is a limit to what I can put up with... stop it! You have said more than enough! Now is not the time to settle old scores... not here."

She turned to the crowd and feebly said, "Forgive us..." Then she took a sheet of paper from her coat pocket and began to read in that same tear-ravaged voice, "My husband... my love... you are no more..." She folded up the paper and shoved it in her bag.

People were swaying on their feet, exchanging uncomfortable whispers. Kuntz kneeled on the ground, balled up a lump of black earth, and tossed it toward the grave. Yoram moved close to my mother and put his arm around her. Then he quickly took a black yarmulke from his pocket and placed it on his head. In a shaky voice he began to recite. "*Yitgadal... v'yitkadash sh'mei raba...*"

Some of the crowd joined the ritual by saying amen in the appropriate places until he finished the Kaddish prayer. At the end, Yoram took the yarmulke from his head, stuffed it in his pocket, and said to the crowd, "The service is over. All members are invited to come to the lawn in front of my mother's room."

Kuntz remained on the ground tossing clods of earth on the grave as the crowd began to disperse.

I went to him and softly said, "Moshe, get up, enough, come with us... He was your brother, and perhaps he knew more about plants than he did about people... But it doesn't matter. Now get up on your feet and come with us." And he reached up and grabbed my outstretched hand.

*⁎⁎

It was starting to get dark as we moved down the path from the cemetery to the kibbutz grounds.

In her room, I pulled my mother close. "Mom, don't be angry at Kuntz. Your lot in life is better than his. You have us, while he… what does he have left?"

My mother, still tearful, shook her head sharply.

"Don't be angry at me… but I thought it would be more comfortable for everyone if I didn't sleep on the sofa in your apartment. I reserved a cabin in Moshav Beit Hillel."

My mother looked up at me with swollen eyes. "Uri, why are you always running away? From your family, the kibbutz, from Israel… My sofa isn't good enough for you anymore? Everyone does what they want around here, no one cares what I think… What do I know?"

I squeezed her shoulder and said nothing.

After dinner, Yoram called Alfred and asked that more chairs be brought to the lawn in front of my mother's house. A woman from my group in the children's house volunteered to get fruit and other refreshments from the kibbutz kitchen. By the time night fell, my mother's room had emptied.

I stroked her hair and kissed her on the cheek. "Good night. I'll be back in the morning. Sleep tight."

My mother brushed my hand with her fingers then retired to her bedroom.

29

The mourning period calmly proceeded on the grass in front of my mother's house in the kibbutz. Like the bellows of an accordion, visitor traffic gradually inflated from the morning hours, was fully expanded by evening, then deflated until the last of the visitors left at night, with the cycle repeating itself on the following day. In the evenings, my mother's room-and-a-half apartment was crowded with visitors, and every plastic chair on the lawn was taken. Kibbutz members took turns providing a daily supply of sandwiches and fruit. The neighbors baked cakes, and two of my mother's friends served food and refreshments. The shiva machine was working smoothly.

Winter was drawing to a close, offering us comfortable weather, and the branches of the massive carob tree in the yard provided ample shade and protection from the sun. The awkwardness that prevailed at the funeral was gone, and sitting together on the grass was pleasant. The reason for our gathering seemed to have been forgotten, and the crowd would often turn into a cheerful social outing. Kuntz had come to his senses and was the first to arrive each morning, take his place in a plastic chair on the grass, and wait for the visitors.

After that, he worked up the nerve to enter my mother's home and sat beside Yoram and me, a glass of tea in his hand. He completely ignored his behavior during the funeral. "Did your father ever tell you about our life in Germany?" he wondered aloud.

I placed a hand on my uncle's shoulder and gave it a warm pat. Kuntz, so used to rejection, was surprised by the gesture and hurried to take advantage of this unexpected opportunity. "I also have some fond memories of Berlin," he said in a confessional tone.

My mother scowled at Kuntz's attempts to improve relations with Yoram and me. She used a few moments when the room was empty of visitors and told her brother-in-law, "You can continue to air the dirty laundry once everyone leaves, not now. We've been through enough."

My mother had not forgiven Kuntz's behavior during the funeral, and she tried to ignore his presence while at the same time following his every action from the corner of her eye. Her hostility did not deter him.

"What have I done to upset her?" he asked Yoram and me. "All I want is to tell you two a little about our family and the kibbutz's history. Soon, there will be no one left to tell you about it."

My mother just glared at him silently.

Kuntz leaned toward me and said, "All right, if it upsets you… I didn't come here to argue with anyone."

Yoram snapped at him, "Kuntz, after what happened at the cemetery, no one cares anymore. Just say whatever you want. Dad's no longer here to stop you."

Kuntz was insulted. "I'm sad to say that my differences with your father were entirely unnecessary. If it had been up to me, it would have ended fifty years ago."

My mother's face had turned crimson. She addressed Kuntz with a shrill voice. "Enough, please… just stop, I can't stand it anymore."

Kuntz stood up and faced her, his hands held palm up, outstretched before him. "What do you want from me? I'm a bereaved father, childless, my wife hardly recognizes me, my brother was angry at me until the day he died; I have already been given my punishment."

We all kept silent. Kuntz's words had touched my heart; it was difficult to see him so vulnerable. He addressed Yoram and me in a bitter voice. "Your father was as stubborn as a mule. He gave up on our relationship and instead clung to the communist ideals. Today, every child knows Stalin was a murderer and a loathsome dictator. I was willing to forgive, I tried everything, but he wanted nothing to do with me until his very last day."

My mother was weeping by then, and Kuntz was on the verge of collapsing. "I have no grievance with any of you… I blame no one. I unburdened what was in my heart. From now on we must live as a tight-knit family."

I took pity on my mother, but I felt sorry for Kuntz at the same time. I took my mother's hand in mine and stroked it. Yoram gently asked Kuntz to leave the room.

"I understand your pain, but this isn't the time or the place; the wound is too fresh. Mom needs time to recover. All I'm asking is that you take it down a notch. Go home and rest. We'll see each other tomorrow."

Yoram walked Kuntz outside to the grass, where my uncle welcomed a couple who had just arrived from Ra'anana. Kuntz had no reason to hurry back to his empty house. He sat in one of the chairs, his eyes darting about, inspecting the crowd. During the days sitting shiva, Kuntz was constantly surrounded, which eased his loneliness. He was always the first to come and the last to leave. He told anyone who would listen about the past, almost obsessively. I thought perhaps this was my chance to finally learn the nature of the controversy that had driven the wedge between my father and him.

Late one evening, I went to Kuntz's apartment hoping to find him awake. My uncle welcomed me in wearing ancient pajamas with faded green stripes. He let loose a sigh that came from deep in his chest.

Then he shuffled into the kitchenette and prepared two glasses of tea, placing beside them a few cookies that looked far from fresh.

"Those were beautiful days of hope and renewal," thus Kuntz began the tale of his first days in the land of Israel. "We lived in Kibbutz Mishmar HaEmek's old barrack neighborhood. Each room contained four iron beds with canvas mattresses stuffed with straw. We woke early and went to work then spent a few hours at school and returned to work on the farm in the afternoon. I was seventeen, and the world never looked clearer or more beautiful to me.

"We happily worked hard during the day, and at night we danced and spoke of Israel's present and future."

The pioneering conditions did not bother Kuntz in the least, and being part of the group compensated him for not having a family. "I had some good friends in the group: Zeev Schwartz, Menahem Baumgarten, and Zvika Cohen. I knew them all from the Berlin movement. Our main source of nourishment was not food but discussing the principles of communal life and socialism. The most eloquent among us was Zvika Cohen, who was a gifted and emotional speaker. That and his fluency in Hebrew made him our leader. I suggested a new rule — speaking was allowed only in Hebrew. Until then, all arguments had been conducted in German, occasionally mixed with some Hebrew. Menahem Baumgarten supported my suggestion, Zvika and Zeev enthusiastically agreed. Only Max Tishler insisted on continuing to speak German.

"He told us that his mother tongue would always be German, the language in which Heine, Nietzsche, Heidegger, Kant, and Goethe wrote. Max maintained that Hebrew would never be able to replace German. I disagreed. Only those who could read the writings of Yosef Haim Brenner, Shmuel Yosef Agnon, Haim Nahman Bialik, and Shaul Tchernichovsky could be considered true Israelis. I said to Max that in Israel, even the dogs need to bark in Hebrew. Max did not abandon his principles; he wrote and spoke fluent Hebrew but chose to write his suicide note in German."

The argument over Hebrew didn't end then; it occasionally resurfaced. At night, Kuntz read only Hebrew books so he could improve his proficiency in the language. Like many immigrants, he wanted to conceal all signs of his foreign origins, abandon any remnants of the Jewish European lifestyle. In Mishmar HaEmek, he and his friends wore khaki shorts and sandals, and kaffiyehs covered their heads.

The question of personal identity was an important and central issue. Kuntz decided to Hebraize his last name but found it difficult to choose a new one. He sought a Hebrew name that would embody Kuntzmacher, but all his attempts were unsatisfactory. First, he translated Kuntzmacher into Kossem, the Hebrew word for magician. Then he tried another option: Moshe O'se Nissim — miracle worker. Finally, he chose a third option: Moshe Nissim. Max Tishler nearly had a stroke upon hearing the change Kuntz wanted to make. He believed original family names mustn't be changed. He explained his position to Kuntz by stating that he must preserve his last name for the sake of future generations.

Zeev Schwartz, his silent friend, pointed out to Kuntz that these were two first names. "Moshe Nissim is a name that reminds me of a worm — it's hard to tell the head from the tail."

Menahem Baumgarten had another argument: HaShomer Hatzair was a movement based on freedom of choice. It did not believe in God and preached socialism. To Kuntz he said, "A member of HaShomer Hatzair can't possibly have Nissim as a last name. Our secular movement does not believe in miracles."

Tzvika Cohen ridiculed the fruitless argument between his friends. "Changing one's last name is hardly important. What's important is the way in which a man chooses to fulfill his life's ambitions and principles. I come from a family of Jewish priests, the Kohanim, but I still see myself as a communist. My worldview does not require me to uphold the commands of the Jewish religion."

Zeev Schwartz translated his last name to Schory. Hilda Hein-seldorf changed her name to Yael Harduf. Menahem Baumgarten boasted the proper Hebrew name of Ganani. But even after all his friends had Hebraized their names, Kuntz continued to deliberate and could find no new last name to suit him. A few years later, when he was selected to go abroad on behalf of the kibbutz, Kuntz simply omitted a few letters from his last name to give himself a fitting name for a farmer and a man of toil. The name appearing in his passport was Moshe Kotzer, the new last name meaning "harvester" in Hebrew. But his former, foreign last name had never fully left him, and in Kibbutz Mishmar Hatsafon everyone continued to simply call him Kuntz.

Night had begun its gradual retreat when at last I stood from my chair, squeezed my uncle's hand, and prepared to leave. Despite the early morning hour, I bid him goodnight and left in the hope of catching a few hours of sleep in my rented cabin. I drove to the moshav thinking about how my uncle had become an object of pity for me. He had no more life in him, only memories.

I had a hard time falling asleep on the uncomfortable cabin bed. Finally, I slipped into a fitful sleep. In my dream I saw a jackal standing about ten meters away, raising his head toward a full moon and howling. I could see his sharp fangs. The jackal — or maybe hyena — looked at me with gleaming, scheming eyes. From afar, I heard the ringing of the kibbutz bell, used to alert members in case of fire. My army boots stood by the bed. I wanted to put them on quickly but couldn't fit my feet inside. I tried to untie the laces in vain. A company of jackals stood on the hill overlooking the kibbutz hous-es and began to creep its way toward me. The jackals echoed the ringing of the bell with their long howls. I knew that if I could scare the leader, the entire pack would run off. I picked up a stone, but it slipped from my hand. I continued to look into the jackal's evil eyes. He was closer now, within biting distance. I felt helpless, shivering and paralyzed with fear. Drool dripped from the jackal's mouth, and his red tongue lolled in preparation of an attack. My Uzi wasn't far, resting on the table. I tried to reach it, but my legs refused to obey me; I was petrified and could not escape. The sound of the bell hanging from a pine branch by the infirmary sounded loud and close, and then I woke up.

My cell phone alarm was chiming loudly. I turned over, still terrified. I wanted very much to go back to sleep, but I knew I had to go to the kibbutz.

My mother welcomed me with a sour face. "I heard you spent all night with Kuntz!"

I knew nothing I said would make any difference, so I sat in the kitchen and together we silently sipped our first coffee of the day. She was in a grim mood. Realization that her life had drastically changed must have begun to slip into her consciousness. My father had been her pillar, an island of security, with his supposedly indifferent attitude toward nearly everything in life. In their relationship, my mother was like a raging storm breaking against an ever calm surface.

Her shoulders began to gently heave and her voice when she spoke was trembling. "Your father was my only friend, you know?"

I said nothing. What could I have said?

30

Ruhale, the kibbutz secretary, was among those who came to sit shiva. Her freckle-spattered face gave her a younger appearance. Her red hair was bundled into a braid, which swung from side to side like a pendulum when she walked. She wore a shapeless dress covered with a floral pattern embroidered by hand. The dress fell below her knees and was intended to conceal her sizeable body. She asked for a small glass, made her own Turkish coffee, took a bite of cake, and ceremoniously addressed me.

"Uri Dolev, my dear, it wouldn't hurt you to stay a little longer here, yes? I'm hoping you haven't forgotten how eagerly we are all waiting for the play you are to write for the kibbutz's birthday celebration. I, for one, cannot wait to see some written pages."

The request, which had surprised me a few weeks earlier, now seemed ridiculous and completely irrelevant. But my stunned reaction only served to encourage Ruhale.

"We're counting on you. You are a man of the world who knows everything about the media. Your beautiful army radio pieces filled everyone in the kibbutz with so much pride. A little bird whispered in my ear that you have a wonderful career in Germany as well. You may have left the kibbutz, but the kibbutz will never leave you, yes? Well… perhaps you have remembered me by now?"

There was something familiar, something from my past, both in

Ruhale's gaze and her special way of speaking, but I simply could not fathom where I knew her from.

"Perhaps you could remind me how we know each other?" I suggested.

"Let's just drop it for now. It's a long story and not very important. Your presence here was not exactly planned… yes? But we need to talk, so I'll allow myself to make good use of this opportunity. So long as you are here, I think you might be able to start helping us, yes?"

I kept wondering where I knew this woman from. I racked my brain, yet the harder I tried, the more elusive the memory became.

"I want to announce to the members in our next secretariat meeting that you are starting to work on our play. Uri, you simply must understand. This is a large celebration with many participants, yes? Write lots and lots of little parts. You know how it is with us. It's just like the Olympic Games, never mind the results, participating is the main thing!"

I'd stopped listening to Ruhale's words as my mind feverishly sought an answer. *Who is that woman?* And then, she was conjured up out of thin air, like an old forgotten tune rising and loudly playing itself like an old, familiar friend.

"Rachel Tenenboim… Rachel… from the Jewish Agency?" I said aloud.

"Yes, it's me. Remember how we met at the Sokolov House so many years ago? I was young and beautiful, yes? You too are no longer the rash young man, and your memory isn't what it used to be, apparently. It took you quite some time, but you ended up remembering anyway."

She chuckled and shook her head. "You were up to your neck in trouble. This wasn't a very pleasant case… yes? I understand that things have somehow worked out for you, that is all I know."

How had Rachel Tenenboim, a Jewish Agency accountant,

become Ruhale, Kibbutz Mishmar Hatsafon's secretary? I kept the questions hidden in my heart, biding my time for the right opportunity to present itself. The sense of comfort and confidence the kibbutz had granted me was instantly shaken.

Ruhale winked at me, and in her eyes, I saw an involuntary flicker I hadn't noticed before. "What do you think, Uri, about you and I going to the archive tomorrow? We'll take a little glance at the documents of the past. You artist types call it inspiration, no? Read a little, it will lead you in the right direction for your play's opening. But I must apologize in advance, the archive isn't in the best of shape, yes? Max Tishler, before he died, left a terrible mess. Temporarily, I am in charge of the archive too.

"Like I said, you've been idle long enough, now's the time for you to start working. So, we're all set — tomorrow at nine I'll meet you at the archive." Ruhale summed it all up and left the lawn with her long braid swinging behind her.

After she left my mother told me, "Ruhale is a good girl; she rescued Alfred from his bachelorhood. He isn't exactly right in the head as it is, but without Ruhale, he would have been committed just like his sister. For the life of me, I can't understand what she sees in him, but whatever it is, he's won the lottery."

***

The sharp smell of mold assaulted us as Ruhale opened the archive door. The house that had served as the kibbutz archive for years was a disgraceful mess. Manila folders were scattered in disarray on stacked iron shelves that seemed on the verge of toppling from excess weight. The bathtub, which had once served Gurnischt, was full of old newspapers. The bathroom was loaded with holiday decorations. The main archive room had no desk or computer. More folders were piled up in a jumbled heap in a corner. Each touch resulted in a plume of dust.

I stood at the entrance, and Ruhale Tenenboim pranced about frantically in the musty room.

"I had no choice but to take over Max Tishler's work myself. I was amazed to discover that even here in our kibbutz there are super-stitious people, afraid that Max's bad luck would rub off on them. I couldn't find a volunteer to manage the archive because no one wanted to set foot in this place. Max simply left for Berlin one day, leaving total chaos behind him. I still don't understand why he had to go all the way to Germany to kill himself."

"Why did he commit suicide, anyway?" I asked while picking up an old kibbutz leaflet from the floor with a Haim Gouri poem and a drawing of a young woman picking oranges on the cover.

"Well, it was because of the cabins. It was all because of the rental cabins," Rachel Tenenboim said.

"What does Max's suicide have to do with rental cabins?"

Ruhale, full of vigor, picked up some old folders from the floor. "In the secretariat, we decided to renovate the archive and turn it into another guesthouse. You see, Uri, our rental cabins bring us income, while the archive only causes us more expenses. Gurnischt thought that the past was more important than the future. He was insult-ed, and his fury released something spiteful deep inside him. He took everything he had worked so hard to gather over the years and tossed it on the lawn in front of the dining hall. Then he turned on the sprinklers. My Alfred chanced to see him in the act. He grabbed Max and dragged him to the infirmary. On the way, Gurnischt told him that he should have burnt the archive.

"In the infirmary, Max was given a tranquilizer. My Alfred res-cued lots of important paperwork and documents from the grass, but some of it was soaking wet. I've been trying to put some order in this mess for a few months now."

She sighed and shook her head sadly. "Gurnischt was a hard man,

like a flint stone, always arguing with everyone until fiery sparks resulted. Everything was sensitive with him, always full of complaints.
It isn't easy here. Each meshuggeneh kibbutz member has his own
hidden lunacies. He had invested so many years in this archive, and
because of this silly business, he turned a treasure into a pile of trash.
Good thing the meeting minutes from the kibbutz's early days were
unharmed.

"And after all that, he went to Berlin, of all places, just to hang
himself like that. Like I told you, a meshuggeneh."

Rachel found a small ladder and climbed up to reach some folders, complaining nonstop. "I have to work like a mule here. Everything is scattered on the floor. We need to scan everything into the
computer, but there's no budget for that. You have so many photographs from the early days of the kibbutz here and movies from
the fifties documenting holiday festivities and kibbutz plays. A real
treasure trove."

I spotted a large photo album bound in green cardboard on the
floor. As the kibbutz secretary continued to kvetch, I picked up the
album and looked at the photographs taken during the building
of the kibbutz — the ceremony of laying the cornerstone, a white
tent at the top of the hill. Humi Schory and Menahem Ganani, both
wearing undershirts and flat caps, rolling a large basalt rock. Alfred
and Max riding back-to-back on a single donkey.

My thoughts drifted to an image of a view that had been etched
into my memory: On the road leading to Ashdod, not far from the
turn leading to Kibbutz Palmachim, there is a hill as round as Mount
Tabor. At the top of the hill stands an old house, its windows broken,
its roof riven, its walls made of bare concrete. A single pine tree grew
next to the house, stark against the blue of the sky. Once, I had parked
my car by the side of the road and took a picture of that beautiful
hill, which reminded me of my childhood views. When I looked at
the photograph I had taken, I was disappointed. My romantic image

of the hill was nowhere to be found in the flat photograph.

Ruhale stood on the ladder and arranged the folders on the shelf, while I continued to wonder how the sister of a security services senior official had ended up in the kibbutz archive. Curiosity wouldn't let go of me.

I casually asked, "Rachel, your brother, is he still a state employee?"

She turned her gaze on me, and a smile rose to her lips. "Uri, you can be a little less formal and call me Ruhale; I've been a kibbutz member for many years. As for my brother, things weren't that easy. Luckily for us, he had the good sense to leave the state security services years ago. People like him don't last too long there. They kept holding him back, not because he wasn't talented, but simply because he always said what was on his mind and refused to suck up to anyone. Today he has the last laugh. He's a successful businessman living like a king in Singapore."

"And how did you ever get to the kibbutz and to Alfred?"

Ruhale stopped working for a moment and gave me a surprised look from the top of the ladder. "Like I told you… it's a long story… and not very important. I'll tell it to you, but not now. When we have more time on our hands."

***

"Things are always complicated with us," Kuntz tiredly told me one day while we were sitting shiva. "In the early fifties, years after World War II ended, Alfred went away for a few days. When he came back, he told me that he had found his sister. He had understood that his sister had perished in the camps, but it turned out she had come to Israel and was immediately committed to a mental institution in ancient Acre. He went to visit his sister at the asylum once every few months and continued to do so for years.

"At the end of the seventies, when our financial situation had improved a bit, Alfred's visits became more frequent, and he went to see his sister at least once every two weeks. Everyone in the kibbutz respected him for that. And at the same time something had changed in him. He was full of vigor, stopped acting rudely, and became more pleasant to those around him. We noticed that Alfred returned from his visits to the madhouse with a smile on his face. We felt that caring for his sister had filled his life with new meaning."

Kuntz paused, and a small smile turned up the corners of his mouth. "In 1980, Alfred's sister passed, and it was then that his secret came out. Rachel Tenenboim showed up in the kibbutz. Apparently, Alfred and Rachel had met a few years earlier. It was a chance meeting in a coffee shop by the asylum. All those years, Alfred had religiously maintained his regular schedule of traveling to Acre. He left the kibbutz every Friday and went on to Ruhale's apartment in Tel Aviv immediately after visiting his sister. On Saturday evenings, he would return to the kibbutz full of smiles."

My uncle grinned at me and shrugged. "Who would have believed that Alfred, the terminal bachelor, would find a young native-born girl for himself?"

***

Gossip has always been a constantly turning engine in the kibbutz. When suspicions arose against me in late 1978, two investigators went to Mishmar Hatsafon to get a better handle on me. Following the visit, gossip about my entanglement with the authorities spread like wildfire. Alfred immediately told his girlfriend about the story that was on everyone's lips in the kibbutz. Ruhale had turned to her brother, and when he was somewhat dismissive of the allegations, she decided, along with Alfred, to help me. Apparently, the romantic relationship that had formed between Alfred and Ruhale at the time had connected me and Rachel as well.

"Alfred is a perfect example of just how complicated kibbutz members are," Kuntz said. "Look, Uri, with us, members are judged according to their work. In that regard, Alfred is diligent; he spends his days and nights working. True, he has some unpleasant features to his character, and his treatment of Henka was disgraceful, but we're all human, we each have our weaknesses and we, especially in the kibbutz, aren't very tolerant!"

As children, we were always afraid of Alfred because of his explosive temperament. A loud, vulgar man who interfered with everything. Kibbutz members treated him with a hint of contempt mixed with revulsion. Humi Schory, a quiet, timid man, detested Alfred and described him in the following manner: "He has a tongue like Munchausen's and a mouth like a rattler."

***

My father always liked to take pictures. His first piece of equipment was a box camera he received from a British soldier in exchange for his Doxa watch. Over the years, he bought more cameras, but he continued to take photographs with his box for decades. He had a lengthy process before taking a picture. He religiously calibrated the light meter, fitted the right lens, located us at just the right distance, moved objects that did not fit with the frame, measured, and remeasured. By the time he pressed the camera button my mother would have lost her patience.

Once, while we stood waiting for him to photograph us, she told him, "You take pictures just like the Jewish landlords used to pay the moujik, the peasant working for them. By the time the moujik got his money, he no longer had a taste for it."

My father ignored my mother's criticism, continued to fiddle with the light meter, and remarked, "A quality photograph requires patience, precision, and perfect timing. Now stand still, Yoram, don't look in my direction, try to act normal, don't pose, this is better. Uri, lower your chin a little, I just need to adjust the lens, and that's it. There, you see? That didn't hurt."

The development and printing processes would go on for many nights. My father locked himself in the kibbutz darkroom, printing each photograph several times until he got the result he sought. It would normally take a few months before we saw the photographs. In most cases he was rewarded for his toil, and each photograph justified and reflected his strenuous efforts. My mother arranged our photographs in a lavish album with a leather binding boasting a copper embossed picture: a farmer holding a hand plow dragged by a bull with tremendous horns. The album contained one photograph I remember especially well.

It was probably taken on a summer day during the early fifties — a black-and-white photograph — Yehiam Gruenwald hugging me, both of us sitting on some balcony rail. Yehiam is laughing, holding a large mug in his hand, his face smeared with chocolate. He and I both have our hair trimmed, wearing matching outfits: a white undershirt smeared with chocolate stains and shorts held up by suspenders.

There were more photographs, taken during Purim, in the kibbutz's early years. Udi Ganani dressed up like a cowboy, Yehiam as an Indian, and me as a Spanish bullfighter. A convoy of tractors, children holding baskets full of first fruit, flower wreaths on their heads. My mother, Yoram, and I against the background of the fishponds. And a photograph of my father on the floating excavator used to dry the Hula marshlands. The photographs had turned into permanent, pleasant memories accompanied by a sense of yearning. Images of simplicity and clean happiness. No one ever documented the sadder moments.

***

The founding generation found it difficult to express disillusionment. Perhaps, I thought, we members of the second generation were the biggest disappointment of their pioneering enterprise. The founders were giants of culture and knowledge. They chose to settle far on the outskirts of the Hula Valley, where they struggled with laying out the land, the anopheles marsh mosquitoes, and the harsh climate. They did not give up but held on to the little they had, finding satisfaction in a hard day's work. The kibbutz veterans wanted us, their children, to create a new and better world. Their lives were simple compared to ours, but they weren't simple people.

They had arrived with nothing, carrying ideologies in their backpacks. They had a way, a direction, and a purpose. Stubbornly, they marched on toward the destination they had set for themselves while still in Europe. Their ways were coarse, direct, driven by the fuel of their vision. Mishmar Hatsafon was a pressure cooker bubbling with complicated and entangled relationships — the trunk of an old olive tree, furrowed and scarred with scratches and bruises. In the kibbutz, everyone was tied to each other. Family ties, ties of friendship that went back to the days of the movement in Berlin, working relationships, and amicable ties based on ideology. Tight knit, fitted into a narrow frame, relationships of love, fondness and attraction, rivalries and hatreds all coexisted.

Most kibbutz members preferred to keep their past to themselves, archive away their childhood, conceal their previous image in the basements of memory. They never allowed us children, born in the kibbutz, to set foot in the world they had left behind. They were afraid of overexposure like a photographic negative fears exposure to the light. They wanted to protect the kibbutz children, afraid we might get burnt by the secrets of their past. They glorified the present and dreamt of the future.

31

My many years away from the kibbutz had created a deep need in me to try to understand and recreate it all. I was flooded with childhood memories. I spent hours sitting on the archive floor, reading with fascination meeting notes from Mishmar Hatsafon's first days. I marveled at the ability to document every little thing, to debate every subject with boundless seriousness. I was surprised to discover that my uncle Kuntz possessed a distinct voice that had made him stand out as a daring speaker who had filled the kibbutz's ideological discussions with fire and brimstone. In a special leaflet printed to commemorate the kibbutz's fiftieth anniversary, I found an article about soul-searching and reckoning written by Kuntz:

"We were confident in the virtue and righteousness of our way. We believed that clinging to this harsh basalt ground would make a country grow out of it, and we weren't wrong. Our fiery belief filled our hearts to the brim, so much so that it blinded us and prevented us from seeing the dangers ahead. Today, Israel is the most powerful country in the Middle East. The Syrian border is far from our kibbutz, our camp is flourishing and, supposedly, all our hopes have been fulfilled. But the kibbutz movement has lost its glamour. We have been pushed into a corner in the country we fought so hard to create with our sweat and hard labor. Zionism today is a flaccid and abandoned member. An insignificant dead weight. Most of our sons and daughters have long left our home. The kibbutz founders have grown old, some have passed, and those remaining are not long for this earth. Their past is behind them, and the future... who does it belong to? Today, crony capitalism is all the rage. Privatization is the instant solution for every problem; a privatization renouncing the basic principles of the communal house we have created. Lacking any other choice, we accept it as one accepts idolatry, because it represents the only reasonable option of preserving what we still have. As far as I am concerned, there is only one certainty: the dream we have all woven together has come to an end."

Kuntz's pointed and precise words expressed a sense of bitter disillusionment and a realization that the kibbutz communal dream that had accompanied him throughout his adult life had shattered against reality. My heart filled with pity for that wise man.

***

As a child, I too regarded the kibbutz as a haven. The kibbutz fence was vital and was there to defend its dwellers from the city people seeking to destroy it. If, as a child, I had been asked to prepare a list of "bad guys" and "good guys," I assume my list would have been similar to that of all other children of my generation in Mishmar Hatsafon. The Germans would be at the top of the bad guys list, followed by the Americans, then the city people, and the British. Ben-Gurion and Menahem Begin would be added to the bad guys list. Syrians and Egyptians would be situated at the bottom of the bad guys list. Arab Israelis were absent from that list; we had paid them no mind at all. The good guys list was topped by the Russians — they had saved the world from Hitler — workers of the world, Warsaw Ghetto Uprising leader Mordechai Anielewicz, writer and partisan leader Abba Kovner, and Hungarian footballer Ferenc Puskás.

In a chilling and multifaceted contradictory way, the kibbutz and the ghetto were perceived as possessing a similar pattern in my mind. More alike than different. A disturbing and horrifying resemblance. The ghetto, like the kibbutz, was sealed and secluded. A place where everyone was alike, with dire dangers lurking on the outside. Our lives in the kibbutz were happy, washed with sunlight. The fearful darkness existed only outside the kibbutz fence. As a child, I knew little about what had taken place in the ghettoes of Eastern Europe but was well aware of the constant threat endangering our own ghetto.

***

The deeper I delved into the documents in the kibbutz archive, the more fascinating my conversations with Kuntz became. I told him a little of what I had discovered about the kibbutz's history. Kuntz was thrilled with this. An inner dam, sealed for many years, had opened in him.

Kuntz referred to the day in November 1945 on which the kibbutz was established as one of the most significant days of his life. He took a chair — I supported him while he climbed on top of it — and unearthed an old notebook from the topmost shelf of his closet.

With sparkling eyes, he read to me: "In the east, the first light of morning was now traced. Black, heavy clouds shrouded Mount Hermon. A rain-filled and cold morning rose over the Hula Valley. When I opened the tent flap, I saw that heavy rain was falling. Happily, it subsided later in the day. I had not expected to see such a downpour. I wanted this, our first day on the ground as a kibbutz settlement, to be washed with a beautiful, glowing Israeli sun. A soft breeze blew between the reeds growing in the Hula marshlands. A herd of buffalo hunkered in the water. The hairy beasts slowly chewed on their cud. A large, black buffalo waded his way through the dense foliage of the lake. In the thicket, two gray herons spread their wings. A flock of coots swam in the lake, creating an arrow formation. The little ripples it left in its wake rolled along until breaking against the trunk of a fig tree whose branches dipped in the water. A blue-winged kingfisher wheeled in the sky, seeking a first morning prey. The rain did not dampen my spirit, I knew we would overcome all obstacles."

Later, Kuntz described how he crawled outside his tent early in the morning, put on long pants, a gray shirt, and high-top work shoes. The founding members of Mishmar Hatsafon boarded three trucks, which drove up the treacherous road leading to the hill on top of which the kibbutz was established. A short ceremony for the laying of the cornerstone ensued. Beneath a large pistacia tree, Yael Harduf stood on an upturned wooden crate and read the foundation charter in a loud, clear voice. At the end of that brief formality, everyone rolled up their sleeves, and the pioneering group set up the first tent and foundations for a watchtower. Toward evening, the erection of two shacks was completed, with several tents circling them. A watchtower, made of wooden beams, stood in the center of the camp, its legs leaning on concrete foundations poured that very day. The hill was surrounded with barbed wire fences marking the boundaries of the new kibbutz.

At night, in his tent, Kuntz wrote in his notebook: "This is a dream come true. The black basalt rocks have become the foundation of our newly erected home. We have redeemed this piece of land to turn it into the center of our lofty goal. I am drunk with emotion over this, our first day on the ground. We all sang with a single, mighty voice, and our tired feet were swept away in dancing."

Sometime after several houses were standing, a group of new immigrants arrived and joined the young kibbutz. Among them was a woman possessing an exceptional beauty. "I could barely sleep that night," my uncle wrote. In tender, poetic language he described how he had fallen in love with Henka. "Cold air snuck into the tent. I lay in the narrow iron bed and thought of Henka. I took courage and invited her for a walk outside the hill fence. We exited through the narrow gate and walked by the wadi channel. Cyclamen flowers blossomed between the rocks, the foothills were covered with a red blanket of anemones and the air was filled with the smell of wet earth and the scent of daffodils."

Without a shred of embarrassment, my uncle Kuntz read to me what he had written about his beloved. "A beautiful sunset painted the Hula Valley with a soft, pleasing light. We sat together on a black basalt stone hanging over the wadi cliff and watched the last light of day over the valley. Sunbeams glittered in her fair hair, which fluttered in the wind, and the soft light bathed her face and emphasized Henka's beauty. The water gushing in the narrow wadi channel disturbed the silence. A northern wind blew from snowy Mount Hermon, and the evening chill engulfed us. Henka rested her head on my shoulder and tears choked her throat. I handed her a bouquet of wildflowers I had picked. I was hoping to make Henka my wife. Shortly after, we moved in to live together in a communal tent, in two separate beds."

Daily life in the new kibbutz was as hard and gray as the basalt stones scattered in the yard. The farm continued to evolve, and Kuntz's friends sought additional sources of income. Following a long negotiation, Alfred purchased two cows and a calf in the Arab village of Salhiya. In return, he paid the village sheikh with ten sacks of cement, iron stakes, two hoes, and a shovel. Both sides were convinced they had struck an excellent bargain. Alfred returned to the kibbutz driving the cows and calf with a long stick.

In the kibbutz general meeting he announced, "I know something about cows. I tricked that Arab peasant and bought the calf based on its weight in meat. But the calf represents a long-term investment; he is of a fine stock. By this time next year, we will have a stud on our hands. Our two cows will give birth to new calves every year. Before long, I will double the size of the herd. You need foresight when you make a purchase. We will have a large dairy barn right here in the kibbutz. Our cows will provide milk for the entire Galilee, you'll see."

A tin shack with an asbestos roof served as the dairy barn, surrounded by a large yard. He named the calf Hercules and cared for him tirelessly. Alfred became attached to Hercules and allowed no one else to tend him. While Hercules chewed the hay in his feed trough, Alfred would talk to him, encouraging the calf to grow and mature into a healthy bull.

Henka went to work in the dairy barn. Twice a day, mornings and evenings, she would milk both cows: Poa and Yahaloma. Toward evening, Kuntz would come to check on Henka.

"Working beside Alfred wasn't easy for Henka," Kuntz told me. "Every time Hercules jumped on Poa or Yahaloma, Alfred would clap his hands. Once, while I was visiting Henka in the dairy barn, Alfred taunted me. 'Look at the strength he has… a genuine Hercules. Look at the size of his hosepipe, poor Poa, he comes of a good stock. What do you say, Kuntz, maybe you could learn a thing or two from him?' He laughed and winked at me. Henka rose from her milking stool with her face flushed and left the dairy barn in tears. I was ashamed for him, there was no point in answering."

Kuntz told me that he had run after Henka to calm her down, she told him, "Here in the kibbutz, there are members who behave like the peasants in Europe's most primitive villages. Pity that one rotten orange spoils the heap."

Kuntz explained to me, though, "We couldn't judge Alfred too harshly. He had gone through hell during the war. It was only by a miracle that he did not lose his sanity. His parents had left him and his sister with their neighbors in a small village on the Austrian border. Their flight led Alfred's parents all the way to China, and he never heard from them again. When the Germans reached Alfred's village, he escaped to Hungary and hid on a farm. He spent several years living with the cows in the dairy barn. The farmer that hid him allowed Alfred to continue to live in the dairy barn like one of the beasts. And that was where he spent most of the war years, sleeping on a bed of straw side by side with the cows he took care of. No one exchanged a word with him for years. The villagers treated him as if he were one of the animals. Toward the end of the war he left the farm and joined the partisans in the forest.

"When he arrived in the kibbutz he was introverted and barely spoke, but a few years later everything burst out, and he began to tell stories. No one knows which of his stories are true and which are simply fairy tales. Perhaps he is exaggerating a little, and perhaps he isn't. After everything he went through, Alfred is possibly the healthiest of us all. Look at Max Tishler; he couldn't take it anymore and ended up killing himself. We have all swallowed our pasts and kept silent. Alfred may be exaggerating, but at least he vomits it all out."

32

Armed with the rich information I had read about the kibbutz's pioneering days, I continued to visit Kuntz while we sat shiva.

On my next visit, after a little small talk and some tea — plus a little cognac for Kuntz — he resumed his tale. "We were an isolated hamlet in the beginning. Not many believed we would survive when the War of Independence broke out. The kibbutz contained only a few dozen members and six children. The attack on the kibbutz began at dawn. To be honest, we were caught off guard. Hundreds of villagers tried to break through the kibbutz fences. One of the members was killed in that initial attack and buried at night in the kibbutz yard.

"We had no ammunition, so each bullet counted. I shot one single bullet during that attack, and I'm not even sure I hit anybody. The next day, during one of the breaks in the fighting, I was sent with Menahem Ganani to meet the Haganah commander, David Ben-Gurion, who had come to Safed for a visit. I explained to the 'old man' that we had nothing to defend ourselves with. He wasn't very impressed. While I spoke, he paced back and forth in his room at the Hotel Canaan, busy with his own thoughts. Occasionally, he smoothed his white mane of hair with one hand and peeked out at the street through the cracks in the shutters.

"At one point, Ben-Gurion interrupted me mid-sentence. He

turned to me, stuck his thumb into a belt loop on his khaki pants and asked me, 'Friend, please lower your voice; the hotel walls are thin. We will do what we can to help. Now get back to your kibbutz because that is where you are needed.'

"I was never a big fan of his, and I still hold the same opinion."

His disappointment with Ben-Gurion was followed by a much larger one — the gulf that opened between him and his kibbutz founding member friends. Kuntz blamed it on a speech he gave during one of the general members meetings about the movement's political path. "I emerged from that meeting with my tail between my legs," he said.

Kuntz's final words gave me even more incentive to seek additional details about that general meeting in the archive. Ruhale came to my aid, and after a few hours she found the minutes of that fateful kibbutz general meeting, preserved by Max Tishler. It was only when I read those pages that I fully understood the intensity of the emotions that drove the veteran members during those days that followed WWII.

The first to speak during that assembly was Holocaust survivor Shmulik Finklestein, and this is what he told the members: "In this troubled time, we have lost our way. The War of Independence still claims its victims, and we have forgotten all about the principles of equality and the brotherhood of nations. And I say to you all — we must never forget! It was only a few years ago that entire nations lost any semblance of humanity. We cannot allow something similar to happen to us. Even during a time of war, the spirit of man must triumph, and we must show consideration and understanding to those who are foreign and different from us. Once the dust settles over the battlefield, we will be required to live side by side with our Arab neighbors. Unless we maintain purity of arms, we will not be able to lead this country."

When Shmulik finished, Alfred the dairy farmer erupted. "You are like a herd of cows, one man jabbers a pile of rubbish and the rest of you follow. Nothing will come out of this conversation, only a royal headache."

While reading the notes, I found myself envying the visceral intensity of the early kibbutz members.

After Alfred's outburst, Kuntz was next to speak. "Our blind loyalty to the Workers' Party of the Land of Israel has made us keep silent. This was a mistake. We were wrong to keep silent and have caused much damage to the party. I regret to say that Ben-Gurion has taken advantage of the situation.

"They say that a movement forms in peaceful times and is tested during times of turbulence. That did not happen to us. We sat on the sidelines, and our inaction has gravely harmed the party. We mustn't yield to the Workers' Party of the Land of Israel's threats, even if this brings division and discord. We members of the United Worker's Party have always supported the establishment of a binational state. The division of this country was a good idea, but one that has been rejected by the Arabs. We have extended our hand in peace, yet they rejected it. The time has come for us to take actions that will affect our future in the land of Israel."

Kuntz outlined the foundations of his aggressive doctrine then made a statement whose echoes refused to subside in our kibbutz, even years following that meeting. "We need to conquer all the territories of the land of Israel, from Jerusalem to the Jordan River. In the conquered area, we will establish an Arab country alongside Israel, one that will maintain a just and long-lasting peace with us. We cannot accept the current division plan and have Kibbutz Ma'abarot or Netanya live in constant fear that Israel might be torn in half. I object to any negotiations with Abdullah, king of Jordan. The war must be used to conquer territories, so we can create in those territories a new Arab country that will be our ally."

Kuntz's words created an uproar in the dining hall, and many members asked permission to speak. Max Tishler, in his picturesque language, wrote a remark about what followed: "The whole chicken coop woke up. Even the littlest mice emerged from their holes."

Alfred's outrage echoed in the dining hall. "Kuntz, when did you become such a big hero? We don't even have rifles and you want to conquer Jordan and Syria? Maybe you should have joined Jabotinsky's revisionist extremists!"

Kuntz was dragged into an argument with Alfred, and in the heat of things shouted at him, "You shut up! Be quiet and let me finish. Everyone knows you're a professional when it comes to blowing lies into the air!"

Menahem Ganani, with his sense of humor, joined in. "Alfred is actually better at blowing farts into the air." That remark was also documented by Max Tishler.

During the rest of the meeting, Kuntz did his best to convince his friends. "I suggest an enlightened occupation. You all know my negative views of imperialism. This is an occupation of necessity, just to establish a new Arab state that will coexist beside Israel. Two countries for the two nations, side by side. This is the only way to maintain fair neighborly relations. A cease-fire now will be interpreted as surrender."

Shmulik Finklestein interrupted him. "Kuntz, my friend, I survived Auschwitz's inferno and came here to create a society based on equality and decency, not to become an imperialist. There's no such thing as a just or humane occupation. Elderly people, women, and children will be killed in this war you are suggesting. We are fighting for our independence here. Israel's soil is already drenched with unnecessarily spilled blood. I will not agree to the killing of innocents; we saw enough of that in Europe."

Alfred shouted from the back of the dining hall, "Kuntz will end up eating his own hat for his stupid suggestion. Go to hell, you imperialist!"

When I told Kuntz what I had read in the archive, his face clouded over. "That night, a chasm opened between me and my friends. It was that discussion that laid the foundation of my argument with your father. But I was misunderstood. I thought we should establish a democratic Arab country as our neighbor, and everyone attacked me because of the idea of occupation. Today, Uri, the entire world supports the establishment of an independent Palestinian state. History has proved me right.

"My friends all drifted away from me. I was suddenly considered a reactionary, called an imperialist. I've spent my entire life preaching the preservation of humane ideals and compassion because in war, justice and purity of arms are pushed aside. We all like to use lofty words, but the truth is simple: When the guns begin to shoot, moral values go down to the bunker. Don't let anyone tell you stories, we have all violated the purity of arms code. During the War of Independence there were horrible cases involving the killing of innocents, the torture of prisoners, rape, and pillage. The solution I had suggested was the lesser of two evils.

"That night, in the tent," Kuntz continued, "the storm subsided. We were there by ourselves, Henka and I. She knitted by the light of an oil lamp while I read an old newspaper Zvika Cohen had brought from his trip to Haifa. A few days after that general meeting I came back home after a long day of work in the field and found Henka in labor. Our daughter was born, and we named her Haya. When we returned from the hospital, we placed her in the baby nursery. Good thing Haya was born then because she brought me closer to my friends again, if only temporarily. We had Moti six years later and named him after Mordechai Anielewicz, leader of the Warsaw Ghetto Uprising. The party leaders all attended the *brit milah* circumcision ceremony. Abba Kovner, the partisan leader of the Vilna Ghetto blessed the newborn that he would grow up in a country that would know no more war."

Even Abba Kovner couldn't have known how ridiculous his blessing would prove to be.

***

My mind kept going back to my conversations with Kuntz. I continued to search the archive for information that might lead me to the event that had severed my father's relationship with his brother. Finally, I found the notes about the Prague trials that Max Tishler had taken pains to hide.

The Prague trials began toward the end of 1952. One of the defendants was Mordechai Oren, a member of Kibbutz Mizra and a well-known figure in the United Workers Party's leadership. Mordechai Oren had many friends in Mishmar Hatsafon; Tzvika Cohen was the closest. Kuntz had met with Oren as part of his activities for the party. Mordechai Oren went to Czechoslovakia for a visit and was arrested on suspicion of espionage. In the show trial that followed, all the defendants were convicted. Rudolf Slánský and others were sentenced to death after "admitting" their actions. Mordechai Oren was sentenced to twenty years in prison.

In Israel, the trial's outcome was received with astonishment. The United Workers Party leaders, Meir Yaari and Yaakov Hazan supported Mordechai Oren's claims of innocence. The left-wing faction, headed by Moshe Sneh and Yaakov Riftin, supported the Czech judges' decision. In Mishmar Hatsafon, most members were of the opinion that the Prague trial was staged. Mordechai Oren's sentence was perceived as a failure in the communist movement's way. Tzvika Cohen supported Sneh's position and declared, "The trial proved that Mordechai Oren was a spy."

The Mordechai Oren affair became a bone of contention. Arguments between supporters and detractors were infused with personal tensions, and the political discussion quickly turned into harsh personal rivalries between kibbutz members. Kuntz was convinced Mordechai Oren was falsely accused. During one of the kibbutz general meetings he said, "We live in a place founded on a collective ideal. A member who is unwilling to accept the majority's decisions cannot continue to be a part of the collective." His words were directed at his good friends Menahem Ganani, Humi Schory, and Tzvika Cohen, who all supported the Czech authorities. His position was also held by Shmulik Finklestein.

A third of Mishmar Hatsafon's members refused to accept the party's hostile position toward Czechoslovakia and Russia. My father openly opposed his older brother and joined Tzvika Cohen's camp. The ideological argument seeped into daily life.

Tzvika Cohen, Kuntz's friend from as early as his Berlin movement days, told him, "Czechoslovakia wouldn't prosecute a man for espionage for no good reason. The facts that came out during the trial speak for themselves. This was a proper trial, and we must respect its outcome."

Kuntz replied, "Mordechai Oren is a Zionist and not a spy, and that was his only fault. This is an anti-Semitic trial. Do you honestly believe Mordechai Oren has sold his soul for money?"

Tzvika snapped back at him, "Mordechai was convicted of spying for a foreign country. A black flag now flies over his every action. If I need to choose between friendship and values, then I choose to follow my ideological beliefs."

The argument disrupted life in the kibbutz, with arguments erupting in the dining hall and in the various committee meetings. The controversary tore families apart. Yaakov Hazan, one of the heads of the United Workers Party, arrived in Mishmar Hatsafon to try to reinforce solidarity. At a general meeting held in the dining hall, he called for the strengthening of the collective ideal among all kibbutz members. Shmulik Finklestein and Kuntz sat beside him.

Shmulik said to the members, "We are allowed to have different opinions, but decisions are made in a democratic vote, and the community in its entirety is committed to accept the majority's decision. That is the essence of democracy. We will not allow a minority to force its views upon the rest. We will stand tall and hold off such destructive tendencies with our very bodies."

The following morning, the kibbutz yard was in an uproar. Tzvika Cohen, one of Mishmar Hatsafon's founders, openly supported the Soviet Union's position. He negated any possibility that the United Workers Party would take a position that would defy Czechoslovakia's communist party, which had initiated the trial. Tzvika called for a secret gathering of his supporters, held in the hayloft by the dairy barn. That meeting served to further kindle the fire of controversy because it was held without the secretariat's approval. Many members saw it as an open rebellion against the elected kibbutz institutions. Tzvika Cohen charismatically continued to encourage members to object to the party leaders' stance and gained new supporters every day. Shmulik Finklestein and Alfred demanded that punitive measures be taken against those opposing the official party policy.

In the minutes, I found a quote of words Kuntz had spoken during one of the kibbutz meetings: "There is cause for taking measures against Tzvika Cohen, who undermined the kibbutz's and the party's democratic institutions."

During that same meeting, my father answered his brother, "Freedom of speech and opinion are the cornerstones of democracy and of our kibbutz. Forcing opinions is against our principles. We mustn't ostracize members just because they hold a different opinion."

***

Time and again, I asked Kuntz about that period of the Prague trials. He scratched the top of his head and pouted uncomfortably — the look of a man who has just swallowed spoiled food. "I have refrained from scratching the wounds all these years" — he placed his thumb under his chin and seemed to be sinking into deep thought — "those were terrible times. We all failed back then. The friendship that joined us together was gone. We acted mindlessly, so many emotions... for nothing. I will give you an example that demonstrates the situation we were in.

"Every Friday, a festive dinner was held in the communal dining hall, a unique Kabbalat Shabbat ceremony in which all kibbutz members would sit together at tables covered with white cloths. Our Shabbat eves were celebrated by a new tradition that exemplified the essence of our communal lives. Henka and I wore our finest clothes. As always, I wore a white shirt and Henka wore a dress. We sat at a table with Tzvika Cohen and his wife, Sar'ke. Tzvika did not speak a word to me. He took Sark'e's hand, and they both made a big show of leaving and moved to another table. Henka was deeply offended and left the dining hall in tears."

Life in the kibbutz continued despite the harsh controversy. Max Tishler, even though he did not support Kuntz's position, made a birthday present for four-year-old Haya in his carpentry shop. Max arrived at Henka and Kuntz's house. From behind his back he took out his surprise, a green truck with a red cabin, its wheels made of four tire bearings he had found in the garage. Max handed Haya her present and broke into song: "See how large and green is our little car, it will travel very, very far..."

"That whole argument had gone too far," Kuntz said. At the mention of Haya, lost to cancer a few years before, the last spark of joy vanished from his eyes.

Many of Mishmar Hatsafon's members held opinions that were even more extreme than Kuntz's. In one meeting, Alfred said, "Sometimes, a good smack across the buttocks will do the trick. If I see an animal straying from the herd, I give her a good whipping, this way she doesn't forget who is boss.

"There's no room for communists in our kibbutz. They are Stalin's fifth column and are capable of anything. An underground resistance has formed right under our noses. I do not trust Tzvika and his gang of bandits. His people have secret stashes of weapons hidden across the kibbutz. This will end badly. I'm warning you!"

Alfred asked Chaim Harduf, who was responsible for kibbutz security, to replace the locks on the armory. Many members treated Alfred's words with grave seriousness. One night, a cardboard sign was hung on Tzvika Cohen's house door: "*Raus* — communists, go to Russia." Kuntz found himself at the heart of the controversy. He feared the self-destructive tendencies that could lead to the kibbutz falling apart. Much to his chagrin, my father, his younger brother, continued to support Tzvika Cohen's positions.

A year passed in constant arguments. Hostility between the opposing sides deepened. A cloud of mutual suspicion and personal rivalries hovered over the kibbutz. Bitter arguments flared over every little trifle. The ill-tempered Alfred took a pitchfork, had Chaim Harduf join him, wielding a hoe, and together they set out for the field to have a physical confrontation with Tzvika Cohen. Max Tishler and Humi Schory stopped the impassioned members at the kibbutz gate.

Max cried out to Alfred, "Jews, have you lost your senses? Alfred, you are a Holocaust survivor. Will you raise your hand against other Jews? This is exactly what the gentiles want, to see us fighting each other while they dance and rejoice."

Max noted in his archive notes that grave violence was prevented only thanks to his words. Unfortunately, at the same time, a trial of Jewish doctors began in Moscow, and each side dug itself deeper into its ideological trench. The tense atmosphere worsened with news of the Soviet Union's leader's death. Stalin's supporters mourned the death of the "light of nations." Rumors spread in the kibbutz about a private memorial service held in the dictator's honor. That memorial service further inflamed the controversy.

Tzvika Cohen gathered his followers for a meeting in a toolshed by the garage. He read an emotional eulogy in honor of the Georgian leader. At the end of the ceremony they raised a toast of vodka, obtained by swiping a bottle from a grocery store in Haifa. Those gathered swore to jealously uphold Stalin's legacy.

Alfred demanded that Chaim Harduf, who was in charge of kibbutz security, give him the keys to the armory so he could take arms and repel the Stalinist takeover attempt. The secretariat refused his request. Alfred organized a small group of friends, who equipped themselves with knives, clubs, axes, hoes, and pickaxes. Kibbutz Mishmar Hatsafon was facing a violent altercation.

During the weekly secretariat meeting, Alfred issued a call to action. "We need to pick up scimitars and pitchforks and throw the communists into Hercules' pen. Don't be cowards like Kuntz. I have two pistols and ammunition. We need to speak to Tzvika Cohen and his bullies the same way we talk to the Arabs; they understand nothing but brute force."

The escalating animosity between the two sides found Kuntz on the opposite side from his friends from the movement in Berlin: Menahem Ganani, Humi Schory, and Tzvika Cohen. More than anything, it disturbed him that his brother had joined those who supported Russia. Kuntz tried to find a compromise, but his positions were rejected. He was perceived as soft and hesitant, a compromiser. He ended up disdained by both sides.

As an act of desperation, he tacked an open letter to the dining hall bulletin board: "We mustn't drive away people from the kibbutz. Division is a tragedy. We must all demonstrate patience and tolerance, otherwise we will be headed for catastrophe. These are the families and children of the founding members we are discussing here, those who built the kibbutz with their own hands."

I found Kuntz's letter filed in the archive under a title written in

Max Tishler's own hand: *"Authentic documents from the kibbutz's early days."* The national kibbutz leadership made an official public statement proclaiming Mordechai Oren's innocence and that the libel against him and the Jewish doctors was anti-Semitic in origin. The United Workers Party's political leadership saw in the small settlement of Mishmar Hatsafon in the upper Galilee a testing ground for its ability to withstand the opposition rising from within. A general member assembly gathered to decide the issue.

Yaakov Hazan, one of the party leaders, was called to speak before the Mishmar Hatsafon members one more time to support the party's official position. Opposing him was Dr. Moshe Sneh, who tried to convince the members of the right-mindedness of Tzvika Cohen's way.

Tzvika said in the assembly, "This isn't about anti-Semitism but about the imperialist way of the Zionist movement."

Shmulik Finklestein spoke for the secretariat, expressing its position. "Members who undermine the cause of Zionism are undermining the country and the kibbutz as well. Those holding such views cannot remain members in our kibbutz."

Tzvika Cohen's disapproval of Zionism determined his and his supporters' futures in the kibbutz. A fateful vote was held, and the members largely supported the banishment from the kibbutz of all those negating Zionism. Tzvika and his adherents were asked to leave Mishmar Hatsafon immediately.

The morning following the decision, Tzvika Cohen's wife and my father went to see Kuntz. Sar'ke told Kuntz that her husband was in a state of deep depression. He was lying in bed and could not stop crying. My father told his brother, "The secretariat's decision to drive out members is a selection just like in the camps!"

Kuntz and Tzvika Cohen went to Tel Aviv for a reconciliatory meeting with Yaakov Hazan, to try to mend the rift. Yaakov Hazan agreed that Tzvika and his family could remain in the kibbutz, as long as Tzvika signed an official letter of remorse. Tzvika agreed to the terms. He signed a statement in which he retracted his accusations against Zionism.

During the long drive from Tel Aviv to Mishmar Hatsafon, Tzvika Cohen regained his senses and returned to his former political positions. Back in the kibbutz he published an official statement: "I was gripped by a temporary moment of weakness and Yaakov Hazan forced his position on me. I have more rights in Mishmar Hatsafon than all the party leaders put together. And now they want to drive us out of the kibbutz we built with our own hands simply because we refused to relinquish our ideals. In their audacity, they forced me to agree that my twin brother would be exiled from the kibbutz as well. I cannot possibly agree to that. The shameful mark of this act will forever blemish those who drove us away. Tomorrow, we shall leave the kibbutz with our heads held high, never to return."

The communist movement's newspaper, *The Voice of the People*, reported the banishment of the kibbutz members in its main headline. Max Tishler filed two copies of that issue in a special folder. A brief description of that most traumatic event in the young kibbutz's history was recorded in the secretariat documents. "In the early morning, all the families and members who refused to accept the kibbutz's authority gathered by the dining hall. Their belongings were loaded onto two trucks, one belonging to the kibbutz and the other to an Arab from the village of Halsa. The families along with their personal belongings were taken outside the kibbutz gate."

The banishment was accompanied by arguments with the remaining members until the very last moment. A group of members headed by Alfred watched those departing, making sure they did not take anything that belonged to the kibbutz.

I could not locate even a single photograph of that dramatic event in the archive. Three couples changed their minds at the last minute and remained in the kibbutz; they signed a letter of remorse that was deposited in the secretariat. The three couples were Rina and Mena-hem Ganani, Humi Schory and his wife, and my mother and father.

The departure of one-third of Mishmar Hatsafon's residents left a painful, open wound. The banished families refused to even visit the kibbutz for many years. Kuntz and Tzvika Cohen, friends since childhood, had not exchanged a single word since. Tzvika continued to be a left-wing activist for many years. In time, he was appointed as a history professor at the Hebrew University in Jerusalem. Even many years later, the insult and anger refused to leave the families of those members who'd had to leave. When Tzvika Cohen passed, Shmulik Finklestein and Kuntz received a message from Sar'ke not to come to the funeral or the shiva. My uncle and my father main-tained a cold relationship for long years. Even the intimate, friendly relationship between Kuntz and his friends Menahem and Humi would never be the same. An atmosphere of suspicion and hostility continued to reign in Mishmar Hatsafon. The kibbutz had changed. Its members trod its paths carefully, doing their best to avoid one another. Friends had become strangers. Each carried his personal burden resulting from that bitter argument.

33

Equipped with the knowledge I had accumulated in the archive, and determined to hold a harsh confrontation with Kuntz, I walked into his room. He was sitting at his desk and nodded his head when he noticed me. Over the years, I'd never understood why my father and his brother insisted on adding fuel to the smoking embers of that foolish argument, an argument over ideology that evolved into personal hostility, sweeping our entire family into an unnecessary tempest of emotion. I sought a way to relay all that to Kuntz.

"Well, how is your mother doing today?" Kuntz asked. Then he jumped up from his desk chair in a panic; the portable heater beside him had nearly singed his trousers. "It's so hot," he said and shook his trousers with clumsy dancelike movements.

He sat in an armchair across the room, buried his head between his hands, and released a heavy sigh. He pulled a handkerchief from his pocket, took off his glasses, and cleaned them for much longer than necessary. Next, he glanced at his watch. I was beginning to think he was off in another world. All at once, he lunged out of his chair, rushed to his desk, and rummaged through a pile of paperwork, muttering to himself. When he stood up, he held a single sheet of paper in his hand.

He walked over to me and with a broken voice I had never heard before said, "I've been cleaning up and found this eulogy I wrote for my good friend Zeev Schory, who died suddenly and still in his prime. Two years later, our Moti was killed on Yom Kippur and then… Haya got sick, and now my brother is also no longer with us." *And what about your mother and father*, I thought.

"Now who do I have left? Henka? You know her condition. I am here on my own… This is it… I have no one left to speak with from my heart." Kuntz dropped carelessly in the armchair and motioned for me to sit next to him. "Strange. When Humi died when he was only fifty, I thought nothing could possibly be worse. Then my whole world fell apart after my son died in battle. I was able to deal with the pain only because my mind was occupied with caring for Henka. And when Haya became sick and passed — I thought I could at least share my grief with my brother. I was wrong."

I had gone to see Kuntz in a fighting mood but found my uncle shrunken and depressed. All my fiery intentions instantly cooled off. Instead, I pitied him and wanted to cheer him up. I thought of hugging him but did not want to embarrass him. Kuntz stood by the window, looking out. The streetlights were on, shining down on the asphalt path separating the two large grassy areas surrounding the dining hall. Every year the kibbutz built a huge Sukkah on the lawn, the temporary hut for the holiday of Sukkot, large enough to host all the kibbutz members. It was there that the festive tractor procession, celebrating the harvest holiday of Shavuot, ended each year. And once a week, every Tuesday evening, a movie was shown on a screen sewn from white sheets.

Silently, I began to walk toward the door and was about to leave. Kuntz stopped me and said, "What's the rush? What could be so urgent? Stay with your ancient uncle a while longer. Fear not, old age isn't contagious. It creeps up on you, slowly, without drawing attention to itself. One day, you will discover it is already upon you, and there is no escape. Old age isn't such a terrible thing. Loneliness is more difficult…"

Kuntz scratched the top of his head and looked into my eyes. "Humi died from a heart attack. I still remember that morning when his wife found him dead in his bed. I received word of his death at the secretariat. I made all the proper arrangements like an automaton. I went down to the dining hall and took all the notices off the board. In the middle of the empty notice board I pinned a large note: 'Zeev (Humi) Schory is no longer with us.' I hung a smaller announcement in the corner of the board, telling members that the screening of the movie *The Umbrellas of Cherbourg* was postponed to a later date.

"Humi's passing saddened me deeply. Without Moti and Haya, my life felt pointless. Difficult days followed as Henka diminished before my eyes. The wheel of fate, apparently, kept turning and turning."

***

I had secretly hoped to see Nurit at Humi Schory's funeral. That is why I, too, remembered that day perfectly. At 2:00 p.m., the kibbutz members gathered in the library with the family. Many members attended, most still wearing their work clothes. Humi's coffin, built in the kibbutz carpentry shop, was resting in the library's entrance hall. There was no forgetting the ugly incident that took place as the members crowded around.

Hilik Zisman, who became a kibbutz member after his military service, felt every inch of the coffin with his calloused hands, blackened from working on a tractor engine. He walked about the coffin, examining it from every side. When he was done, he loudly proclaimed, "You should be ashamed of yourselves! The boards of this coffin are rotting! You're trying to save money while burying Humi? A man who gave his very soul to this place? Who allowed the idiot carpenter to do such a terrible job? I would cut the stupid ass' fingers with an electric saw. Just look at that, it looks like cheap Arab labor!

An idiot could have done a better job. We'll be lucky if the coffin doesn't fall to pieces when we lower it into the grave."

The members swayed uncomfortably on their feet, and Menahem Ganani, who stood beside Hilik, grabbed him by the elbow. "Hilik, this is undignified. Lower your voice; we have guests from outside the kibbutz here."

This only served to further enrage Hilik, who made a big show of wiping his oil-smeared hands on his filthy pants and told Menahem, "You have forgotten what Meir Yaari said: 'The working hands must always come first.'"

Menahem lashed right back at him. "You think I've forgotten, you sniveling brat? Who do you think you are? You youngsters have short memories. It is because of you that we have a salaried carpenter in the shop. Max Tishler no longer works there because you complained he is slow and cannot keep up with the demand. You have no respect.

"He was a true craftsman who learned his trade in Germany. You threw him out of the workshop and called him 'Gurnischt' — nothing. Now Max spends hours sitting in the archive, and you brought in a cheap hired hand who barely knows how to put two planks together."

For a moment, it seemed like the angry exchange would turn to blows. Alfred was called to hold back Hilik and prevent him from harming Menahem.

"You, Menahem, like all veterans, are nothing but a deadbeat," Hilik shouted while Alfred grabbed him and held him tight. "All you ever do is talk. You're all the same. Humi was the only one who knew how to keep his mouth shut and kept working in the field to his last day. The good ones are always the first to die.

"What do I care? You can bury me without a coffin; I don't need your favors. In the city, they just place the body on a stretcher and toss it straight into the grave. The worms don't care about the coffin, and I'm sure Humi wouldn't have cared either. But since they went ahead and built a coffin, they should have done a proper job of it."

Max Tishler and Kuntz joined Alfred to help separate the two. Kuntz placed a hand on Hilik's shoulder. "Enough. This is undignified. Humi was a friend to us all."

Hilik refused to settle down. "Here's another one who does nothing but talk and t—"

"Humi was my friend from way back to our days in the German movement. He was the best at what he did, and no one would dispute that. He treated everyone in a simple and refined way, spoke quietly, and never made an uproar in his life. It would be undignified to bury him with shouting and screaming."

Hilik calmed down a little, but after Alfred had eased his grip, he added a final jibe and told Kuntz, "I'm sure you'll have many more refined words to say about Humi, who could never stand the sight of you. I only wish all veterans were like him; you should have cloned him. It would have made the kibbutz look much better today."

They settled Humi Schory's coffin on a cart hitched to a tractor, and the funeral procession headed toward the cemetery. Humi's wife, who was afflicted with chronic depression and rarely left her home, walked behind the coffin leaning on her daughter. Nurit had come home to the kibbutz for the first time since leaving for Sweden those many years before. Many guests from the Galilee area kibbutzim had come as well as friends and relatives. They all climbed the dirt road on their way to the first cemetery, built at the foot of the hill where the first foundations of the kibbutz had been built. Now the hill was abandoned, and the cemetery remained far beyond the kibbutz fences. The procession walked by sabra shrubs, fig and carob trees, the last remains of an abandoned Arab village.

A guest from outside the kibbutz whispered, "Why was he called Humi if his name is Zeev Schory?"

Alfred explained, with a small smile, "During one of the kibbutz's first Purim costume parties, Zeev Schwartz dressed up as Othello. He smeared his entire body with brown shoe polish. It took him three days of scrubbing to get it off. After that, we all called him Humi, which means brownie. He had already changed his last name from Schwartz to Schory, but that nickname, Humi, clung to him. He hated when people called him that, but what could he have done? He could not shake off the name even after his death."

***

The funeral procession continued past the rainwater pool for irrigating the fields, which was used as a swimming pool in the summers with its icy cold water. The tractor drove down a muddied dirt road, past the memorial to kibbutz member Aharon Buchner, who had been murdered in 1958. The monument's base was covered with moss, and the fence surrounding it had been torn. Two dusty pine trees grew on both sides of the monument. Menahem Ganani stopped by the monument and looked at the patinated brass plaque. Aharon Buchner had been shot in the back by Syrian soldiers who had crossed the border. Aharon was a single man who had spent most of his time shepherding the kibbutz's cattle herd. He used to bring the herd all the way up to the Syrian border. A friendly relationship developed between the shepherds on opposite sides of the border. Aharon told them about the kibbutz, and they in turn told him of their difficulties in earning a living and their wish to return to their abandoned village. The conversations were conducted in Arabic, which Aharon had learned.

A small, silent local peace agreement was reached between the German-born Aharon and the Syrian shepherds. At the end of each workday, Aharon Buchner would walk the kibbutz sidewalks singing, "A shepherd am I. I play my flute as I lead my herd down the route…" He sang the tune in his raspy voice over and over, as if passing fingers over prayer beads. His naivete cost him his life.

One sunny January morning all the shepherds sat down to have a cup of coffee brewed on a small campfire. The Arab shepherds sat on the hill terrace on the Syrian side of the border, while Aharon leaned against it with his feet resting on the Israeli side. A few Syrian commandos came from the nearest outpost, made a detour through the wadi, and infiltrated Israeli territory. The unarmed Aharon, who feared nothing, was shot at close range. The rattling gunfire and whistling bullets were heard all the way in the kibbutz yard.

Chaim Harduf, who was in charge of security, gave the instruction to get the children to the shelters. Massive gunfire continued for several hours, preventing the kibbutz members from rescuing Aharon. It was only toward evening that the area settled down. With the UN's intervention, a few members retrieved Aharon Buchner's body and brought it to the kibbutz infirmary.

Years later, my mother told me, "It was a terrible sight. They set Aharon on the treatment table. He wore rubber boots, heavy with mud. A rope served as a belt for his blue work trousers. His khaki shirt was drenched with blood and perspiration. A single bullet had pierced the back of his neck and bored a hole straight through his forehead."

I remembered that Yael Harduf had come into the children's shelter and said, "Children… be quiet. They found Aharon Buchner dead."

At Aharon's burial, Kuntz's eulogy sent a shudder through the members with his succinct words: "Aharon had lived his life in loneliness, the girls did not find him to their liking…"

A few days later, Alfred and Haim Cohen snuck to the basalt stone hill terrace marking the border and brought back Aharon's *tembel* hat. A dark bloodstain marked it, a silent testament to Aharon's murder. A heavy sorrow descended on Mishmar Hatsafon, but it quickly seeped away into the mundane routine, leaving behind only a thin trail of memory of the orphaned youth who had escaped Nazi Germany.

***

The recent rains had transformed the path to the cemetery into a gooey, black paste. The tractor bearing Humi's coffin spattered clods of earth in its wake. Guests from outside the kibbutz were unprepared for the mud and found themselves hopping across puddles, unsuccessfully trying to stay clean. The grave had been dug beside Ronnie's, Humi's son, who had died of illness at the age of three. In the morning, a kibbutz sapper had placed small packets of dynamite in a few locations in the rock, to blast the upper layer of black basalt. A hired hand from Kiryat Shmona and a young man from the kibbutz had toiled for several hours digging into the rocky soil to deepen the grave so it could contain the deceased's coffin. A wintry show of daffodils, cyclamens, and anemones painted the small, cypress-encircled cemetery. Between the graves grew Pines, Pistacia, and Oak trees. In the center, my father had planted a fine boulevard of red-trunked Arbutus trees. The valley view spread before all arriving at the cemetery gate.

A light drizzle began to fall, and I heard Chaim Harduf whisper to his wife, "I just hope Kuntz doesn't use battered clichés and say that even the skies cry over Humi."

At the cemetery entrance, Hilik Zisman carefully supervised the removal of the coffin from the cart. The coffin was placed on several ropes prepared in advance to make it easier to lower it into the grave. The initial attempt was a failure; the coffin was wider than the grave. The crowd in attendance fidgeted nervously, embarrassed for the family. Humi's widow began to sob, and Nurit wiped away a tear as well. In her long black coat, she looked more alien than ever against the backdrop of the funeral. I took a few steps to be closer to her.

Hilik, Alfred, and Menahem Ganani grabbed the tools left nearby for covering the grave and began to widen the pit with great vigor. The sound of pickaxes and curses — issued by Hilik between blows — echoed in the cemetery for several minutes. Another futile attempt to lower the coffin into the grave followed. Once more, the hoes and pickaxes pounded the rocky soil to enlarge the grave. Again, the coffin was lifted and brought to the open grave.

Suddenly, a piercing, pain-filled scream was heard. The effort had proved too much for Alfred. The rope dropped from his hand, and the coffin fell with a great crash, one end in the grave and the other sticking up like a mast. Alfred lay in the mud, clutching his chest and desperately trying to breathe before losing consciousness.

Someone shouted, "We need a doctor. Where is Bruno Zucker?"

A few members lifted the unconscious Alfred and laid him on the marble slab covering the nearest grave. Dr. Zucker struck Alfred's chest several times then performed mouth-to-mouth resuscitation while telling those around him that Alfred had had a heart attack and needed to get to a hospital right away.

Humi Schory's funeral was paused, and his coffin remained absurdly stranded — half in the grave and half outside. The attendees who had surrounded the open grave moments before now gathered around the doctor and Alfred, who was sprawled on a gravestone. The members spoke loudly among themselves, completely nonplussed by the events.

"It's all an act," Hilik commented nervously. "I know him too well from the time we worked together in the dairy barn. He should go work for the national theater."

Dr. Zucker continued his efforts to save Alfred, and a few minutes later succeeded in stabilizing his condition. Alfred regained consciousness, pale as a sheet, his bald head dripping with cold sweat, and breathing hard. A few members picked him up and carried him outside the graveyard. He was laid on the cart that had held Humi's coffin, and the tractor took off toward the kibbutz with Dr. Zucker and another member following on foot.

Max Tishler turned to a guest standing next to him. "That Alfred… always has to play the big hero. Once, he drove his bicycle down the hill from the veterans' neighborhood to the dining hall. He lost control and smashed into a big pine tree that grew by the infirmary. A volunteer from Denmark found him. The bicycle's front wheel was bent completely out of shape. Thick, greenish-white liquid ran from the top of Alfred's bald head and trickled down his face. The volunteer panicked and began to scream for help in English; she was terrified that Alfred had fractured his skull and was about to expire momentarily.

"In the Safed emergency room, the doctors found Alfred's head to be unharmed. The liquid that had trickled down his head was bird droppings. The common belief that bird droppings bring good fortune was not borne out. Alfred broke two ribs and his collarbone. Furthermore, the younger dairy farmers took advantage of the opportunity and got rid of Hercules, the kibbutz's old stud. They bought a new, young stud and sold Hercules, who could barely move by then, for a pittance to some meat merchant from a neighboring Arab village. Hercules was sent to the slaughterhouse that very day.

"Alfred just doesn't get it. Just like Hercules, he has depleted his youthful strength. Just a show-off, he didn't even have enough strength to carry the coffin."

The rain came down harder, and Kuntz realized he had to shorten the burial service. With a great deal of effort, a few of the younger members freed the coffin then straightened it and squeezed it into the grave. Hilik and a few other young members worked frantically to fill the grave with large basalt stones and baskets of wet earth. Kuntz decided to forgo what he had written and briefly eulogized his good friend. The gathered crowd sighed with relief. The funeral was finally over. The kibbutz members quickly dispersed, stepping over and around puddles.

Max Tishler went straight to Menahem Ganani and said, "That Hilik is a disgrace. Is this what comes out of our educational system? Two slaps across the face, that's what he should have gotten… what is he carrying on about? Humi had said nothing for years, too ashamed to talk. Everyone in the kibbutz spoke behind his back about his slutty daughter, where was Hilik then? Now he's suddenly trying to educate us all."

Menahem tried to silence Max with a gesture, but Max would not be stopped. "This isn't right. They buried Humi without a shred of dignity; what a disgrace. If this is how they treat the veterans here, I'd rather be buried somewhere else."

"Don't exaggerate, Max, it's not that bad here," Menahem answered impatiently.

Gurnischt only grew more upset. "Why does Kuntz always do the talking? And what was his rush to finish the service like that? There were other members who wanted to say a few words. What is this, piecework? A rushed job?

"So disrespectful, the way they pounded Humi into the grave. They should be ashamed of themselves. Instead of giving Humi his due, Alfred stole the show. I've made up my mind. When my day comes, I am not going to be buried here!"

"Just leave it for now, Max," Menahem snapped. "No one is in a hurry to bury you. We still have a few years of going uphill. Now's not the time for arguments. Alfred had a heart attack, and Hilik has never been the sharpest pencil in the box."

Max Tishler continued to growl. "I won't be buried like that. Believe me, Menahem, I know Alfred. Everything's an act with him. He's an idiot, just like that hired carpenter who built the coffin. I went to the carpentry shop this morning. Good thing I checked it. I added a few screws to the joints in the lower part, made a proper job of it. If I hadn't, the coffin would have broken open. I used the opportunity to send a note with Humi to my dead parents and sister. He was a good man; I think he'll get to heaven."

The cemetery was nearly empty. I looked over at Nurit. Her rain-drenched hair emphasized her beauty. She bent over the grave and arranged the many bouquets piled on it, ignoring the lashing rain. When she finished arranging the flowers, she squeezed under her mother's umbrella, held her tight, and they marched down the path, which was quickly turning into a small stream. I was hoping Nurit would stay in the kibbutz for a while. Outside the cemetery I watched Kuntz awkwardly wobbling down the path. He pulled up a stalk of wild oat growing by the path, tore off the top, placed the green stalk in his mouth and chewed it thoughtfully. Humi was the last to be buried in that cemetery.

***

On my way out of the cemetery I recalled the first funeral I had attended; I was only in the fifth grade then. Our teacher, Tova Zisman and the chief nurse, Yael Harduf, watched over us when we accompanied Ronnie, Humi's son, on his final journey. Yael feared we were too young to attend a funeral, while Tova thought it would be best to have us face the harsh reality together and that an emotional final parting from Ronnie Schory would turn us into a tight-knit group.

After the funeral, Humi Schory came to the lawn in front of the children's houses, and Nurit ran out to meet him. Humi took his daughter's hand, and together they climbed up the slide in the yard to get some privacy. They stood with their backs to us, Nurit glued to her father's side. Humi did not hug her; he merely placed his hand on her head and slowly stroked her hair. I remember watching them and crying.

***

The day after Humi's funeral, I met Nurit in the dining hall. After dinner, we walked together toward her parents' home, chatting pleasantly as we walked.

"Wait here a minute," Nurit told me when we got to her mother's apartment.

She went inside and returned a moment later. We continued to stroll along the kibbutz sidewalks until we reached the room she had been given for her stay. Nurit hesitated then invited me inside. We rushed together, cautiously fumbling, removing layer after layer of estrangement that had separated us over the years. It was the only time we made love.

I tortured myself for having taken advantage of her vulnerability following her father's death. I thought she had slept with me merely to find some momentary comfort. We lay glued together, silently. I stroked her shoulder, and she gently rejected me and covered her naked body with the blanket. An uneasy silence followed. We were two strangers once more.

A nocturnal bird called out an incessant monotonous cry. Nurit curled up with her back to me and sobbed for a long time. When her crying stopped, she went to the closet and dressed in a light robe. She came back to the bed, gently stroked the back of my neck, and asked me to go. I left her room sad and embarrassed. The disappointment stung for long after I left. In my heart I knew Nurit remained unattainable. We had taken a wrong turn somewhere, and there was no going back. Her image remained with me for a long time, then the years had passed, Nurit had withered, the yearning remained, until it too had finally changed shape and was lost. A few weeks after Humi was buried, Nurit returned to Sweden.

34

During the shiva I was restless and preoccupied. I found there was something terrible in it all: My father had had to die in order to clear a place for me. His death had opened a flood of emotions I'd thought were securely damned up. Occasionally, I found myself observing my surroundings like a stranger.

The lawn in front of my mother's room filled and emptied of people in a kind of arrhythmic motion. Binder, Hatuka, Kadmi, and the rest of my friends from the commando unit reported to the shiva. Some had grown old, others had grown paunchy, their hair had thinned and whitened. The youthful spirit of mischief, once an integral part of the commando unit's mannerisms, was gone. Gidi Turner was the only one who acted the same. He walked about, clapping everyone's back and gathered the commando unit into a circle. Out from his backpack came the eternal arak bottle, spiced with herbs and honey.

"Dolev," he announced loudly, "get an onion. We'll raise a toast in your father's honor. I'm sure he would have liked to join us."

My commando reconnaissance unit friends filled the grass in front of my mother's house with the cheerful atmosphere of a nostalgic reunion, which I was not comfortable with. I asked Gidi not to overo it; I was afraid my mother might get insulted by our ridiculous reservist rituals, which had long grown stale in any event. Gidi was not to be deterred that easily.

"Dolev, can I tell the guys about that night years ago, when you came to me and told me you were suspected of being a spy? You sure fooled us all. Well done. Why do you think Dolev is living in Germany now? It was all an elaborate stunt pulled by the Mossad. They pinned him with an espionage case just to quietly plant him in Berlin without anyone suspecting him.

"Well played, Dolev, you got yourself a dream job, and at the country's expense, no less. You bastard, and to think how much I pitied you back then."

Toward evening, Yehiam Gruenwald, my old friend, arrived. I was very happy to see him walking toward the gathering. Gidi, who had been having a lively conversation with Binder, saw Yehiam and greeted him with his typical enthusiasm.

"Well, look who's here, Mr. Gruenwald himself. What a surprise. I haven't seen you in ages." Gidi nearly crushed Yehiam in a hug and asked him, "How do you even know Uri Dolev?"

Yehiam was embarrassed by Gidi's exuberance. "We… grew up together… in the same group."

Gidi dragged Yehiam off to the side, and they spoke together for a few minutes. Until then I'd had no idea that Gidi and Yehiam knew each other. Sometime later, I found out that Gidi, who managed a small metal factory, suspected one of his managers was doing some industrial espionage for his competitors. The employee was sent for a polygraph test at Yehiam's institute in Netanya.

The guys from the commando reconnaissance unit eventually went their separate ways. The girls — now women — of the Cypress group joined Yehiam, who had arrived with all my old classroom friends by design. I could hardly recognize some of them; time had marked them all. Only Udi Ganani was missing, the memory of his image untouched by time — strong, handsome, and inexplicable. I wondered how all those who had once shared every important moment of my life for so many years had become so completely irrelevant. The passing years had engendered an estrangement, embarrassment, even. We were connected simply because we were born in the same year. Other than Yehiam, I had not kept in touch with any of my classmates and hadn't seen most of them in years. In my mother's apartment we exchanged tentative embraces and shared experiences in the subdued atmosphere.

Yehiam sat in the armchair that used to be my father's regular spot. His hair had gone gray and fell almost to his shoulders. He awkwardly tried to hide his potbelly while stroking his almost fully white beard. A strange look was in his eyes, and he mostly sat looking at his cell phone. I went over to him and suggested we go outside to talk. Out of all my friends in the Cypress group, Yehiam was the only one for whom I'd felt an occasional pang of yearning. Our friendship had known its share of ups and downs over the years, but we had maintained our relationship despite the passage of time, a sense of intimacy and understanding that did not always require words.

We walked leisurely up the path away from the commotion on the lawn. Our feet carried us to the area of the small garden by the two graves next to the northern tower. We sat on the bench by the stream, just as we had as children.

"We shared some beautiful times here. We had a childhood like no other," I said.

"Uri, it's all the same at the end of the day," Yehiam answered coolly.

"What do you mean?" I asked.

"What's there to understand? We'll all end up at the same last stop."

The warm familiarity I was used to with Yehiam had been replaced by an impatient series of growled responses. I attributed it to the changes we had each gone through, or perhaps to the fact that the intimacy of our youth had eroded over years of separation. We silently sat on the stone bench after that until I disrupted the silence.

"With us, death treads in his slippers, walking the kibbutz pathways in utter silence. Now and then, he goes out in search of a new victim, wearing his old-fashioned rubber-soled plaid slippers with a zipper up the middle. Have you ever noticed that death has been hanging around here for years? It sprouted from the seeds of the death camps. The veterans thought they would be able to escape the fate of the Holocaust in this new place, but that fate followed them here and shows no intention of leaving."

Yehiam did not reply; he continued looking at the water flowing in the stream.

There are three cemeteries in Mishmar Hatsafon. Death had crept almost unnoticed into the life of the kibbutz. The Holocaust, wars, work accidents, and diseases. Death had visited every single one of the kibbutz veterans' families.

"Death feels right at home here. I don't know why, but he's comfortable in the kibbutz. He came for a visit and forgot to leave."

Yehiam looked at me, puzzled. "What are you talking about, Uri? The kibbutz is no different from anywhere else in the world." He waved a hand as if flicking an irksome fly.

"Don't you think Mishmar Hatsafon has suffered an unreasonable number of tragic incidents?" I asked.

Yehiam viewed the world in a calculated way. As far as he was concerned, everything had a reason. To find it, one merely needed to look close enough.

He snorted and shook his head at me. "Uri, the kibbutz is no different from any other community. There might have been a little overenthusiasm from people who thought they'd invented something new, but at the end of the day everything is the same — relationships, resentments, desires, loves, and jealousies."

Yehiam got up from the bench and turned to leave but paused

when I called out to him. "I don't know; I think slippers bring bad luck. I threw the new slippers I got from the kibbutz in the trash, just to be on the safe side. Slippers will fool you. They're warm and cozy. They make your feet feel just fine, creating an illusion of safety. But they slowly kill you unnoticed."

Yehiam kept quiet. I couldn't hazard a guess as to what was going on in his head. As for me, I was thinking about our dead friend Udi Ganani.

***

As children, on a trip to Manara, Yael Harduf sat us down on the edge of the cliff and said, "Look down, there is the Hula Valley spread before you in all its glory."

She took a few oranges out of her bag, peeled them and handed each child a few slices. The sun was in the middle of the sky, illuminating the fields of the valley, which spread all the way to the Bashan mountains. Udi Ganani pointed at Mishmar Hatsafon and said, "From here, you have the best view in the world."

Yael heard Udi and said, "Beauty is in the eye of the beholder; we each find it in different things. There are those who say that a human being is the most beautiful thing in the world." The tough-minded Yael Harduf had tears in her eyes, and we all sat quietly.

"I don't care what anyone says," Udi sulked, "this place has the finest view in the whole world."

***

Nurit Schory came back to Mishmar Hatsafon to live thirty-one years after leaving. She never started a family in Sweden, and her wandering was over. Her elderly, depression-prone mother lived in the kibbutz on her own. Nurit was given a small apartment not far from her. She opened a pottery studio in the clothing shed that had been unused for several years. For a minimal sum, Nurit rented half of the shed's space. In her small workshop, she created plates, cups, and other pottery ware that was sold to the kibbutz members and the various visitors who frequented the guesthouses. The income was enough to cover all her expenses.

Slowly, Nurit fit back into the kibbutz social life. Other than her green eyes, no trace of her youthful beauty remained. She had rounded with extra weight, and she often walked about in paint- and clay-stained coveralls. The once wild social life of the popular bachelorette had been exchanged for long hours spent in her studio, the rare visit of a friend, and many hours of voluntary loneliness.

I met Nurit for a brief conversation during my father's shiva. Like most kibbutz members, she had attended out of politeness and a sense of obligation to the community. Nurit lowered her head while speaking to me, and I sensed her relief when my mother joined the brief conversation. Before long, she said goodbye and left. That evening, I passed by her apartment and heard the gentle sound of a violin. She had given up playing at the age of seventeen, and the sounds thrilled strings in my heart that had rusted long ago. I stopped, enchanted by her playing, and a sentence of stage direction written by Chekhov for *The Cherry Orchard* came to mind: "Like a breaking harp string." That was how I felt for Nurit Schory. Life's race had made me lose my longing.

35

The sun had set, my friends had gone, and I left my mother's house to get some air. I found myself walking toward the nursery and the children's houses. A black pole was planted at the intersection bearing directional signs: one pointed the way to the nursery home, another pointed at the children's houses, and the last showed the way to the dining hall. Someone had added "RIP" by the words "Dining Hall" with a black marker. The old dining room had been severely damaged during a shelling in 1958 and now served as a pub for the kibbutz's younger generation. The "new" dining hall was beside it — a decidedly ugly structure made of concrete, an elongated building with narrow windows and a low ceiling, as bulky and graceless as a medieval fortress. The planners had learned the lesson of past shelling from Syria; the dining hall ceiling was sixty centimeters of reinforced concrete.

The old dining hall had served as the focal point of kibbutz social life, so a huge shelter had been built underneath the new one, able to accommodate hundreds of people in case of a shelling attack. The shelter had been used by kibbutz members as a club — a pleasant place where they could drink coffee and read newspapers and magazines from all over the world. The dining hall had hosted the kibbutz general meetings, holiday parties, weddings, and theater shows. Menahem Ganani and Max Tishler had once suggested to the general assembly that the gray dining hall roof be covered with red tiles, to lend the proper rural appearance to the central kibbutz building in the same color as the May Day International Workers celebration flag. When it was discovered that the aesthetic addition would cost the kibbutz a small fortune, the tiled roof was met with vehement opposition from the treasurer.

"This is just a waste of money. We'll build a red roof when the ideology pays the bills," he argued.

The general members assembly rejected the suggestion.

***

We were twelve, when one day our teacher marched us, bathed and wearing our finest clothes, down the stairs leading beneath the dining hall to the kibbutz members' club to meet some guests from abroad.

When we reached the club, a crowd of eager kibbutz members was already waiting for the guests, and there was a table laden with juice and malt beer bottles, cookies, and small sandwiches. Two strangers came down the serpentine stairwell leading to the club, different in appearance from anyone I had seen. It was midsummer, yet the man wore a white suit and a red tie. His white hair was neatly parted and combed to one side. Round, gold-framed glasses rested on his nose. A beautiful woman stood beside him, much taller and with a high-cheeked Asian face. Her hair was tied back with a light-blue silk kerchief. She wore a turquoise dress, the kind of dress I'd only seen at weddings, and transparent nylon stockings that ended in high-heeled white leather shoes. She was stylish, made-up, distinguished, and cultivated. A stark contrast to the women of the kibbutz. The lady from abroad looked like a fairy-tale queen to me, and I could not take my eyes off her.

The conversation with the guests was conducted in French, a

language which, obviously, I did not understand. Their escort turned to us, the children, and said that the lady and gentleman would like to ask us about life in the kibbutz.

"How frequently do you see your parents?" the gentleman asked in French, and the escort immediately translated his words.

I pointed at my parents and said, "Every day."

"For how long?" I was asked.

"Two hours in the afternoon, sometimes more," I replied.

"And that is enough?" asked the lady in a severe tone.

"Yes," I said.

"Where do you sleep at night?" she asked next.

Nurit replied, "We all sleep in the children's house."

"And do you miss your parents?" the lady wanted to know.

"No, we're used to it," Yehiam said and then added insolently, "I don't understand this stupidity, each child here sees his parents every day and that's enough."

Yehiam's words were translated for the woman, who responded with a wide smile.

Even though the male guest was shorter than his companion and even slightly stooped, his impressive presence and self-confidence made everyone listen to his every word with awe. The gentleman leaned forward, rested his chin on his open hand, and asked us to detail our daily schedule. His request seemed odd, but I gave him a full account.

After going over our work and school schedule, I told them, "We go to our parents' room in the afternoon. They have already finished working and showering. We have a snack together, play a little, and just before seven in the evening our parents walk us back to the children's house, tell us good night, and leave."

"And do you feel lonely in the children's house?" he wanted to know.

Hilik Zisman joined the conversation. "Why should we feel

lonely? We all sleep together, the whole group, and there is always a night watchwoman."

The woman asked, "And what if you wake up in the middle of the night from a scary nightmare without your parents next to you?"

Nurit answered that question. "There's a night watchwoman. And when that happens, she gives us a spoonful of sugar with a little water to calm us down."

Hilik Zisman added, "We're not cowards like those city children."

I couldn't help myself from sharing a story. "I once went to visit our relatives in Haifa. We had dinner before their father came home from work. When we got up in the morning, he was already gone." I summed everything up this way. "We're much better off than the city children. Their parents are always tired, and they hardly see them at all."

The gentleman exchanged a few words with the woman, and the translator explained that the guests indeed had gotten the impression that the two hours we spent with our parents could be viewed as "quality time" — a term which I did not understand back then. Once the distinguished guests had gone, Tova Zisman proudly told us our two visitors were renowned philosopher and playwright Jean-Paul Sartre and his wife, author Simone de Beauvoir.

***

The dining hall had fallen into disuse during the privatization era and lost its former glamour. The large building in the center of the kibbutz stood as empty as a huge monument, calloused and ugly. The regular morning, noon, and evening communion of kibbutz members had ended. No more meetings and discussions, gone was the sound of arguments around the work roster supervisor. The dining hall now only served as a gathering place for memorial services in the veteran members' honor. And there had been no shortage of funerals and memorial services in recent years.

A loud commotion of ear-piercing squeaks and flapping wings invaded my musings. New residents, recently arrived, had taken over the trees. A flock of parrots landed in the branches of the old carob tree. With high-pitched caws, they competed for the best positions. I looked at the flock of parakeets and admired the way the members ceaselessly screeched and made war with each other, flying from the carob tree to the Margosa tree and continuing on, screaming, to the large oak tree. The parakeets had taken over the landscape, chasing away all other birds except the crows, which had turned more aggressive and violent as well.

It seemed the kibbutz had really changed — every man for himself. The individual was pushed into a corner; there was no more room for wagtails in the yard and goldfinches on the oleander branches. The kibbutz youths, like the parakeets, struggled for every morsel of property, the outcome of privatization, which had watered down the ideals of long ago. Mobility scooters drove past me down the trail, not much different from the electric vehicles used by the world's richest men on golf courses. In the renewed kibbutz, such vehicles were the trademark of the veterans, a clear sign that old age and difficulty in walking had reached here as well. In the veterans' neighborhoods, special electrical sockets had been installed to recharge the scooter batteries. So not only had the treetops changed, the sidewalks had a completely new look. Next to the scooters, private cars could be seen, densely parked along the kibbutz paths.

An old mulberry tree still towered over the children's houses. We used to climb its scarred trunk each year to pick the purple fruit and gather fresh leaves for the silkworms. There was a small swimming pool next to the mulberry tree. Now it was full of brown earth, planted with grass and flowers. I remembered how Tova Zisman had taught us to swim at the age of five. The first time I was able to swim unaided, I had nearly drowned, until I finally managed to cross the pool, feeling extremely heroic.

Udi Ganani saw me and said, "I can swim back and forth five times straight without breaking a sweat."

***

On Friday, we finished sitting shiva and went to the cemetery. Coming back, I asked myself when I intended to go back to Berlin and was unable to come up with a clear answer. My mother made dinner and asked that Yoram and his family stay for the weekend. During dinner, I told everyone I was going back to Berlin the following week.

"What's the rush? Stay a little in the kibbutz with me," my mother asked.

I suggested she come for a visit in Berlin come spring. She refused and wouldn't even hear of it. "I'm not going anywhere without your father," she said.

I asked my brother, Yoram, to try to persuade her. I thought maybe my mother would listen to him. Before leaving, I visited the archive one last time. I was looking for information about my parents, and Henka and Kuntz. I tried to understand how they had led their lives in the kibbutz while most of their relatives had remained in Europe during the war. I discovered that while Europe was ablaze, the kibbutz members were kept busy trying to find sources of income. Because of the war, the export and harvesting of oranges had stopped. There wasn't any work, but there were plenty of oranges.

The members busied themselves with maintenance work on the existing buildings and the creation of a small agricultural farm. One of the leaflets reported that Menahem Ganani, who was responsible for the vegetable garden, had managed to sell the leftover produce at the local market in Halsa. The temporary camp provided members with vegetables, eggs, chickens, and even goat milk. When making a living had become more difficult, salvation came from an unexpected source: Humi Schory and Tzvi Cohen were hired to work as temporary laborers paving the Wadi Ara road.

Stealing for the benefit of the kibbutz was a matter of daily routine. In that regard the members had the morals of a rubber girl. During one of the general meetings, Tova Zisman said, "Swiping is permissible as a last resort, but one needs to obtain the kibbutz secretariat's approval first."

I had always known that a large number of Mishmar Hatsafon members had volunteered for the Jewish Brigade and the Palmach and had always wondered why they were the first to join the military organizations. That eagerness to volunteer seemed strange to me in light of the pacifist worldview of the kibbutz founders.

My attempts to find any information about Kuntz's past in the Palmach went nowhere. Max Tishler wrote down and documented and added to the archive every note that remained on the secretariat desk or in the dining hall during the members meetings. Secretariat decisions were obsessively documented over the years. I found an ocean of words hidden in the ancient folders but nothing about the Palmach or the Jewish Brigade. I assumed that when it came to security issues, Max Tishler had chosen an underground mentality and that in this case, the security considerations overcame his desire to collect and document every piece of local history.

Perhaps he had feared a surprise British army inspection; Mishmar Hatsafon had various underground illegal weapons hideouts. These weapons hideouts — the *slikim* — were a source of great pride, and the members who knew of them kept their existence a secret even from their closest friends. At the end of the nineties, Chaim Harduf agreed to reveal the location of the largest *slik*, hidden in the kibbutz yard near the pigsty. Police officers, invited to the kibbutz from the neighboring city of Kiryat, Shmona were surprised by the number of weapons and their mint condition.

Mishmar Hatsafon members zealously guarded all aspects of security issues. In the archive, only a hint of their security activities was found in a single members committee report: "Kuntz's request to work at the British army airport by Ein Shemer during his Palmach service has been approved." The committee explained this approval by pointing to the kibbutz's cash flow problem. A large map was hung in the dining room with flags marking the advancement of the allied armies. The German army had reached as far as the borders of Egypt. In Kuntz's diary, I found a single reference to the question of drafting members for security activities.

Kuntz described the sensitive situation from his own standpoint. *"My family has remained in Europe, and news of its situation is fragmented and does not bode well. A few members, German speakers all, gathered in the forests surrounding Kibbutz Mishmar HaEmek. We trained to establish a special force of fluent German speakers. Our goal: set out on missions behind enemy lines, make good use of our fluency in the language, blend in and cause damage to the advancing German army. Our aim is to parachute into the enemy's home front and act as a fifth column. While training we speak only in German, which I find extremely difficult. I consider Hebrew to be my language now, and I prefer it over German a thousand times."*

Menahem Ganani had joined the Jewish Brigade, Tzvi Cohen joined the German division, and Kuntz chose to volunteer in the Palmach. He gave up the German division to stay in Israel, be close to Henka, and maintain a close relationship with the kibbutz. In my conversation with Kuntz, I got no confirmation or additional details.

Kuntz told me, "Those who nostalgically lean on their past actions are admitting their current failures."

With those words he justified the fact that he never attended the Palmach veterans reunions and meetings. He explained to me, "The Palmach handled Ben-Gurion with silk gloves and never came to terms with him over his decision to dismantle the organization.

After the establishment of Israel, the Palmach veterans preferred to play down that fact for political reasons."

***

When the shiva had ended, I said goodbye to my mother. It was an uneasy farewell. After a commotion-filled week and countless guests, she would suddenly be on her own in an empty apartment. Without my father. She realized the future held many lonely days in store for her. Once more, I suggested she come to Berlin as my guest, but she firmly rejected my offer.

"We'll talk about it. Don't forget to call me when you get home."

The fact that my mother had reconciled with the idea that Berlin was now my home filled me with a strange melancholy.

I went to Tel Aviv for a couple of days to decompress before heading home. By the end of that week I felt the familiar distress that accompanies Saturday evenings — the end of the weekend. For several years, I recognized that murky mood that began to creep its way in during the Jewish day of rest's afternoon hours. "Saturday night blues," I called that feeling, without understanding its genesis. Friday afternoon ushers in the "angels' hour." It comes in through a hidden door, bringing with it a uniquely pleasant feeling reserved for Fridays in Israel. The blues originated in the military service — the knowledge that the weekend was over, and you needed to head back to base. "Every weekend has its Saturday night," we used to tell each other in the army. The Saturday night blues seeped into our civilian life and became an inseparable part of Israeli culture. The crashing wave of Friday family life slowly receded throughout Saturday, clearing the way for the counterstrike of the mundane.

36

Germany welcomed me home with freezing temperatures and clear skies. I returned to my quiet apartment on Kollwitzstrasse and tiredly dropped into my beloved leather couch by the fireplace. I took a little nap, lacking the strength to even prepare coffee. I remembered my father and began to cry, large tears coursed down my cheeks. His presence had always been eclipsed by my mother's. His quiet ways that verged on indifference had an intensity to them somehow. His inflexibility had often irritated me, a kind of tough austerity in which everything was obvious — what was right and what was permissible. He used to utter regular slogans like Moses preaching from the top of Mount Sinai:

"No combination is deadlier than diligent fools with too much time on their hands."

"Flattery doesn't come with a value added tax."

"Television is a type of air pollution."

Beneath my father's thick skin, another, different character was hidden — sensitive and attentive to others — but that aspect was difficult to see in him, much like the cactus, the desert queen of the night, whose magnificent blossom opens for a single night and disappears in the morning.

"The world is in the small details."

"Not being on time is disrespectful and inconsiderate to others."

In his company, I had learned to love classical music and to recite the names of wild plants. I was taught to be accepting and respectful of others, to be meticulously neat and tidy, and, above all, to always be on time. Punctuality was something my father and Kuntz agreed upon. Kuntz would go out of his mind whenever a schedule he'd planned would go awry. My father's penchant for punctuality had successfully made its mark. I'm chronically punctual; being on time is etched into my consciousness. Anytime I'm late, my heart starts racing, I get upset and start sweating like a man on the verge of a heart attack. My behavior could sometimes be intolerable for those around me.

I remember how, at the age of fourteen, I was late for harvesting at the apple orchard. Because of me, the ride to the orchard was delayed for about five minutes. In the evening when I visited my parents, my father scolded me, "Uri, remember, you should always get to an appointment a minute early. I really do not like the fact that you were late this morning. Look what you did; the whole company of apple harvesters was delayed because of you. You were only five minutes late, but multiply your delay by the thirty people who were going to work in the orchard, and you'll see that the kibbutz lost two and a half hours of work. If someone else was late for a mere few minutes each day, the kibbutz would lose over five workdays per year. God is in the details. Unless you are strict, the result could be a catastrophe." He slowly enunciated each syllable of the word — ca-tas-tro-phe — so I understood the full import then said to me in a fatherly tone, "Please try it next time — a minute early."

***

During my first kitchen duty, my aunt, Henka, noticed that I was unable to get a handle on the dirty dishes before me. Pans, pots, kettles, plates, and cups — all in a single chaotic pile. Henka stopped her own work, wiped her hands on her apron, placed them on her hips, and said, "Uri, without some sort of method you won't be done washing dishes until the moon hangs in the sky. Just stop for a moment and look at what needs to be done."

She rolled up her sleeves and began to organize the sink. "Order comes first. Each of the dishes has its own family — the plates family, the cups family, and so on. You need to sort the dishes into groups. The pots, cookware, and pans are soaked in boiling water and a little soap. The soaking takes off fat and food residue clinging to them. Cleaning large items like that without soaking could take hours. Once they are properly soaked, all that's left to do is scrub the stubborn spots. The utensils should be put together in a large bowl, then use hot water and soap again. Place the plates on top of each other in a single pile beside the sink. Scrub the first plate in the pile with soap and put it aside. Don't rinse it just yet; let the soap do the cleaning. This way, plate by plate, you should systematically work your way. Do the same thing with the cups. Once you've taken care of the plates and cups, the soaked utensils will be almost clean. There is an order to things."

Each kibbutz dining hall had a huge dishwashing machine, a long track winding its way like a toy train's. Hard plastic baskets, faded from being washed and rewashed, sat on the conveyor belt. Each basket had a designation — plates, cups, and utensils. When you finished eating, you put your dirty dishes in the appropriate basket. The conveyor belt went round and round after every meal. Only at night did the machine stop. Thus, revolved the life of the kibbutz, an endless cycle of members' nourishment. And perhaps a new Jewish identity, one involving place and boundaries, estrangement and immigration, the individual versus the collective, reality confronted with utopia. That giant machine was like an independent territory with its hidden and revealed areas. I used to watch the dirty dishes making their way until swallowed into the dark, intimidating washing channel from which noises and steam issued. At journey's end, on the machine's exit side, plates, cups, and utensils were ejected washed — as clean as the kibbutz members on a Shabbat eve.

In my mind rose the image of the kibbutz dining hall in winter. A special device for washing one's boots was placed at the entrance — a hose with a large scrub brush tied to it. Gurnischt would spread wood shavings on the dining hall entrance floor, which he would bring in burlap sacks from the carpentry shop every day. Along the wall, the green camouflage raincoats were hung, remainders from the American army. The kibbutz revolved about the Formica dining hall tables, members on kitchen duty pushed stainless steel cars with large, food-filled containers, passing through the tables. I thought of my father, on kitchen duty just like every other kibbutz member, pushing a cart with a steaming pot of soup. If one of the younger members had said, "Give us more meat with the soup," my father would stop his work for a moment, look at the hungry youth and always repeat the same joke, "Kid, you should look for the meat in your life rather than your soup."

***

My father's death brought about the beginning of the end of my wandering. My stay in Berlin began to feel uncomfortable. I wanted to go back to Israel. The big city of Tel Aviv appealed to me, but the time I had spent in Mishmar Hatsafon made me reconsider. The option of building my own house in the kibbutz tipped the scales. I told myself not to procrastinate. Make a decision and act on it. I called Ruhale the evening I made up my mind. The phone rang and rang, until a familiar scorched manly voice sounded on the other end.

"Good evening and season's greetings." I was surprised that Alfred had answered.

"Can I speak to your wife?" I asked.

"You want to speak with my wife? That's a little complicated," Alfred continued cheerfully. "Since she became the kibbutz secretary, even I have a hard time getting hold of her. And who, if I may ask, wants to speak to her?"

I was quiet for a moment. "Uri Dolev. I'm calling from abroad. I'm returning her call."

"Oh… Uri, very interesting."

I heard noises in the background, and Ruhale was almost instantly on the line. "Uri Dolev, how wonderful. What a pleasant surprise. How are you? Well, how goes the writing of our play? I hope all that digging in the archive helped you. Are you finished? We've been patiently waiting for a very long time, yes?

"But you've caught me in the middle of an important meeting. Why don't we talk a little later? I'm not going anywhere," she said with a burst of energy that I couldn't comprehend.

Before she hung up, I managed to tell her, "I'm coming to Israel next week, we'll talk about it all then, all right?"

"Excellent," she said, and the conversation was over.

∗∗∗

I went back to Israel.

Happily, Ruhale asked to meet me in Tel Aviv, in a café not far from the national Kibbutz Movement offices. I had a hard time falling asleep the night before our appointment and kept tossing and turning in my hotel bed. Every time I was on the verge of sleep, a thought came unbidden, followed by a string of other thoughts that did not allow me any sleep. Lying in bed, I recited my opening sentences for the coming meeting with Ruhale. I reviewed my wording, organizing my various arguments. Each time I thought things were in perfect order, I recalled an additional small detail, and the whole process began anew.

I tried to think of other things. I strained my mind to divert it from the endless cycle. I even tried reasoning with myself to fall asleep. I counted slowly, but found myself reciting the words I would have to say to Ruhale instead. Despite my great tiredness, I was unable to fall asleep. I so much wanted a soothing sleep, and the more I desired it, the more wakeful I became. I got up, opened my laptop and checked emails and news websites, got back into bed, kept tossing and turning and not sleeping.

At 3:30 a.m. I got up to urinate. I stood in front of the toilet and waited. Leaning against the wall with one hand, I tilted my body forward, ready to perform that simple action. I stood like that for several minutes, finally sitting heavily on the toilet seat. This had happened before. A physical blockage, the result of holding off too long, prevented me from urinating comfortably. I was annoyed at my rebellious body — first the thoughts that prevented me from sleeping, now I had to sit like an idiot on the toilet bowl, unable to perform the simple act of urinating.

"What is happening to me? What is the meaning of this rebellion of every part of my body? Get a grip, don't allow external forces to take hold of you. Clear your head and empty your bladder," I quietly told myself.

But my body persisted, an independent machine no longer under my control. No matter how much I pleaded, it refused to comply.

"Relax, focus, let go, take a deep breath," I encouraged myself.

I reverted to an old, popular remedy. I turned on the faucet and let the water flow in the sink. I laughed, upset with myself. A no longer young man sitting naked on a cold toilet seat, waiting for his body to yield and stop torturing him. I leaned my head on my hands and took deep, slow breaths. I turned off the water in the sink since it wasn't the solution. I lifted myself off the toilet, got a pen and paper from the night table and wrote down the main points I wanted to discuss with Ruhale in an orderly manner. I went back to the bathroom. I sat on the bowl and read what I had just written. While reading, a powerful stream of urine surprised me, lashing at the sides of the bowl as if it did not belong to me. Finally.

I washed my hands, got back under the covers, and immediately fell asleep.

In the morning I put on a pair of jeans, a black t-shirt, a sweater, and sneakers. Satisfied, I took a cab to the Dobnov café. I arrived half an hour early. I ordered a bottle of soda and a small latte, took a newspaper supplement left on a nearby table and began to read.

Not far from the café, in a small public garden, a homeless man settled on a bench. His extraordinary attire immediately attracted my attention. He wore a pair of once yellow sneakers and two t-shirts, a short-sleeved white one on top of a long-sleeved black one. His hair was fashioned into long dreadlocks that looked greasy from dirt and neglect. His black beard grew as wild as a hippie's. A supermarket cart leaned against the nearest bench, full of various colored plastic bags stuffed with his belongings. The man held a red leash tied to a small dog, whose fur looked like a brown variation of its owner's hair. The bench appeared to be the homeless man's regular place of residence. He settled on one end and placed his belongings on the other. He fumbled in the plastic bags and took out some clothes, which he set out on the bench. He placed the bags in an orderly manner beside the clothes. From one, he removed a small stainless steel bowl, released the leash from his hand, and allowed his dog to investigate the garden. He filled the bowl at the drinking fountain, placed it beside the bench, and returned to rummaging in the bags. He took out a toothbrush, returned to the water fountain, and brushed his teeth without toothpaste for a few minutes. All that time, he completely ignored the café's patrons, some of whom, like me, stole quick, uneasy glances at him. When he finished brushing his teeth, he cupped some water in his hands and washed his face, then he splashed some water on his hair, smoothed it back with his hands, and returned to sit on the bench. He took a bundle of old newspapers from one of the bags, turned his face to the sun, and started reading.

***

The first time I saw street beggars was when my parents had taken me to Jerusalem. Against the backdrop of our comfortable life in the kibbutz, begging was inconceivable. As far as I was concerned, they were the world's most miserable people. The image of a street beggar I had regularly seen many years ago is still etched into my memory. He used to sit on Allenby Street, corner of Sheinkin, not far from the Carmel Market. He would arrive every day early in the morning, lower a large sack from his shoulder, and sit with his back against a tree. He was wrapped from head to toe in several layers of clothing that resembled hospital gowns worn one on top of the other. His clothes were all of the same white cotton, the uppermost garment covered with oil and dirt stains. A sailor hat made of the same white fabric rested on his head, and his feet were in cloth slippers whose soles were black with street grime. He used to sit for hours by that tree, sewing new clothes from the same coarse cotton fabric.

A pile of the white fabric was beside him, a needle and thread were gripped between his fingers, and a pair of black scissors dangled from a shoestring tied around his neck. He used to sit there all day, busy with his slow, ceaseless sewing, making shirt after shirt, pants, hats, and socks. An aluminum bowl for collecting alms rested beside him. Passersby looked at the strange sewing man and tossed him a coin every now and then. The tailor — as he became known — never raised his eyes to see who had tossed a coin into his bowl and never stopped sewing.

At noon, he took out a small container and a metal spoon from one of his bags, ate his food, and once finished, went back to sewing until the evening. When it grew dark, he gathered his fabric and vanished until the following day. Many stories circulated regarding his origin; some said he had lost his children in the Holocaust. In the camps, they said, he had sewn the prisoners' striped uniforms and thus survived.

***

I slowly sipped my coffee and continued to watch, entranced by the homeless man's every movement as he sat on the bench. I occasionally peeked at my watch and eventually saw that my appointment time with Rachel had come and gone. As usual, this made me feel restless. "Ten more minutes," I said to myself, that's when I would call the kibbutz secretary.

"How are you, Uri?" Ruhale startled me, having rushed over to my table from a different entrance.

I quickly rose and invited her to sit down.

She waved her red ponytail. "Do you mind if we switch places? I need to sit with my back to the wall, to see who's coming in. This makes me feel safer." Her usual robust voice betrayed some fear that was not evident on her face. She wore a too-tight green dress that clung to a sloped belly and a full bosom that wasn't properly packaged. A bold necklace of lacquered leaves joined together with a silver-tone chain hung around her neck. Rachel had grown old as well, but she made a noticeable effort to adopt a contemporary style. Before sitting down, she pulled me into a sticky, clumsy embrace and kissed both my cheeks as if we were a couple of old friends delighted to see each other again.

"Wow, having a wild time in the city, Uri! The espresso generation fills up the cafés, yes? Well done, living like a movie star, a man after my own heart," she announced.

At the table next to ours, a young man raised his eyes from his laptop and glowered at us. Two girls sitting nearby exchanged glances and moved farther away. I asked the waitress for another cup of coffee and asked Ruhale what she would like to drink. She did not require my mediation.

Ruhale grabbed the waitress' arm. "Listen, sweetie, do you happen to have some good old-fashioned malt root beer?"

The waitress shook her head.

"All right, so bring me... an apple cider with no ice, and a little added vice, maybe — a croissant, of the type that has chocolate inside, yes? If I'm in the big city, I might as well enjoy life," she added with a wide smile. Only then did Ruhale relax her grip on the waitress, who remained rooted to the spot, stunned for a moment.

"Well, Uri, is your task complete? Do we have a play on our hands? The kibbutz members are getting impatient, we want to start rehearsing immediately, yes? You know what we say in the kibbutz, Uri: time is running short; and our work is never done. One needs to jump into the cold water and start swimming, yes? There's no learning without effort, right? We mustn't fool around with time. If I had to fool around, well, there're better things I can think of... just kidding... The only fooling around I do is with my husband."

I hadn't expected the conversation to go that way, without any unnecessary introduction, straight and to the point. I found myself stirring an empty coffee cup, digging for some last remnants of white and brown foam, as I sought a way out.

"Look, Ruhale, I thought we could talk about a different matter first. A theater play is a complicated matter... I thought... that we need to talk about it," I stammered with embarrassment.

Rachel, in a decidedly cheerful mood, threw back her head and sent her red hair waving. "What could be so complicated? We are working people. We take on a task and simply get going, yes? We plow, sow, and reap with joy. We kibbutzniks rise early every morning and get to work.

"Uri, don't forget all the preparations we still have to go through once your writing is done. This isn't a simple thing. We need to cast each member in the right role. There's always someone who gets insulted, yes? In other words, a kibbutz play is like a military operation!"

I shifted in my chair with discomfort. "With your permission, Ruhale, if you don't mind, before discussing the play, I would like to talk with you about building in your kibbutz extension, will that be all right?" She didn't seem to hear me.

"You've nothing to fear, Uri, we are very experienced in successfully producing plays. We don't want much, just a simple play presenting Mishmar Hatsafon in all its glory, a local history, yes? The kibbutz needs a milestone. We definitely know what we want. We have an idea, but the cake isn't properly baked yet; you're here to put things in order. You see? This isn't so complicated."

Rachel took a sheet of paper from her bag and outlined the play's structure as formed by the culture committee. "So, it goes like this, act one — the establishment of the kibbutz in the Galilee and the first attack on the kibbutz. In act two — the drying of the Hula lake, working and developing, celebrating the harvest festival. Then comes the final act, a grandiose finale — a kibbutz wedding with the participation of all the actors, the members. See? It really isn't complicated. We have the recipe already. All we need you to do, Uri, is bring the raisins, yes? Well, what do you say?"

I cringed with embarrassment. Seeking any assistance, I focused my eyes on a young couple sitting and facing each other, each absorbed in his or her cell phone.

After some hesitation I said, "Ruhale, I heard that you've started building a new neighborhood, an expansion of private houses in the kibbutz. I would like to look into buying such a unit. What exactly do I need to do in order to proceed?"

Rachel shifted in her chair, smoothed her red hair with her fingers, and stared at me. "With us, everything is very simple, there's a protocol. There are several requirements that must be met. Of course, kibbutz members get priority, yes? But... not just anyone, there's an admissions board, we are very strict about admitting only those who suit our rejuvenating community. Obviously, we need to maintain our unique character.

"This isn't only about money. We're not just talking about selling lots, yes? This is a social revival. You need to file an application. The admission committee examines each case individually, understand?"

Rachel suddenly turned impatient. "I suggest we discuss this some other time. I came here with a clear mission to advance our kibbutz theater play. About the expansion, I suggest that you set up an appointment and come to the field, get a better impression, see if it suits you. Right now, I need to focus on arranging our kibbutz jubilee celebrations."

I deliberated. I obviously needed Ruhale's support if I wanted to build my home in the kibbutz. I wanted to go back to where I was born, to live beside my mother. The community life of the kibbutz did not interest me at all. I assumed I would be able to find the golden mean uniting these two wishes: going back to my birthplace and the kibbutz's desire of revitalizing the community.

"Ruhale... I wanted to honestly tell you, I can't write the sort of play you expect me to write." I quickly added, "You're right... I understand your desire for a festive play, a kind of milestone. I... it's just that I'm not the right person to write it."

Her mouth hung open, speechless. But of course, that didn't last. "Wait, I can't believe my ears. What are you telling me, that you're changing your mind... now? Uri, I don't get it, you let me get a whiff of the honey, and now you're snatching the jar from my hands and locking it in the cupboard?"

I knew the worst was now behind me. "Understand... this just doesn't work out for me. Not that I haven't tried. I considered many directions. This is my own private failure, what can I do? I just wasn't able to pull it off! You saw how I tried to find some guidance based on the facts I found in the kibbutz archive.

"Mishmar Hatsafon has lots of wonderful accomplishments to be proud of, it's just that I'm not the right man for the task of chronicling them. You need an assured success. If you ask me, you can't take any risks and experiment with writing your own play for such a significant event. Why don't you put on *Fiddler on the Roof?*"

I said these last few sentences in a gentle, flattering tone. I had hoped to placate her, and while the frenetic, redheaded kibbutz secretary had gone still and silent, it was clear I had not succeeded. She crushed the remains of the croissant, allowing the crumbs to fall from her fingers and scatter on the table. I could see that she was disappointed to the roots of her soul.

"Look, Ruhale, *Fiddler on the Roof* is a fantastic musical. I'm sure you'll have an emotional, heartwarming event. Old and young sharing moments of joy and sadness. Diverse parts, singing and dancing. And the main thing, it's a play that requires a large cast — just like the Yiddish theater of old. Such a play would be ideal for your kibbutz jubilee."

Rachel leaned back in her chair, anger pulling down the corners of her mouth. "What will I tell the members now? That Uri Dolev suddenly doesn't feel like writing their play? Yes? I really don't understand you. When first we spoke, you were full of enthusiasm. What suddenly happened? Is this about money? Look... we can work things out, don't be shy. We'll find the resources if we have to. We can't start over now. The cart is off and rolling, can't turn the wheel back, yes?" Disappointment was reflected in her every movement.

In a calm voice, I tried to explain one more time. "This isn't about money. I just don't see the world the same way you do anymore. I love the kibbutz in my own way but know I won't be able to create a good play."

Rachel looked at me with a sour face.

"Ruhale, perhaps you shouldn't be too quick to rule out the *Fiddler on the Roof* option?"

She made a dismissive motion of utter negation with her hand. "Stop calling me Ruhale already, come on, who do you think you're fooling? *Fiddler on the Roof* is like a TV dinner, yes? Lacking any personal taste or flavor. What could I tell the members now?" She took a much-needed breath, and when she spoke again, she was uncharacteristically gloomy.

"Everything has gone to ruin. Everyone was so excited about a son of the kibbutz, a man of the wide world… one of our own, writing something special just for us.

"Is this your final decision?"

She looked straight into my eyes and realized no further persuasion could sway me. She recovered, leaned across the table at me and said, "Just so you know, Uri Dolev, I always headed your supporters' camp, even back then… long ago, when you were suspected… I went to talk to my brother, on my own initiative, so he could pull you out of the mud. Now, what thanks do I get? I have no more trump cards to play, yes?

"I thought I was going back to the kibbutz today with your play in my bag. I'd already scheduled a members meeting to plan the rehearsal schedule. Now we'll have to start over. We're back to the starting point. I find your attitude very, very frustrating, yes?"

The homeless person was still sitting on his bench in front of the café, petting his brown dog. I flagged down the waitress and paid the check. Then, impulsively I suggested, "Why don't you ask Yehiam Gruenwald? He used to write for the kibbutz newsletter, and I think he has both the talent and the ability. He's the man you're looking for."

An involuntary spark of anger flared across Rachel's face. She sat up straight in her chair and when she spoke, her voice took on a steely tone that took me aback.

"Yehiam Gruenwald? Tell me, Uri, have you lost your mind? He hates the kibbutz. There's no way in hell, yes? Yehiam Gruenwald does only what suits him. That is really a bad idea; we'd be better off with *Fiddler on the Roof*. I don't understand what went through your head, Uri. Yehiam Gruenwald?"

Rachel pushed back from the table with a loud noise and picked up her bag.

"You should reconsider. Yehiam grew up in the kibbutz just like me, he's more sensitive, knows all the details, and genuinely knows how to write."

Rachel waved her hand angrily and raised her voice. "Yehiam is out of the question and that's final! There's nothing to discuss. We know him. We know what he's made of — he's an egotist, a lousy egotist, yes? Max Tishler once said that Yehiam was a failure of the communal educational system. Gurnischt spoke a lot of nonsense in his time, but in this case, he was one hundred percent correct."

The café patrons stole glances at us. Trying to soothe Rachel, I moved closer to her and quietly said, "Come on, Ruhale… it isn't like Yehiam ever committed a crime or stole anything from the kibbutz. I've known him for years. He had the courage to voice some critical opinions, which ticked off quite a few members. He gained the reputation of being an oppositionist at the time that being an oppositionist was considered a crime in the kibbutz. The rest of it is just gossip because he stood up for himself."

Rachel's face turned almost as red as her hair. "The cat's out of the bag at last, Uri Dolev. With all due respect, you haven't lived here for years. You have no idea who Yehiam Gruenwald is. Trust me, kibbutz members aren't idiots. I know him well. Yehiam only ever thinks about his own benefit, and that's nothing compared to what my Alfred thinks about him."

I put a hand on her arm, uncomfortable with her outburst, but she got even more upset. "Pity, Uri Dolev, now I see your true colors. I don't deserve this. I was always on your side, yes? Turns out I was wrong. Many members warned me, said that a cunning snake was hiding under your pleasant behavior, yes?

"My husband is straight and to the point, no monkey business. And he never trusted you… right from the start. I kept protecting you. I told Alfred he mustn't judge you based on the rumors, yes? Surely you know that even your own classmates, like Hilik Zisman, are certain you dealt in espionage for money. This explains your meteoric success abroad and how you've gotten so rich. How do they say it? You have a can of frogs in your closet. You understand what I'm talking about, yes?

"But I never believed the stories about you, up until today. Now… I'm not so sure anymore. You and Yehiam complete each other, quite the pair, like Tweedledum and Tweedledee… Max and Moritz. Each of you with his own tricks, yes? The communal education system wasn't always successful, apparently. Forgive me, I'm talking straight from the heart, no monkey business, yes?

"I guess those who thought you betrayed security secrets to an enemy country were right, you have betrayed Israel! In the kibbutz, the members haven't forgiven you yet. And I was the only one who kept defending you. Now it's all clear to me. I guess everything they said about you was true. It wasn't a coincidence that got you into trouble, and then, at the first opportunity, you jumped right off the wagon and ran away to Germany. Everyone in the kibbutz knows you went to hide in the Nazis' country."

Rachel hoisted her handbag over her shoulder and without shaking my hand stormed out of the café, her red horsetail waving behind her. I remained seated for several more minutes. I looked at the poster on the wall, a print of a painting I had seen at the Tel Aviv Museum several years before: two little girls with pigtails wearing pink dresses printed with colorful butterflies. One girl holds a suitcase, and they both stand at the heart of a green European forest clearing. They are surrounded by a dense group of tall trees, dark and menacing. On the horizon, a ray of sunlight glimmers, a blinding beam emerging from the crowded woods, offering a little hope.

Oddly, I wasn't insulted by Rachel's harsh words. I accepted my punishment as someone who refused to toe the line.

"The cat's out of the bag." I rolled one of Rachel's catchphrases on my tongue. I acknowledged her anger with understanding. Hers was a world that contained no other colors in its palette besides black and white. If I had complied with her request, the suspicions against me would have been unfounded. Because I had disappointed her, they received confirmation. I felt relieved, in a way. For the first time, I was explicitly told what people in Mishmar Hatsafon felt about the whole affair.

How easy it was for Rachel to label me a spy and a traitor, just as Yehiam was labeled as egotistical, and Nurit as insane. I emerged from the café into the fresh air. I went to the bench, took out a hundred-shekel bill from my wallet, and handed it to the stunned homeless man. The cloud of distress that had enveloped me since my return to Israel had vanished.

37

On the shortest day of the year, December 21, I called Yehiam Gru-enwald to wish him a happy birthday. I told him about my meeting with Rachel Tenenboim and my decision to reject her request to write the kibbutz play. I also told him I had suggested him as my replacement.

Yehiam burst out laughing. "Are you nuts, Uri? Even though she barely knows me, Alfred's wife hates me with a vengeance. She really can't stand me."

"What does she have against you?"

Yehiam chuckled. "It's a long-forgotten affair, from years ago. There was this kibbutz meeting in which a motion was made to stop bringing volunteers from Scandinavia. It specifically discussed the female volunteers. I stood and announced that the motion was plagued with hypocrisy.

"I'm sure you can imagine the uproar in the dining hall. All the horny old devils who drooled day and night around the female volunteers suddenly turned into moral men of principles. I said that the female volunteers were easy prey and that the male members' high morals went down their pants as soon as they saw one sunbathing without a bra. A few female members, headed by Rachel Tenenboim, thought that the volunteers brought about moral deterioration. As far as they were concerned, those shiksas from Scandinavia were no better than prostitutes. They demanded that the volunteer initiative be stopped immediately."

I smiled. "That's the only reason she hates you so much? Aren't you exaggerating a little?"

Yehiam cleared his throat. "I'm sure she has more reasons. Anyway, when I told them I was leaving, Rachel and Alfred didn't shed any tears. I couldn't stand them, and they couldn't stand me." His voice was full of derision.

"Well, Rachel settled for describing you as an egotist who hates the kibbutz," I said. "As for me, she angrily accused me of handing classified information to the enemy and betraying my country."

There was a long silence. "What did you expect, Uri? You cooked this mess and now have to suffer the consequences," Yehiam said almost solemnly.

"What are you hinting at, exactly?"

"Do I really need to explain, Uri? You chose to go places that respectable, decent citizens stay clear of, that's what I mean."

I was surprised, even angry. "What are you talking about?"

"If you lie down with dogs, you get up with fleas, that's what I mean. Don't play the innocent guy here, Uri, you knowingly hooked up with the most radical left-wing organizations, those hypocrites who, under the pretext of being morally superior, have no qualms about hurting their own country. Those are your friends, and these are the facts."

"Excuse me, what facts?"

"Uri, you can cut out the playacting and hide-seek-games, Uri. I'm familiar with the circumstances of your arrest. I had my doubts at first, thought it was a one-time slip, a youthful whim, but then the facts came out, and I learned the bitter reality. You willingly attended meetings that took place in an apartment on Zrubavel Street in Tel Aviv. In that apartment, people cold-bloodedly planned to hurt their own country. You had no qualms about joining up with the worst and most radical of this country's self-haters. Those who practically handed out instructions for sabotaging this country's security. Your presence there speaks for itself."

I could barely swallow. "And what do you have to do with all that?"

Another silence followed. "What does it matter now? Your name was on the list of those gathered in that apartment. That's a fact, right?"

"Right, I was in that apartment… but I never did anything to endanger state security!"

"So, you admit to being present at the meetings that took place there. I was shocked when I saw your name. And don't give me any stories; you knew exactly what went on in that place, you weren't there by accident. You've always flaunted the flag of self-righteousness and morality — they are so weak and miserable, we're so strong and ruthless. You were always one to bang your head against the wall."

"And you knew and said nothing? Stood by the sidelines without doing anything while I was fired for no reason? They ruined my life, and you didn't even have the guts to say anything to me? And all those years, I believed that you were my best friend," I spat at Yehiam.

He lashed right back. "Even if I wanted to, I couldn't have. I was hired to analyze the polygraph results from some of those involved in the case; I signed a confidentiality agreement. All the suspects' names went through me. Yours was the only one I knew. I reported to the interrogators that we were from the same kibbutz and knew each other well. I—"

"What else did you tell them, exactly?"

"Only the facts: that you had an exceptional memory, so this could prove dangerous… that you're a stubborn man who doesn't know when to let go, that you're self-righteous, and that we all grew up receiving radical left-wing education."

I had begun to tremble, and sweat coated my palms. "A dangerous memory, that's what you had to tell the Shin Bet interrogators about me? Why didn't you ask me what I was doing there?"

Yehiam didn't answer, and I carried on, "I was only there to hand an article to an editor who lived at that address. I knocked on the door and went into the apartment. I saw a lot of people I didn't know in the living room, and the air was thick with cigarette smoke. The editor wasn't there, so they asked me to wait for him, and I stood by the door for a few minutes. I was never a part of any scheme. I never belonged to any organization. I had no idea what they were talking about. I waited fifteen minutes, the editor came and took the article, I said my goodbyes and left. That is the sum total of my great betrayal!"

"That's one way of describing it. The facts I have are different." I couldn't believe how calm, how cold he was.

"You snitched on me! You tarnished me with a traitor's reputation for life. I got fired because of you. We grew up together. We've known each other for twenty years, and you chose to believe this nonsense! You turned your back on me without a second thought. You threw me to the wolves!"

Yehiam hung up after that. I had so much more to say to him, but it all had to remain pent up in me, without an outlet. I lay on the bed, angry and deflated. When I realized stewing over my betrayal was not doing me any good, I left the hotel and ran along the streets until the air was wrung from my lungs. I went to the shore and collapsed on a boardwalk bench to catch my breath.

***

The mystery of the informer was solved. The friendship I had considered the most significant in my life ended with a poof, leaving no mark behind. The years-long tradition of the December 21 phone call was over. To Yehiam, this was insignificant either way. My annual call, as I had discovered, had been nothing more than a nuisance for him in recent years. I was determined to put it behind me. I wanted to "go with the flow," a new expression I learned during my visit in Israel.

**

After getting back to Berlin, I sped things up. I had already decided — I was going back to the kibbutz. I had the financial ability to pay for the building of my new house. I was certain I would be admitted; after all, I was a son of the kibbutz, and my mother was still a member. I walked about my Berlin apartment, wondering which of my belongings I should take to Israel. I loved my beautiful apartment, whose window looked out over the plane trees of Kollwitzstrasse. It wasn't easy for me to let it go, so I decided to keep it — a beloved refuge to which I could occasionally escape. The idea that Berlin had become my second home amused me. What would my father think of me?

38

Three years after my father's death, I moved into my new house in Mishmar Hatsafon. I roamed the rooms to get a feel for my new home. I hung a few paintings I had brought with me from Berlin. In the living room, I hung the first original painting I had purchased years ago. It had accompanied me everywhere I went, and now it seemed to have returned to its natural place. The painting depicts a man standing on top of a brown hill with his back to the viewer. He wears a red sweater, and his hands are in the pockets of his gray pants. The man in the painting reminds me of my brother, Yoram — a kibbutznik at the end of his workday, although I suppose he could easily be a bank clerk taking a break from his work. His face is unseen, only his wide back is visible. He looks toward a distant field, where, at the edge, there stands the blurred figure of a woman in a bright dress, possibly returning her father's gaze, or her lover's. The painting is deceptive, it contains everything and nothing. Seemingly it merely shows two people in a pastoral field. Still, one cannot help but feel a sense of restlessness, a great storm that is about to break, possibly separating the two forever. In the painting, I also see a hopelessness, a missed opportunity, maybe. Something slippery and evasive, a tender threat that something terrible might happen at any moment. And a small cloud hovering over the uncertain future.

I sat in my armchair, gazing at the painting, then my eyes looked to the horizon, all the way to the Bashan Mountains. The slopes were painted with the orange palette of the setting sun. The last sunbeams gleamed on the leaves of the oak and pistacia trees, which had flourished since we'd won the land from Syria. Each tree in its own solitude; one pistacia looking from afar at an oak bending one of its newly grown branches at the abundant orange fruits of a jujube tree. I closed my eyes and a soft sleep enveloped me.

✳✳✳

The following day I took a trip to my childhood home. On the kibbutz access road, I ran into Kuntz, a hoe on his shoulder, black rubber boots on his feet. He neither spoke to nor looked at me as I slowly marched beside him. He trudged along in his boots, and only when we were reached his house did he speak.

"Loneliness is especially difficult here. I have no one with whom I can exchange a single word. I'm here only to take care of Henka and watch over the graves."

Kuntz's schedule began at the crack of dawn. In the morning, he went to the swimming pool, the front gate key in his pocket. The rainwater pool had been neglected and eventually closed. Its floor was green with algae. My uncle did not mind the dirt and cold water. Each morning he would undress down to his underwear and swim for an hour. Then he showered and went to the nursing home to feed Henka her breakfast. Next, he pedaled his ancient bicycle to the deserted dining hall and waited for the car that brought the newspapers from Kiryat Shmona. He distributed the newspapers in the members' mailboxes then rode back to his apartment. At 2:00 p.m. he rested for about an hour, and when he woke from his *schlafstunde*, he took a hoe and some other tools and went to the cemetery to care for Moti's grave. Come evening, he returned to the nursing home to take Henka out for a walk and have dinner with her. Back home, he listened to classical music and read a book, until it was time for bed.

I went to visit him that Saturday night. Kuntz, as always, prepared a cup of tea and poured a little cognac in it. He complained, "I wake up so early and the water in the pool is freezing." On the living room wall Kuntz had hung three black-framed photographs: a picture of Haya aged thirty-five, her smile revealing pearl-white teeth, her eyes looking peaceful, and her hair caught in a breeze; a picture of Moti in his army uniform with a parachutist's badge, a sturdy young man with a boyish face, close-cropped hair, a slight, optimistic smile, holding his weapon against the background of a snowy Mount Hermon; the third photograph showed Haya and Moti hugging on her wedding day.

Kuntz took a gold pocket watch from a desk drawer. "I got it from my father when I left Germany for Israel. He got it from his father when he left Poland for Germany." Kuntz opened the watch cover and glanced at the time. "Too long… too late…" he said without explanation.

I wondered who he was thinking about — his father or his son, killed before he could inherit the watch. He took an envelope from his dresser and with a trembling hand removed a brown parchment certificate. He flattened the crumpled edges. The unpleasant odor of mold wafted up from the parchment. Kuntz held it like a treasure map and read its German script to me.

"This certificate confirms that Moshe Kuntzmacher has paid HaShomer Hatzair one shekel, whose value is 1.5 German marks. Shekel certificate No. 03806." The certificate was issued in June 1935. "I was only fourteen when I officially joined HaShomer Hatzair," he added.

***

Kuntz took off his clothes and remained in his underwear. He went into the small bathroom, left the door open, and stood in front of the mirror. Leaning on the sink, he examined his face for a minute. Even though it was late, Kuntz took the shaving brush out of the cabinet, placed a new blade in his razor and tightened the screw. He arranged his shaving instruments on the sink the way he probably had for over seventy years. He passed his left hand over his face, feeling the stubble, turned on the faucet, and waited for the hot water to flow into the sink. He regarded himself in the mirror. What little hair remained had gone white. His forehead stretched up to join the bald top of his head, pockmarked with the wounds of time.

He fingered a small scar on his chin and told me, "This is a souvenir from a soccer game in a Berlin schoolyard."

He let the water run for a few minutes, then he dipped his hand in to check the temperature and was burnt by the steaming water. Kuntz emitted a feeble cry that was lost in the walls of the empty apartment. He looked at me, rubbed his fingers, and held them under some cold water to ease the pain. Then he squeezed a generous portion of shaving cream on an old brush with sparse bristles. Kuntz wet the brush and smeared shaving cream on his face with measured, circular movements. With one finger, he removed a layer of foam close to his sideburns, held the razor and with smooth, measured movements, from the top down, shaved his face. At the end, he stretched the skin of his cheeks and checked his work. Then, exactly as he had the first time, he repeated the ritual.

With one careless movement he nicked himself near his left ear. Kuntz washed his face, then pressed a transparent stone to the cut. He held the stone against the cut for a few minutes, and when the blood flow stopped, he examined himself in the mirror. All that time, I stood beside him, silent and ignored. His gray underwear hung loosely over his thighs, emphasizing his weight loss. Endless wrinkles furrowed the skin around his eyes and on his forehead. The skin of his chin drooped like a melon peel hung to dry in the sun. I pitied him and didn't know if it was decent of me to see him in his decrepit state.

He meticulously washed the shaving utensils, carefully cleaning every part, then placed them side by side to dry. From the cupboard over the sink, he took an after-shave cream tube, applied a small amount to his hands, and rubbed his face so the cream would soak into his skin. Next came a small bottle of aftershave. He shook a few drops into his open hand, then patted his cheeks several times. The fragrant aftershave stung the open cut and a bead of blood appeared. Kuntz folded a sheet of toilet paper and stanched the blood. After showering, he put on his pajamas and I handed him a cup of tea.

"In Berlin, I used to earn money as a flower shop delivery boy. I rode my bicycle and delivered arrangements to offices and homes. Once, after I finished all my deliveries, I had one unclaimed bouquet. I gave it to the prettiest girl in HaShomer Hatzair; her name was Rina. She kissed me on the cheek and married my good friend Menahem Ganani."

I nodded, and Kuntz slowly sipped his tea.

"I've no more strength in me. Today, in the garden, I saw that my greatest enemy, the Prosopis plant, has taken advantage of the situation and claimed a large territory. You know, Arabs villagers around us used to call the Prosopis 'the poor people's date.' The Arabs, like the Prosopis, tried to hold on to this land forever. In the struggle over the land we have claimed victory, but we seem to have lost to the Prosopis. In the early days of the kibbutz, whenever I saw a Prosopis I would destroy the branches with a hoe then dig with a pickaxe to expose its roots. Finally, we burnt the roots so no trace would remain. And now, the Prosopis has spread in every corner of my garden. Its pink fruit has ripened, and it stares at me, mocking me through eyes like a dead carp's.

"Good night, Uri, go to sleep."

***

It was a clear night. I thought of Kuntz, who monotonously carried on, trying to maintain the routine of his empty life. His breakfast reminded me of the days of austerity: a cup of instant coffee, a slice of bread and jam. In the evening he settled for a glass of tea, a bit of white cheese, and a hard-boiled egg. The menu changed only if he was invited to eat with a neighbor or if some female member came with a pastry and left it in his apartment.

Kuntz had grown old, his passion extinguished. He took naps in front of the television, listened to classical music, and read a little. Little by little he followed the paths Henka had trod before him, continuing along without noticing the loss of reality. He continued to enjoy good physical health, easily riding his bicycle up and down the kibbutz paths, while many members his age had to use their mobility scooters. The grandchildren, as they grew older, became distant from Henka, who could not even recognize them anymore, and avoided Kuntz's apartment in the kibbutz. Once a month, he went to visit his grandchildren, was their guest for a single night and day, and returned to the kibbutz.

His neighbors, a young couple new to the kibbutz, complained of Kuntz's inexplicable and unprovoked temper tantrums. He would go to the community manager's office, screaming that his new neighbors were trying to steal from his garden and had stolen tools from his shed. Once, he was found after midnight roaming the lawn by the dining hall stark naked. The next day, I asked him what happened, and he explained, "I ran out of hot water, so I went to bathe in the public shower but couldn't find it. Perhaps it was stolen?"

I didn't remind him that the public shower had been closed for thirty years.

His mental condition rapidly deteriorated, and his angry outbursts worsened and became an offensive nuisance. The medical health committee consulted with the kibbutz doctor, and Kuntz was prescribed sedatives. He was permanently relocated to the nursing home, in the room next to his wife.

The community manager turned to Henka and Kuntz's grandchildren, their sole heirs, and asked them to clear their grandparents' apartment so it could be rented. When they came to the kibbutz, I joined them on their visit to Henka and Kuntz in the nursing home. Moti, a tall young man named after his late uncle, led his two younger sisters. The three of them spent twenty minutes in Henka and Kuntz's company, silent, looking at each other, waiting for a mutual sign of agreement that would allow them to rise and leave. At the end of that obligatory visit, the grandchildren made their way to Henka and Kuntz's empty apartment, and I walked along with them.

My mother was sitting under the carob tree on the pleasant end-of-summer, sun-washed day. The grandchildren went over to her and said hello then crossed the sidewalk to Henka and Kuntz's modest apartment.

My mother called me over. "Stay with them. Make sure they don't throw everything away."

The apartment had stood empty and locked for a long time. The unrelenting odors of mold, dust, and rot permeated the abandoned rooms. Spoiled fruit rotted in a bowl on the table. Yellowed newspapers were piled beside it. A few unwashed cups and plates remained in the sink. The grandchildren opened the windows, letting fresh air and sunlight in. Everything in the apartment wore a thin, gray coat of dust and dirt; each moved object brought about a cloud of dust, miniscule particles that scattered in aimless flight, transfixed in a ray of sunlight coming through the window.

Haya's children looked around the apartment they all knew from their childhood and gathered a few photo albums from the shelves. The youngest of the grandchildren sat on the couch and looked at photographs of their mother. The first pages contained black-and-white photographs of a chubby baby wearing a Queen Esther costume; Haya as a young teenager wearing a swimsuit and smiling at the photographer; Haya and Nurit Schory at the foot of the stone sentry by the Nahal Amud stream, both wearing *tembel* hats, white kaffiyehs around their necks, blue shirts with white lace, and shorts. After a brief look at the photos, the grandchildren wasted no time. With chilling nimbleness, as if assigned some work by strangers, they gathered all the belongings in the apartment into big plastic bags and carboard boxes. They put all the clothes from the closets into a large pile to be donated to one of the associations gathering used clothes for the poor and for refugees.

They placed the hundreds of books in boxes: German literature, the finest of German culture, Hebrew literature, translated world literature, poetry, philosophy, and nonfiction books about social issues and socialism, along with sheet music of the works of famous composers. Indiscriminately, these were all removed from the shelves and tossed inside the boxes. The books were never rescued.

Kuntz's record collection contained hundreds of classical pieces, various albums purchased with much effort and with what little funds were available. Bach violin concertos, compositions by Mozart, Beethoven, Schuman, Sibelius, Britten, Tchaikovsky, operas by Verdi, waltzes by Strauss. The record shelf had bowed under their weight over the years. All the records were piled on the carpet, awaiting their fate. Moti and his sisters debated what to do with the collection Kuntz had accumulated since the seventies. I picked a single record off the pile — Bizet's *Carmen* performed by Maria Callas. The rest of the records, without too much sorrow, were thrown into several orange garbage bags. At the last second, I was able to salvage a record player and a tape recorder Kuntz had purchased in Haifa to record birdsong, the howls of jackals, the singing of his children, and his own playing of various musical instruments he had built with his own hands.

Evening drew closer. Haya's children were in a hurry to finish clearing the apartment to get back to their own house in Givatayim. Moti found Kuntz's gold pocket watch. Amused, he opened and closed the cover of the beautiful watch, secured the gold chain to a belt loop, and tucked it in his pocket. All the rest of Kuntz and Henka's belongings ended up in the trash bags. The trio made a final inspection of the apartment, checking the remaining belongings, and choosing to leave most of them on the yellowing grass. A small pile of human history rested in front of the apartment. The items were now in the public domain, orphaned of their past, freed from the weight of memories stored in them, a useless pile of memories fading away for the lack of any demand or interest. Objects that despaired of finding a new owner and accepted their fate of becoming extinct. After several hours of strenuous work, Henka and Kuntz's apartment was stripped naked. A few gray stripes were seen on the walls, marks left by the various furniture, a loose electric wire without a lamp, thick drapes that desperately needed washing, a pair of old slippers, a gray flat cap that had known better days. In a mere four hours, Henka's and Kuntz's belongings had turned into worthless trash. It seemed that the grandchildren refused to tie themselves to their grandparents' fate. The numerous garbage bags were hurled into a large trash container standing by the sidewalk, emitting a hollow sound that was absorbed by the rusted iron as they fell, its echoes fading unremembered within a split second.

Afterwards, I went to my mother's apartment and found her in a very emotional state. "I… don't have much left either. I guess this is what the end looks like…" And she wouldn't stop crying.

Epilogue

A sense of long-absent contentment settled in. The anger and insult that had fueled my life had evaporated. A youthful vibrancy returned to energize me. I fell asleep easily and slept well. My dreams still contained moments of terror and fear, yet something had purified inside me, clearing a path to healing and acceptance. I attributed this general improvement to my return home. Being close to my mother filled me with happiness, and I visited her often. She was in good health despite her advanced age.

Few of the kibbutz veterans were still with us. One funeral chased another, and soon none of the kibbutz founders would be counted among the living. Their dreams are all smaller these days. Happiness is in a glass of tea, a day full of sunlight, the aroma of jasmine that suddenly fills the air, a stroke or a kiss given by a beloved grandchild. I made sure to have dinner at my mother's apartment every Friday evening. One evening, before we sat down to eat, my mother asked, "Come with me to Kuntz. It's his birthday today. He is ninety years old, and I am the only one who remembers."

I held my mother's hand and, letting her set the pace, we walked to the nursing home. I barely recognized the ancient couple sitting by the entrance: Henka and Kuntz, each in a wheelchair. Their children had died long ago, while they continued to bear the burden of life, unknowing, awaiting their turn without comprehension. A cruel fate fills them with enough physical strength to go on living, postponing the end, refusing to release them from the agonies of bereavement.

Just like in their first days as lovers, Henka and Kuntz were now constantly together... but in another vicious trick, they could not recognize each other. The Philippine caregivers dressed and sat them in front of the nursing home to enjoy the view and the pleasant air. Breathing human statues, living monuments in the shadow of a boulevard of plane trees whose leaves fell in an autumn that had come too early.

I rested a hand on Kuntz's shoulder and asked, "What gift would you like for your birthday?"

He gave me a hollow stare, but then his eyes lit up. "The 'Internationale'... sing the 'Internationale' with me... let's sing it together like in the old days…"

I looked at my mother, and we both tentatively began to sing: "Arise ye workers from your slumbers, Arise ye prisoners of want…"

Kuntz held Henka's hand and joined us in a rusted voice, "So comrades, come rally, And the last fight let us face. The Internationale, Unites the human race…" and a large smile brightened his face. He urged Henka to join the singing. She smiled and moved her lips voicelessly. For a single moment, in the darkness of their faded lives, happiness flickered on the faces of my uncle Kuntz and my aunt Henka.